Ruslan

Barbara Scrupski

Ruslan

A NOVEL

CROWN PUBLISHERS
NEW YORK

Published by Crown Publishers, New York, New York. Member of the Crown Publishing Group, a division of Random House, Inc.

www.randomhouse.com

CROWN is a trademark and the Crown colophon is a registered trademark of Random House, Inc.

Printed in the United States of America

DESIGN BY ELINA D. NUDELMAN

Library of Congress Cataloging-in-Publication Data
Scrupski, Barbara.
    Ruslan : a novel / Barbara Scrupski.—1st ed.
1. Russia—History—Nineteenth century—Fiction. 2. Passing (Identity)—Fiction. 3. Women soldiers—Fiction. 4. Poor women—Fiction. 5. Nobility—Fiction. I. Title.
    PS3619.C77 R87 2003
    813' .6—dc21   2002153021

ISBN 1-4000-4761-7

10 9 8 7 6 5 4 3 2 1

First Edition

For my mother and father—
who gave me the world.

The novel *Ruslan* takes place in an imaginary nineteenth-century Russia of no specific time, in which all periods of the century, from the beginning to the end, coexist. The "tsar" referred to in the story is a symbol of Russian imperial power and does not represent any particular ruler.

PART 1

There is no food in Russia: wizened peasants, their faces as wrinkled as old apples and as red, kneel on the frozen ground and scrabble with their fingertips at projections, lumps and bumps that might conceal a beet, a carrot, a turnip white and sad as the sky above their heads. But whatever is found is not eaten, rather drunk in the form of clear and bitter alcohol distilled, it seems, from the winter air itself. It burns their throats like liquid ice but warms the stomach and spreads like sleep in their veins until they lie down and dream. They dream of beets as big as houses, edible dwellings whose walls drip sweetness. They dream of eggs as small as pearls, smoky in color, or luminous as fire—a load of treasure contained in the belly of a fish. They dream of snow that stays on the tongue and fills the mouth as sour white cream, and stones that, boiled and halved, reveal a magically edible flesh. They dream of mushrooms. While miles away in icy rooms with ceilings that merge with the sky, seated at snow-covered tables set with ice and silver, the slant-eyed ladies feed on diamonds brought from the luscious south (the Caucasus, Black Sea) and warm their tiny, cold feet against the muscular calves of imperial guards, then, lowering their lashes, dream of something else, of something more than that, for this is not enough (the slap of a stallion's balls against their upturned buttocks).

This is the Russia of the mind, half heard of, half remembered—the detritus of a culture, of a history exploded and drifting like ash across our consciousness, the decades of its greatest century jumbled together, out of their timely order, so that

Pushkin (but isn't he dead?), strolling up one of the spectral boulevards in Russia's great white city of the north, nods to Chekhov coming down the other way, tips his hat. So. Imagine St. Petersburg in all its titanic splendor, its icy might—a city built on water, mist. Imagine its windows, myriad points of light in the winter sky, and imagine in one of those windows a girl who is almost a woman. We see the impoverished slimness of her arms, hear her grunts of effort as she stretches herself toward the whorls and clouds of frozen gold that drift across the ceiling just out of reach above her head and then drops her arms in despair. Dressed in faded black, she might be a servant of this great house, driven to madness by the disparity between its grandeur, its spaciousness and the narrow poverty of her own destiny (a garret room, a sixteen-hour day). Alone in this room, her eyes frozen in intent, she gazes up again at the intricate golden sky. A knife glints in her hand. She tests it against her finger and, finding it sharp, grunts with approval, pushes back her sleeves. What is she doing? Stop her! No!

And indeed, a servant comes rushing into the room to do just that, protesting, weeping, clinging to her skirts, for our young countess, teetering atop a giant ladder, forearms bare as a wash-erwoman's, is reaching up again about to peel the plated gold from yet another of the ceiling decorations of this once-great home. She has to. There is no food in this house. Praskovia, the house serf who is clinging to her skirts and pleading with her mistress not to further damage the splendor of the palace, has had nothing but black bread and weak tea without jam for days, a consequence of her mistress's careful economy, and if we look around the room, we see that it is empty. The furniture has all been sold.

Countess Alexandra Korvin's father, the old count, has died a year ago, leaving debts as massive as the family's fortunes once had been. For the past year, the year of her mourning, the countess has seen no one—has not attended one ball, one musicale, one tea, one dinner or Christmas party (not to mention has not been seen at the golden Maryinsky sitting in the family box, which has been sold). "What a lovely girl," whispered the rest of Petersburg society when they met at those balls, musicales, and teas, "so gracious, so serious, so willing to observe the proprieties and proper customs—unlike the rest of our youth. Unlike, say, the Bezinsky boy. When his father went, he bent over the bed, not to kiss him, but to assure himself that old Sasha—what a rake!—was really dead. Then he went straight to his club, ordered oysters and champagne, and danced for joy on the dining table among the crystal and the china, kicked it all to the floor. The scratches of his boots are still there." They imagined that Countess Alexandra Korvin had been resting in darkened rooms, overwhelmed by her sorrows, that the countess lived in a twilight world of memory and grief, and indeed, when she was seen walking by the Neva, pausing from time to time to regard its dark waters, her face was congested by thought, grim with concentration.

But she was thinking about money. She had not been resting in darkened rooms, but rather standing straight in their antiseptic morning light, arms folded, voice caustic, directing the servants to remove this chair, this table, to wrap this porcelain vase, that crystal box. Tradesmen and dealers came and went much later in the day, in the muffled blackness of the night, to shield the house's shame from prying eyes as they stripped it room by room.

"We still have that forest in Lithuania," the countess had stated firmly to Trenyakov the lawyer that Friday after the funeral. Sitting at her father's old carved desk in her simple black mourning outfit, she'd come into view only intermittently, a piece of a face briefly visible in the cracks between the crumbling walls of paper that teetered on top of the desk, always on the verge of crashing to the floor. "The deed is here somewhere."

Trenyakov, a connoisseur of art, was thinking that she looked rather like fragments of a Greek sculpture from the Archaic period, those pieces of her that he could see: a splendid nose, a superbly modeled chin. Alexandra had to repeat her statement with greater force before Trenyakov started in his chair and automatically agreed.

"Oh, so we *do* have the forest in Lithuania, which means we must still have the hunting lodge in Mazuria with those ten thousand acres rich in game and fish."

No, not Archaic—her features were more refined. The elegance of her elongated eye was Etruscan in feeling. Or Minoan perhaps, reminiscent of the purity of its architecture with the perfect balance of the arched brow above, the superb carving of the entire bony socket a testament to a designer of the most refined tastes. Even this small piece of her was so perfectly turned and shaped, it revealed the harmony of the entire larger structure.

"And the shoe factory and the coal mines in the Ukraine. All those western holdings that he probably forgot about, forgot to sell. I know the deeds are here," she continued, confident, commanding. Trenyakov heard her ruffling through the papers, scrounging, digging, scratching like a starving yet industrious and hopeful mouse. He couldn't bear it.

"Countess"—he hung his head—"five years ago."

The countess, distracted as she scrounged among the papers, separated a stack from the larger pile and began to thumb through it. "Five years ago what?"

The lawyer began to explain. Five years before, the count had found himself in some difficulties, financial in nature, involving some rather aggressive creditors entirely without scruple, which he had requested his attorney to help him solve.

The countess understood at once. Her shoulders sagged, her mood deflated. And what had it all been spent on? She understood that too. For instance. A townhouse for a pretty singer, just the latest in a long succession of women whose townhouses could be found all over the city, opulently appointed and housing all manner of ballet girls, aspiring actresses, milliners, even impoverished daughters of the aristocracy, whose task it was to fill his empty bed and heart (he had lost the countess's young mother at her very birth), though none of them, while succeeding at the first, ever succeeded at the second even in the slightest. Or the expeditions round the world, from which he returned with trunks of treasure—golden masks of Aztec priests, stacks of Turkish tiles, Greek pots, Indian ankle bracelets beaten out of silver, even an actual Indian temple dancer, still living in the city on the count's largesse, still jingling and glittering through the dark Russian winter afternoons as far as the countess knew. And then there were the animals: a crate of fantastic birds, iridescent, cobalt-crested with golden throats and fire-tipped wings, who wilted and died upon meeting their first blast of arctic air; an infant elephant who had wandered—dejected, bewildered— through the inner courtyard for a month or two before contracting pneumonia and being shot, with many tears, by the count himself.

"And just how," the countess had to ask, though she really knew the answer, "were they resolved?"

Trenyakov was silent.

"The estates, the factories, the mines. Everything. Correct?"

"Your father was a most extraordinary man," he said finally.

Oh, a most extraordinary man. When he and her mother had

returned from their wedding trip—three years of extravagance that took them to a mountain peak in the Himalayas and into a ferocious gale around the Cape of Good Hope—he had had the titanic marble staircase of the palace torn out and replaced with one of lapis lazuli, a color that reproduced with *exactitude,* he exclaimed to all who would listen, the opaque intensity of azure to be seen in the water off the shores of a certain island in the Cyclades at seven o'clock of a fine spring evening just as it is getting dark. The semiprecious staircase flowed from floor to floor as if the sea itself had been brought inside the house, and its fantastic richness of color commemorated as well, he said, the color of her mother's eyes as they had looked that one night as they had walked together on the sand and stared out at the reaching sea. He had promised his wife at that moment to make for her a road of the sea so they could walk right up to the moon, and this he had duly done, but then his young wife had died.

"All of it," said Trenyakov, "and there are debts."

A road to the moon! A hundred thousand souls—every serf they owned—it had cost, his road to the moon! And the land that went with the serfs; all their holdings, a small kingdom. Everything gone.

Trenyakov, a stubby man of middle age still living with his mother, watched the countess cover her face, watched the tears drip down between her fingers, and would have liked her to cry in his arms. But his hair was too thin, he reasoned, for this ever to come to pass.

"For every problem there is a solution, Countess," he said. It was something his mother was always saying. The money, he wanted to say, had been well spent, spent to walk upon the sea, he would have liked to whisper leaning over her, to smell her hair. But he was too fat. He shifted uncomfortably in his chair.

"For every problem there is a solution, Countess," he repeated.

"A road to the moon." She gripped her scalp with sharp fingernails, released it, and shook her head. "An elephant!"

Trenyakov felt that his whole life had been pointed toward this moment, when he could be of service to a beautiful woman. The taunts of his fellow schoolboys at his fatness and at the fact that his mother had been a serf and his education paid for by the otherwise indifferent master who had fathered him, the nights of study when his mind raced the setting sun in order to absorb the contents of a page before the lines of print melted in the dark, the stench of the tannery across from his rooms in Moscow, the distaste of the girls he'd tried to court and that time at his friend Yuri's afternoon tea and what he'd heard Yuri's sister say about him—all this did not matter. He would be of help to a beautiful woman.

First, he stressed, honor. If she wished to keep her palace, which was heavily mortgaged, she must honor her father's debts.

"But how? With what? With this?" She smashed the wall of papers, sent it flying. Trenyakov dropped out of his chair and fell to his knees.

"Sell what you have, your furniture, your art, your library," he said as he crawled along the floor retrieving the papers, encountering to his astonishment the tip of her shoe as it peeked from beneath her shadowy skirts and wanting to cradle this special treasure he had found in the palm of his hand, but contenting himself with merely sniffing deeply of its fragrant leather.

"I'll start with that staircase," said Alexandra, the shoe vanishing into the shadows as she rose to her feet. "I'd gladly take a hammer to it myself."

"Oh no, dear Countess, you must leave it be," said Trenyakov, rising now himself with reddened face and taking a handkerchief from his sleeve to mop his gleaming head. Heavily, he sat again, then popped up abruptly to hover by his chair until the countess settled him back into it again with an irritable wave. "How will you get from floor to floor?"

The countess had to admit the question was a reasonable one. How would she get from floor to floor? By the servants' back staircase?

"Besides," continued Trenyakov, "you may someday wish to sell the palace, and then, without its famous staircase—"

"No," said Alexandra.

"But if you did—"

"Never! I will never sell the palace!" The countess threw herself down in a cracked old leather chair across the room. The dust spurted into the air and settled round her and over her, so that she herself looked as discarded, rejected, unsaleable as the chair would be found to be when she would later try to sell it too.

"If you marry well," said Trenyakov, twisting in his seat to face her, "you won't have to sell the palace."

"Who would marry me now?"

Oh, anyone, he wanted to say, me. Instead, he proposed his plan. Strip the palace of its ornaments and furnishings in secret. No one need know what had happened. With the money she could not only pay her debts but finance a season in Petersburg's marital hunting ground, where she would be sure to find success and a restoration of her fortunes and good name.

"Absolutely not!" she had cried, jumping from her chair and beginning to pace the room. The disgrace of fortune hunting— why, she would be nothing better than a whore!

Nevertheless, Alexandra did as he prescribed. She really did not have a choice. It had taken one year of private meetings with dealers and the sounds of transport wagons clattering into the inner courtyard in the small hours of the morning, but she had done it. So what to do now?

The debts were paid, but there was very little left, and the countess, economizing harshly, was trying to stretch the small supply of rubles as far as they could possibly go for as long as she could make them last. Thus her attempt to supplement her income by peeling as much of the delicate gold leaf from the ceiling decorations as she could.

Alexandra looked up again at the ceiling. No money, no food, no furniture, no proper clothes, most of her opulent wardrobe having been picked through already by sharp-eyed dealers in the secondhand. She could continue to strip the house of its decorations. But what would this solve? It would be only a matter of time before every scrap of gold in the house was gone. Then there would be nothing but the staircase.

And how long before the staircase, too, was gone, its absurd magnificence gnawed to dust by hammers and saws, its preposterous splendor broken up in pieces and carted away so that she was stranded, forever, on the ground with no way of reaching higher? What then?

The countess gathered her skirts, climbed down from the ladder, and handed the knife to the weeping serf, who hurried away to hide the precious object in the kitchen, where there weren't many of them left.

All right, the countess said to herself, no peasant nonsense about love.

She went out of the empty room and up those foolish, gleaming steps and locked herself in the shabby room she had taken for her own because it was small and cheap to heat. Standing in front of a large mirror (worthless, cracked) that the serfs Praskovia and Matryona had carted up the stairs, she examined with a critical eye the goods she had on offer. Just a body. Why men were willing to pay for *that,* with money or with marriage, was something she would never understand. What was it exactly they saw in it? The indented waist that fit their hand so neatly? And the breasts that were the object of such frenzied preoccupation—were hers large enough to absorb anyone's permanent attention? Or would he come to the end of them too soon? The opulent thighs and but-tocks favored by nineteenth-century tastes, as sumptuously uphol-stered as their furniture, were in her case discouragingly flat, as if they'd never been properly stuffed to the point of plushy comfort. Perhaps if she ate more . . . but how was she to do that now?

The Princess Rusavsky, for instance—now there was a woman, everyone said. Her breasts bulged up from her décol-letage like fresh-baked loaves of heavy bread, her arms were solid fat, white as lard, and it had been whispered by the lady's maids, who formed an underground system of satisfying secret news, that she had no need of a bustle—the extravagant backward projection achieved by lesser ladies with complicated mechanisms involving metal and springs was, in her case, solid flesh.

Alexandra pushed her breasts together, hoping to achieve the plump-loaved effect, but achieved only the impression of kneaded dough—she could not even make them meet in the much-admired mysterious cleft, the very ravine of femininity in which, she supposed, men desired to lose themselves.

She resolved to eat more but knew that it was probably hopeless—she was one of those women, unlucky by the stan-dards of her time, who just could not keep the weight on, no matter how many blinis she might consume, no matter how fatty the carp at dinner or how many Spanish oysters she slid down her throat.

But there had been no Spanish oysters for some time, and there promised to be none again if she did not accomplish her purpose.

RUSLAN

[13]

Alexandra began to dress herself once more. It was difficult without Matryona, her lady's maid, who was never to be found when wanted, but Alexandra did the best she could, applying the flat, bone-reinforced stretch of cloth to her midsection herself, reaching round with breath sucked in to try to tighten it to the proper point of exaggerated femininity, and tying the strings securely round her waist. Her dress went over her head and she fastened it awkwardly up her back, missing a button here and there—but so what? There was no one to see her. At least her lack of attributes was safely hidden now.

With her clothes on, she had more to offer—perhaps. She supposed she was intelligent. This was not necessarily a plus, if she considered her father's tastes in women axiomatic. Though, strangely, he had attended to her education with a fanatical zeal. Apart from the usual languages, the drawing, the dancing, the music, the instruction in the use of the globes, she had been trained in some rather odd accomplishments for a woman of her era and station. An expert marksman at her father's insistence, she had spent many a morning in the misty autumn air of the Mazurian hunting lodge, the butt of a double-barreled shotgun punching bruises into the tender flesh beneath her collarbone as the ducks, pheasants, and grouse rained down from the sorrowing Polish sky. She knew also how to clean and hang a variety of game, from pheasant to elk, whose scent she could not only detect from a distance but differentiate. Her father had called her his "bird dog"—not something she was sure she should be proud of. She could imitate the calls of exotic birds but would never do so in public. Handling saber and epee with equal dexterity, she regularly beat her fencing master. She rode sidesaddle when in the company of others and astride when alone or with her father. Most oddly of all, she knew how to construct a leather shoe, having been instructed by an Italian master imported for just this purpose for reasons Alexandra could never fathom, but which she supposed had something to do with the Ukrainian shoe factory the Korvin family owned. And she smoked a cigar with all the style of a genuine connoisseur.

However. The eccentricity of these accomplishments must, she knew, be concealed. Russian noblewomen, perhaps like women everywhere, were allowed to display their eccentricities only after marriage, when they were at last allowed to expand their personalities to fill the shadowy outlines that had hung about them as young girls. Marriageable young women, in order to reassure the skittish male, had to pretend to be blank—a page that the man could write his fantasy upon. Of course, the woman could scribble over what he'd drawn as much as she liked after marriage, when it would be too late. But for now, Alexandra must conform. And if she was to play this part convincingly, she must, like a bad actress, inhabit her part offstage as well. Alexandra was about to smoke her last cigar.

s for why Alexandra, at the advanced age of twenty-three, had not already been entered in the marriage stakes, the answer is that the count would not allow it. He would not see his daughter led snorting into the ring like a broodmare to display herself before the appraising stares of Petersburg's men while they smoked and chattered amongst themselves, assessing the breadth of her hips, the health of her teeth, and the size of her father's purse, bulging, they hoped, with munificent dower funds. The question of her marriage was a matter of complete indifference to him when it did not inspire in him outright hostility. He hadn't even been willing to present her formally to society ("What society?" he had sneered). Any suitors she had attracted in the course of her rather quiet social life had been gently but firmly discouraged, and when she'd asked her father why, he'd spoken bitterly of the sufferings of love—of its birdlike, fleeting nature, quickly flown, of the tiny island of transcendent happiness he'd inhabited while his wife had lived, his life before and afterward a sea of empty darkness, and how it had been his very passion that had destroyed her mother's life. He had watched his love die raving in a hot fever of delirium, writhing on the sweat-soaked, bloody bed where she'd only lately given life—a tiny glowing body made of flesh—to love itself. He did not wish to see Alexandra suffer as her mother had. He did not wish to see her suffer as her father had.

Alexandra, knowing that love would have nothing to do with the marriage she was planning, was not concerned. And as for the risk of childbirth (in this century a very real one), it would be the price she paid for the restoration of her fortunes, and, if she and the child survived it, a compensation for a loveless match.

However, the young countess was uncertain of her path. She knew nothing of the nature of men or courtship or society, and so she set out to consult the one person in St. Petersburg she thought might be able to help her—the "princess," who was no princess at all, as everyone knew, but a *grande horizontale,* that is, a woman who made her living by men and the most illustrious of her father's discarded mistresses.

The smoke of that last cigar was still coating her tongue with its taste of final comforts when Alexandra climbed into the droshky and pulled the lap robe across her knees. She did not look at the white stream of buildings that flowed past the carriage. She did not hear the soft sound of the horses' hooves as they padded through the snow at an easeful trot, snuffling through their large, moist nostrils. The muttering of the old Hungarian coachman, whose back confronted her with a potato-like solidity as he relaxed up front with an active and meditative finger up his nose, did not penetrate her consciousness a bit. Instead she was looking inward, rubbing her soft sable muff against her lips, seeking to soothe herself, for the princess had always frightened her.

It had been years since she had seen this woman, whose scrutiny had shadowed her childhood. On those days long ago when she was appointed to visit the princess, she had first been vigorously scrubbed—Alexandra remembered particularly the roughened, nubbly sensation of the washcloth-covered finger as it drilled at her tender ear. Then, dusted sweetly with talcum and dressed as a sugarplum, beribboned and velvet-bowed, she was driven alone to the princess's palace, there to be devoured by the princess's savage gaze as the tiny Alexandra, feet dangling high above the floor, rattled her enormous teacup nervously but managed never to spill a drop. Why her father had felt obliged to present his daughter for periodic inspection by the city's most notorious demimondaine while declining to associate with the woman himself ("When he's through with them, he's through," Praskovia had explained) had been one of the great questions of her childhood, but one she did not dare ask. The visits had ceased at about the time Alexandra began to lengthen to her present near-towering height, when the form of her features began to sharpen and shift toward an approximation of beauty that the princess, famous for her competitive vanity, apparently could not bear to see.

However terrifying a presence the princess was, however, she was acquainted with everyone of importance in the city and knew the labryinth of its social world inside out, though the fabled beauty that had assured the princess her place in society, had floated her up into the very cream at the top of the bottle, had surely faded by now. The princess had not been seen in public for quite some time, and Alexandra wondered if the ruin of her fantastic symmetry of form was the reason why. There had been rumors of an illness, but who knew if they were true?

The carriage stopped. Drawn up and out with a lift of Istvan's hand, Alexandra landed lightly on the pavement and looked up at the cold face of the palace, no warmer now than when she had stood before it as a child. Ushered into the vestibule by a dried old serf woman whom she also remembered from her childhood, Alexandra unwrapped her head, removed her gloves and coat, handed them to the serf, and waited as the old woman hurried up the stairs to announce her.

The countess's attention was drawn to an onyx bowl on a small gilt table, its purpose to receive the flurries of visiting cards whose "dropping" absorbed a great deal of aristocratic Petersburg's frivolous days. You dropped one on so-and-so, and he dropped one on you, and the cards, like flakes of snow, were dropping all over the city right now, right into these empty bowls, the height of the pile they made determining one's triumph on the social battlefield, or utter defeat. Curious to see who visited the princess, Alexandra drew out one of the stiff cards and was startled to see its edges had curled and browned with age. A name she did not recognize was printed on the card, a crown embossed underneath, and something illegible was scribbled in French on the back. Alexandra began to gather the cards from the bowl, each as weathered as the one before, and on them she recognized the names of the dead and their invitations to dances long over, to dinners long eaten, to afternoon garden parties in a long-faded sun.

Footsteps sounded on hard marble steps like light rain. It was the old serf, out of breath but alight with happiness that her princess was about to receive a guest. Alexandra dumped the cards back into the bowl and followed her.

What Alexandra saw in the room at the top of the stairs was not the princess, surely. But it was, of course. And for once the princess, seated proudly in the very same chair Alexandra remembered from the past—the long-ago past—did not smile with satisfaction that her own beauty was still supreme after casting that same appraising glance over the figure, now much larger, that stood before her.

Pleasantries. There were social pleasantries—the princess's issuing forth from a face more than faded, but half dead, and Alexandra secretly wondering when the tea would be brought and if there would be something to eat.

"The effects of a stroke," the princess said matter-of-factly, waving her hand in the direction of what was impossible to ignore. "I hope I don't frighten you, my dear."

Alexandra could not assure the princess that her fabled beauty was undisturbed, as would be required by social formula, so she merely shook her head and looked away, an uncomfortable smile appearing that she would have liked to direct at the princess, but which she could somehow not, so the smile remained a bit too long on her face and then died away into the silence that had descended on the room, which seemed suddenly enlarged and empty. A clock ticked weakly somewhere, and the two women, whose relation to each other was so irregular that there could be no social model to provide them a premade form to follow, sank into their own thoughts until both were revived by the sound of the serf's footsteps coming quickly down the hall, bringing tea.

"Why are you here?" the princess suddenly said in a hostile tone. The serf, leaning over the table where she was setting the tray, dropped her head in embarrassment at the princess's gaffe and looked sidelong at Alexandra, whose face had gone blank in surprise.

"Vain as I am—as I used to be, with reason—I am not so vain as to believe that you care anything about visiting a broken old woman like me," the princess went on. "There must be something that you want."

There was indeed, and Alexandra, shocked out of politeness, was just about to pour it all out when the princess, mindful of the servant, closed the young countess's opened mouth with a wave of her hand and shushed her, casting her one still moveable eye in the direction of the serf.

A few minutes later, when the servant had gone and Alexandra, tearful though her mouth was stuffed with jam-filled cakes and awash with cream tea, was unloading all her worries and concerns onto the princess's shrunken shoulders, so grateful for an open ear, the princess fixed her with that one cold eye and asked, "But why come to me?"

Alexandra swallowed and wiped her eyes with the edge of

her hand to prevent the messiness of powder-sugared fingers mixed with tears. She was about to explain when she thought better of it and simply sat silent, carefully holding her teacup, now normal-sized.

"I see," said the princess, her voice sharpening. "You cannot admit to me that my disreputable reputation makes me the perfect confidante."

It was true. Alexandra dropped her chin. Whom else could she tell? Whom else could she go to for aid? The entire success of her scheme rested on its secrecy. Alexandra's own closest friend, the Princess Andreyev, secure at the very pinnacle of the social world and padded too comfortably in money to worry over any possible fall, could certainly be trusted with the secret, but not with Alexandra's tattered pride. This was why Alexandra had refused all invitations from her friend, who had been eager, when the required period of mourning was over, to salve her grief with parties, balls, or intimate evenings by the fire with tea and crumpets from the English Shop (their favorite childhood treat). The Countess Korvin had sent back nothing but regrets, and Olga, kind as ever, had left Alexandra to her extended mourning, sympathetic to the countess's desire to remain apart and not guessing that the source of this desire was shame, embarrassment.

"I did not mean to insult you, Princess," said Alexandra.

"No matter. I've had worse. In my position."

And what position exactly would that be? The admission was surprising, and Alexandra wondered if it created an opening for questions she would like to know the answer to. She was eager to learn something of the princess's fabulous career of love, which had been set in motion by a beauty so flaming, so intense that its heat had generated a force powerful enough to propel the princess from the degradation of the brothel (so it was rumored) upward to the triumph of her present station, though it had been said, by Count Korvin himself, with bitterness, that the flame was cold to its core, its heat illusory, an intensification of ice that burned without warming.

There had been no prince, as everyone knew. The princess had simply appeared one day, dropped as if from the sky into the center of society, and begun collecting things along with hearts—carriages, horses, jewels. This very palace. Of course the princess claimed a husband, long dead, of great wealth and complete obscurity somewhere in the enormous south of the country—Armenia, perhaps, or Georgia—and everyone pretended to believe in his existence, for otherwise how could she be received at court? And she must be received. Her beauty demanded it. Her decorative quality was unsurpassed.

But no longer. The princess's flame was diminished, dying, and Alexandra suddenly wondered how much longer the princess could live without her beauty, which, it seemed, had formed her entire soul, because without it her once-great stature had folded down upon itself into the shape of a woman old before her time.

"I cannot help you," said the princess suddenly. "You must marry for love. As I did." And Alexandra saw that the woman had veiled herself again in lies, that there was nothing more to be gotten from her. She hadn't even had the chance to ask her the most important question of all. The audience was ending, the princess assuming the mantle of social convention.

However, the countess was not entirely correct in this assumption, as she was about to discover to her amazement.

"Before you go," said the princess, holding up a hand to keep Alexandra still and lifting the loud brass bell that she used to summon the deaf old serf, "walk over there, yes, to the table over there, and bring me that box."

Alexandra did as she was told and laid the ivory chest in the princess's lap.

"Now here, here," said the princess, rummaging in the box and pulling out a large velvet bag, which she opened and up-ended vigorously, "see how pretty."

There was a pattering sound of dried beans softly hitting the carpet, but what Alexandra saw there were brilliant fragments, bits of stone like the soft shattering of moonlight on moving water—diamonds, a mess of them on the floor and most likely of the finest quality.

"They're not mine any longer," said the princess, her mouth sagging sideways in defeat, "they're yours. You've won, you see, my girl. You've won."

"Won what?" said Alexandra, stunned.

"But I can't bear to make it easy, I can't bear that," the princess said, as if to herself. "Why, your father's heart, my dear, so long ago. And now you've got it all, you might as well have these too. So take them, take what's yours. I did, once. Get on your knees and pick them up."

However prideful she was, our young countess did not refuse to take the diamonds, but scrabbled as desperately on the carpet as any starving peasant digging for beets in the frozen ground, though she hated the princess more than ever for forcing her onto her knees. The diamonds would buy her ease from worry at the price of just a little of that pride, and who was there to see? Riding home triumphant in her carriage, Alexandra hefted the satisying weight of that crunching velvet bag and the years of comfortable independence it contained. But when the diamonds ran out, then what?

Better, she reasoned, to invest them in her future. Just a handful would buy her the most opulent of wardrobes for the coming social season, and now she would appear resplendent in the latest vogue instead of somewhat seedy in what she had planned before this windfall—the few dresses she had retained because they were too stained or worn to sell were to be recut, the few old bonnets reshaped, the old shoes resoled, work she'd started on already, sitting sewing with heavy thread and tiny cobbler's nails held hard between her teeth. But now she could throw those worn-out shoes away! Another precious stone and the box at the opera was reclaimed, a few more, and the horses reappeared in the stables munching softly on their dusty oats, and the carriages rolled again in the courtyard. All the outer trappings of her former wealth could be tacked up again to screen the enormous hole that had opened in her future and her past—the emptiness of the palace, restoration of its former glories requiring more than many handfuls of these gems.

But prudence asserted itself. Alexandra weighed the bag again with a lift of her hand. It was not so plump as all that. Better to leave the horses where they were and abandon the carriages by the road than to risk a single stone more than was necessary to accomplish her purpose. For how long would it take and how long would the diamonds hold out? The clothing, a new outfitting, was as far as she could go. Perhaps the box at the opera could be reclaimed, for appearance's sake, and that was all.

More particularly, she would need a chaperone, a sponsor, the princess having so rudely refused the task of presenting her at court, not even suggesting a suitable candidate to perform this service in her place. The next day Alexandra called for Trenyakov, who came immediately after breakfast, blinking sleepily, with a spot of butter on his tie that his mother (scrubbing dutifully with tongue between her teeth) had not been able to remove, so that the spot of grease remained in the center—like the ghost of his breakfast, Alexandra thought exuberantly when she rose to greet her lawyer.

He bent over her hand, straightened up, and answered her question after no more than a moment's thought. Not looking at her (but Trenyakov never looked at her directly, for whenever the impulse struck, his lids clamped down in a violent tic that expressed all the desperate shyness of his soul), he spoke.

"The woman you choose," he said, "must be an utter fool."

Alexandra looked at him with appreciation. How clever he was! She'd grasped his meaning instantly. Someone so obtuse, so scattered and distracted, she'd never notice the hollowness behind the showy surface, this Potemkin village of a show of wealth.

"Undoubtedly, the woman you want would be—"

"Madame Lavorine!" She finished his sentence.

A woman legendary for absurdity, Madame Lavorine for years now had enjoyed an unparalleled popularity among the Petersburg elite. It was impossible to be in her presence for more than five minutes without finding oneself possessed, in comparison to the ridiculous creature, of the greatest wit, the most acute judgment, the most blinding mental power. She was therefore deeply loved, invited everywhere, petted and praised, and her girlish curls shook with her giggles as she looked out over the shifting sea of admirers that lined up before her comfortable chair to pay respects.

So she came, in response to Alexandra's scribbled note on the cream-colored board engraved with the Korvin family crest (this lurid symbol, a screaming eagle with stiffened tongue protruding obscenely from its straining beak, had rather frightened Alexandra as a child, seeming to represent something about the world she as yet only dimly sensed). She came with her bouncing curls, trembling hands, and protruding, boiled eyes, dense with stupidity and social greed—for more distinguished invitations, more spectacular intimacies. The Countess Korvin would be a feather in her famous ruffled white cap.

Madame Lavorine sat on a stiff-backed chair across the tea table in the one reception room that Trenyakov had advised the countess to maintain in its original, opulent state and was stiff with desperate deference as Alexandra, sitting businesslike in the opposite chair, described to her the problem.

"I would," replied Madame Lavorine, "be most honored if I could be of some service to you, Countess, but why," she added, "call upon me? Surely there are other ladies of your circle who would be more suitable for your purposes?"

"Oh no," said Alexandra, raising her voice in an attempt to underline her sincerity, "no one could be more suitable," a sentiment Madame Lavorine accepted with delight, more readily than the princess, who had asked the same question but did not take its implied answer as a compliment.

"Well," said Madame, figuring, eyes wandering the ceiling above her head, "the season opens next month with the New Year's Ball at the Winter Palace. I will present you there." And so it was arranged. The Countess Korvin would be presented within the month. Once the season began, there would be engagements every day, and so all the preparations must be made beforehand, the fittings done at once. Alexandra spent the next month swimming in rivers of satin, suspended in clouds of tulle, washed by foamings of lace, but with aching feet and head.

Standing near the window in her small room late one afternoon and wearing nothing but her underclothes (the pantelets slightly yellowed but still quite serviceable), Alexandra gulped for breath as the brand-new corset gripped her waist in its bony fist and the dressmaker poked with pins and measured with tapes and gossiped like a gushing fountain spurting forth all the delicious secrets of her clients. But Alexandra was not really listening. She was looking out the window, where the sun—the exhausted red of a winter's dusk—was beginning to meld with the molten horizon, and the structures of the city, sketched in charcoal and standing out sharply against the smoldering clouds, were soon to be smeared and smudged to formlessness. A man in a deformed old student's cap loitered below by the river, a silhouette cut from the terrifying sky. He stared down at the black river as if considering a leap inside its annihilating waters, and Alexandra wondered what he might have done in his life to warrant such an impulse, what guilt might have driven him to contemplate that act, or what misery she could not comprehend.

"And then he took her to Café Paris," the dressmaker was saying, driving a pin into Alexandra's side so that the countess caught her breath, "where they took a private room and did not come out until the morning. Luckily her husband had been out all night himself with that dancer and didn't come home until eight, which was two hours later." The dressmaker jerked hard to bring two seams together tight as skin, and Alexandra's head bobbled lightly on its stalk.

"But then it turns out the blackguard Ulyanov was through with the countess anyway because," the dressmaker went on, words squeezing out among the pins she gripped between her teeth, "the next night she sees him at the Europa with one of her very own maids, dropping oysters down the girl's silly throat. Naturally, she drags the stupid creature home again, but only to throw her out so she can walk the street the way she deserves, and then the countess gets her pistol . . . "

Alexandra had seen the man in the cap before, standing in the same spot staring down at the river, and he all alone seemed to represent the great seething mass in the darkness below, the nameless ones whose thin lives melted inside the city like paper gone to pieces in the water. In the system of cheap lodgings that honeycombed the city, in those dark warrens of the poor, reeking meals of nameless boiled things were devoured in half darkness while the million voices groaned and sighed and wept.

The dressmaker, crouching on the floor to pin the hem, was rattling on. ". . . then Ulyanov rips open the door, bold as you please, and climbs right in the carriage, where the countess sticks the pistol in his gut—with pleasure, she told me—about to blow a hole in him the size of the one that got our dear and sainted Pushkin, causing his belly to swell to the size of a horse's rump before he died of the putrid gas, and that wife of his, Natalya, playing the modest widow as if it weren't her fault in the first place, what a slut! And do you know that she padded her bosoms? I know, because I made her gowns myself. She also had very big feet. So anyway, the countess is about to pull the trigger and really enjoying herself at the thought of how he'll suffer, when he grabs it! And grabs her too! And well, apparently, they were in that carriage all afternoon again and all's forgiven, even though I told her—"

"Stop," the countess whispered as she tottered gray-faced on her heels, about to faint. The dressmaker gaped upward past the long expanse of satin skirt, and Praskovia the serf, who had been perching on top of the stove that warmed the room, dropped to the floor and began a menacing advance while Alexandra plucked frantically at slippery satin to try to free herself of the suffocating tightness of the gown.

"You," said the serf, jerking the dressmaker onto her feet. The trembling woman, who did not know what she had done, knelt again and began to gather her things as the serf stood over her, continuing her tirade. "Stop filling the little countess with your filth," Praskovia shouted, though she herself had been enjoying the story immensely and was hoping for more explicit details, even filthier, which she begged as soon as she had closed the door behind them, details the dressmaker happily provided as Praskovia led her past the doors of the palace, cleverly closed against any prying eyes, and down the hall to the servants' staircase at the back.

The dress lay puddled, shining, on the floor, but its bodice, stiff with silver encrustations, stood up on its own, an elaborate empty form. Alexandra quickly loosened her stays, breathed deeply, relieved, and wiped her hot forehead. The hours of standing on her feet and the unending clatter and chatter of the dressmaker's tongue had made her temples pound. The whole process of these fittings was a torment. Careful with her aching head, Alexandra lay down on the cot she used for a bed in this shabby room, which she hoped the dressmaker had not realized was the countess's very bedroom and boudoir, in which she had been living, a mouse in a hole, for nearly this whole last year while her beautiful bedroom, large as a ballroom, stood empty far below, stripped of its painted paper, its silk hangings, its carvings, its mirrors, its baubles of silver and gold. She lifted her arm and applied it to her forehead, hoping to soothe herself, but not succeeding.

Christmas was coming, but it would not be the extravaganza of past years, the rooms of the palace drenched in scarlet ribbons, swimming in points of golden light, soaked through with the scent of wintry forest and of smoking food, but a shadow of the holiday, an empty outline. Still, the day must be marked, honored in some small way, and so she had determined at least to purchase a goose, a small one, prudence-sized. Perhaps an extra potato or two. A few nuts. An orange for each member of the household—herself, Praskovia, and Matryona, the two serfs she hadn't sold, though their squabbling made her doubt the wisdom of that act. And Istvan, who did not live at the palace but spent his days there, ate his meals in the kitchen. There would be but a taste of Christmas this year for this much-reduced household, one frugal mouthful—and how long would it be before those reassuring bits of glittering stone vanished like snowflakes on water one by one, disappeared one by one like the household serfs she had sold one by one, and she was herself pulled under to poverty, tumbled and tossed and swept away to melt inside the city's teeming tide?

On a January night sometime in the great Russian century, Alexandra held herself carefully as she rode through the icebound winter streets, her stiff carapace of silver, pearl, and crystal tinkling and crunching with every bump of the hired conveyance as it fought its way among the other conveyances all heading toward the colossal glow that filled the sky above the city.

As she stepped down from the carriage into the sunlike dazzle of the Winter Palace, the countess seemed to shrink to the scale of an insect—an ant, a gnat, a dragonfly in her iridescent veils—joining the mass of other tiny creatures that swarmed at the base of the white, blue, and gold façade, streamed through its mighty doors, skittered across the shining floor, and began their buzzing, whirring ascent into the airy upper regions of the palace. Russia lived here, and the building had been constructed with that very fact in mind.

Madame Lavorine toddled and wheezed at Alexandra's side, struggling up the endless stairs. While they climbed with all the others, the older woman pointed out to her charge many of the more prominent personalities of Petersburg and, savoring each unsavory detail, whispered their disgraceful stories in the direction of Alexandra's ear. Why, there goes Princess Sherbatkin in a fascinating creation surely by the House of Larin—a gown of skintight flesh-colored silk appliquéd with artificial autumn leaves encrusted with a frost of diamonds. See how her graceful body sways like a tree in the October wind! The princess, though, was seldom seen in the capital, preferring to spend her time at German spas or Italian villas where the supply of dark-meat, dark-eyed peasant boys was plentiful and fresh, a most refreshing change for a palate wearied by pallid Slavs.

Alexandra, who was watching the undulant backside work its way up the stairs ahead of her, failed to see the romance in the sight of a woman gotten up like a tree, but perhaps, she thought, she should be more flexible in her judgments.

"And there's Count Parsegian." He was stuffed like force-meat into the casing of his white uniform, the cleft of his back-side markedly visible under the fabric. "Don't you know of him, Countess?"

Alexandra, watching plump haunches tightening and loosen-ing, fatly jiggling as the spurs on his polished boots and the medals on his tunic jingled gaily, didn't and didn't want to. He was a man of rather specialized tastes, Madame Lavorine explained, who was said to enjoy the charms of "fat boys" like himself. In search of these plump young men, he roamed the cap-ital and the countryside in his carriage with a cooperative coach-man, and though frustrated by a recent famine in the neighbor-ing provinces, he was willing to work closely with whomever might show potential of reaching the desired state of portliness. To this end he had imported the finest chefs of France, who ded-icated their art entirely to rich cream sauces poured over heavy meats, and milk desserts fortified with sugar and nuts to increase their fattening power. Why, the count's guests were likely to encounter at least one of the count's protégés at any time, con-suming diligently under his patron's affectionate eye.

"Charming," said Alexandra.

"And there's General Kropotkin." *He* kept a second family by one of his serfs, with whom he lived quietly in a parody of respectability, in bed at nine each night with his glass of warm sugared milk and his sunburned serf woman plumping his pillows while his other wife and family in the house across the street gazed mournfully at the empty seat at the head of the dinner table and said nothing. And Dr. Marsinko, known for his comprehensive collection of pornography, which, after dinner, his male guests would sneak up the back staircase to take an eager peek at. And Countess Rogatov, who had had a son by her cossack footman, a fine strong boy!

Hundreds of backsides ascending the stairs, all of Petersburg, it seemed, displaying its exuberant salaciousness in a crowd of jiggling, wriggling behinds.

"Don't you know any nice stories?" the countess hissed to Madame Lavorine as they rounded an enormous corner and started down a mirrored hallway, their slippers clicking sharply on the diamond-hard floor.

Madame Lavorine, who didn't appear to have heard her, went on with her recital, but Alexandra had stopped listening, her ears attuned to the sound of babble that flowed faster and faster toward her as she was carried on the rushing tide toward the ballroom.

As she confronted the entrance to this enormous room, Alexandra's eyes, accustomed to the soft candlelight in the hallway, were assaulted by the blinding glare of noon, her eardrums pierced by a thousand voices chattering loudly. Her lids snapped down. Her hands twitched as she resisted the impulse to cover her ears. She swayed, as if about to faint, and steadied herself with a gripping hand on the older woman's shoulder. Burned into the insides of her eyelids were strange imprints, odd shapes: dark-glittering waterfalls suspended in the air, titantic trees of ebony, natives roasted black by a tropical sun. But these colors reversed themselves when she confronted them with open eyes, and all was white chandeliers and white pillars and ordinary Russians white as winter.

The women, coldly jeweled and gleaming like reptiles, were slithering through the crowd, while the men, just as cold, were raptorlike, with crested, beaklike helmets tucked under their arms, their chests slick with ribboned decorations or heavy plates of gold embroidery that signified their rank at court. Alexandra wondered what comfort these slippery, scaly creatures could find in each other's arms, what softness in either sex.

Although she was herself safely armored in her stiff, encrusted gown, the young countess hesitated. She stood still in the doorway, looking confused, and though Madame Lavorine urged her forward with a well-intentioned poke in the small of her hardplated back, the countess did not budge an inch. The veil that streamed and floated out behind her, required of all ladies at court, seemed to her an obscene parody of bridehood, and none of the men who skittered and buzzed across the floor seemed in the least appealing, seemed obscene as well, unnatural. Her feet shifted beneath her, ready to turn and run. The serfs would be sitting in the darkened kitchen, safe in their warm circle of light from the oil lamp above their heads, and perhaps there was something nice and dark baking in the oven—a loaf of moist black bread, a plum cake with those ovals of soft purple pulp embedded in its eggy sweetness—or they were still mixing and melding with butter, eggs, and sugar, and they would offer her a taste from their thick fingers, as they used to do when she reached up on tiptoe to see inside the bowl.

"You're making a spectacle of yourself," said Madame Lavorine, prodding her again. "Go in, go in."

The featureless enameled faces of the ballroom were turning toward her, their scrutiny multiplied in the mirrors a thousandfold. But now one of these faces shifted shape, took on features, and the countess saw her friend the Princess Andreyev lift her arm and wave from far away across the hall. Comforted, relieved, the countess stepped inside the room, but her horror was only renewed, for Olga herself, friend of her childhood, did not look Olga-like at all. As the princess, head down, the hem of her heavy skirt slightly lifted for unimpeded movement, was making her way through the maze of bodies on the floor, she appeared suddenly to Alexandra as a stranger and, like a stranger, was perceived not as an entire whole impression of a personality, but as a disparate collection of physical traits. Alexandra, seeing in her a rival in the fight for marriageable men, could not stop herself from comparing Olga's attractions with her own.

Is she prettier than I am? Alexandra asked herself, her anxiety mounting. More graceful? Better built? Are her hands as fine? Her neck as long? Alexandra was horrified at these questions, but unable to control the direction of her thoughts. The creamy pinkness of Olga's cheeks, which had always suggested to Alexandra that her friend breakfasted regularly on roses, was now envied rather than admired. The lustrous dark hair, subject of many compliments from the countess on long summer afternoons of earnest girlish talk, looked so much more striking than her own pale locks that it made the countess grind her teeth. However, the fact that Olga's waist was clumsy filled her with an ugly joy. The shortness of Olga's neck was also reassuring.

Oh, once they had been the truest friends! Meeting at first at children's parties, they'd approached each other awkwardly, probing for the thread between them that they sensed was there already. A common dislike for Kolya Rittenberg, discovered, caused a wrinkling of their small noses at the mention of his name, which name they repeated to each other rhythmically until they'd attained a kind of hysterical joy. The revelation that frosted tea cakes looked like snowballs was shared, and this strengthened their bond, which was then cemented by Olga's observation that if one rode on a snow-white horse through the snow dressed in white, one would be invisible—a stunning fact that convinced the child Alexandra that here was a mind to be cherished and explored.

Now Olga snatched up her gleaming skirts in both of her tiny hands and ran the last few steps, but skidded on the slippery polished floor and whoops! was caught in Alexandra's arms. She was awkward Olga again, and beautiful for that.

"So glad! You're out at last! Been . . . so long!" said Olga, out of breath. Bobbing to Madame Lavorine, she seized Alexandra's hand and pulled. "Come. You must come now. There's someone for you to meet!" Back across the floor they went, Olga with hiked-up skirts dragging at the white-gloved hand she gripped in hers, Alexandra trotting, pulling back against her, mouth moving quickly, protesting, laughing. Madame Lavorine toddled after them.

And there he was. O sweet Olga, to introduce her to such a man! To choose him for her, as if she understood it all. How had Olga known what she was looking for? That she was looking for anyone at all?

Standing beside Olga's father, the Prince Andreyev, with his noble, graying head, was this other man entirely, a man who clearly looked down at the world from the height of a superior perch, a man of a perfection so exalted that he seemed another order of being entirely and not a man at all. A glittering star studded his gold-embroidered chest, a mark of his distinction, and his elegant torso was bisected by the black and orange ribbon of the most prestigious order of the empire.

Alexandra bobbed to the prince and turned in the direction of the man so quickly that she teetered on her heels and put out a hand to steady herself, which the man immediately, chivalrously, grasped. Bending over her white-gloved fingers, he caught her eyes in his. His lips opened in a smile and showed glowing, perfect teeth.

"State Councilor Gregor Rybynsky," said the prince, and Alexandra knew at once by the way the old prince said the name that this man was intended for Olga, not for herself, as she had thought in that first fraction of a moment, and she wanted him even more.

A pair of tremendous doors at one end of the ballroom creaked slowly open, and the inhabitants of the ballroom stopped rustling, chattering, laughing, gossiping, flirting, and criticizing their friends. They fell silent. A tiny man appeared in gorgeous costume, banged three times on the floor with a golden rod, and the orchestra began to play "God Save the Tsar." Then the crowd was in motion again as the assemblage stood on tiptoe, stretched their necks.

The imperial family flowed out from the darkness. Small sparkling objects, they seemed to be made entirely of crystal, as if they looked out at the world from behind a protective plating of glass. These miniature people mounted the steps of the dais and settled into their seats beside the throne. Above the silk-hung dais, the double-headed eagle—emblem of the empire—hovered, shimmering as it struggled with titanic golden wings to hold its tremendous weight aloft, and its wings shifted the air in the ballroom, so a cold wind blew at the hair and faces of the thousand nobles. The veils of the women lifted, floated a moment round their heads, and settled down again. The tsar and his empress now seated themselves on their thrones, and, sensing this movement, the eagle turned its heads, slowly revolved these giant structures to fix on the imperial pair its lidless, doubled eyes. It stretched its crippled talons out; its beaks began to strain, to open wide, its tongues to vibrate, throats to swell with rage.

But it is not yet time. And so the dancing music began.

When Rybynsky did not ask the Countess Korvin to dance but instead went to Olga, Alexandra stood sullen beside Prince Andreyev and stared as the couple took their places on the floor. The old prince, who had known Alexandra from childhood, began to chat amiably in her direction but, finding a distracted response, retired after a few minutes of disconnected talk, settled back into his gold-embroidered chair, and took stealthily from his pocket the miniature card game he had brought to play with. Alexandra stood at the edge of the dance floor sweating lightly, her crackling bodice feeling unbearably tight, wondering if her dress might be too tastelessly elaborate, her headdress too vulgarly aglitter with diamant and pearls of paste, aching at the sight of Olga in her perfect gown, Olga with her perfect man as they pranced through the stately polonaise.

But Alexandra was not stranded long. The polonaise had ended, and she was trying to catch Rybynsky's eye, hoping he would ask her for the next of the dances, when she perceived in another area of her vision a white figure coming closer. Golden epaulets shimmered vaguely, along with a uniform of the cleanest white, indicating an officer of the Imperial Guard. She dropped her head to see the glittering buckles on his shoes and raised her eyes again as a white-gloved hand opened in her direction.

"May I?" said the gentleman, bowing low to Madame Lavorine, and then to her, while the older woman introduced him by a complicated name that the countess was too distracted to catch.

"I'd rather not. If you don't mind," said Alexandra sweetly. The next dance had not yet begun, and perhaps Rybynsky would come over after all. She stared over the stiff gold shoulder board of the man with the complicated name and concentrated hard, trying to send a mental message to the councilor that she wanted very badly that he should take some notice of her. But he seemed to be intending to give Olga the coming waltz—they were standing on the dance floor still.

The officer, rejected, looked surprised. "At a ball, one must dance," he said.

Alexandra smiled her excuses. The officer murmured his regrets. Alexandra could feel the chill from Madame Lavorine but didn't care. She watched the officer, Prince Something, walk slowly away, as if looking for a place to slot himself inside the crowd. She felt sorry for him, but why waste time? He was much too short for her. There was something about him, though, that interested her—an air of distinction, nobility, purity of heart—and she was curious to see what he would do. He hesitated a moment, then joined a conversational group composed of men in stars and sashes. A heavyset young man in spectacles came rushing up to him, grabbed his arm, murmured something into his ear, and indicated with his shoulder the presence of a girl standing not far away. The girl, very young, looked unhappy and somewhat wilted, though still fresher than the rose that decorated the tight dark swirl of her up-turned hair, and she seemed, in her embarassment at appearing *décolletée* at what was clearly her very first ball, as pure as the white of her simple dress, her breasts merely a breath, a suggestion of the fuller womanhood to come. Alexandra envied the girl her freshness—at twenty-three, the countess herself was considered slightly faded, having sat too long on the shelf in strong sunlight, so to speak—and Alexandra watched with a pang of regret as the officer in white approached the young girl, who raised frightened eyes but allowed him to slip his arm about her waist and lead her to the floor.

"What have you done?" hissed Madame Lavorine. "When a man like that asks you to dance, you say, 'Yes, please.' "

Alexandra was affronted at Lavorine's presumptuousness. She stared at the little woman. Lavorine lowered her head before the imperious glare and trembled, bit her lip. Nevertheless, Alexandra would now take care to avoid looking so often in Rybynsky's direction, for fear that Lavorine might notice and comment on *that,* and it would not do for her interest in him to become material for Lavorine's foolish tongue.

"Well," said Madame Lavorine cheerfully, bouncing back, "no matter. You will certainly have many chances, a young lady as lovely as you. A young *countess,* that is. Forgive me." Eager to restore the young noblewoman's goodwill after her slip, she began to fuss with Alexandra's hair, to exclaim over its thickness, its smoothness, until Alexandra jerked her head away.

Lavorine ignored the second insult and rubbed her hands. "There's someone special I would like you to meet," she said. "Forget the other. You were right, absolutely right to refuse his invitation to the dance. He's prideful, disdainful, arrogant, conceited. Everyone says it."

No matter, thought Alexandra; the waltz had begun and she had missed her chance. Rybynsky and Olga were whirling round the floor.

"He's an older man, a widower, very lonely, very rich," Lavorine explained as they began to make their way across the ballroom, strolling its outer edges while the older woman bowed right and left to those she knew, stopped to chat, and she knew everyone, so their journey was long. Not so foolish as Alexandra and her lawyer believed, Madame Lavorine had guessed instantly the young countess's predicament and her requirements and, hoping it would improve her own prospects if she could make a lucrative match for the girl and obligate the couple to herself, had marked out a number of wealthy subjects as possible candidates for the appealing young countess's hand. But especially this one.

"Count Kolygin," Madame Lavorine announced when they had reached the man, when he had turned around, "may I present . . ."

Oh dear, thought Alexandra, much too old.

Count Kolygin was actually quite an attractive man and certainly still serviceable, even handsome in his wan, worn, melancholy way. But Alexandra, clasped in his arms on the dance floor, did not listen to a word he said. What attractions he might have possessed paled in the distant glow of Rybynsky's perfection, and so to whatever he said to her while dancing she replied blandly, generally, not caring if her answers matched his questions and secretly hoping that her obvious indifference would discourage him completely.

But she did not have time to discover whether or not this was so, for when the count led her back toward her waiting chaperone, there was already another candidate at Madame Lavorine's side, ready for presentation to the young woman. Having seen the countess's barely disguised disdain of Kolygin, and her refusal to dance with the well-connected, brilliant prince, Lavorine had marked her as a pretty tough customer, a hard sell. But still she tried, bringing forward to face the countess's determined indifference the young, the old, the dull, the bright—but all of them rich. Occasional glances in her direction from the magnificent Rybynsky excited Alexandra to extravagant heights of rejection, refusal, resistance as she turned up her nose at even the handsomest and youngest, finding, perhaps, a nose that was too highly arched, a hairline too obviously thinning, or eyes a hint too close together to compete with Rybynsky's perfection.

However, she danced with every one of them until the soles of her feet, rubbed raw, felt as if the skin were coming off in strips, until her throat was dry and her belly empty. Alexandra hid from her latest suitor, one Count Myznikov, by concealing herself behind a potted palm and then adding herself to the grouping of the fabulous Ouspensky sisters, all six of them standing in a row like pearls of graduated size but identical shape. The countess was confident that Myznikov, who had weak eyes and wore spectacles, would not distinguish her from them, which he did not. She watched as his eyes wandered over the crowd until he shook his head and walked away.

Alexandra immediately made her way to the buffet. Holding her plate, her silverware, and her napkin, she bent greedily over the table, surveying the iced delicacies with smoke-burned eyes, deciding which to choose and wondering how much she could pile on her plate without incurring the disapproval of the social arbiters, who were watching from all their chairs in all the corners of the room. The liver puree looked good, rich and eggy, but it had been molded in the shape of the Russian eagle, and the countess was reluctant to be the first to attack and dismember it, not wishing to be considered unpatriotic. There were poached eggs floating in burgundy wine, and they looked delicious, these little islands of white in their wine-dark sea, but she was certain the wine would make her bilious, and her bodice was so tight she didn't want to risk it. There were also assorted cold meats, sliced and arranged to form the peaks and valleys of the Caucasus Mountains, pale breads, dark pickles, and an enormous sturgeon with its belly eaten out so that its spine was exposed, but with still quite a load of meat on it—the fish must have weighed a hundred pounds.

"The sturgeon is delicious," said a voice at her side. "Why don't you try it? Let me help you."

Alexandra jumped so suddenly her silver knife and fork clattered on the china plate. "I *beg* your pardon," she said.

"No need to beg my pardon," said the man's voice in a tone that had something faintly insulting about it, something she could not put her finger on. "When one is as beautiful as you, anything is acceptable."

"It is you who should beg *my* pardon," said Alexandra, though there was that something in his voice that indicated to her that she shouldn't be speaking to him at all, "since you addressed me without an introduction first."

She knew she really ought to walk away, but she was curious. What was it about his voice? Why did it offend her? However, she did not want him to know that he had excited any sort of interest, any thought or response at all. This would only encourage him, opening her to further and deeper incursions into acquaintance with someone she was sure must be in some ineffable way . . . unsavory. It was not entirely true that he could not address her at a ball without an introduction, but she'd said it anyway. It was that something in his tone, that . . . too-familiarity! That was it!

Still, she was curious. She wanted to see what the man behind the insinuating voice was like. Glancing up at the mirror behind the table, she flicked her glance in his direction and was caught. His reflection smiled at her.

She turned instantly round so that her back was to the mirror.

A hussar, of course. And what a peacock! With his spit-polished boots, his thighs decorated with whorls of gold embroidery as if to celebrate this part of his anatomy and draw attention to that something in between them, with the neck and sleeves and bottom of his tunic where it met his crotch all roughly furred in a border of extra-masculine hairiness, with the shoulder boards exaggerating the width of his shoulders and plaques of gold braid marking the male flatness of his chest, he was positively offensive. As was his oozing manner.

Madame Lavorine was making frantic signals from across the room. Alexandra hurried toward her, still carrying her empty plate.

"Oh my dear," the woman whispered, gripping her charge's arm, "you mustn't be seen speaking to him at all."

"Why's that?" Alexandra asked, sensing the answer, but wanting to hear the details.

"It's Mecklenburg-Ulyanov. The dissolute. The rake. And he hasn't a ruble to his name, at least not rubles that really count."

"Then what's he doing here?"

"His mother was a Mecklenburg, so unfortunately he has to be invited everywhere. Which only gives him further scope for his activities."

Alexandra, to whom the name was vaguely familiar, searched her memory. Ah yes, the oysters, the revolver, the countess and her maid. Fascinated, she resolved to watch, wishing to see the rake ply his trade amongst the women at the ball, but she was unfortunately frustrated in this ambition by a commotion that was taking place in the center of the room.

Someone who did not belong had appeared among them. The crowd gave him a wide berth, moving back and away. Alexandra herself stepped back, but she was still close enough to be frightened by the eeriness of the transparent eyes, incandescent with visions, and to smell his feral odor, and to see the light from the chandeliers glancing off the slick and oily scalp, from which unraveled skeins of tangled hair, black as the fur of a bear. A dirty peasant blouse hung from his starving frame, and broken peasant boots were on his feet. Slyly he looked about him at the assembled nobles, then opened his mouth and cried:

"Again I say, a terrible storm cloud hangs over Russia, disaster, grief, murky darkness and no light. A whole ocean of tears, there is no counting them and so much blood. The disaster is great, the misery infinite."

His shouts were still resounding through the hall when the crowd began in one motion to chatter again, to laugh, to flirt, to criticize their friends, to eat and drink. He does not belong here; it is much too soon for him. Finding no response to his anguished warning, he melted into the crowd and disappeared.

The moon was still white in the tall winter sky when Alexandra, barely tired, returned from the ball so late that it was early. Climbing the stairs to her bedroom, dragging her skirts heavily up each separate step, Alexandra listened with pleasure to the soft sounds her dancing shoes made in the spaciousness of the hollow palace. She had taken off her headdress in the carriage, impatient with its weight, and she held it in her hand as she ascended, the veil that floated behind her forming a layer of morning mist through which she seemed to be wading.

Praskovia was sleeping on the floor in front of the room Alexandra now called her own. The countess prodded the rug-wrapped bundle with the pointed tip of her silk shoe, and Praskovia sat up grimacing.

"Where's that Matryona? Get *her* to help you. She's supposed to be the lady's maid," said the serf.

But Matryona was nowhere to be found, as was usual—probably sleeping on the floor in the kitchen in front of the low fire—and Alexandra was too tired to wait for Praskovia to go and get her. Mumbling her complaints and adjusting her head scarf, which had been forced down over her eyes during her sleep, Praskovia followed her mistress into the tiny room.

"Praskovia, tell me," said the countess as the serf loosened the strings that held the bodice tight around her waist, "how do you make a man fall in love with you?" Praskovia, who had already buried two husbands though still relatively young, ought to know.

"Well, little mistress," said the serf, "it's quite simple. You

simply act as though you think he's the most wonderful man in
the world, but you don't care if you never see him again. They
love it, can't get enough." While the countess held each arm out
straight, the serf tugged at the fingertips of both of the white
kid gloves and then skinned the long pieces of papery leather
from Alexandra's arms.

"But why would they like that?" said the countess, pulling
her arms out of her flaring, fortified sleeves so that the bodice,
now split in back but still holding its tubular shape, flopped forward. "Wouldn't they rather prefer to be treated as though they
were the most wonderful in the world and you wanted to see
them all the time?" Praskovia pulled the gown down around her
mistress's thighs and Alexandra stepped carefully out of it.

"Oh goodness no," said Praskovia from behind her, now loos-
ening the strings of the corset. "You see, they want your attention every minute, but when they get it, they get tired of it. If
you make them fight for your attention, and only give it sometimes, they're happy as little pigs with apples. If we gave our pigs
apples every day, would they be happy? No, they would turn up
their noses and squeal for something even better."

Thinking, Alexandra stood half nude in the center of her
room, rubbing her fingers up and down in the long grooves the
bones of the corset had cut into her flesh. She shivered in the
cold, though the stove was lit. Praskovia knelt and began to strip
the countess's stockings from her legs, rolling the fabric down
toward the ankles, and Alexandra rested a hand on the serf's
shoulder as she lifted one foot and then the other. Her slippers
hit the floor where Praskovia tossed them.

"But Praskovia, what if you think he really *is* the most wonderful man in the world? How do you pretend you don't?"

Praskovia slipped the yellowed nightgown Matryona had set
out for the mistress over the waiting head (at least the lazy

Matryona had done *that*). She prodded Alexandra over toward the bed, threw back the covers, and settled her inside it.

"Practice," she replied, vigorously stuffing the covers round Alexandra's shoulders so that she was packaged good and tight and ready for sleep.

However, Alexandra was not ready for the night to end. She wished it could go on and on. Praskovia was already snoring outside the door, but the countess turned on her side, propped her cheek on her hand, and looked at the moon, which had come up close to the window and seemed to be looking inside. Alexandra threw open the covers, leaped from her bed, and ran toward it, but the moon backed away, receding into the distance, and Alexandra, fingertips resting on the frosty glass, looked down at the empty winter street below. Or not so empty. The man was loitering there again at the edge of the river, his misshapen cap visible against the lightening sky. He was not facing the river this time but had turned in the direction of the Korvin palace. Alexandra could not see his face from the window. It was hidden from her, tucked under his cap, as if he were looking deep inside himself. Then he raised his head, looked up, looked right at her. To him, in the graying light of just before the dawn, the figure in the window high above, with its colorless hair and misty raiment, seemed an emanation of his anguish, a visible haunting. He drew back his lips in a rictus of pain, and, head down, hurried on his way.

Oh, but Rybynsky had danced with her at last. Feeling his arms around her waist again, she blushed and pressed her cheek against the glass, which was cold and still smelled of the stars that had already vanished in the milky morning sky.

Her appearance at the imperial ball was adjudged a resounding success. At least this seemed to be the case from the flurry of invitations that now blanketed the Korvin palace. In the hope of seeing Rybynsky, Alexandra accepted every one, and although he did not appear at any of the dinners, dances, teas, musicales, or evening card parties she attended in the next week or so, the possibility of his sudden advent, at any time, in any place, created around these small events an atmosphere of unbearable suspense. All of her surroundings, the entire city, glowed with his unseen presence—somewhere. And Alexandra, rushing toward her next occasion in her carriage, would sink deeper under the load of heavy furs, safe in the bath of warmth that reached up to her neck, and exult in the iciness of the air against her face, opening her mouth to taste on her tongue the flakes of snow that fluttered down from the heavy sky and wet her eyelashes delightfully.

Old Istvan, the Hungarian coachman, who always seemed to have a cold, would be snuffling and squeaking to himself in his odd native tongue (the harsh and alien language of insects, she had always thought) as he pursued an imaginary quarrel with his wife, all the while punctuating his more important points by blowing mucus loudly into the sleeves of his enormous coat. And even this made Alexandra happy.

One day several weeks after the ball, Alexandra was standing in the front hallway taking off her wraps, her sealskin coat, after returning from a luncheon. She had no engagements in the afternoon and was looking forward to a quiet cup of tea and a long rest before the evening's ball when Praskovia came running out of the kitchen.

"Another one!" cried the serf, brandishing the white paper in the air as if in triumph, proud that her mistress was so popular, a fact that would do a great deal to restore her standing among the other household serfs of the city, who assigned rankings based on the number and quality of invitations received by their masters.

Impatient to know whom it was from, Praskovia snatched a chair from its place by the wall, slammed it into the center of the hall, and pressed her mistress into it. She took up her place behind the chair and thrust the invitation into the countess's hand.

"It's from Olga," Alexandra said as Praskovia settled her chin on her mistress's shoulder. "Are you ready?"

Praskovia nodded, digging her chin into Alexandra's collarbone several times. Praskovia could not read, but she enjoyed trying to match the letters she recognized with the sounds her mistress made when she pronounced the words.

"It was good to see you at the ball," Alexandra read out loud, pronouncing each word with careful clarity and showing Praskovia with her finger how each written mark corresponded to a sound.

"It was good to see you at the ball," Praskovia repeated solemnly, proud of her fluency.

"I'm having a skating party tomorrow afternoon at three."

Praskovia repeated these words to herself firmly and slowly.

"I'm hoping you can come."

Alexandra realized that since this invitation was from Olga, it was likely that Rybynsky, Olga's "special friend," would certainly be in attendance at the party. Suddenly, she felt Praskovia's presence as an intrusion, and although it made no sense to hide a letter from one who could not read, she shielded the rest of the note from Praskovia's eyes and finished it silently. Praskovia, insulted, flounced across the hallway and slammed a door behind her.

Alexandra suspected Praskovia could learn to read properly if she really wished to. These reading lessons had been going on for many years, and Alexandra was beginning to wonder if they weren't just an excuse to be nosy, since Praskovia's reading was never practiced on books or newspapers, but only on social correspondence. As if Alexandra didn't tell her everything in any case.

The door opened a crack and Alexandra saw a section of Praskovia's face.

"There's not much more, all right?" said the countess. "Just where the party's going to be. All right?"

Praskovia opened the door wider. "Where is it, then?"

"It's at Olga's! Where else would it be? We'll be skating on the river out in front."

"Where's that?"

Alexandra, irritated, told Praskovia that she knew very well the location of Andreyev palace. She had been allowed to accompany her mistress there many times in order to pursue her "friendship" with one of the Andreyevs' stable boys. Praskovia protested that she did not remember ever having been there, that she would love to see the splendors of this famous building, and that she was not aware of any stable boy at all.

"You did too go there," said Alexandra, pointing out that she had been there on countless occasions and that there had indeed been a stable boy who, by the way, had been much too young for her.

Praskovia pulled the knot of her colored kerchief even tighter under her chin as if to emphasize the importance of the issue. "I need to go again, "she said, "to refresh my memory. I'm sure Matryona can describe every room in detail, she's been there so many more times than me. How come you never take me? How come you always take Matryona?"

Actually, this was quite true. The countess had indeed brought Matryona to Andreyev palace far more often, but the younger serf was her personal maid, and a lady always took her personal maid along to any sort of event (except for dancing) that involved physical exertion, or any kind of athletic activity, to stand by with needle and thread to repair rips in clothing, or to carry extra equipment like shoes or skates, towels, smelling salts, cologne, perhaps an umbrella in case it started to rain. This privilege meant a great deal to Matryona, and if Alexandra took Praskovia instead this time, there was no telling what the repercussions might be. Matryona was of a spiteful temperament. The result could be something truly ugly.

"What if I send you along with Istvan to Olga's to let her know I'll come? That way you can refresh your memory quite well."

"I'll only get to see the outside," said Praskovia. "If I went with you tomorrow for the party, I'd get to sit in the kitchen and maybe Oksana would show me around."

"What if I let you come in the sledge with us tomorrow and then come back with Istvan to pick us up? I can't bring you both."

This concession indicated weakness. Praskovia, sensing victory, set her mouth more sullenly than before and allowed tears to form in her eyes, reaching up theatrically to wipe at them.

"All right," said the countess. "You can both come."

"Matryona always gets to go by herself," Praskovia stated flatly.

"So you won't share with Matryona?"

"Does Matryona share with me?"

The booming bells of the city had just rung three that next day when Alexandra climbed up into the sledge. How she missed her red troika! (The third horse the troika required would have strained her budget more than the two-horse droshky, and so the beautifully painted thing had been sold). Praskovia, eager to justify her presence at her mistress's side, fussed so violently with the countess's fur robes that Alexandra pushed her away. From a window upstairs, the defeated Matryona gazed down at the little party in the carriage with open malice, and Alexandra knew that she would pay for this infraction of Matryona's "rules." However, Alexandra was forced to admit to herself that she had quite deliberately, by taking Praskovia in Matryona's stead, stirred up the hornet's nest that was Matryona's mind, always buzzing with imaginary grievances and intricate plans for revenge. She was curious to see what would happen. And too, Matryona had been especially lazy and sullen of late. Perhaps she ought to transfer some of Matryona's other favorite duties to Praskovia as well, just to keep things on the boil.

The conflict was of many years' standing and had been going on so long that Alexandra could no longer remember its beginning. Like rival countries, the two women existed in a permanent state of psychological war, which only occasionally broke out into open conflict (when Praskovia dropped a boiled carp onto Matryona's head, for instance), but once had escalated into an actual physical skirmish complete with biting, kicking, and slapping. The object of their rivalry, a handsome groom brought in from the Fedoskino estates, grew tired of them both and ran off with a scullery maid from a neighboring palace.

"Happy now, Praskovia?"

"Yes, little countess. You are a good mistress. I kiss your hands a thousand times. I spit on that Matryona."

The serf, sitting proudly under her own fur rug as the sledge scraped its way through the icy streets, began to look happily round her, crying out with joy at the sight of this or that shop that she knew, or excitedly identifying a servant buried under a pile of bundles as "old Ivanka who belongs to Prince Vishnyevsky!" or "Nikolasha the footman at Chernenko palace, who lost his little finger last year while skinning a rabbit! His brother had six toes. It's God's justice to even it out."

The skaters were already out on the river in front of Andreyev palace. There seemed to be quite a large party, perhaps a hundred, and therefore plenty of men to flirt with, so Olga would not suspect her. Alexandra felt guilty, however, when a figure encased in white fur waved to her from the ice, then turned and skated toward the embankment.

Face nestled in a hood of exuberant fuzziness, cheeks bitten red as apples by the cold, Olga gazed up the steps to the street where Alexandra was descending from her sledge and smiled with joy. Looking down at her friend, noticing again the too-large, too-protruding front teeth that Olga had always been embarrassed by and which Alexandra had always told her gave her "character," Alexandra hoped there was no truth at all to her suspicion that Olga and Rybynsky were "attached," or on the verge of announcing an engagement. Perhaps Rybynsky's intimacy with the Andreyevs was simply a result of the prince's need for advisement in the pursuit of his philanthropic goals, which were famous throughout the empire.

Yes, that was it. Who better than a councilor of state for that?

"I haven't seen you in so long," said Olga, sitting beside Alexandra on the steps that led down to the river while Alexandra stuck out one foot and then the other to Praskovia, who was screwing the new silver skates to her mistress's soft white kid boots.

Olga, huddled inside her snowy furs, leaned against her friend and rubbed her head affectionately against Alexandra's arm.

"You saw me two weeks ago," said Alexandra, drawing back.

"I know, but not like we used to be. I missed you so much during your mourning, and"—Olga's voice diminished to a whisper—"there's so much to tell you." Moving her head closer to Alexandra's, she raised her mouth toward Alexandra's ear.

"Let's skate," said Alexandra, jumping to her feet. Without

looking at the surprise on Olga's face, she took the princess's arm and pulled her onto the ice. They skated together briefly holding hands, their blades whispering together on the ice though they themselves were silent. Something was different between them, Olga felt, but she was too shy to ask the reason for Alexandra's coldness (could it be only distraction? a residue of grief? or had she herself done something wrong?) and decided sadly that it was probably that they were growing up, their girlhood gone, or going.

A hundred young people were circling on the metal-colored surface of the river, all sailing smoothly along the silent ice, twirling in a blur, or, linked into couples with braided arms, swaying back and forth in rhythm as if in time to music only they could hear. Braziers with hot red coals had been set up at intervals along the embankment, and servants, buried in coats and scarves, their breath a smaller version of the swirls of smoke that lifted from the braziers into the cold gray sky, served steaming hot tea from the samovars and a selection of greasy meats and melting cheeses on bread. Ato, the Andreyevs' African butler, presided over the wintry scene in all his sepulchral dignity, his burnished skin, with its undertone of gold, standing out against the poverty of color as a testament to the power of an absent sun.

Alexandra had detached herself from Olga, insisting that her friend attend to her guests (Olga skated off with a hurt and troubled face), and now she searched for Rybynsky among the men whose identities were muffled under caps or hidden behind stiffened, upright collars, or sunk inside their bearish furs. She found instead Ulyanov, that dissolute, that rake. He must have been watching her all along. Having noticed her glancing in his direction, he gave an irritating wave, and, as if she had beckoned him, set off down the river in her direction.

In fact, Alexandra had been avoiding him these past two weeks, though meeting him incessantly at musicales, at dinners, at dances, at teas, at evenings of cards. For some reason she could not understand, Ulyanov seemed to be pursuing her, but each time he had approached her, the countess had delivered him a ringing rebuff in the form of a cold silence drawn out to insulting length followed by a turning of her back. What interest such a man could have in her was something Alexandra failed to understand—she was neither married nor a servant nor an actress (his favored prey, so far as she had heard)—but he continued to pursue the acquaintance doggedly, accepting each of her snubbings with a kind of cheer, an almost . . . merriment.

Alexandra was not the best skater, but in order to evade him, she began to make her slightly wobbly way in the opposite direction, hoping that he would get the idea. He did not. An excellent skater, he reached her in moments, his arrival announced by the harsh scraping of his skates as he skidded to a stop.

"I'm sorry," he said breathlessly, bending over, hands on thighs, "I was so rude to you last night. I didn't say hello." More soberly dressed for skating, he was wearing a heavy black woolen duty coat (the military were not allowed to appear in civilian clothes) and no hat.

"I'd call that, rather, courtesy," she replied, but the flippant effect she had hoped to achieve was undermined by a particularly vehement wobble of her ankles such that Ulyanov had to put out his hand to steady her. She jerked her shoulder away, but this unsteadied her further and, after waving her arms in the air in an attempt to keep her balance, she fell heavily on her backside.

Ulyanov, who had deliberately failed to try to steady her again, watched her fall with a blank expression.

"Are you going to help me up or not?"

"You made it clear to me you wanted no help." Alexandra, looking up, noticed that his nostrils moved while he talked in a very unattractive way. This made him even more repulsive than he was already.

"I want it now, your help," she said.

"No," he said, crossing his arms and ankles, "absolutely not. Do it yourself." Alexandra admired his ability to stay upright on one foot while expressing himself so emphatically.

"Why are you being so rude?" she said, wobbling as she tried to rise but only fell again.

Ulyanov raised his eyebrows but said nothing.

"Then I suppose I'll just sit here," she said.

"I suppose you will." With a scraping of skates, he was gone.

Alexandra was now forced to try to get up by herself, a nearly impossible task for a skater of her ability. First, she positioned herself on all fours and, digging the toes of her skates into the ice, tried to rise, but she slipped down again and banged one knee quite painfully. Then she sat heavily again, braced her hands at her sides, and tried to raise herself that way. She managed to reach a half crouch before her feet slipped out from under her again. Once more she went onto her hands and knees and, by flailing her arms, reached the crouching position and tried to straighten up. Then, magically, she found that the slipping blades had bitten deeply into the ice, her feet were fixed firmly, and she rose triumphantly to stand easily upright on her skates.

"The reason," said Ulyanov, still holding the back of her coat, "that I refused to help you is that *you* were the rude one. Not only have you been rude to me on every occasion of our meeting, a fact I chose to overlook, but you further compounded your offense to my courtesy by expecting me to help you up as soon as you asked me, right after you had rejected my previous offer.

It is this feminine arrogance—'don't help me when I don't feel like it, but help me when I want it,' and men are supposed to know which one is which without your telling us—that we find so irritating. You seem to think there are different rules for you, just because you're women. It is this attitude that is holding you back."

"Holding us back from what?" asked Alexandra, still happily upright and too grateful to throw off his hand. This conversation interested her in any case.

"Equality."

"We don't want equality," said Alexandra haughtily, "we want superiority."

"I'd say it would be more prudent to try to achieve equality first." The question of women's rights was a particularly popular topic these days in fashionable salons, discussed and argued over endlessly in the abstract while everything went on pleasantly as before with no change at all.

He released the back of her coat but caught Alexandra's hand before she could fall forward. "Here," he said, crossing hands with her, "let's skate," and so, in what felt like a near embrace, they set off down the ice, and Alexandra marveled at how easy it was to skate this way, how smoothly she was gliding across the ice.

"As I was saying, equality first, then superiority."

"We are already superior," said Alexandra, glancing at the buildings that stood on either side of the river, at the people who waddled and trudged on dry land while she glided and floated her way along.

"How so?"

"In moral terms."

"Oh really? Look there." He skated her toward the river's edge and stopped. A woman was standing with her arms on the railing of the bridge, looking down at nothing in particular, as if she were waiting for someone. The woman's face was startling, composed of smears of vibrant color—red for the mouth, sooty black for the eyes, spots of pink on the bright white cheeks.

"So?" said Alexandra.

"Just wait," he said, still holding her hands in a way that began to make Alexandra uncomfortable. She noticed for the first time that they were quite far from the others, who were small figures in the distance. She glanced back at the woman on the bridge. A man had stopped to talk to her. He leaned his arms on the railing. Alexandra could see from the woman's lowered eyes and slight smile that she did not know this man. The woman then nodded, and the two strolled together across the bridge, the man's hand on the woman's back, and disappeared.

"I think you are disgusting," said Alexandra, snatching her hands from his grasp and turning to skate away from him.

"Just what I mean," he called after her. "When we're right, you find a way to change the subject!"

The short skating practice she had had with him must have restored some of her former skill, or maybe it was just sheer force of will, but Alexandra had pivoted deftly on her skates and already put a goodly distance between herself and the rake Ulyanov before it occurred to her that she could not remember how to stop or slow herself and was about to collide with a couple skating leisurely, distractedly down the ice, holding hands and talking softly, too absorbed in each other to see that she was rushing toward them, an unstoppable projectile looming suddenly out of the winter afternoon. Whoops! With a scraping sudden turn, Alexandra succeeded in avoiding them and came to a skittering stop, chips of ice flying at her face, but still managing to keep her feet. She was certain she could hear Ulyanov laughing in the distance. Her face warm and red, she inserted her hands inside her muff and began to skate carefully in the direction of the embankment, where she thought she might find Rybynsky.

Somehow, Ulyanov had managed to draw her into an intimacy as instantaneous as it was inappropriate. How had he done it? Simply by doing it. He had behaved as if this intimacy already existed, and Alexandra wondered if this was his standard technique. And of course she had not gotten rid of him at all. She heard the sound of his skates behind her.

"I'm sorry," he said, skating up beside her, "I offended you. I spend so much time in the company of men, I forget sometimes how a gentleman talks to ladies."

"Ha!" said Alexandra, "You call yourself a gentleman."

"On the other hand," he said quite mildly, "maybe you're just too easily embarrassed by the facts of life."

Alexandra's mouth dropped open. Had he really said that? She decided that he had, and to escape him again she began to move her skates vehemently over the ice, again without looking where she was going. This time, she could not stop herself and collided with Rybynsky himself, who had been standing not far away from her.

She blushed deep red. That Ulyanov! She would gladly kill him for this, and if she had been a man, she could have indeed. The insults he had delivered already, far out of proportion to any she had delivered herself, would have required her to challenge him on the spot.

Alexandra watched as Rybynsky walked away from her. Of course he was not wearing skates—he was too dignified to indulge himself in that childishness. Even his response to her collision with him had been measured. He had looked at first surprised, raising his eyebrows slightly. He had steadied her with his hand, nodded, touched the brim of his high silk hat, then walked away, turning his head once to look back at her with an expression she could not interpret. What did it mean, that glance? Surely it must mean that he thought her a silly creature, utterly ridiculous. Oh, everything was ruined now.

Or perhaps not.

Alexandra turned back to Ulyanov, who was standing nearby staring down at the ground and poking sullenly at the ice with the tip of one skate. She skated up to him, tugged on his sleeve, and gazed upward into his eyes as if she thought he were the most wonderful man in the world.

Practice, Praskovia had said. And who better to practice on than someone who didn't count?

Looking down into her upturned face, it occurred to Ulyanov that her eyes looked, at that moment, as if they were inhabited by stars. Correction—the entire evening sky, with its luminous blue and brilliant moon, was represented there inside her eyes. Moreover, he thought, were he to be able to gaze indefinitely into those starry depths, he would have no need of evening skies or summer mornings. No need of the scent of new grass, or the comforting sound of rain on a gray afternoon, or the warm lights of home shining out through the dark on some cold and tired night.

Actually, this *was* his standard line. He had used it many times on many women, especially the part about the home shining out through the dark, which had worked every time. He had simply never expected to meet a woman to whom it would actually apply. He had not expected this at all. Stunned, he simply stared.

It was true he had pursued the countess off-handedly. There were no respectable women among his feminine acquaintance— they had always seemed a waste of time—and he had sought to remedy this situation of late. He thought he might marry someday and had decided he needed experience in how to behave with marriageable young ladies. The countess had seemed a suitable candidate to practice on, nothing more. In truth, he had not been strongly attracted at all. She was not really his type—a bit too tall, a bit too thin, nothing to get hold of. So how had this happened? The eyes that were looking up at him contained an entire world, and he felt himself falling into it with a bump.

"You were right and I was wrong. I was rude and you were kind," she said, still gazing up at him, and Ulyanov was not able to tear his eyes away as much as he might want to. "I think you're quite wonderful."

Too far, Alexandra. Not so fast.

Ulyanov narrowed his eyes and succeeded in blocking out the stars. He was himself so practiced in romantic insincerity that it was easy to recognize when someone else was practicing it on him.

"No you don't," he said. "What do you think you're up to?"

"I do!" Alexandra protested.

But Ulyanov, relieved to have this excuse to save himself from falling farther, was sailing away across the ice. She was playing with him, as if he didn't matter. He had done it so many times himself with women he didn't care about that he knew the signs. So. To soothe his wounded pride by asserting to himself that at the very least he exceeded this annoying person in strength, power, and especially skating ability, he first pounded powerfully at the ice with his skates and gathered enormous speed, then leaped into the air, spun round, landed back on the ice, and sped away.

That didn't go well at all, thought Alexandra. It seemed she had succeeded only in hurting his feelings. Not that he had any, she was sure. A dissolute? A rake? A seducer of women? He should certainly be punished, and she had somehow clearly achieved that end, though she wasn't quite sure how she had done it. However, the punishment had driven him away, and now she had to get him back. Practicing on him had been so pleasant. She wanted to do more of it. Not to take advantage of the opportunity would be wasteful. She had her future to think of.

Ulyanov was standing near the embankment, balanced on his skates, a cigarette between his gloved fingers. The countess skated up to him.

"It seems I've offended you somehow," she said, wobbling slightly, "and I didn't mean to. I meant only to say I think you're very nice."

Smoking, he only looked at her, suspicious, cool.

"Come skate with me, please," she insisted, pinching the sleeve of his coat between two fingers and tugging gently. "I need your help."

"Get someone else."

"But you're my teacher," said the countess, catching on. "See how much better I can skate now since you helped me?"

Oh, the appeal to his masculine vanity! Within the minute, he was skating carefully backward holding her hands, instructing her in a pedagogic tone, and staring with great solicitousness at her skating, slipping feet as he suggested she not keep them so close together and try to get some flow into her stride.

They encountered a face in the ice. A not uncommon sight in winter, these were suicides who had taken their final leap, or drunks who had stumbled and fallen into the river. Frozen like flies in amber in the solid water, these blurry faces gazed up through the ice until the spring, when the bursting bodies were fished out and disposed of. A young man skating with a girl always hoped to find one. It was an opportunity for comfort, a chance to get his arms around the girl.

Alexandra was duly horrified and Ulyanov duly comforting,

but he did not put his arm around her. The rake Ulyanov, seducer of hundreds of women, was suddenly too shy.

In fact, the young countess began to enjoy herself so thoroughly in the company of Ulyanov, who was behaving not like a rake at all, but more like the young captain of hussars and the nobleman he also was, that she forgot her pursuit of Rybynsky entirely. Until she looked up. Olga was skating alongside her perfect man and skating far more imperfectly than Alexandra knew she could. In fact, Princess Andreyev fell against her companion several times—Olga, the champion of them all! Alexandra dropped her eyes, not able to bear the sight of Olga in Rybynsky's arms, if only briefly, and it suddenly occurred to her that while the Princess Andreyev skated beside her paragon, the Countess Korvin herself was being seen in the company of a person of questionable status, unquestioned vice, and no fortune to speak of.

Her hands felt trapped. The countess pulled them free. Ulyanov looked at her, puzzled.

Alexandra saw it all! How all of Petersburg would turn out for the wedding of the wealthy princess and her distinguished consort, glittering wedding crowns held above their heads as they were blessed with all the riches life could offer, while Alexandra sat head in hands with blackened eye (Ulyanov would surely beat her) at a table with a torn and tea-stained cloth as a passel of dirty-faced children dressed in rags scurried screaming round the single dingy room that was their home, and the rake himself, unshaven, threw another glass of vodka down his throat and held out a boot for her until she got down on her knees and pulled it off to reveal a moth-eaten sock, and no one was coming to visit her, not ever.

"Let me get you some tea," said Ulyanov, uncertain of what had caused the sudden drop in temperature. He shivered lightly in the cold of his partner's demeanor and skated away.

When he returned, Countess Korvin was talking to the princess and the councilor. She paid no heed to the glass of tea Ulyanov offered her, talking on and on with an animation he had never seen in her before.

Boldly, Ulyanov took the countess's hand and inserted the glass of tea.

The countess failed to notice. She accepted the glass of tea as if from the hand of a servant and did not even thank him. Her face was turned up to Rybynsky's as if she were reveling in the warmth of a summer sun—her face reflected its radiance.

I will make her look at me like that again, Ulyanov said to himself. If only he could think of how.

It was nearly midnight, and Alexandra was not yet asleep. Her muscles groaned, complaining of their exertions on the ice, and though she kept turning herself and readjusting her relation to the sagging mattress, each new position only uncovered a new and different area of ache. A cigar would be just what she wanted to help herself relax. Of course she had tossed them into the trash some time ago, but somewhere in this enormous structure, with its myriad nooks and crannies, there might be a box she had missed.

She sat up painfully in bed and with her dangling feet felt for the slippers that Matryona, on her hands and knees, always placed in perfect alignment beside the cot. However, it seemed that Matryona had struck her first blow in the campaign of vengeance at her mistress's latest slight—the floor was empty, cold and hard against the tips of Alexandra's questing toes.

The countess smiled in the dark.

Now, of course, she was forced onto her hands and knees herself (how clever of you, Matryona, to put your mistress in your place!) and with the frayed edges of the coverlet brushing against her head, Alexandra lay flat on her sore belly and felt for the slippers under the bed. There was nothing but thick mats and pads of dust, which Praskovia had obviously been sweeping under there. Alexandra wondered if this too was part of Matryona's plan, for Praskovia would have to be spoken to and would weep with embarrassment while Matryona stood smiling by.

The countess wanted that cigar. Oh rich dark taste of Cuban nights, warm emerald air, sun-saturated seas—a tiny ember of the tropics glowing amidst the ashes of this gray winter night. Renewing her courage, the countess thrust herself more deeply under the bed, emerging seconds later empty-handed and spitting dust.

The slippers were under the window, all the way across the room. They shone at her in the moonlight. She had to cross the cold floor on bare feet to get to them. Oh clever Matryona!

She pattered across the room, slid her feet into the slippers, lit a candle, pulled a ragged white robe across her shoulders, and left the bedroom, stepping carefully over the bundled serf in front of the door. Stopping in the wide hallway, she thought carefully of all the places she might have overlooked in her previous quest to rid herself of the smelly things. However, since all the rooms but the one reception room had been stripped of their furniture, there were no drawers to peek inside and, well, in a moment of weakness just last week she had rifled the tables and chests and cupboards in that reception room in any case.

Still, she sensed that there must be someplace she had overlooked. A room she had not been inside in many months? Aha! Her father's bedroom. Although it too had been stripped, she had left a few things of sentimental value only and could easily in her grief and hurry, her eagerness to close the door behind her, have overlooked a cache of tobacco hidden somewhere in the room. Keeping her hand cupped around the sideways-bending flame, she started off in that direction.

She stopped. Of course the room would be locked. She remembered clearly the turning of the key. This key would be on Praskovia's belt. Carefully she proceeded backward with her candle.

Setting down the candlestick, Alexandra knelt on the floor beside the mound that was the sleeping serf, a shape that inflated as it softly filled with air and then collapsed again with a hissing sound, as if a balloon had been punctured. The countess pushed her hand beneath the bundle, feeling for the heavy ring of keys, but just as her fingers touched the hard, sharp bits of metal, her hand was caught, Praskovia instantly half awake.

"What . . . doing? Do you want?" Praskovia mumbled.

"Shh," whispered Alexandra, "it's only me. I'm looking for something I need."

The serf, reassured by the sound of her mistress's voice, descended into sleep again while Alexandra unbuckled the clinking load of iron and brass and slid it out from under the woolen coverings—a collection of keys to empty rooms, only one of which was still kept locked. Her father's bedroom.

It was on another level. So down the wide steps that flowed between the palace floors she went, shivering in the palace's bitter cold, the weak candle pitiful as proof against the enormous dark, and then along the hallway, so that a watcher outside in the street, on looking up, would have seen a pinprick of light floating slowly from window to window and thought that there might indeed be a ghost in this house.

It was something the countess often wondered herself. So often, when she was thinking of nothing, her mind empty and open, she thought she felt her father's presence, heard him calling to her from a distance. His voice was urgent if unintelligible, as if he had an important message to deliver and was forced to shout across the barrier between the two worlds. Remembering the gruesome illness that had taken him, his pitiable final hours, her fingers trembled as she tried key after key in the bedroom's lock. The jarring jingling of the keys sounded enormous in the hollowness of the palace, and Alexandra wondered what restless spirits the sounds might rouse, what tormented souls, invisible, might fill the dark around her. It was Russian to believe in ghosts, and Alexandra, not easily frightened, was frightened now. She swore softly at her trembling fingers. A sizzle of fear went up her spine. And then there was a click, a crunch, and the doorknob turned.

In the small circle of light thrown by her candle there was not much to see. But even in the light of day there would not be much more—the room had been stripped of its valuable paintings and furniture, its books and art objects, even its silver toiletries. She walked to the bed and stood over it with the candle. Illuminated on the pillow was the stain of that final, fatal hemorrhage, now faded to a shadow of the thick black fluid that had gushed and spurted from between his bloodied teeth, coated his chin. Alexandra put the candle down on the bedside table with its empty lamp and sat on the bed, pulling her legs up under her, hugging her knees against the cold and squeezing shut her eyelids to trap her tears.

Those last months he just could not get comfortable. Irritable, he had ordered his new manservant, a boy picked out from one of the estates south of Moscow especially for the enormous size of his arms, to carry him from chair to chair, as if he might discover just the right relationship between thickness of upholstery and angle of wooden back to ease his struggle. Then it was found that he was most comfortable aloft, and a sort of sling had been constructed—a silk sheet was tied firmly to the bedpost, the other end in Prokhor's fist, and the count, suspended in the air, was rocked gently for hours, until he was able to fall asleep. At the end, lungs liquefied, reduced to a mass of random cells inside his chest, he was laid on the bed to die, in the interest of a final dignity.

What was left of him now? Only the foolish staircase made of semiprecious stone, and his clothing, all of it very fine but which she couldn't bear to sell, though it would have brought a pretty price—the high silk hats stored neatly in their leather boxes, the fine-grained gloves and buttery leather of his custom-made shoes, his sparkling shirts, cold and slippery as glass when she'd pressed her face against them as a child, but turning quickly warm against her cheek. All these were locked inside his wardrobes in the dressing room, which was locked as well. Of course, his furs had gone and his jewelry. What more was left? A few volumes of poetry in French (his favorites, though the rest of the massive library had gone), a few trinkets of no substantial value (a crystal egg he had kept in his pocket because he liked the way it felt in his hand, a lacquer box or two, a stray razor found to be silver-plated). And the *object,* the construction of which had ruled his life, and from which she had already picked the precious stones he had pasted there so meticulously, obsessively, all through the years he had worked on his memorial to that one moment of transcendence on the island long ago.

She had not been able to understand it: the hours he spent bent over a desk fitted with mirrors to magnify the power and precision of the light as he went about the task of reconstructing the past, of fixing and freezing time. Oh, the cries of delight when he achieved an accurate effect or remembered another detail to include. Jewelers came and went with their small bags, large cases, and they disappeared behind his door, emerged again shaking their heads, muttering about how they couldn't cut that small. In fact, it had never really been completed. He had continued to add to it right up to the moment when the last stages of his illness began to sour his soul, exhaust his spirit.

The staircase had not been enough. He had been compelled to re-create the entire scene surrounding the event, the glittering, glowing penumbrum of that exquisite instant, no more than a second wide. One day when she was still small, he had opened the box in which it was kept and shown her. Standing on the tips of her toes to see inside, she was suddenly grown enormous, as if she were aloft, floating in space and looking down at the luminous features of a night on earth, with pearly moon and peaceful sea and sparkling sand, the stiff leaves of cypresses shivering and shimmering in the wind, an angel's-eye view of the world.

The sensation had lasted only a moment before she realized it was merely a model, a reconstruction of that small Greek island he had spoken of, done in precious and semiprecious stones. She had been impressed that his love for her mother had been so enormous he was driven to create this—*thing,* but she would rather he had talked about her, and that he never did, except in terms of an abstract perfection of form and character, as if the woman had been a living avatar of virtue, a godhead of beauty, never a human being. Alexandra wanted to hear him tell her what her mother's laugh had sounded like, the color of her hair, her quirks, her tastes, her words. Little stories about her. But her father kept these details to himself, as if they were too precious to be exposed to the roughness of the ordinary world outside his mind. All he would say was that her mother's soul was as beautiful as her face, both so exquisite and fine that words could not do them justice. Many portraits had been painted, but none had captured her radiance, and he had had them all destroyed.

The reproduction of his precious moment was still there inside its box, but there was almost nothing left of it now. Just a few bits of glass, some wood and broken wire, a twisted skeleton of his memory stripped of its luminous flesh, by her. By his daughter. By *their* daughter, in her greed. She ought not to have done it—it had pained her so to destroy it, as if she were tearing his heart apart. But the creditors had had to be paid.

She often asked herself if what she had done was right. The

loss of her wealth and standing ought not to have mattered to her. She ought to have accepted the sinking of her position, the disappearance of her luxuriant world, and been content with riches of the spirit, as she was sure her mother would have done. Hadn't the woman given her very life for her daughter in final proof of her otherworldly goodness? Well, Alexandra thought, she would never equal the perfection of her mother's soul, match her in any of the feminine virtues in which she had excelled and which her father had held up to her as a mirror that reflected Alexandra back to herself distorted, askew, utterly imperfect, and unworthy.

She never did get her cigar. She hadn't even bothered to look for it. Locking the door behind her, she climbed the stairs back to bed. The next morning, while Praskovia was giving her her bath, she was still thinking.

"Praskovia," she said suddenly, after not having responded to any of Praskovia's remarks for quite some time, "what could make a person love another person so much that her memory would rule his life, that there would be nothing else for him?"

"Only God knows that," said Praskovia, vigorously scrubbing behind her mistress's ear.

"Did you ever meet my mother? Did you ever see her?"

"Oh yes," said the serf, soaping up the washcloth and then dropping it onto Alexandra's head, "she was very beautiful. That's all I remember. I only saw her once or twice when he brought her to Fedoskino from Mstyora, which was where they spent their time. Where you were born. Where she died. So I didn't get to see her again."

The countess's head wobbled under Praskovia's energetic scrubbing of her scalp.

"But why did he love her so much? Was it because she was so good? So perfect?"

"How would I know?" said Praskovia, irritable at being asked a question she did not know the answer to.

"Was it because she was beautiful?"

"In my experience," said Praskovia, "beauty seldom has anything to do with it. And goodness, certainly not. I told you what the secret was. Why must I tell you again?" Praskovia was eager to get on with the story she'd been telling about the Chibikovs' old butler and the goat he was devoted to. He kept it in his room, ascribed to it supernatural powers, and claimed that the arrangement of hairs on its coat, which changed daily, could predict both the weather and the outcome of the St. Vladimir's Day Memorial Horse Race, an event around which he centered his life. Praskovia started in on the story again, beginning where she'd left off.

"Shut up, Praskovia, I don't care about the goat. I want you to tell me how you know when a man loves you. How he acts."

Praskovia dumped a bucket of cold water over her mistress's head and watched with satisfaction as Alexandra's hair melted down over her face, hiding it entirely. These questions were annoying her, particularly the ones about the mistress's mother. It made her feel as if her mind were being stretched and poked about in—the sensation was uncomfortable.

Alexandra parted the curtain of hair that covered her face and went on asking. "Is it the way he looks at you? Or things he says? Or things he does?"

"Never trust anything they say to you," said Praskovia, helping her mistress to rise from the tub and wrapping the long body in several enormous towels that had been warming on the stove. "They have the tongues of serpents, double, forked. And no connection between their mouth and brain. Their mouth is connected to something else." Praskovia smirked to herself at this joke, confident that the mistress would not understand. "Oh, they have wonderful words, words like smoke that makes pretty shapes in the air and then it's gone, just made of air. They smell good, too. Don't get too close. Wham—like a snake they wrap around you, whispering pretty things in your ear with that special voice they use so soft and low, and you lose your head completely, and next thing you know he's sitting at the table with his knife in his fist looking up at you with that confident look that means he knows you'll bring his dinner and he knows you'll wash his clothes and no need for pretty words for you, no need for words at all, he thinks."

Alexandra, sitting on the bed wrapped in her towel, her hair hanging in separate strings already beginning to crystallize in the cold, wasn't listening.

"Do you think," she said, "that if a man looks at you a lot, it means something?"

Praskovia, kneeling on the floor to dry each one of her mistress's wet little toes before they iced over, was now launched on a recital of her marital woes—the one husband who'd died of drink, the other who'd stuffed himself to death sitting at the table cutting slices off the Easter ham until his belly was big as a boulder and just as hard, and he hadn't left any meat for her at all.

Alexandra was thinking of Rybynsky. The glances he had cast her way first at the ball, and then at the skating party. These glances, meaning something she couldn't put her finger on, were burning holes in her consciousness, and she thought about them constantly. As for Olga, he was attentive to her but detached, and the countess saw no sign of passion or even affection for the princess, though some mysterious connection between them seemed definitely to exist. But those burning glances! Burning or not, however, they always cooled when she came closer until his eyes had turned to ice, impenetrable. His manner with her was just as pleasantly detached as it was with Olga. Oh, what did it mean?

She caught Praskovia by the skirt as the serf stood up with a towel slung over her shoulder.

"What does it mean when a man looks at you as if he desires you, and then when you respond, he behaves as if it didn't happen?"

"Oh," said Praskovia, "it could mean he's shy. Or it could mean he's teasing you. They play the same games that we do, you know. Perhaps he's trying the secret on you."

Rybynsky shy? Alexandra didn't think so. She had never seen a man more glacially solid in his self-assurance, more poised, more graceful of manner and speech. Never had she seen a moment of uncertainty or awkwardness. He seemed, in fact, to look down on the world from the stratospheric height of a mind unmarred by common emotions or common thoughts. A tease? His dignity would not allow that. He was certainly not the sort of man to find amusement in the idle picking and gathering of unwanted hearts. Unlike that other one.

As for that other one, who was at this very moment sitting at a desk in his home across the city staring thoughtfully at a piece of paper that lay on the desk before him, he was similarly wondering about why a certain person had looked at him a certain way and then pretended it meant nothing. Except that she had gone on to look at someone else that way, and he was wondering how to get her to look at him instead and why she had stopped it in the first place and what he could do about it.

I drink too much, Ulyanov wrote on the paper in front of him. Brow pursed with effort, he stared at what he had just written, feeling that he had struck another blow at the badness in himself.

Already he had set down on the paper the following:

1. I am vain.
2. I am lazy.
3. I have no ambition.
4. I have no self-discipline.
5. I am unchivalrous toward women.
6. My mind is prosaic and ordinary.

When, he felt, he had identified and catalogued all of his personal faults, he could begin to carve away at them, like a sculptor, and then the new Ulyanov would be revealed—a smooth white marble figure staring into the distance, noble and serene, pure in mind and heart.

Startled by footsteps, Ulyanov hid the list with his arm.

The maid Lukasha had appeared in the room. Standing with her hands behind her back, some hair that she had carefully arranged to escape attractively from underneath her kerchief curling round her temples, she gazed at him with her slanting eyes and breathed as heavily as she could so that her breasts would push forward at him, giving him the right idea. It was just two weeks since he had gotten the right idea on the table in the library, her feet kicking wildly at the air and her bare bottom squeaking rhythmically against the polished wood. It had been too long since then, she thought.

Since Ulyanov had discovered the meaning of life at the age of fourteen in the hay barn on one of his family's estates outside Moscow, there had been many like Lukasha. To discover the various variations of women had been the chief goal and amusement of his life: the sounds they made, the odd expressions that came over their faces at the climax, the amazing differences in size and shape of breasts, some small and pointed and angry-looking, others helplessly sagging as if they could not support their own load of beauty, others balancing perfectly aloft the rib cage, a miracle of design—it was enough to make him believe in God. And since his family, modestly rich, owned five thousand souls, half of them female and many within an appropriate age range, which in Ulyanov's case was fairly wide (fifteen to fifty), he had had quite a range of comparison for his investigations. But of course even these were not enough. There were seamstresses, factory workers, ballet girls, women of the streets, unhappily married women, and so on and so forth. It had always seemed to Ulyanov that he was embarked on a quest of true profundity, the actual point of which had never become quite clear to him, but the nameless object of which pulled him toward it with the greatest urgency. Women seemed to hold the key to something, but to what?

Now his head jerked up with the violence of revelation. He realized at that moment, with intense emotion, that his search for some essence of meaning amongst the many women had been fruitless: the key to something that women held was not some general quality distributed amongst them all, but was exclusive to one and one alone. A woman with thoughts and emotions and spiritual longings just like his! A partner, a mate, an entire world enclosed within another human being!

Ulyanov placed his hand on his forehead, as if to trap the

thought inside his head, not lose it, while in the meantime the predatory Lukasha had begun to insinuate herself along the floor, sliding along on hands and knees toward her master, or more specifically, toward that part of the male anatomy that was, at the moment, her own special goal.

"You have headache," she said, continuing to slither toward him with greedy eyes, "Lukasha fix it," but then Lukasha's command of the language had never been strong. She had been imported from one of his family's holdings somewhere in the Crimea, and God only knew what her native language actually was. It apparently did not utilize the first-person pronoun. Of course, the utter simplicity of her thought patterns as revealed by the truncated vocabulary had always excited Ulyanov most of all—she had seemed all body and no mind, and that was just fine with him. But now, in the fullness of his revelation, it occurred to him that not only Alexandra herself but indeed all women were full human beings, with thoughts and dreams like his, and so, as Lukasha's kerchiefed head descended into the portion of his trousers she had just unbuttoned, he gazed down at her with a new and utterly spiritual interest. He wanted to know things about her. He wanted, in short, to start his new program right at this very moment.

"Lukasha! Stop that!" he said.

Lukasha did not stop.

"Lukasha, please!" With some difficulty he managed to detach her. Buttoning himself quickly back into some semblance of dignity more consistent with the new, reformed, spiritual person that he now felt himself to be, he gazed down into her shocked and hurt little face.

"Not like? You not like Lukasha?" Manipulative tears began to form in her eyes. She had not given up. Her hand reached his thigh again and began to creep upward and over.

"Of course I like you, Lukasha." He snatched her creeping hand and held it. "Lukasha, tell me"—he struggled to frame his question in such a way that she could grasp it—"how you feel about life? What you think?"

Lukasha looked up at him, puzzled. He had never tried to have a conversation with her before. It was shocking. She released his hand and sat down on the floor with a bump. Now that she thought of it, since he had always treated her like the sum of her body parts, she had always treated him this way as well. He had always been simply the master, with one particularly fulfilling body part attached. Never someone she thought of as a human being. With thoughts and dreams like her own. And now, looking up into his face, which looked down at her with an expression of willed, self-conscious interest, desperate to prove to her that he cared, Lukasha found that she did too. And she saw that his eyes were as blue as the sea and the sky, and his face shone like the sun for her, and this fairy-tale way was how she suddenly saw him, for it was all she had in her head to work with—only the folktales of her indeterminate homeland, along with six different recipes for black bread, the lyrics to five or six little songs, the responses of the mass, and a knowledge of how to clean silver with spit.

"Lukasha," he said urgently into her bewildered eyes, "tell me what you are thinking."

But how could she? In her own language in her head, she was thinking thoughts more lovely than she could say. She hid her face in her arm. No one had ever asked her what she thought. And no one had ever looked at her with interest but him.

"All right then," said Ulyanov, slumping back in his chair, "if you don't want to talk to me, then go," and he was suddenly the master again. Frustrated, he prodded her with his foot, resisting with some effort the impulse to kick at the little heap on the floor, which had not even appreciated his attempt to be spiritual with her! What a stupid little slave she was, not to try to understand!

As he watched with hateful eyes, Lukasha crawled a little ways away from him, then scrambled to her feet and, throwing her apron over her face, ran from the room.

Or perhaps, he thought with a sigh, not *able* to understand. Perhaps he'd asked too much of her. Turning back to his list of faults, he took up his pen and added another:

8. I am cruel.

"Cruel! Cruel! Cruel!" he repeated to himself. He needed a drink, but he could not have one. It was not part of the program for the new Ulyanov.

But still. He needed a drink.

Jumping up from his chair, he began to pace the room. Alexandra! Why wouldn't she love him? Cruel, he was cruel and vain. But he could take care of that. Pay less attention to his appearance, give Lukasha some very nice present to atone. That was a start. But what else was there?

A lot of things, actually. Dissipation? Corruption? He'd indulged in every thinkable vice and some unthinkable ones as well. Not only was there the vodka he loved so much (either clear and cold as ice, or fragrant with the spring smell of juniper or elderberries) but brandy, cognac, armagnac, claret, port, fine wines from France and Portugal—how alive they made him feel inside his mouth with the effort to absorb most completely their exquisite and varied tastes!

And there was opium, too. Oh, to be lost in the rich blue haze of it, a girl's plump bottom burdening his lap, her breasts filling his palms while his mind dissolved into the smoke above his head, and he was no longer body and soul and mind but pure sensation—pleasure! Oh, the things he had done in his search for pleasure, disgusting things, impure. Two women at once—how many times? Many. And sometimes three or four. While he lay alone in his bed at the country estate, they would climb up the trees, these serf girls stronger than the women of his class, up the trees and into his room they came, smelling deliciously of sweat from their work in the fields, and he rubbed his nose in their softly furred armpits, and their breasts dropped in his open mouth like ripe fruit, and their liquid limbs formed a serpent around him, writhing. Oh, the soft sounds they made when his fingers touched them in soft, secret places—the small peeping cries of surprised little chicks all furry and moist, coming out of their shells, confused.

He thought about Lukasha. Perhaps he ought to reconsider, call her back to him. Just once more. Just once.

But no!

That Rybynsky. What a stick. But Countess Korvin had clearly admired him, and what Rybynsky could do, could be, so could Mecklenburg-Ulyanov. Rybynsky clearly did not give in to pleasure. He was too dignified. Ulyanov thought a good stiff drink would have done the man good, but Ulyanov's own particular brand of manliness was obviously not to the countess's taste; she preferred Rybynsky's priggishness. And perhaps she had a point. A real man was not a slave to sensation or anything else. A real man loved one woman truly, and treated all others with respect, did not exploit them for his pleasure. Instead he protected and served them all.

Ulyanov decided to begin his program by going to church. He would cleanse himself. Start again. Reexamine his faults. Castigate himself thoroughly. Perhaps a whipping would do him good. Or maybe he should give away all his possessions, put on a dirty cassock, and become one of those holy idiots the Russian people were so fond of, the ragged ones who wandered the end-less roads of their giant country in search of the thing all Rus-sians searched for, though they never seemed to find it, but con-tinued wandering round and round as if that were the very point, to absorb the vastness of the country, to feel small in the eye of God.

On the other hand, perhaps that was too extreme. Just a sim-ple trip to the cathedral would be a start.

Ulyanov was just having his coat put on in the vestibule when his mother, who had been lying on her divan in a small room off the hall, called out to him: "Andrei! Where are you going?"

He had to listen hard to hear her. Her lungs were weak, dis-integrating, not strong enough to provide her voice with any volume.

Ulyanov remembered then that he had promised to sit with her this morning, and although the urgency to begin his pro-gram had already driven his arms into the sleeves of his coat with exceptional force and was about to propel him out into the cold, brilliant morning, which would surely illuminate every last dirty corner of his soul so that he could more accurately see his faults before reaching the cathedral, the weakness of that voice defeated him.

"Nowhere, Mother," he called out, removing his coat and handing it to the puzzled footman, who had been about to place the gold-trimmed shako upon Ulyanov's head. The footman smiled lewdly to himself as he walked away, wondering who it was that Ulyanov had been intending to see and how large her thighs were.

It was just as well, Ulyanov thought, stepping from the hall-way into the soft-carpeted room in which his mother had been sheltered for many years, where, as if to further cushion this fragile person from the harshness of the world around her, the walls of the room were lined in rose-pink silk upholstery, the windows firmly shuttered against the violence of even the weakened winter sun—the whole small space translucent, as if she lived, protected, inside a seashell.

She had come into the world askew and was, as a result, crippled in her legs. Now afflicted with consumption, she lay always on a small divan. Her eyes were radiant as he approached her, as if she were still amazed at his presence in the world, that he walked and talked, this large, strong body so unlike her own, which she had woven of her very own cells nonetheless. Her head listed to one side on the pillow. She closed her eyes, tired now. She rested her hand on his knee.

Just to sit quietly together, talk a little—this was what she liked. It was all she had the strength for. It's just as well, he thought, taking her withered hand from his knee and holding it. He might as well be here as in the cathedral after all. He might as well look at that face as the face of the Virgin—they were equally pure, equally unworldly. Might as well look at those crippled limbs as the twisted limbs of Christ upon the cross. To witness his mother's pain was punishment enough for now.

The Maryinsky Theater! A fabulous Fabergé egg, intricate, gold-encrusted, it hatched the Russian Ballet and its myriad of stars—Kschessinskaya, Preobrazhenskaya, Pavlova herself, who might be among these dancers as, moist and shining, they break forth, shake their limbs, bite their feathers, and spread their wings to dry before pouring out across the stage on pattering, sharp little toes to gather in groups, cheeping softly, all downy and white. Mist from the silvery lake drifts among them, a painted castle in the distance, a cardboard moon above.

Ulyanov was not watching the swanlets on the stage. Unusual for him: typically, his eyes would have swept the crowds of these peeping, tender birds to fix on one, or two perhaps, who might be taken somewhere afterward to be stripped of her feathers and eaten in quick little bites or, better, slowly with relish. Tonight he did not see them. He was staring at Countess Korvin across the auditorium, where she sat, attractively presented, in her velvet-lined box. A very jewel she was, all of her.

First she leaned back. Perhaps bored. Then she leaned forward, interested. Then she dropped something and dropped from sight herself, only the top of her head visible above the golden horizon of the box, and he had to content himself with looking at that for the moment. Then, upright in her seat again, she fussed with something in her lap. It seemed to be the cone of candied chestnuts from which she had been eating diligently all through the act. He imagined he could hear the paper rustle, hear the soft crunch of the chestnut crumbling between her teeth. What ecstasy to be inside that mouth.

It had been several weeks since he had seen her at the skating party. He hoped this was time enough for his transformation to be complete. In the meantime, he hadn't wanted to encounter her and so had avoided all the teas, dances, receptions, balls, and concerts where anyone who was anyone in Russia ceaselessly met everyone else, as if there was strength in numbers and they could drown out with loud chattering the rumble of the approaching century beneath their feet.

He had avoided, in addition, in this time of metamorphosis, the shadow world of which he'd been so fond—the demimonde, where princesses who were not princesses dined with lovers who did not love them, and the guests at table weren't witty but drunk. Gaming houses, opium dens, bordellos specializing each in one odd predilection—Ulyanov had loved them all.

However. For two weeks he had gotten up early, exercised vigorously, shined his boots himself, and gone humbly on parade with his regiment instead of getting someone else to do it for him. For two weeks he had read diligently in the most edifying volumes he could find. For two weeks he had avoided Lukasha, though she followed him everywhere now like a dog and just as silent. For two weeks he had drunk only milk, to freshen a complexion grown stale in the smoke of too-late nights, to clear away the dirty sediment that had settled to the bottom of his soul. For two weeks he had read to his mother every night. And for two weeks he had thought of nothing but the Countess Korvin, who at this very moment was stuffing another chestnut into her bulging cheek.

Now the act was over, and it was he, Ulyanov, who was on. The interval! The gaslights flared, and the audience began to boil, to chatter and rise from their seats. The countess, with her odd companion, rose from her seat as well and, fanning herself, chatted a moment before disappearing through the door behind the box, where Madame Lavorine attempted to remove the cone of chestnuts forcibly from the countess's tenacious grip, and a tussle ensued before Madame Lavorine emerged triumphant, protector of proprieties

Ulyanov leaped from his seat. The countess could not only be seen in her entirety somewhere outside in the crush of the crowd, but actually met and spoken to. He rushed out into the corridor, where he found himself bumped about in the stream of people flowing down the double golden staircase in a quest for refreshment.

The extravagant curls that had once tangled in the metallic threads of his stiff military collar and had announced to the world that martial discipline was for him a joke had been neatly snipped. And then there were his fingernails. Long and pointed, these had been for him grace notes to his sartorial splendor, to that spirited symphony of gilded tunic, mirror-shiny boots, and dashing pelisse—the fur-trimmed extra tunic worn slung over the shoulder as if he'd simply tossed it there and it had magically stuck. Good too, these long nails, for getting into those hard-to-reach places, those feminine crevices and culverts where women tried to hide their vulnerability to pleasure from his skillful, determined fingers. But the nails were gone now, too.

From where Ulyanov stood at the bottom of the stairs holding two flutes of champagne (one for his beloved, one for her companion), he had a clear view of the descending throng on both sides. His glance skipped back and forth between the two staircases to be certain he did not miss the countess's appearance amidst the happy crowd. However, his attention was distracted for the moment by the appearance of one woman who not only silenced that section of chattering crowd in which she moved but repelled it, so that she existed within an empty space of her own making, literally alone in the crowd. This woman—infamous for having left her husband and son for a young officer—was one Ulyanov had had his eye on for some time, as he considered it a challenge to his skills to distract her from what was considered a great, if scandalous, love, and wouldn't it have been a feather in his cap to get her away from that dull-minded, if handsome, oaf? However, where this woman had once glowed for him with the magnificence of her defiance of convention, now she seemed, in her isolation, a light that was flickering and about to go out, her once opulent beauty worn away by contact with hard, disapproving stares. She wore the sickly smile of one who apologizes for her presence in the world and hopes not to offend by merely living; her dark pansy-colored eyes shifted and flicked nervously about her, as if looking for some shelter in this relentless driving rain of condemnation. Her attendance at the performance had already caused a scene, when a respectable married lady in the very next box had protested so loudly about this woman's presence that the entire audience had heard it. What a humiliation.

And what had been her crime? Hardly the adultery—perhaps the main form of entertainment for married aristocrats—but merely the honesty that had led her to abandon an empty marriage. Ulyanov was about to speak to her, at least to catch her eye to make her see that there was one person who was willing to acknowledge her, but he lowered his eyes to the ground. What good would it do her? They would only say that she was sinking even lower now, that her lover was tiring of her and she was looking for another, and then another after that, or two at once. Ulyanov's notice would only add another layer of grime to a reputation as sullied as his own. And too, in an odd way, Ulyanov began to wonder if they weren't right after all. It was not something he could articulate clearly to himself, but her rebellion against the social order, her concentration on the self and its own desires, detached from its responsibilities to others, was perhaps deserving of a certain opprobrium. This thought, so alien to his entire worldview, in which pleasure seeking, pure enjoyment, had been the chief value and end in life, disturbed him. It seemed so harsh, unkind. Puritanical. He wondered if he was truly metamorphosing after all, and was suddenly uncertain of whether he really wanted to.

Still enclosed within her lonely space, the woman disappeared from sight. Again his eyes traveled to the top of one stairway and found it empty of *her*. Then he shifted his gaze to the other, and there she was.

She was wearing a butter-yellow gown so smooth and creamy and tight it looked as if liquid satin had been poured over her like hot candy and allowed to harden to a crispy gloss. He was sure if he bit into her he would find her filled with cream.

This feeling, he thought, gazing up at the radiance that was Alexandra—who, unaware of the emotion she inspired, paused at the top of the stairs, peered down at her bodice with distorted, fattened chin, and flicked a crumb of sugar from the surface of her glossy breast—is not as spiritual as I would like. I am sliding into old and well-worn grooves.

Distracting himself from his too-lustful thoughts while he waited for the countess to descend, Ulyanov practiced gallant phrases, inventing and discarding them one after the other, as none was good enough—he had used them all before. For Alexandra there must be something new that he could say, something extraordinary to impress her, but he could think of nothing and so, when she was about to step down off the last step and onto the marble floor, Ulyanov simply came forward with the glasses and held them silently in her direction.

He swallowed and jerked his chin, trembling with the effort to think of something good to say, but the words were jammed up against each other in his head, his mind at a standstill. The

champagne glasses shook in his hands. The pale liquid inside
them vibrated, fizzed.

Alexandra looked down at him, severe. It had been several
weeks since she had seen him—what a relief! She had assumed he
had slithered back beneath his rock, but here he was again, and
looking awfully strange. His face was red and moist, and he
seemed unsteady on his feet.

"You look sick," she said, "you ought to go home. I don't
think those"—she pointed haughtily to the glasses of champagne—"are going to do you much good. Especially not if you
drink them both yourself, as you seem to be intending." She
tossed her head in what she hoped was a sprightly way, happy to
have insulted him well, hoping it would drive him utterly away.
Rybynsky was nearby, a glow at the edge of her eye. She hoped
he had noticed her in her stunning dress, in which she was hard
to miss.

So what else was there to do, Ulyanov thought as she swept
past him in a buttery swirl, but drink them both himself? Which
he did, savoring the bubbling burn.

Now Ulyanov saw that she was gazing up at Rybynsky again
as if *he* were the most wonderful man in the world, and Rybynsky turned away from the circle of male admirers, important figures at court, in politics, finance, to focus his cool gaze on her.
Rybynsky was not trembling. He was not holding empty glasses
like a fool. Rybynsky's mouth opened, and Ulyanov was certain
that a perfect arrangement of sentences was issuing forth in
words that were cut like diamonds, that glittered in the light.
Ulyanov noticed that Rybynsky bent over the tall countess with
an assurance, a confidence in his eligibility, that Ulyanov was not
certain he would ever be able to achieve with Countess Korvin
no matter how much milk he drank.

And they were standing too close together. Yes, while he,

Ulyanov, had been undergoing his metamorphosis, blind and groping for new life inside his milky chrysalis, there had been some developments. He had let Rybynsky overtake him in the race!

The countess was laughing at something Rybynsky had said. Apparently, the witty statesman had produced a mot so brilliant that the countess, slender hand on slender stomach as she giggled violently, was forced to hold herself together just in case she came apart. Now Rybynsky was serious again, his elegant hands dancing in argument, which the countess followed with her eyes in a kind of awe. Then Ulyanov saw their gazes meet and intertwine, as if about to draw the two together like a tightening string.

Ulyanov turned, strode, and exploded out the door, where he was smacked in the face by an icy wind. Though he could feel the tip of his nose sharpening in the cold, he did not care. The skin on his face seemed to harden and crack. The champagne glasses froze to his fingertips, but he tore them off, tearing skin, and shattered them against the side of the building. All this hurt less than she did.

He stood there breathing hard. His breath kept exploding from his lips, turning white, widening into glassy webs, and drifting out of sight, carried away on the night winds. He looked up at the moon. It was cold and perfect and reminded him of *her*.

Something touched him on the arm. With its white felt boots, plump, quilted coat, and the head-muffling scarves covering its forehead and nose, it merged with the snow, so all that was visible of its features was a pair of large dark eyes that looked up at him with enough heat to melt all of Russian winter.

He jerked his arm away.

"Lukasha, go home," he said, wanting to get rid of her so he could get back to the moon. Since that day in the library, Lukasha had followed him everywhere, watching his every move with an intensity uninterrupted even by a blink. Now here she was again.

"Go home!" he shouted, raising a hand to strike her.

Lukasha flinched but stood her ground. "Lukasha stays!" she said.

Ulyanov dropped his hand. "Lukasha will go," he countered.

"Lukasha stays."

"No," he said, grasping her by the shoulders and pushing her in the direction of home, "Lukasha will go," but Lukasha slipped away and stepped behind him, where he could not get at her, and Ulyanov realized that this struggle could go on all night. He could not have her stand in the cold outside the theater waiting for him, as she clearly had, while he sat warm and toasty in his seat. The performance bored him anyway, and what else was there for him to see? Not Countess Korvin. He could not bear to look at her.

"I will go home too," he said.

"Then Lukasha goes home," she said, her eyes slanting more sharply in what Ulyanov recognized behind her scarves as a smile of satisfaction at the knowledge she had beaten him.

Not bothering to return to the theater to retrieve his cloak (to do so would have meant to see *her*), Ulyanov took off down the street in leggy strides. He did not call for one of the hired cabs that loitered by the theater with cabbies mountainous in their coats, who shouted insults at each other from their seats while their horses, shivering, stamped at the clotted ice and spurted smoke from their nostrils. He preferred to walk. Violently walk, walk away from that countess-person as quickly as he could.

The gold tassels hanging from his belt turned brittle in the cold and clattered against the metal of his sword. Lukasha hurried behind him, keeping up for a time, then slipping and falling on the ice. Hearing the soft thud, Ulyanov did not turn around, but simply waited, then continued striding.

Lukasha was worried about his ears. They might freeze and drop off in the cold, leaving him odd-looking, though still handsome enough for her. Still, she did not want even one precious part of him damaged. Running with all her might, Lukasha peeled one of the many scarves from her neck and, on reaching him, threw the cloth in the direction of his head as he pulled away from her again and grew smaller down the street.

The scarf managed to cling to his shoulder, and Ulyanov, noticing it, stopped. He snatched it off and looked at it, frowning. He wanted nothing between himself and the punishing cold, but before he could toss the scarf to the ground, Lukasha ran up, took it from his cracking, reddened hand, and, standing up on her toes, for she was very small, tried to tie the scarf around his head with clumsy mittens.

Ulyanov tore it off again and tossed it in her face. This action made him feel both better and worse at once. To see her flinch gave him pleasure. He would have liked to do it again. And to slap her hard would satisfy him even more—the small body tossed headfirst into a snowdrift, buried there, with kicking little feet.

But he would only have to dig her out again and hold her as she wept, as he was doing now, with stroking hand, and talking to her softly.

"Lukasha," he said, leaning down to place his mouth against the muffled ear, "you mustn't follow me around like this. It's not good for you. It's too cold."

"Lukasha is not cold," she said, teeth chattering.

"Oh, I think you are," he said, pulling her closer, and he raised his arm to signal the cab that had been clopping alongside them all along, seemingly aimless, but waiting for its moment as the driver muttered to himself about the foolishness of walking in the cold, the risk of "white-nose," the danger to fingers, toes, and other more important parts.

Lukasha had never been inside a cab before. In fact, she had never been inside any sort of conveyance whatsoever, except for the creaky old cart that had brought her up from the south, and that was too long ago to remember. Like all Russian peasants, she walked everywhere, from church to church, from town to town, from cities to distant country estates when the masters were on the move. At these times, while carriages and carts went trundling past them bringing provisions from the city palaces, the serfs, crowds of them, village-sized, would walk the muddy roads of spring, their felt boots sinking deep, or trudge the harder roads of autumn going back, summer gone and the social season in the capital about to begin.

Lukasha had never had a gentleman take her by the arm and, with a gentle heave, support her ascent into a carriage. She had never had a gentleman drop a lap robe across her knees, tuck it firmly. Ulyanov did these things unthinkingly. She was a female person riding in a carriage and, because of this, approximated a lady. And he was a gentleman—a nobleman, in fact. So now, as Lukasha sat up very straight on the stiff hard seat, hands folded shyly in her lap and amazement on her face as she watched the buildings of the city rush by her with astounding speed, Ulyanov, lounging in boredom, sat smoking across from her in the dark interior of the cab.

Now that he thought of it, she might make a lady at that. His eyes watering with the smoke from his wrinkled cheroot, he narrowed them at her, bringing her into sharper focus. In her white winter outfit, all fluffy and plump, eyes shining in the dark, she looked the most exquisite little peasant doll. Failing

Countess Korvin, he might marry her. Why not? It was not unheard of. It had been done. Why shouldn't a nobleman marry his serf? Certainly he did everything else with them. Even when not formally wed, some masters conducted close approximations of married life, with supper and tea and wife, slippers before the fire and children tucked snug in their beds with a story, except that all of them were chattel, property. Rather like mating with one's couch. Or falling in love with one's boots. Which, he had to admit, he had actually done, removing them from their box that very first time and seeing his face reflected in their military shine.

If not marry her, perhaps create a lady. At the very least, a person.

"Lukasha," he said, blowing a smoke ring, "tell me what you are thinking."

Startled by the question she had been hoping he would ask since the time he had asked it before (since then she had really thought of nothing else), Lukasha trembled. Oh, since he had asked her what she was thinking, she had been saving up so many thoughts for him! So many questions and observations about the world. That the rising sun looks like the oranges we get at Christmas, with ripe juice seeping out into the dawn. That in the winter, when it snows, it is like the stars are falling down on us. That dreams are caused by ghosts that live in your head, which sleep by day and come out at night to play in your empty mind. And why are toes just like fingers but shorter?

However, now that he had asked her to tell these thoughts to him, they tumbled from her consciousness and were lost. Groping through her mind, she could find none of them. She blinked, squeezed her eyes shut, and pulled her shoulders toward her ears as if in expectation of a blow.

"For God's sake," he shouted, "I'm not going to hit you!"

Tears began to form, pooling at the bottom of her eyes.

"Have I ever? Have I ever hit you?" he demanded. The truth was, he hadn't, but had nearly done it many times.

Lukasha shook her head. Then she dropped to the floor of the cab, and on her knees kissed the shiny toe of one of his boots where it hung in the air.

Ulyanov sighed, forcing a stream of smoke from his tired lungs. He would never make a person of her, much less a lady, he thought, looking down at the little heap. But at least he could treat her like one.

He lifted her from the floor, replaced her on the seat across from him, and for the remainder of the journey home chatted pleasantly about the weather to the uncomprehending little face. Then, amused at his own charade, he walked her up the winding, creaking steps to her tiny room at the top of the house, where she slept with three other serfs in one small bed, and left her, with a dashing click of his heels and a kiss on the hand, astonished at her door.

In front of the colossal golden doors of Andreyev palace on the Neva was an uproar. It was Sunday afternoon, the day on which the Prince Andreyev, wealthy beyond the wildest dreams of Western magnates, opened his door and purse to anyone who came to call on him for help. The petitioners jostled and bumped their body parts against each other while staring at the beneficent doors with eyes made runny both by winter cold and tears of hardship, human misery.

The door opened a crack. A cry went up; the ragged crowd surged up the steps and threw itself against the door. Ato, the elegant African steward of the house (also butler, majordomo, and valet to the prince), regarded these assembled human dregs, the filthy bottom residue of Russia's poorest, with the coolest brown and ivory eye. How he hated them. Across the windy steppes they came on frozen feet, or crawled on hands and knees; starving, they trudged up from the deserts of Asia and down from the savage Siberian snows. Ato wondered if they would ever stop, but he knew that poverty, misfortune, the games of the gods would never stop, and so they would continue to come until they had drained his prince of all his tears and left him dry and shriveled, old before his time, worn out by the weight of other people's sorrows.

How hungry they were for pieces of his prince's heart! It was not the money Ato would deny them, not at all—the prince had more than enough, so much, in fact, that he looked for ways to spend it all. The prince's weekly beneficence, however, did not even begin to absorb the better part of all his cash. So many times, as Ato was putting him to bed, the prince would drop his chin in despair. "Oh, Ato! What am I to do with it all? The money must be spent. The world must have some good of it! But try and try as I do, I can never seem to get rid of it. They tell me to invest it, gather interest, but then there will only be more!"

Ato closed the door against the stricken faces and turned away. The prince was happy today, and Ato would not disturb him. Certainly, knowing it was Sunday and his "giving day," the prince would be distressed to know that Ato's austere heart had denied this suffering, ignored it. But the prince, absorbed in the planning of his daughter's name-day party three weeks hence, had not seemed to notice what day it was at all, and Ato would not remind him. Laboring under the illusion that this extravagant "do" would, perhaps for good, unburden him of his riches and thus the load of other people's sorrows (for if he had no money, they could ask for none), the prince was crouching feverish over his golden desk, scribbling furiously his lists of provisions and plans for entertainment. In fact, Olga's name day would not occur until July, but the prince dismissed this fact, reasoning that his daughter's appearance in the world was an event of such importance it merited multiple celebrations, and if Ato had allowed it, the prince would have celebrated her birth with extravagance at least once a week.

Proceeding down the hallway, Ato passed the prince's study but did not glance inside. He knew what was on those lists. Hot spices of the Orient, a glare of summer sun upon the tender palate. Fruits of the south, fragrant melons, apricots, glistening plums and grapes, exotic pineapples and bananas that would scent the odorless empty winter days, traveling up from their tropical homes much as he had, swaddled in cloths and coddled in hay, until they reached their final destination, the after-dinner plate of a guest at the family estate, Pandemonium, where the great house party—a thousand guests—would take place.

Islands of summer in the cold were what the African sought, and toward this end he had nudged the tastes of the prince so that Ato himself might experience again the nutritious equatorial sun for which his very bones had hungered these many years. Continuing down the hallway, the magisterial African wafted past a series of reception rooms until he reached the door into the colossal courtyard. Looking through the glass, Ato stood transfixed with pride, for there it was, his masterpiece.

Ato had designed it himself. A cathedral of the sun, with an intricate system of prismatic windows that focused the weak rays of winter light into swords of heat that carved the cold away. It was thus summer in the summerhouse all year long. And the young mistress, the Princess Olga, was entertaining her many friends inside right now.

Amidst the lush vegetation, figures in white were seated at tables, their faces moist and ruddy with the heat. Some of the guests were playing tennis on the fine clay court; others were drinking lemony summer drinks. And through the center of the summerhouse there flowed a stream upon which a punter punted, pushing a boat back and forth inside this imported season, this artifical English summer afternoon, a flake of green lost in the vast white winter outside the glass. Perhaps this Anglophilia, the very rage among the Russian nobles, was a comfort to them in some way, as if England's very smallness, drabness, reasonableness were a shelter for them to hide in from Russia's enormities, enormousness.

Olga had merrily insisted that all of her guests attire themselves as English gentlemen and ladies, in straw boaters, striped blazers, dresses of thistledown white. For those guests who did not own these outfits, she provided them, and now Ulyanov, irritable in his blazer, which was far too small for him, leaned against an oak tree and sipped at a china cup. The cup was tiny, so ridiculously posed between thumb and forefinger, and the sips of milky tea he took were effete and small, which made him feel unmanly—how different from the harsh black Russian version of the drink, which burned his throat so brutally as it flowed from the finger-scorching glass in deep masculine draughts as he stood in muddied boots in a field and gazed at the bloodied birds or bristly boar he had bagged in the morning's hunting, breath smoking in the cold gray autumn air—now that was tea!

Rybynsky, Ulyanov noted with envy, was the only man in the group not gotten up like a fool to please his hostess. He stood, severely, casually, infuriatingly elegant and assured, his cup of tea resting gracefully in his palm, talking to the countess while Princess Olga, their nervous hostess, distractedly wiped her forehead, sure she had forgotten something, done something wrong. Was the tea properly weak and watery? Was the sandwich bread cut parsimoniously thin and lined with wilted watercress? Were the biscuits crumbly enough and not too sweet? Were the strawberries small and somewhat hard? And where was the clotted cream? She so hoped the servants would not substitute the hearty, heavy Russian sour stuff for that delicate condiment.

Ulyanov in his blazer was watching the Countess Korvin with falcon's eyes. It was not that he was interested in the woman any longer. No! He was merely observing her scientifically, to see how a properly brought up Russian young lady dressed, walked, spoke, leaned forward with concentration to catch her companion's least drops of studied wit, laughed, brightened her eyes, softened her speech, smiled fetchingly. The fact that Alexandra did none of these things with particular grace, however hard she tried, escaped his passionate attentive-ness, for he had set Alexandra up as his womanly ideal, and at this very moment Lukasha, back at home, was marinating in a bath of heavy cream and roses bought in bulk at the florist's with which Ulyanov hoped to bleach away the peasant duskiness of her skin, soak out the bacon stink of the kitchen, tenderize her hardened fingertips, and render her fresh as a newborn child, ready to be created in the image of Countess Korvin, although she was much too short.

Thus, he studied his model, who was now trying to suppress an impending sneeze. Too late. It rattled her tiny teacup and brought tears to her eyes.

"It's just . . . it's just . . . it's just that—" Another sneeze erupted into their discussion of what Russians were always dis-cussing, that is, how it was possible to live in Russia, Russia being impossible to comprehend, to get one's mind around. The attempt to understand it had set heads aching and thoughts churning from one end of the empire to the other, and the fevered discussions and ferocious arguments ground on and on in elegant drawing rooms and peasant huts alike, in army barracks, offices, cafes, across fences in the countryside, in autumn fields where serfs, putting up their scythes a moment, shouted at each other, shook their fists. The nationwide debate did not even stop for Sunday worship, but went on in whispers under the gilded onion domes while the interminable mass grieved on and on, the priests' hysterical laments echoing through the hollow churches the sound of a special Russian sorrow.

"Santé," said Rybynsky, placing a hand on Alexandra's arm to steady her as another sneeze exploded, rattling her teacup again and bursting a tiny pearl button from the back of her dress. The button soared through the air and dropped to the ground not far from where Ulyanov was standing. Instantly, he was upon it.

His teacup sat on the ground as he crawled through the heavy grass, parting it like hair in his quest for the tiny object. Success. The bead pressed hot against his palm. Surely she would be enormously grateful to have it back.

"I can't imagine," said Alexandra airily, though suddenly aware of an eager presence at her side, "why you think it is possible to conduct a reasonable, satisfying life in this country. Simply to avoid insanity we have to delude ourselves we're somewhere else. Right now we are in England. It is clearly the only way." Ulyanov stood near her, breathing a little too loudly.

"On the contrary," said Rybynsky, raising an eyebrow, "it is impossible to live anywhere else. Truly, that is, to live." He gazed at her over the rim of his raised teacup in a way that made Alexandra sip quickly at the air herself.

They are sinking into each other's eyes, Ulyanov thought, and, doubting that the countess would be interested in knowing at this moment that a button was missing from her dress, he dropped it quickly into his pocket, intending to examine it later, pore over it, stroke it, press it against his cheek.

However, now that he thought of it, he did not like Rybynsky's tone, nor the provocative nature of that remark. There was clearly some insinuation, some suggestion of insidious intimacies, passions of a nature one did not mention in a lady's presence. Chin thrust out, aggressive, Ulyanov stepped forward.

"Truly to live—what do you mean by that, sir?"

Rybynsky slowly turned his head. "Simply that there is an extravagance, almost a violence, a vividness of emotion to which we Russians are prone, which cannot be had in any other civilized country. As you yourself so clearly demonstrate."

Ulyanov was now uncertain. Had he just been insulted? Or not? Rybynsky's benign expression had not changed. It was detached, reasonable, dignified as ever. But one corner of his mouth betrayed a tiny twitch, and that was enough.

"I challenge you," said Ulyanov flatly.

"My point exactly," Rybynsky returned, and, turning his head, addressed the countess. "This excess of emotion, this snatching at daggers, this overflow of energy is quite marvelous, don't you think, Countess? In Western Europe they haven't had it for years. I do not think it would be overstating the point to call them decadent, by the most classical definition of the word."

My second will call on you, Ulyanov wanted to say, but he said nothing, understanding now how deftly Rybynsky had side-stepped his attempt to call him out to a place where Rybynsky's intellectual agility would be of no use to him, where raw nerve, a steady hand, a clear eye determined a man's standing as a man. However, it was those unmanly mental skills that had slipped the eminent councilor past the danger of facing the possessor of those manly skills, which, Ulyanov suddenly realized, might not be so valuable after all, especially when he saw the way the countess was looking at Rybynsky and ignoring himself, superior in masculinity though he was.

Which had been Rybynsky's unstated point exactly, he saw. For whose arm did the pretty countess cling to? Toward whom did she bend?

He, Ulyanov, champion of a hundred duels (well, actually, not that many, but quite a few), was only foolish in the count-ess's brittle eyes, which were looking at him now with distaste. All his favorite things about himself were nothing when set beside the councilor's dazzling apathy, his absence of emotion. Even the heat of Rybynsky's gaze upon the countess was not all that heated, to tell the truth. Ulyanov hadn't noticed that before. And yet why did she look at Rybynsky so thirstily?

Of course. Ulyanov himself had played with too many
heated hearts, his own as cold as ice, not to know the power of
indifference, the cruel attraction of the one who does not care, or
only cares from time to time, the infliction of the torments of
uncertainty, the precisely administered, exquisitely excruciating
crushing of the ego that brought them to their knees, gazing up
at him with streaming tears and groping hands, and happily.
And hadn't the countess done just that to him? And wasn't he at
her feet? So happily, too?

To hell with her! His attempt to make the countess love him
by simply, kindly loving her had been a failure. So why not
return to the ways he knew best? He would turn her own indifference back on her.

A mark was what he needed. A woman whose social anxiety
and fear of sexual failure gave off the delicious fragrance of a
flower open to his needle-sharp but gentle probe, a woman on
whom he would land gracefully, most lightly, to drain from her
the ego-expanding elixir on which he had always lived. And he
saw one now, a perfect one, who stood to the side watching the
countess and the councilor with clear dismay, though she was
trying hard to hide it. Left out. Ignored. Just what the old Ulyanov liked.

And most gratifying (oh, how rich this was), she was Rybynsky's own intended, as everyone who was anyone knew very well,
though the engagement was as yet unannounced.

Ulyanov oozed toward her, radiating delight at her existence—the indifference would come later; it was the dousing of
that warm and nourishing light that drove them mad. Poor
Olga. Not a pretty girl; even the luscious complexion that was
her chief beauty had gone gray in her distress, rendering her
invisible. Ulyanov noticed that her hair was too carefully done,
her dress too elaborate, as was usually the case with plain girls, as

if they thought that by applying decorations they could distract from the lack of beauty elsewhere.

Princess Olga looked up at Ulyanov from where she stood wilting against the glass wall and tried to smile, but she succeeded only in cracking her face apart in the middle.

"Dance with me," said Ulyanov with a bow. Olga, unnerved by the suggestion—to dance at an English tea—laughed out loud. And laughed again when Ulyanov swung her off her feet, set her gently on the ground, and began to dance with her to the tune of his own humming.

"We mustn't," she said breathlessly, "people are watching."

"Let them watch. I hope they do." He swung her again, her feet flying, and, settling her back on the soles of her shoes in the soft summer grass, waltzed with her.

The color had come back to Olga's cheeks. She had a face again. However, this face was now looking up at him with brimming, liquid eyes in a way that told him it was time to stop. Soon it would be too late. Although there was a heart to be captured here, twisted, broken, wrung dry of all its riches, emptied out, devoured whole, he found to his amazement, his dismay, he hadn't the heart for it.

Ulyanov's own indifference to the countess lasted but an hour or two. The suppression of his love was choking him. He had to get it out before he died of it. And what better way than a letter?

That night, while Lukasha went on soaking in her odor-removing, complexion-softening bath, Ulyanov sat down at the desk in his study and, taking from the drawer a piece of that special scented paper he used for all his romantic missives, contemplated the blankness of the sheet. Then he snatched it up and crumpled it. To use the same paper he usually did—why, this would taint the purity of his emotion. What paper would be proper to use to write to her? What material? The petal of a rose, a bit of precious silk? No, paper would have to do. But not this, not this—he'd written to serving maids on that (and to tell the truth, this stationery had served him very well, especially when he had remembered to perfume it). No, to Alexandra he would write on . . . his mother's paper! Nothing could be more pure or more symbolic of the seriousness of his feelings than creating a link between this precious, saintly person and this other saint (not saint exactly, he would have to amend that, but that was the general idea).

Ulyanov jumped up from the desk, ran into his mother's library, rummaged in her rosewood secretary, and departed with a handful of stiff vellumlike paper, enough to do the job with extra sheets in case he needed to rewrite. Back at his desk, he settled himself again and chose a pen. A drink would be nice at this important moment, to help his thoughts to flow, but no, he was starting a new and purer life.

He dipped the pen in the ink (would that it had been his blood, he thought, or better yet, his tears, but then the writing would not show up) and allowed it to hover in the air above the paper while he thought. Should he call her Countess Korvin or Alexandra? Did he wish to show respect or warmth and intimacy?

My dear Countess Korvin, he began in his best handwriting, having reached a compromise, the "my" added to the "dear" expressing a slightly greater degree of warmth than the usual "dear." More he could not venture. It would not do to be too familiar with such a (he could not stop himself from thinking it) ferocious woman.

Ought he to plunge directly into a declaration of his feelings? Or lead her gently into the center of his heart? He did not want to shock her. On the other hand, he did not want her to mistake the power and depth of his emotions.

I hope my forwardness in addressing you directly will not prejudice you against my suit. He liked that. It sounded intelligent. It hinted at what was to come but still kept something in reserve. It was ever so slightly roundabout.

We have not known each other long. Looking at the sentence carefully, reading it over and over to see how it went with the previous successful clause, he decided it took him in the wrong direction. He drew his pen vigorously through the line. Then he crumpled up the piece of paper and threw it on the floor. He took another.

My dear Countess Korvin, he wrote again, *I hope my forwardness in addressing you directly will not prejudice you against my suit.* He read it over. And over and over. No. It was wrong. All wrong. Too many words, too formal. It made him sound timid. Unmanly. He crumpled up the piece of paper and threw it on the floor. He took another.

Alexandra, he wrote, and sat back to look at the name. He loved her name. It was majestic. The way the beautifully balanced *A* rose up like a mountain, a tower, a flame. The slender *l* beside it. He sat looking at what he had written for a long time: *Alexandra.* Then he crumpled up the sheet of paper and threw it to the floor. He took another.

For hours he struggled with the letter, writing it over and over and over again, trying to express to her what he felt. But it was impossible. No words could do it justice. He had failed. Still, he had emptied his heart out onto the page, and this had given him some relief. The problem was that his heart filled right back up again.

She would surely laugh at him. He imagined her taking the

letter, sitting back in whatever exquisite chair she might choose inside her magnificent gold-encrusted palace, opening it, laughing, and tossing it to the floor. Correction—first she would find it among the many, many other such declarations she was sure to receive each and every day, and *then* she would open it and laugh and toss it to the floor. How foolish of him even to think of sending it.

No, he must take the risk! Grabbing another sheet of paper, he scribbled, *I love you,* signed it *Andrei Mecklenburg-Ulyanov,* folded it, wrote *Countess Alexandra Korvin* with a flourish, and ran out into the hall to find the footman Porfiry, who was sleeping off a satisfying drunk in the chair next to the coatrack. He shook Porfiry awake, pressed the letter and some paper rubles into his hand, and pushed him out the door, shouting, "Take it to Korvin palace!" at the old serf as he made his way drunkenly down the steps. "And wait for an answer!"

No answer came. An hour later Porfiry was back, shrugging. Ulyanov suspected that Porfiry had not actually found his way to Korvin palace but had gotten even drunker with the money for the cab. And suddenly, Ulyanov hoped he had done just that, but he did not ask because he did not want to know the answer.

Three weeks later, on the morning of the great name-day party at Pandemonium, Istvan the coachman sat in the kitchen of Korvin palace angrily eating potatoes, smashing them against the plate, expressing his emotions in a way that the mistress would see and understand, if only she were here.

The problem was not really that potatoes were all there was to eat any longer in the household. He could forget the fatty slabs of boiled beef in caper sauce, the rich and oily soups that had warmed his cold belly on a winter's night, or the flaky fried fish on a winter's morning such as this, its crisp and silvery skin melting in his mouth. He could forget the stable of a hundred shining horses, the fifteen grooms and thirty stable boys who kept them that way without his having to lift a finger except to say "Baba has had a workout today. Look after her." He could even forget the supply of compliant serving maids, so appreciative of his tales of Budapest and ready to reward his descriptions of that wild, romantic city with an animal vigor of affection appropriate to the spirit of the Magyar. They too, like the horses, had been sold.

No, what he could not forgive was that she would not let him drive her. For how else was he to have all this again? For weeks he had hungered for this trip, remembering the kitchen at Pandemonium, the berries and cream, the pickles and salted cabbage, the fresh chicken and veal—a whole week of it! And the varying textures of what's-her-name, who had, in exchange for a description of the mad mosaics on the roof of the Matyas church on Buda hill and of the majestic bridges across the Danube, allowed him to explore the geography of softness down here, up there, back this way, and so forth. For a whole week the mistress was scheduled to be there. There was no telling what he could accomplish with what's-her-name in a week! And an entire week away from the whinings and scoldings of the worn-out wife who lived in a tiny room off Prishibodiev Street and actually expected him to come home to her every night! If only the mistress would let him drive her!

She would not. He was to drive her only to Andreyev palace and leave her there to be taken down to Pandemonium in what he knew to be an improperly sprung old coach by that old cheese of a Platon Platonovich, the Andreyevs' third coachman and a man whose idea of sensual pleasure was to venture out without a scarf over his face in the very coldest of weather in order to enjoy the crackling of the frozen hairs inside his nose. To waste a week at Pandemonium on such a man! Istvan cut a potato carefully into quarters to make it look like more and smelled it before eating it.

Someone was speaking to him. He thought it might be Matryona. Of course, he had been deep inside the experience of the potato when she entered the room, or he would have made the effort to sit up straighter in order to flatten his sagging bag of a belly and present to her the tautened torso of a true Magyar—heir to the steppes, wolf of the wide-open spaces. That was him.

Matryona was standing in the doorway with her arms crossed in such a way that her breasts plumped up invitingly beneath her food-stained white blouse, her muscular, work-thickened hands and forearms promising skill and vigor in amorous combat. At least this was how she appeared to Istvan at this very moment as he sat transfixed, open mouth filled with half-chewed potato, by the seductive apparition in the doorway.

But she's never paid any attention to me before! Istvan protested to himself. Could it be that he was only imagining her slant-hipped come-hither stance, the erotic glint in her penetrating, shadow-lidded stare?

Apparently not, for now Matryona inserted a finger in her mouth and closed her eyes, sucking deeply on it in a sexual promise that could not be mistaken for anything else, and it did not occur to Istvan to ask what he might, inadvertently, be promising in return as he rose from the table, shuffled over to her in his boots, knelt on the floor, and raised her skirts. He forgot all about the trip to Pandemonium, though Matryona herself clearly had not, and if Alexandra, who was upstairs packing trunks with the favored Praskovia, who once again was to accompany her on a journey without the resentful Matryona, had known that at this very moment in the kitchen the Arpad wolf was galloping triumphant through the swamps and fetid forests of Mother Russia, yipping, slavering, grunting, she would have known that the vengeful Matryona was planning something big.

Alexandra did not know. At this very moment she was standing with hands on hips, a puzzled expression on her face as she looked at the opened trunk, trying to remember what she had forgotten, which was, of course, impossible if one has truly forgotten it. In any case, she had so little that it was easy to remember all of it. Alexandra only hoped that the collection of gowns, dresses, shoes, fans, and second-rate jewels so painfully acquired from her small store of funds would hold out well enough during the week-long stay to create, with the necessity of three changes of clothing each day, an impression of sufficient wealth and luxury. Count Kolygin would be there, his presence specially arranged by Madame Lavorine, and although Alexandra had not relinquished her pursuit of the splendid Rybynsky, practical considerations required that Kolygin's suit be strongly entertained at least. After all, he had not been unpleasant at all. A widower, yes, and quite old—fiftyish, she believed—but handsome in his grief-gaunt way. It would be easy to imagine herself loving him if Rybynsky did not work out.

"Praskovia," said Alexandra to the serf, who was kneeling on the floor by the open trunk vigorously stuffing an otter-skin muff into a space between a tissue-wrapped petticoat and box of gloves, "do you think it is possible to be in love with two men at once?"

"Absolutely," said Praskovia, "or even three or four. I once knew a girl who was in love with an entire regiment of infantry."

"I don't believe you."

"Oh yes, little mistress, she loved them all. Her little hut was always surrounded that summer as they paced around in the dust and kicked at the chickens and peered into the windows and banged on the door, impatient for their turn at love. They were very happy together, Ippolita and her regiment. They were always the same, but always different, she used to say, one man with many faces, so to speak, and she could never tire of him, as she did of her husband. Many, many women would have envied her. When they went marching away waving their muskets and blowing kisses at their sweetheart, Ippolita threw herself into the Oka, but it was one of the tributaries, very shallow there, so of course it did no good. She only got wet."

"I don't think you'd call that love," said Alexandra. "Wouldn't you call that something else?"

"Of course it was love. What else would it be?"

Alexandra declined to say the word. Praskovia dropped the lid of the trunk with a bang and snapped the clasp. Taking Alexandra by the hand, Praskovia led her to the silver icon hanging on the wall, a candle burning beneath it, where she removed her peasant kerchief, folded it neatly, placed it on the floor, helped her mistress down to rest her knees upon it, and directed the countess to pray for a safe journey, for the guidance of the Lord and all the saints, and for the continued health of all the household, "but not that Matryona."

There was building going on at Pandemonium. There was always building going on at Pandemonium. By now, the manor and its outbuildings—the stables, smokehouses, gazebos, and teahouses with windows opening on choice vistas, cobbler's sheds, tanning sheds, greenhouses, mausoleums, temples, pavilions, cow and threshing barns, blacksmith's forge, wheat and oil mills, offices, workshops, galleries, and churches—occupied some one hundred acres, but still it was not enough. Even the greenhouses and gardens, which demanded round-the-clock surveillance by an army of careful serfs, some of whom were charged with the nurturing of one single tree, which they watched and watered all night long, muttering gloomily to themselves between sips of warming vodka—even this was not enough to make a dent in the prince's resources. Nor the private museums stuffed with antiquities Dravidian, Tibetan, Scythian, and Greek, nor the churches (their bulbous domes pressed with pure gold), nor the castles brought from Ireland stone by stone had provided the prince relief from the burden of his wealth. His one great hope, the private railroad linking the palace on the Neva with Pandemonium and the family's holdings all over Europe and Asia, had utterly failed to drain his resources. And the schools and hospitals he had endowed across the length and breadth of Russia were so modest in their demands—a few pounds of rye flour and a pencil or two, else the luxury would damage the soul—that he had begun to seek greener pastures in Germany and France, but these countries, misunderstanding, were fearful that the prince might expect some political or economic quid pro quo for his barbaric country and had refused his benevolence. Forced to turn to the tsar for help, the prince had offered to build a new fleet and underwrite the expenses of the army, but the tsar, suspicious as any peasant refusing the gift of a cow, certain there must be something wrong with it or that some evil trick was in the offing, had adamantly refused.

However, the railroad was out of service at this time due to a dispute between the peasants who kept it running and their prince. A section of track had been displaced by a shifting of eroded soil, but the peasants—convinced the occurrence was a sign from God, the flip of a colossal finger at man's technological hubris—refused to repair it, arguing that such an act constituted a disrespect toward the will of the Almighty that was outright sacrilegious. The prince could not budge them, and so the entire enormous party, the very cream of Petersburg, a group a thousand strong, was being carried away from the city in carriages fitted out with runners and thus turned into gigantic sleds, which skimmed over the surface of the frozen river that wound like a gray ribbon through a landscape of ice-burdened trees that bent and twisted and groaned under their load of winter, sped past the drab and greasy huts of the peasantry that squatted on the banks, and once sent scurrying with a frantic waddle and a honk a fat domestic goose who had stepped out onto the ice on careful red feet. The crack and moan of the river's ice, about to collapse under the weight of hundreds of carriages, the snorts and frightened whinnies of horses as they slipped and scrabbled at the glassy surface beneath their flat hooves, lent a certain excitement to the journey, the travelers knowing that an icy death could come at any moment, but this was all part of the fun of Russia in the winter.

The sun could not penetrate the tough white skin of the sky. Unnecessary, however, for Pandemonium itself, with its acres of light, was visible for miles down the river and provided the glow of another sun, one that would not go out, and so the travelers had been for hours on the verge of this other sunset, as if time had stopped until the carriages rounded the bend into the night and the enormous estate, with its lighted buildings, its welcoming bonfires set on distant hills, appeared as a visible series of stars, a constellation fallen to earth and glowing hot along the ground.

The carriages stopped on the river. The guests, emerging into the cold, were being handed down.

"Do not forget what I told you," Madame Lavorine urged, clutching Alexandra's elbow just as the countess was reaching for the steaming glass of tea that was being presented to her by a liveried servant as she alighted from the carriage. She took a sip, singed the roof of her mouth, and became aware of the entire structure of her upper digestive system as the tea burned its way down her throat and dropped like a hot coal into the center of her stomach. Still, it was welcome after the cold dim hours in the coach, with Madame Lavorine chattering all the way about Count Kolygin and his oddities of taste and behavior, personal characteristics of which, she felt, Alexandra must be made aware so that she might manipulate his emotions more effectively.

However, Alexandra, again in the grip of what she believed to be the idealism of her in fact imaginary love for Rybynsky, was willing to accept Praskovia's cynical technique for exciting male passion when it applied to Rybynsky but felt horror at Madame Lavorine's equally cynical instructions when applied to the wealthy count. Alexandra decided that Lavorine's advice was heartless, condescending to the male, and ultimately degrading to the dignity of the human spirit, and she told her so.

"Pish-tosh," said Madame Lavorine, "you don't know men at all. The sad truth is that they don't much care who they're with, have better things to do, and are quite happy to be relieved of this particular responsibility. They don't know what they want until women tell them. It's time for you to learn that." Throwing her chin up, Madame turned away to accept her own glass of tea, which had appeared in the grip of a white-gloved hand.

Alexandra was astonished at the impertinence of the tiny woman's words, the sharpness of her tone, but she realized with a sudden shock that she herself was not who she had been, and that it was her own precarious position, still masked by her title but unreinforced by wealth, that allowed the woman such freedom, since Madame Lavorine must somehow have divined what no one else knew—that Alexandra was in the process of sinking to that muddy layer near the bottom of polite society that Lavorine herself occupied, only just clinging to the hem of respectability, dependent on the largesse of relatives and friends, barely tolerated, laughed at and pitied behind her back, which position she might share permanently if she did not listen up in the first place.

She was about to give the newly arrogant Lavorine a dressing-down when her eye was caught by the sight of a figure she knew rather well and another she didn't.

It was Ulyanov and a woman whom he was helping down the tiny collapsible stairway of a large, plush traveling coach in the tenderest, most solicitous fashion. The woman, dressed in the richest furs, came forward into the light of a flaming torch and blinked her large, liquid black eyes in bewilderment.

"That woman looks very like an innocent doe in the midst of a forest," Alexandra noted with irritation, grinding her teeth and staring with resentment, until Madame Lavorine, vaguely but intuitively conscious of some danger to her plans for Alexandra and thus herself, grasped her young charge by the back of her coat and began to pull her toward the red-painted troika, one of hundreds, that was waiting to bring them up to the manor house.

"Another of his women. No concern of yours," she said, pushing Alexandra up into the troika, "and you had better watch yourself over the next few days, my dear countess, if you do not want your chances to slip away."

In the reception area of the house, a hallway river-wide, the countess was just having her heavy coat removed from her shoulders by a footman and was holding out her hands to him for the removal of her gloves when Count Kolygin himself emerged from the teeming crowd of arrivals with Madame Lavorine at his elbow, darted in ahead of the footman, and caught one gloved fingertip like a teardrop on his own.

"My dear countess," he breathed, "it has been too long," and bowed low over Alexandra's hand. Looking directly at the scalp he displayed to her, Alexandra noted with reassurance that he still had most of his hair, and she wondered if the desire to establish this fact hadn't motivated his gallant gesture in the first place. He was shorter than she was, she noticed when he straightened up. But no matter, he was still handsome in his ruined way.

The count began to strip the gloves from her hands like a loosened skin. He passed them to the footman, and Alexandra, whose experience of masculine gallantry had been, up to this point, limited to Ulyanov's overconfident bumbling and Rybynsky's glacial, oddly ironic deftness, was impressed.

His eyelids, slightly puffy in a way Alexandra attributed to recent melancholy, lifted slightly to take in her face and lowered again as his eyes swept down the length of her body. Then he smiled in a way that Alexandra was not sure she wanted to interpret.

"One hundred thousand souls," Madame Lavorine whispered in her ear.

*A*to stood, as he did at every meal, behind his prince's chair, leaning over from time to time to offer reassurance that all was well. He watched the prince's hands tremble as they toyed with the golden fork and knife, cutting listlessly, distractedly at his food. Stepping back and raising his eyes to the assembly of guests, Ato noted with satisfaction the precise alignment of the golden salt cellars, bowls of flowers, and candlesticks that were ranged on each of the ten long tables in the enormous dining room, a geometrically perfect arrangement that had taken him hours to achieve as he measured the distance between each object and the wall, believing as he did that this alignment would ensure the continuance of calm and peace for at least this one more night, that such exquisite order could foil at least in part the malicious will of the gods, with their love of chaos, catastrophe.

So. What chaos was brewing tonight, what disorder on the verge of breaking out, which none could see but Ato? The dinner for the thousand was going on in three separate dining rooms, but Ato, anxious, knew that it was here in the silver and red dining room that the gods were at work.

The crux of potential disaster was formed by three couples. First, his prince's daughter and her presumptive intended, the young bureaucrat, the brilliant court functionary. Of Rybynsky's dignity, his simplicity of manner, Ato approved. But this man's mask was thick and hard as glass. Ato feared for the little princess. Next, watching the man of glass from her place far down the table at the side of a wrinkled old man was his princess's friend, the Countess Korvin, yearning foolishly toward that cold, unattainable star. Ato shivered in his heavy furs. And that wrinkled old man at her side wanted to eat her, Ato thought, to eat her youth and get it for himself, so that he would never die. And there was another—the young dissolute with the peasant mistress disguised as a lady—who wanted to eat her too but not to keep from dying, for he was still too young to believe that he would ever die. Though he was scrupulously attentive to the little peasant, the rake's mind was elsewhere, his eyes bouncing from time to time toward the Korvin girl to see the effect he was having. Foolish, foolish, Ato thought. Why don't they eat my good food? Useless to give them good food. They paid no attention to important things. Ato raised one white-gloved hand and snapped his fingers softly. Each one of some three hundred footmen stepped forward in synchronization, extended a hand, and lifted a plate. Another soft snap of Ato's fingers and the next course was served.

An untouched portion of sturgeon mousse had been removed from Alexandra's place and replaced by a ball of minted snow in a long-stemmed crystal flute.

Count Kolygin was watching her so hungrily that Alexandra was inspired to eat something herself. It was unbearably hot in the dining room, and so she dug into the snow with her silver spoon and deposited the coldness, intensified by the burning mint, on her tongue. Relief.

If only Kolygin would stop talking at her, Alexandra thought, she could concentrate on what was really important: discovering who that woman was with the hated Ulyanov (not that she cared) and what exactly Rybynsky's feelings for Olga were (about which she cared a great deal).

"My late wife," Count Kolygin was saying, his hot breath pouring into Alexandra's ear in a way that made her want to slap him, "adored our Crimean estates. The softness of the air! The velvet nights! The rich perfumes drifting into the open windows of our bedroom. I hope I have not offended you by mentioning our bedroom."

If you had, you have compounded it by apologizing for it, Alexandra wanted to say, but simply closed her mouth over another mouthful of cooling snow. Ulyanov was actually feeding the woman spoonfuls of the greenish ice in the most disgusting way, with an expression of tender ardor in his gaze, which gaze, however, collided at just that moment with Alexandra's. They both looked away.

Oh, thought Alexandra with satisfaction. He wants me to see. There is therefore no point in looking. I know what I need to know. So what he said in his letter was true (as true, in fact, as Ulyanov's supposition that she would throw it on the floor, would laugh at it, which was exactly what she'd done).

She turned her eyes to Rybynsky, who sat ensconced in courtly dignity near the head of the table. From time to time he bent his sleek head to Olga's words, but suddenly his eyes met Alexandra's and did not drop away. He held her gaze, but without changing his expression, as if unable to acknowledge this moment of connection. He held her gaze and held it, until the countess shivered and shook. Perhaps we will meet later, the look seemed to say, perhaps in the library, or a corner of the music room, or a niche in the hallway, or on the darkened stairs, even better. Somewhere. Later. And who knows what will happen when we meet?

Any interest, faint as it had been, in the fadedly handsome count who sat at her side dissolved away.

"She loved to make things," the count was going on, smiling to himself, "anything she could make, she would, napkins, tablecloths, shawls, gloves, hats. Slippers. She made tea cozies and Christmas ornaments and shoes. She made shirts. She made trousers. Oh . . ." The count hesitated. "Do you find that offensive?"

"Find what offensive?" Still simmering in the aftermath of that look from Rybynsky, Alexandra had nevertheless turned her attention back to Ulyanov, trying to figure out just who that woman was. There was something strange about her. She did not look at all the type of woman she would have associated with Ulyanov.

"My mentioning trousers. I think an unmarried lady might find trousers offensive."

"I do not find trousers offensive, Count," she said distractedly, still looking at Ulyanov's woman, who sat stiffly in her place at his side, her large, irritatingly soft eyes fixed on a spot far away, and the giant plate of dark fat roasted boar, the mound of meat so high it reached her chin, untouched.

Who was she? Alexandra searched her mind for the answer as the count continued to catalogue his wife's housewifely virtues (jams of all kinds she had made herself, from gooseberry to quince, all berries gathered by her hand and washed and boiled in vats and dripped into jars and set to cool on surfaces throughout the house and the breezes from opened windows blowing the scents through all the rooms so that he might have been living in an orchard, he softly said).

She was foreign. That was it.

A haunch of meat was heaved in front of her, but Alexandra faced the challenge with vigor. For reasons she could not begin to explain to herself, the thought that this woman was foreign provided a measure of relief. There had not been the foreign woman yet who could compete with a Russian woman in her ability to deal with the boar-eating Russian male. Not, she explained to herself, tearing into her meat with her small, strong, white Russian teeth, that it mattered to her at all.

After dinner there were card games, drinking games, charades, dancing, the singing of arias and Russian folk songs, the wailing of Gypsy orchestras. The faces of the guests flickered in the candlelight as they gathered in conversational groups on couches and chairs, or stood beneath tall paintings that covered the tremendous walls, or lounged in doorways, or sat at harps and clavichords idly plucking at the strings, fingering the keys. Laughing, chattering, flirting was going on in room after room after room. As Alexandra slipped in and out among the revelers, her eyes darting over her shoulder to see if she had lost him yet, Count Kolygin followed doggedly, stumbling and tripping among the outstretched legs, all the while explaining the virtues of his wife.

The countess stopped and thought a moment. She suggested a game of hide and seek.

"Delightful!" answered the count. "My wife—"

But the countess had already disappeared.

Alexandra had eaten far too much. She now stood, slightly bent in digestive discomfort, a white-gloved hand on her stomach, her back against the wall at the bottom of a stairwell leading up to the bedrooms on the next floor. If only she could lie down for a moment! Loosen her corset! Take the damned thing off!

The entire existence of food in the world was something that Alexandra wanted to question. What was the point of it? It should not be allowed. Alexandra vowed never, ever to open her lips to food again.

She wondered if she could make it up the stairs, decided not. Slowly, so as not to disturb her burdened stomach, which, she hoped, was working as fast as it could to dissolve and dissipate the load it carried, she inched her way along the wall and out into a deserted hallway filled with the faraway sounds of merriment. Resting, she leaned against the wall again.

It even hurt to breathe. In fact, it was positively dangerous, the extra added pressure from the air in her expanded lungs threatening to split the straining membranes of her stomach. O Lord! O Heavenly Father! Alexandra felt the presence of God. A vengeful God, disapproving of excess.

The turmoil in her belly was subsiding. She could move again. However, she was not yet willing to. Still reclining against the wall, she remained motionless, sunk in the mindless stupor induced by the marinating mess in her stomach.

"Why, Countess Korvin, how delightful," said someone who Alexandra hoped was not the someone that she thought. But it was. Ulyanov was proceeding down the hall in her direction, his mysterious companion following meekly behind.

"Countess," he said, bowing low with an indifferent assurance that suggested to Alexandra that perhaps the letter of declaration had not been sincere after all, and she had to admit she almost found him attractive at this moment, "may I present the Princess Luka Abbabovna Mastradonian of Armenia."

Of course protocol decreed that a countess be presented to a princess and not the other way around. But Alexandra hadn't time to smell a rat before an amazing burning sensation began somewhere around her heart, one Alexandra could not attribute to the overworking of her digestive furnaces. A princess. She was outranked. And a beautiful one too.

He's mine: those were the words that formed inside her head.

"I want to talk to you," said Alexandra, treating the little princess as if she weren't there and taking satisfaction in her rudeness.

"You do?" Ulyanov goggled, forgetting for a moment the carefully cultivated suavity he had only just, with the insurance of an adoring woman at his side, begun in Alexandra's presence to be able to implement.

"Meet me in the small library—the gold one, not the green one—at midnight," she said firmly, and swept on down the hall, her discomfort now miraculously dispelled. But why, she wondered, had she said that? Why had she proposed a rendezvous? It had simply sprung full-blown from her lips, this invitation. Of course, she had no idea of whether or not she would be there. Perhaps something else would come up. Perhaps it wouldn't. But it would serve him right to wait for her. It would put him in his place.

Alexandra turned her thoughts to the question of Rybynsky himself. Where was he? What was he doing? What amusement had he found to prefer to her company?

She could not forget the promise of that gaze across the dinner table, and so she went in search of him, to find out what it meant.

Rybynsky was in the drawing room, resting his hands on the back of Olga's chair.

In the center of the room a Gypsy woman danced and sang, exposing teeth like the kernels of white corn, her skin rich and brown as Turkish coffee. Plum- and lemon-colored skirts swirled around her. She was delectable, and she knew it, and she approached each of the men who stood in the circle around her with a glittering shake of her tambourine, bending forward so that her breasts dropped down like soft pears into the damp thin fabric of her blouse, and each of the men who watched her quivered like a stallion scenting the mare.

Except Rybynsky, who was too dignified for that. He went on talking to Olga, smiling, gallantly turning his ear to the sound of Olga's voice, ignoring the Gypsy's presence as something too vulgar and low to exist within his sphere.

Again his eyes met Alexandra's. She turned away, trembling; not knowing where she went, mind swept clean, she drifted with a bump against a table set incredibly with after-dinner snacks. Not quite aware of what she was doing, she grasped a fork, took a plate and began to fill it with pickled beets.

"I've found you at last," said Count Kolygin.

The countess stabbed at a round wet beet so brutally, it skidded across the plate and smacked the count in the chest like a stray golf ball.

"So sorry, so sorry," said Alexandra, alert again and now waving a napkin vaguely in the direction of the stain on the count's white shirt. She looked in Rybynsky's direction. He was talking to Olga again. The countess threw her head back and laughed at nothing, hoping to attract Rybynsky's attention.

Count Kolygin looked down at his shirt and grew sad. "It's only the blood of a broken heart," he said softly. The countess, suddenly ashamed, touched him briefly on the shoulder, comforting. The poor man only missed his wife. She ought to have been kinder to him. Still, she did not relish further discussion of his wife's domestic talents, and for heaven's sake, hadn't the woman had a hundred thousand slaves? Perhaps Madame Lavorine had misrepresented him and his holdings.

"How is it, Count, that your wife did so much of her own housekeeping?"

"Hobby," said the count, still staring at the stain on his shirt front, which, Alexandra had to admit, did look rather as if a full and loving heart had been squashed in a splatter across his chest.

Now Madame Lavorine came rushing up, all sympathy and concern for the count and his shirt. She had armed herself with a wet napkin, which she pressed vigorously against the count's broken heart until it had absorbed some of the stain. Then she procured another napkin, and another, pressing and pressing against his heart until the redness was nearly gone. The count gazed at her with admiration.

"Seltzer," she explained, "best thing for stains. Though for oily substances, your melted butter, your French sauces, your brown gravies, it's vodka that really does the trick. It's the alcohol that sucks the stain right out."

"My wife used whiskey," said the count.

"Whiskey, yes, that works too on oils, but it does leave you with some residual darkness from the pigment in the malt, which is why clear, unflavored vodka is best."

Rybynsky was gazing at Alexandra openly now, with an expression she found difficult to interpret. She left Lavorine and the count to what was becoming a rousing debate over stain removal and moved in his direction.

Alexandra would have been happier if Olga had not risen from her seat and approached her with arms extended, protesting that in her preoccupation with her guests she had forgotten the most important guest of all—Alexandra herself. A much smaller person than her friend, Olga nonetheless managed to press Alexandra's cheek against her shoulder with affection, which action made Alexandra feel worse than ever, though it did not keep her from checking the direction of Rybynsky's gaze. He was, indeed, looking at her again, but now that she had come closer, the heat of his gaze had seemed to dissipate, as always.

"We're going to make an announcement tomorrow," Olga whispered. "I want you to be the first to know, but don't tell anyone, not even Praskovia."

Praskovia, who at this very moment was sitting with her skirts up on a chair in an enormous kitchen at the back of the palace, stretching her bared feet and legs toward the heat of the open hearth while crunching sunflower seeds and spitting the shells into the fire, listening with satisfaction to the spit and crackle as they burned, and at the same time bragging to one of the cooks about the number of pairs of full-length white goatskin gloves owned by her mistress, could not have cared less. But to Alexandra, the news was thunderous. She turned to stone in Olga's arms.

"Lovely, wonderful, so happy for you!" cried Alexandra, forcing her mouth into a smile so wide she felt it would break her stiffened face in pieces. "I only came to tell you I'm going up to bed. So tired, so tired." She rushed away as Olga, who was about to say "But it's early yet," turned to watch her go.

$\mathcal{A}$lexandra stayed at the window a long time before going to bed. Snow was pouring down from the face of the moon. She had forgotten about Ulyanov, who was sitting quietly in a chair downstairs waiting for someone who was not going to come, shifting his glance between the clock and the very same moon outside the window.

Eventually, she went to bed, undressing herself with difficulty, undoing slowly the hooks and eyes, the knots and bows, and listlessly dropping her clothing on the floor. She laid herself carefully in bed and placed her aching head on the smooth linen of the pillow. She had cried long and hard and, though exhausted, was still awake long after Praskovia had come into the room, settled herself on top of the porcelain stove, and narrowed her breathing to a thin, whistling snore. Sometime in the night, long after the moon had moved away from the window, Alexandra fell asleep. She slept long and hard, worn out by her tears.

She was startled awake by the strangeness of the morning light as it glowed through the snow-blocked window. Alexandra jumped out of bed, ran across the room, and, puffing with exertion, pulled up the sash. She punched through the wall of snow with her fist and stuck her head out the window.

Outside, the view was nothing but white, tints of it, different shades. Only the branches of the trees, in delicate patterns of darker white, and the tip of the onion-domed church, with its thin gold cross, showed above the surface of the snow. Delightful, she thought, amazing. Russian winter often brought satisfaction to the human appetite for sudden disaster and upheaval, and this was an exceptional example. All melancholy of the night before, all sense of chances missed and fate gone awry, was wiped as clean as the world outside the window. It was a new day, and Alexandra wondered what delightful dislocations of routine, of expectation, would result.

Anything was possible now.

Descending washed and dressed to the breakfast room, cheeks pinked with the ice that Praskovia had broken from the windowsill and rubbed across her skin in the Russian woman's version of rouge, Alexandra found everyone in the same high mood.

"Have you seen the snow? How terrible! How awful! We'll never get out again!" the thousand guests shouted to each other with joy, their appetites now fully resurrected. They loaded their plates with eggs boiled and fried, poached and scrambled, coddled and creamed, lamenting the certain disruption in the schedule of events. "A hunt will be impossible!" they laughed, adding sausages, ham, haddock, and pickled flounder to their plates. "No skating on the river today, I'm afraid," they moaned, popping gooseberry tarts into their mouths, "no riding, no sleighing, no walks in the woods, no tours of the grounds. No visiting Father Yoshka in the village."

"What are we all to do with ourselves today?" they cried. "And there's no getting home at all!"

But the prince had thought it out. Ato had wakened him at five with the news that the gods had been at play again, that all their careful plans for entertainment were laid waste by the storm. Appearing in the doorway of the breakfast room in his morning dress of Turkish trousers and tasseled fez, the prince raised his hands to the excited company.

"We all have seen the disaster that has visited us in the night.

My plans for you are thus disrupted. But I have another plan! I have decided that we will build . . ."

The assemblage rustled, simmering with excitement at the possibility of something new and unexpected, something they'd never done or seen before.

". . . a palace out of ice. Yes, in memory of our empress who built such a palace out of ice in honor of a wedding, we will build it."

The proposal was a sensation. The thousand guests now nodded to each other their approval of an expectation fulfilled.

"Moreover," shouted the prince above the boiling voices and bubbling heads, "there will be teams of men and women! We will draw for partners! And each will have a special task!"

The company went silent. Stunned at the prince's ingenuity, they bent their heads in reverence as all manner of possible intrigues and new entanglements, irregular arrangements and daring liaisons suggested themselves. The prince's hospitality was as imaginative as it was stupendous. They thanked him heartily in their silent hearts. A remade life! New love! Redemption! Joy!

Alexandra herself had not missed the sly allusion to a wedding, but she dismissed it, excited as any of the others. Perhaps she would draw Rybynsky as her partner. Yes, anything was possible. A clean slate. A new configuration of the world.

In the lottery for partners, the countess drew Ulyanov.

Still holding the slip of paper in her hand, she glanced at it again to make certain she had not been mistaken, then glared at him across the room. She was certain he had fixed it somehow. Surely providence could not have assigned her such a partner, matched her with such a man. Was this God's judgment on her worth? Her soul rebelled at the idea. She was sure Ulyanov himself must have bribed an eager servant.

And for what? Why did the rake pursue her? Certainly not because he loved her, as he had protested in his note (which was, she was certain now, a subterfuge, a fake). No, having devoted himself to making fools of women, he had merely chosen to add her to his list, and the countess wondered what quality she possessed beyond the incitement of her obvious virginity that excited his predatory instinct, the swift and swooping dive in her direction with opened beak and beady eye and reaching claws.

Ulyanov, equally surprised, crossed the room to her and silently offered her his arm. She took it, cursing softly to herself in a way she hoped he might faintly hear, and trotted along beside him in her high-heeled leather boots, a little sable muff dangling by a string from her arm. Her face, under the small fur-trimmed hat that was perched above her eyebrows, was pink with anger. They went out the door and down the steps, which had been swept and salted, so Alexandra's boots made a crunching sound as they crushed the grains of salt under their heels.

The long procession of couples wound through the paths that had been cut for them in the snow. The wet whiteness formed walls on either side of them so high they saw nothing but the snow itself, had no idea where they were going, and could only follow blindly the people in front of them as they made their way through the winter maze that zigged and zagged.

Alexandra slipped twice on the hard-packed snow of the path and had to grab at Ulyanov in a way she was sure would please him. This made her angrier.

At last they reached the end of the maze. An endless field had been cleared of snow and in its center the outline of a building had been marked with sticks and string stretching far in the distance. Mountains of shoveled snow towered around it. The growing crowd of couples, still issuing two by two from the maze of snow, murmured their awe, impressed by the seriousness of the undertaking.

"Well," said Ulyanov loudly, clapping his gloved hands together, "let's start." He stepped over to one of the snow hills and pried a stone-shaped chunk away from it. Others followed his lead. He walked over to the foundation site and dropped the hunk on the snow-packed ground. Others dropped their chunks in imitation.

"Not like that," said Alexandra irritably. She grabbed her own chunk and, kneeling down, rolled it in the snow as if covering a tea cake in powdered sugar. Having thus enlarged the chunk to what she thought a goodly size, she patted and shaped it until it looked like a large white brick—somewhat misshapen, she admitted, but good enough.

"Like this," she said, regarding her handiwork with satisfaction. "Haven't you ever built an igloo? What in heaven's name did you do as a child? Drink and chase women?"

"Actually, yes," said Ulyanov.

The countess was too angry to laugh. She made another brick of snow and packed it on top of the first. Then she made a third and packed it down on the first two, so that she had a tiny, narrow wall. Ulyanov stood aside and watched her work.

"I think we'd be better off if we laid a whole line of them out, a first layer," he suggested, "instead of trying to build a wall only one brick wide. It would fall over."

Alexandra, face already pink with cold, now turned red. She smashed the brick she had been making on the ground and stood up, vehemently stuffing her gloved hands inside her muff.

"That was productive, Alexandra," said Ulyanov.

Alexandra drew in her breath, a big and forceful one, while Ulyanov smiled with innocent delight.

"That's 'Countess' to you, Captain," she said. Turning her

back, she went over and plummeted into a snowbank. There were hundreds of couples now toiling busily round the site, rolling bricks of snow and packing them together into walls. The ridiculousness of the sight of these aristocrats—in their high-heeled boots and silk-lined coats and thin-skinned gloves and little muffs flying round on their strings—working as diligently as peasants made her happy for a moment, until she saw Rybynsky. He had gotten Olga for his partner (surely this could not be chance as well?), and they were working busily together—building, she bitterly supposed, a secret memorial to their soon-to-be-announced betrothal.

Alexandra got up out of the snowbank.

"So why didn't you meet me last night?" she said to Ulyanov's back. He was kneeling on the ground packing a brick into their section of wall. She noticed that his ears had turned red with the cold, for he wore nothing on his head. His light hair, dampened with sweat, was freezing in thick squiggles and curls and looked very like the frozen, floating hair of a gilded angel of the sort that had decorated the ceiling of her palace, but which now, stripped of its gold, resembled nothing more than a ghost of splendor.

"Why didn't I meet *you*?" he returned, suddenly standing, then coming toward her. "Why didn't you meet *me*? I waited in the library for hours." He seemed to have grown until he towered over her, so close she could feel the faint warmth of his body along with its size.

This sudden aggression frightened Alexandra in a way she found indefinitely exciting, indeterminately thrilling, for reasons she could not explain.

"Yes," she said more airily than she felt, for it suddenly occurred to her that he was rather taller than she was and much heavier and much stronger, and could easily break her arm if so inclined. The thought thrilled her even more, but not because she would have welcomed such an action, certainly not. It was simply that he *could and did not*. That this power was under restraint because she was a woman was what excited her, and she had never in her life felt so deliciously, exultantly, gloriously feminine, tall as she was.

"Yes, yes," she blathered, her face turning red and warm, "you're right. I wasn't there."

"Then why," he insisted, "did you suggest that I was the one at fault?"

Ulyanov's eyes were amazingly blue, Alexandra thought. She had never noticed that before. Blue as an angel's eyes, she would think, though he was certainly no angel. As for his question, she had no answer. Why had she? And why had she asked him to meet her in the first place? She didn't know. Some impulse to prod and poke and tease him, to see what he would do. Or what?

A house serf muffled in scarves came squeaking up on soft felt boots with glasses of steaming tea. Alexandra took one in her black-gloved hand and held it briefly to her cold cheek, kept it there until the hot tea began to burn. There were hundreds of these muffled servants squeaking about the building site with glasses of tea for the workers, and Alexandra noticed that tables had been set up in the snow. They were covered in cloths of rustic color and design, as if to underline the peasant nature of the task and thus its utter novelty. Samovars smoked in the wintry air, and bands of serf musicians began to tootle and strum their maudlin peasant melodies.

Ulyanov now subsided into politeness, then collapsed into uncertainty. He offered to hold her glass of tea for her, and when she refused, he fell silent, a blush spreading over his face. Alexandra settled her glass of tea in the snow (which began to melt around it) and went back to making bricks and packing them ferociously into their wall.

Ulyanov knelt down to put his own glass of tea in the snow and started rolling bricks with great industry alongside her. They were no longer making bricks and packing them immediately into the wall, but seemed to have silently come to the agreement that it would be better to lay in a store of such bricks before they set them into the wall. They were now collecting them in a row along the ground.

"So why didn't you?" he said suddenly.

"What?"

"Meet me in the library. You said you wanted to talk to me. What did you want to talk about?"

"Oh my," said Alexandra. "I've forgotten, I'm afraid."

Ulyanov turned his head and thought a moment. "You haven't forgotten. You just don't want to say." He paused. "Why don't you want to say?"

He was breathing oddly now, and looking at her in a strange way. She could feel it though she couldn't see it, bent over her work as she was. She flicked her glance briefly upward to check, and yes, there it was, that odd look she'd seen on his face a few times before. It made her want to laugh, but not with glee, with nervousness.

"Go away," she said suddenly.

"What?"

"Go away," she repeated.

"Why, Alexandra?" His voice was soft. And much too intimate, insinuating, oozing, enveloping, coming closer.

"I don't like you."

Ulyanov said nothing in reply to this, and Alexandra checked his face to see the effect of her remark. Yes, he looked as if he'd been slapped, as if he might be about to cry. Horribly, confusingly, her heart went out to him, but Alexandra snatched it back again, said nothing, and did not even lift her eyes to watch him walk away as his boots squeaked softly on the snow, then more and more softly, then faded into nothing, no sound at all.

The interest of this company in its construction work, sapped by cold and unaccustomed exertion, was soon exhausted, and couples began to wander back to the house in search of less strenuous amusement and lunch. The building site—a jumble of crooked walls half built—was soon deserted.

However, as the guests moved about inside the house, pursuing further the flirtations of the morning as they chose their spots at table, the walls of the palace of ice straightened and strengthened and grew. Clear blocks of ice the size of traveling trunks were chopped from the river and dragged by ropes up the hill to the clearing in the snow. A cathedral of dark and solemn sound enclosed the building site as the peasants sang at their work, and the company inside the house, unaware that the palace of ice was now rising from the ground, assumed that this sonic glory a thousand voices strong had been conjured for their pleasure out of the spirit of Russian winter itself, another spectacular diversion arranged by their solicitous host, who at this very moment had set before them at their luncheon tables a feast of white food to match the day.

Small twisted trees set with silver and diamonds to represent the ice rested on the white of the tabletops as a winter forest in miniature, the unneven driftings of the snow simulated by the packing of straw beneath the tablecloth. White soup was served in crystal bowls, white fish, white chicken, white pork, white asparagus, white potatoes in white cream on more plates of faceted crystal, and from crystal goblets they drank their pure white wine, which tasted of icy winter air. Then, at a clap of

Ato's hands, the winter trees were cleared away and spring was carried in—in baskets of crocus and daffodil and pots with tiny live trees just beginning to show their green buds. Applause. And then another clap of the hands and summer had come. The trees had burst into leaf, gone heavy with fruit, and the guests reached forward to pick the blood-ripe cherries, rosy peaches, musty pears. Another clap of the hands and it was autumn: apples swelled crisp and hard among the leaves and pumpkins and squashes appeared, their plump bellies carved out, hot custards in the hollow spaces. The leaves of the trees, gold and scarlet, loosened from the branches and dropped desolate on the tablecloths as footmen with large feathered fans simulated the winds of October from behind each chair. And then it was winter again, the return of the season signified by the glittering of sugar snowflakes that dropped from the ceiling and coated the heads and the shoulders of the eaters as they dug with their spoons in dishes of ice cream glistening with the snow from the simulated sky above. A marvelous effect, it was agreed by all.

But we've eaten too much! they groaned to themselves (they would never have said it out loud). They had eaten, in a sense, for a year, and they felt that way. So now it was time to sleep, to rest before the evening's ball.

Upstairs in her room again, Alexandra fell facedown on the bed. Praskovia had not arrived to remove her clothing before her nap, and Alexandra had no inclination to undo by herself the finger-defying hooks and eyes on the back of her gown, or the knuckle-breaking knots and bows of the laces that knit the two edges of the corset so tightly over her back that she could sometimes feel her internal organs. Thinking of Ulyanov, she preferred to keep her clothes on. In fact, she found the corset's tightness strangely comforting. Not only did it lend her a sensation of hard discipline and rectitude that reinforced her determination to resist the softening power of Ulyanov's voice, but the barrier it formed between her flesh and his was comforting, as if she were perpetually enfolded in a chaste and protective embrace. Trussed in her corset, she turned on her back, enjoying her mood of strength and purpose.

In a few hours, the engagement between Olga and Rybynsky would be announced. She still had time to scheme a way to substitute herself so that it would be she who stood at his side beneath the sparkling crowns, she who would mount up beside him to look down at lesser mortals from their perch among the clouds.

However, worn out by the exertions of rolling bricks in the snow, by the tensions that Ulyanov's presence so inexplicably imposed on her, by the stress of avoiding Kolygin, and the fact that she really had eaten and drunk too much after all, Alexandra fell instantly asleep.

She dreamed a Russian dream, one dreamed by other Russian girls before her. In this great Russian dream, she is out in the forest at night, dragging herself through drifts of snow, a bear in pursuit behind her. Branches tear at the sleeves of her dress, snatch at the jewels in her ears. She tries to run but is slowed by the drifts of snow. As if she is running through water, her motions stick and freeze. Her heart swells with fright. She falls. The monster, smelling bad, seizes her, carries her away. She is crushed in his arms, smothered in his shaggy breast. Then he's gone. She finds herself inside a hut. From another room she hears the sounds of laughter, glasses clinking, shouts of men at drinking games. Inside the open door she sees a table full of monsters, freaks—at the head of the table, their master. Turning their heads in one motion, they see her, shout, and grind their teeth. "She's mine!" they cry, but their master snatches her away and the monsters fade and dwindle, leaving her alone with him, trapped within his arms, his body over her, around her, his blue eyes staring down at her.

With a sudden start, she woke and didn't know where she was. The room was dark, small, and strange. Where was she?

Ah yes. Pandemonium. The fancy-dress ball tonight. But Praskovia, again, was nowhere to be found, and so Alexandra, happy to escape her dream, Ulyanov's arms, rose from the bed in her sleep-wrinkled dress, her reddened cheek still bearing the imprint of the seam on the pillowcase, and, without the serf to smooth her down and fluff her up, left the room in her rumpled state and made her way downstairs in search of Rybynsky himself.

The house still seemed to be asleep, not even a serf to be seen. The countess swept down empty stairs, through empty rooms, the hissing sound of her dress as it dragged along the floor the only sound that she could hear.

Through a doorway, she saw Rybynsky working at a desk. State papers, they must be, evidence of his membership in that wider, grander world, his existence on that stratospheric plane. He was farther away from her than ever, enclosed within his private space, and though she might easily have stepped inside to speak with him, or even cleared her throat so that he looked up from the desk, she found her throat was dry, her feet were made of marble. Suddenly she thought: Why should he pay attention to me at all? Who am I that he should care for me? Who am I to raise my sights to him? Penniless, unimportant, not even pretty. Not pretty enough for one for whom all the prettiness in the world would never be enough.

She turned to go and then flattened herself against the wall, for here was Ulyanov himself coming toward her. Looking up at the ceiling as he walked, his expression exalted, he did not notice that Alexandra was standing there until he was upon her.

Ulyanov, who had had just a tad too much vodka in the billiard room, where a card game was going on, walked unsteadily. He was thinking of how enchantingly the countess's nose had started to run this morning in the snow. Catching sight of her now, he squinted, uncertain she was really there, thinking she was a manifestation, a dream of drunkenness; then, deciding she was real, he lurched in her direction. As she shrank away from him in obvious distaste, he noticed that she looked enticingly messy in her rumpled dress, her hair sticking up adorably where she had slept on it. It made him want to mess her up even more.

Just a tad too much vodka.

He bore down on her, rested one arm on the wall beside her head, grasped her 'round the waist, and buried his nose in her hair, breathing deeply.

Alexandra found she could not move and almost didn't want to. He was murmuring something soft, his mouth moving softly on her head, across her tender, tingling scalp, his lips adhering warmly, moistly, then pulling away, and she found her thoughts beginning to slur, as if her nervous system were shutting down. Immobilized, mindless, aware of odd sensations in places she did not want to think about, could not think about because her mind had ceased to work, she felt her eyelids drifting shut as she floated back inside that dream where he had held her in his arms, his body over her, around her.

Then he burped. Alexandra's eyes popped open, her mind was functional again, and she wriggled free. Ulyanov, still unsteady on his feet in spite of that refreshing burp, fell back against the wall as he watched her scurry down the hallway heading for the safety of the stairs.

Oh God. He slid down onto the floor and dropped his

swirling head into his hands. What had he done? All hope of convincing the countess of his suitability as a husband was now lost, irrevocably lost. He had appeared before her as a drunken sot, pawed her like an animal, substantiated every claim that had ever been made about the unfitness of his character by society at large. The crudeness of that burp! And he had been trying so hard to be good! He hadn't been drunk in a month! Hadn't visited the girls at Madame Frou-Frou's House of Love! Hadn't touched Lukasha or Pelageya or Aksinya or anyone else! And now he had ruined everything. Even though it was her fault in the first place. Her cruelty had driven him to drink. But he hadn't intended her to see him that way.

He struggled to his feet and lurched back toward the billiards room. Everything was ruined anyway, so he might as well have another drink.

Still shaking, Alexandra reached her room. Praskovia, who had been waiting quite a time, pacing and muttering to herself, didn't notice. She grabbed the dazed young countess, stripped the clothes from her back, and hustled her into the waiting tub, a portable steel monstrosity equipped with wheels. Eight minutes later—Praskovia checked it by the watch she wore suspended from her belt—Alexandra was sitting on the bed wrapped in a towel.

"A record, my lady," Praskovia said, wiping her wet timepiece on her skirt and then advancing on Alexandra with another outstretched towel in readiness to dry the sopping head of hair.

Alexandra's head bounced this way and that under the vigorous scrubbing of the towel as she looked at the costume for the coming ball that Praskovia had set out upon the chair. When the countess had discovered there was to be a fancy-dress ball, she had ruminated long over whether to waste one of the precious diamonds on a costume that would be worn only once. She hesitated over sketches of Valkyries, milkmaids, bibilical warrior-queens, Hellenic goddesses. It was those bellicose bibilical queens that had set her mind traveling in a certain direction, and, suddenly remembering an old costume of her father's, she had begged the keys from Praskovia's belt, made her way back into her father's room, and there, in pieces at the bottom of a dusty wardrobe, she had found it, its angel wings eaten by insects.

For a costume party he had given in Alexandra's childhood, her father had had reproduced the sumptuous fifteenth-century armor, wings, and billowing crimson cape of Bartolomé Bermejo's painting of St. Michael, a full-size copy of which had hung always in his bedroom and which had long been sold. Beneath the dust of the dull armor was a splendid shine, the silk-lined cloak was still good (the moth holes would not show in the complicated pattern of brocade), and the sword and saintly diadem were equally undamaged. It would do perfectly for Joan of Arc, that is, if the armor fitted her, which it did, to her surprise, and perfectly. The feathered wings were too tattered to save, but no matter. To maneuver through a waltz with them would require more physical dexterity than Alexandra felt she could claim.

The French standard—sky-blue field with lilies—had been easy and cheap to make.

Now, as if she herself were being prepared for battle, the countess received on her body the separate pieces of hard, gleaming armor. She watched in satisfaction as each of her limbs was plated in chased steel, shielded against softness, weakness, fear, as if this carapace rendered her an instant man, clothed her in masculine power, manly strength. So. Here she was arrayed for battle, but what was her cause? Not to make a nation, certainly. No, she was to capture a husband, what a bore. The feminine battle-field was small and circumscribed, and though she could put on masculine power, she could not exercise it in any arena larger than the bedroom, the ballroom. Taking one last look in the mirror, Alexandra turned on her armored heel and went clanking out the door, her standard lifting in the air.

But where was the ball itself? Small clumps of revelers decked out in feathered plumes and powdered wigs and laurel wreaths, in senatorial Roman robes and satin breeches and jeweled caftans, wandered from room to enormous room, but found all of them empty. No orchestra, no potted palms, no table set with silver samovars and crystal glasses holding the liquid yellow diamonds of champagne. Where was the ball?

There. The servants pointed out the opened doors in the front of the house, pointed into the darkness. There was the ball. Out there in the snow.

Dance in the snow? Why not? But won't we be cold?

You won't, the servants answered. Go out and look. And they smiled.

The sky split. A boom shook the air. A glitter of fireworks rained down, and the guests began to scream, delighted, and went crowding out the door. They pointed and chattered and laughed at the palace of ice, cathedral-high, that shimmered and glowed in the night, its inner surface streaming with water that melted and dripped in the heat of the flares of fire inside its walls, which thinned and grew clearer with every moment. Through these transparent walls they could see the dark forest with its caps of snow, the silvery river, the huddled peasant huts on the river's other side.

Hurry! the peasants whispered, hurry and dance before it melts and crashes to the ground. There's not much time, they urged the guests, not much time at all. Have fun, have fun till then!

The orchestra had begun to play; laughing, the guests ran

through the snow to meet the music, not to waste a drop of it. Alexandra trooped after them into the towering palace of ice. And there it all was—the orchestra, the potted palms, the tables set with silver samovars and crystal glasses, all warm and glittering in the light of braziers and flaming torches. But the floor itself was made of snow packed down until it was dancing smooth, and the clarifying walls showed the winter night outside, and, looking up past the icy chandelier, they saw through the thin, transparent ceiling the stars, the radiant moon.

Alexandra discovered quickly that her costume had been a mistake. Or rather, it succeeded all too well. In it, she exercised no power at all. If masculine power was denied her, so was feminine power, because though she had left her hair undone to cascade down her back, she was not perceived as feminine in the first place. No one asked her to dance. She retreated, watching as the queens of various centuries and countries danced past, as Dresden shepherdesses and Nordic goddesses pranced their way around the floor. Taller than the average, her feminine bumps and bulges crushed flat underneath the layer of steel, the countess might have been any young man of the aristocracy, shy of the women and feigning indifference near the wall. At other times, however, with meager breasts squeezed upward by the rough grip of the stays and plumping out above her bodice, hips expanded by a stiff-gathered skirt, she was a goddess herself, an Amazonian Aphrodite par excellence. Many men had told her so, and demonstrated their admiration definitively, not least the repellent Ulyanov this very afternoon.

Now he seemed not to see her. She had imagined she would spend her time at the ball escaping him, fending him off, but he was dancing with determination with that woman he had brought, some kind of foreign princess, holding her too tightly in the waltz (cad that he was), bending close, whispering in her ear, throwing his head back and laughing at whatever witticism this foreign princess had produced. *She* had not made the mistake of choosing an unattractive costume, no. This foreign princess with the doelike eyes had arrayed herself as the Asiatic seductress that Alexandra supposed she was, her bare arms strangled in the grip of jeweled snakes, hair trapped in ropes of pearls, a diamond like a drop of perspiration standing out trembling on her forehead but never collapsing, never dripping down. Ulyanov, in the costume of the ancient hussars of Poland (his regiment, the Zamoyskis, was a Polish one), steered her nimbly round the floor and did not even poke any of his fellow dancers with his feathered wings while skipping through a lively mazurka.

Well, good, Alexandra thought, I'm rid of him for now. And she turned her attention to Rybynsky. It was difficult to see him through the crowd, standing at the top of the room, conversing with Prince Andreyev. He appeared in a gap between the dancers, disappeared again behind the whirling figures on the floor. Dignity unimpaired by a silly costume, he wore simple evening dress, elegant black and white, and looked more distant than ever and more alluring.

With a sudden cold contraction of her stomach, Alexandra knew that this was how he would remain. The announcement of his betrothal to the princess would be tonight, and how could she have believed that she could stop it? How foolish she had been to stake her future on this fantasy. What those glances signified was moot; he had never followed up on them, but ever receded, always backed away at her advance. Furthermore, in pursuing him so relentlessly, so exclusively, she might have destroyed her chances with Count Kolygin, just as Madame Lavorine had predicted. After evading the count so foolishly last night and giving him the slip at this morning's breakfast, she had ignored the eager glances he had sent her way this afternoon while making bricks with that Ulyanov in the snow, and then lost sight of him entirely. Where was he now? She searched the room.

There. He was there at the top of the room, standing right beside Rybynsky and the prince. How odd, how strange that he should be there. Why? Did he too have an announcement to make?

The orchestra finished the waltz. The dancers broke apart and leaned against each other, breathing hard. A drumroll. What was happening? Prince Andreyev stepped forward, held up his hand.

"Friends," he cried, "when I told you this morning we would build, I did not lie! See the magnificent palace we have built!"

The crowd applauded themselves for building the thing they had not built.

"And I told you that we would build our palace in memory of one of our old empresses, who had built such a palace of ice in honor of a wedding!"

More applause, and murmurings of "God save our old Empress Anna!"

"But I did not tell you, for this was my surprise, that we built this palace in honor of a wedding in our own time, a wedding which will take place very soon."

Gasps from the crowd.

"Our dear and beloved daughter, Olga, has consented to become the bride of our most distinguished, and youngest, councilor of state, the good Rybynsky, Gregor Gregorovich!"

A rushing forward of the crowd, to congratulate and kiss the blushing Olga, dressed as a vestal virgin all in robes of pristine white, as if she were a bride already, and the dignified Rybynsky, who held her hand.

So there it was. Well, she had always known, and had had fair warning, too. But there was still Count Kolygin, wasn't there? Or was there? Why was he standing there beside the newly betrothed pair? Why was Madame Lavorine herself there next to him? And why did Prince Andreyev lay a hand on Kolygin's shoulder and raise the other to the crowd?

"Friends, dear friends," the prince announced, "there is another couple here whose very recent engagement can only magnify our joy. We have not one but two brides here tonight. One my daughter, Olga, the other our most well-respected and beloved Madame Olympia Lavorine, who has most graciously consented to bestow upon our friend Count Arkady Kolygin . . ."

Alexandra turned away. When? How had it happened? Why? So the foolish Lavorine had not been so foolish after all. She had only paid attention to a lonely man, fussed about his comfort, shown an interest. Lavorine had admired instead of asking to be admired, and if she, Alexandra, were a goddess, an Amazonian Aphrodite, then what was that to him? She might as well have been a statue in a temple for all the warmth that she had shown him, unresponsive as a chunk of marble and as cold.

So who had really been the foolish one?

Making her way quickly, quietly through the crowd, Alexandra slipped away unnoticed. But for one person who followed her. And another who, unnoticed, followed him.

Ulyanov had observed the countess closely enough these past few weeks to know very well what her feelings for Rybynsky were and how disappointing this turn of events must be to her. She had broken his own heart so firmly, so repeatedly, that he was familiar with the sensation, but it was one he did not, in his masculine gallantry, want her to know herself.

After searching quietly through many empty rooms, Ulyanov came upon the countess in an empty drawing room. She had arranged her limbs in an oddly masculine manner—perhaps the only manner that was comfortable for her in the stiff metal casings of her manly attire. She looked very like one of his young recruits who had perhaps just lost a great deal of money at cards or had his awkward suit rejected by an actress in search of bigger fish to fry. What awe he had felt of her instantly collapsed.

Alexandra did not look up when he stepped inside the room. As if she'd been expecting him, was not surprised at all to see him, she continued staring glumly at the wall. Turning a chair around, he positioned himself beside her in the very same attitude—legs straddling the chair, chin pillowed on his arms—and hoped that this mimicking might make her laugh, but it did not. She ignored him.

"I know you are upset," he began, joining her in her examination of an empty spot on the wall. "You shouldn't be. He isn't worth it, you know. In fact, he's quite a bore," he ventured further, surprised by the intimacy of word and tone that both her costume and her attitude were calling forth. Had she been armored in her femininity, he would never have dared to probe so deeply or speak to her so openly of her distress.

Alexandra grunted manfully, avoidant of emotion as appropriate, reluctant to confide, self-protective, lost in masculine pridefulness. Nothing new.

"Please talk to me. I want to help you."

"You can't," she returned, bitter in her tone.

"How do you know I can't?"

"Because you can't."

"I know you loved Rybynsky," he said, "and I know it hurts, and maybe if you talk to me it will hurt you less."

"It's not Rybynsky," said the countess firmly, "and I didn't love him."

I have a chance, Ulyanov thought. "What is it, then?" he asked.

"I can't tell you."

"I see," said Ulyanov, suddenly relaxed, amused—walking on air, in fact. "I can't help you and you can't tell me why I can't help you."

"That's right," said Alexandra.

The next step he normally made in his quest to find out what was wrong with one of his junior officers was to cast a net of possibilities—money, a woman, a disgraceful, career-threatening escapade—and see what he might catch in it.

"It must be something," he said. "It can't be nothing. What could it be?" But of course she was a woman, not a man. He concentrated hard, trying to bend his thoughts in a feminine direction, to see how he might understand her, penetrate her mind. What do women care about? He hadn't the faintest idea. If he had ever been able to figure it out, he would have been more successful with women than he already was, but he was quite successful enough, and so he had never bothered. He always used what worked with them best—the appeal to their vanity. He knew they cared about their beauty, but what else did they care about?

A striking revelation came to mind. Perhaps they cared about the same things men cared about. Why not try it?

"You drank too much. You lost at cards. Your father will be angry," he said, half joking.

Alexandra gave him a look so withering, he felt he would shrivel up into a ball of rubbish and drop to the ground to be swept away with all the other trash. "Don't be a fool," she said. "How can you be so stupid? Besides, my father's dead."

"Well," said Ulyanov hopefully, casting his net again, "perhaps you miss him."

It seemed he had succeeded in his quest to probe her mind, for the countess began to cry, but this was hardly a success. Her mouth began to twist and tremble, and before she hid her face he saw the liquid of her tears begin to gather. It made him frantic. He jumped from his seat, hovered over her, paced round in circles, hovered over her again, but he did not dare touch her. Her shoulders shook and the sound of muffled sobs could be heard from beneath her hanging hair. Ulyanov was wretched, for although he had made many a woman cry, it had always been intentional, a testing of his power, and the stopping up of those sobs, the drying of those tears, had been within his power too. These tears were not within his sphere of influence.

Ulyanov protested frantically that he had said the wrong thing, that he was sorry, and asked the countess what he could do or say to ease her pain. "Please stop. Don't cry, my dear," he said.

The words "my dear," though spoken with hesitation, so quietly he was hoping she wouldn't hear, seemed to soften her further. She cried harder than before, but out from between her sobs words began to struggle, misshapen, indistinct. He thought he heard her say "alone." He thought he heard her say "frightened." And oddly, he thought he heard her say something about money. About not having any. Stranger still, for the Korvins were by common knowledge among the richest of the nobles based in Petersburg, their name long eminent, their status utterly secure. Unlike his own.

"I miss him!" she said distinctly.

Carefully, he connected the words he had gathered, constructed a context to hold them and create a meaning. She felt alone and frightened, missed her father, had no money. Instantly he understood. Her father had left her with nothing when he died. It was all a charade. She was penniless. Ulyanov saw his chance and seized it.

"Alexandra," he said with excitement, staring down at the

drooping head and thankful that he could not see her face, or he might lose his nerve, "you must marry me, then! I will take care of you! I am not very rich, but I'm not very poor. I've got five thousand souls, that's enough, maybe not what you've been used to, but I promise you I will be good, make a good husband to you. I will."

Her face flipped up at him. It was swollen and red.

"You!" she spat. "Marry you? I can't marry *you*!"

"Why not?"

She looked at him as if he were an insect, something utterly repellent, her lips turning down as if she were smelling something bad. This was not going well, Ulyanov thought. He changed his tactics. Go with what you know.

"I love you, I think you're so beautiful," he said hopefully, staring into her reddened eyes in a way that usually worked quite well, and should have worked even better now, the words being true for once. Of course, they did not work at all. If he'd had time to think of it, he would merely have been puzzled. Instead, he was shocked.

"Oh really?" said Alexandra, seizing on what he'd said and twisting it. "I see how much you love me. As much as you love all the other women in your . . . harem—would you call it? For instance, that woman you brought here, the princess. I suppose you love her too. You certainly behaved that way with her. How dare you make declarations to me! What respectable woman could want you? What woman could take you seriously? With *your* reputation!"

What was she talking about? What woman? What princess? Lukasha!

"Her?" he cried, relieved. "She's not a woman! She's one of my serfs!"

But wrong again, Ulyanov, you have only made it worse.

"I should have known a man of your low morals would take advantage of a slave."

"You're wrong, she loves me," Ulyanov protested, digging himself more deeply into the grave of his aspirations.

"Ah, so she *is* your mistress, then," said Alexandra with a sneer, but Ulyanov detected a hint of jealousy, so heightened was his perception at this moment. Aha! Now he felt himself on stronger ground. He had brought Lukasha here to make the countess jealous, and clearly he had succeeded. He wanted to laugh with joy at his own cleverness. It worked! It worked! It worked!

Or had it? Perhaps it had worked too well.

"Listen, darling," he said with urgency, "if that's your reason for refusing me, you're wrong! You're wrong! She's nothing. Not my mistress, nothing. Just a serf who works in the house."

"Then why is she here? And why were you calling her a princess? Is she that to you?"

He wondered if he should tell the truth. He was so close now, drawing near his goal. Lukasha's former status as a mistress—well, really, one of them—over that he would pass, ignore it, the countess would never, ever know. He'd send Lukasha away, to one of the far estates. He would have done it anyway, truth be told. She got on his nerves now, always staring at him, following him around, expecting something, wanting. And he knew enough of Lukasha's persistence, the weak water that wears down a rock, how she was always besting him in their quiet war of nerves, to know that if he gave her time she would wear him down on this as well, that somehow she would get her way. But should he admit the real reason for Lukasha's presence here? He decided not.

"A joke. It was a joke. I wanted to see if I could pass her off...."

Alexandra rounded on him now, tossing thunderbolts from the moral high ground on which she felt she firmly stood. "Oh, I see," she said. "You dressed her up like a doll and played with her, amused yourself, without a thought of her or how she felt. You used her for your entertainment, and in how many other ways I don't even want to think, but she's a human being, a soul, a creature of God."

"So I'm wrong again," Ulyanov said, "and you're so high and mighty, but I didn't see *you* befriending her, my pompous one, or lending her a sympathetic hand. Or were you really jealous? Admit it! You were, dear Countess, weren't you?"

"Jealous of a serf?" she cried.

"Obviously. You've sunk pretty low, Countess, haven't you?"

He was sorry immediately. Her face showed her shock. The remark—all too true in light of what she had told him so tearfully, in confidence—was cruel indeed, and he felt the shame of it as a sickness in his stomach. He could not look at her. He wanted to cry. Alexandra wanted to cry herself, but she couldn't, wouldn't. He must not see that he had hurt her.

"Indeed I have," she said after a moment, her face composed and blank, "if I have attracted a proposal from a man like you. If such as you would dare." The countess, who had risen from her seat some time ago, turned and made her way stiffly from the room, awkward in her armor but still dignified. Ulyanov opened his mouth to speak and closed it again, feeling his lips as thickly stupid, his hands as clumsy paws that dangled foolishly from the end of his arms.

It was not long, however, before he heard a sound and saw Lukasha lurking near the door, peering at him from under the glass diamond he had bought to decorate her forehead and which, in its vulgarity, its lack of authenticity, seemed to symbolize everything that was wrong with him and with his life.

"Lukasha, go away," he said, waving his hand and turning toward the window, "go to bed, whatever, just go away." He heard the pitter-patter of her feet as she trotted across the polished floor on her too-high heels.

Of course everything Alexandra had said to him in that regard was perfectly correct. He had exploited this defenseless person, treated her as an object in every way a woman could be treated, when she was in his charge, his care! It was absolutely true. What kind of man was he? No man at all.

Lukasha was on her knees, her face against his legs, her arms clinging to them.

"Lukasha, stop that," he said. "Get up. Get on your feet. I don't deserve that, especially not me." He changed position, moved his legs to shake her off, but she only followed him walking on her knees. He had the impulse to kick her across the room. Oh God, he thought, was there no escaping his badness, his inner evil?

He turned to face her. Bending over, he pulled her hands from his legs and raised her to her feet.

"Don't do that anymore," he said. "You never have to do that again, for anyone, and especially not for me. You're free," he said, "you're free."

She looked at him with puzzlement and shook her head. She raised his imprisoned hand and began to kiss it.

He snatched his hand away.

"Do you hear me, Lukasha? You're free. You don't have to do that anymore. You don't have to do anything for me. You're free."

"Lukasha is not free," she said, rubbing her cheek against his hand.

"'I'm not free,'" he shouted at her, "'I'm not free.' Can't you

learn to use the first-person pronoun? Say it! Not 'Lukasha,' 'I'!
Say it, 'I'!"

"I," said Lukasha, uncomprehending.

"Say 'I am free!'"

"Lukasha is not free."

"Lukasha, listen," he said, grabbing her by the arms and
bringing his face very close to hers. "You do not belong to me
any longer. You are no longer subject to my mistreatments. You
can do what you want. Tomorrow I will give you money. You
will be driven back to Petersburg or wherever you want to go.
You will have money, I promise you. And you will be free."

Lukasha gazed up at him. "I am not free," she said.

"You will not see me again, you understand? I have treated
you badly, or so I have been told, " he spat the words, "and you
should be happy to get away from me. I am not a nice man."
Ulyanov paused, gazing at the floor. He put his hand up, gripped
his face, and sighed. "So," he said, "you are free."

Lukasha nodded. Her eyes, enlarged by tears, gazed steadily
up at him.

"Say 'I understand.'"

"I understand."

"Good," he said, patting her arm, "good. Now go to bed.
Tomorrow I will give you money and you will go back to Petersburg. You will own your own life. You will not see me again,
lucky for you."

The effort of talking to Lukasha had wearied him, as it
always did. He turned away and left the room. At least he had
done his conscience where Lukasha was concerned, or rather,
Alexandra's conscience, but what difference did it make? In any
case, now he intended to get drunk. Not very drunk. But very,
very drunk.

. . .

The ball did not last very long. The palace of ice began to crumble long before midnight, and Ato signaled to the prince that it was time. Not that his work was done when the last guest had been ushered, unsteady with drink, out of the melting structure and into the great warm house. His work had only just begun. There were the potted palms to remove, the wet and soiled linens on the tables to be stripped, the tables themselves to be carried out, and the porcelain and crystal and silver to be gathered—the half-drunk flutes of sparkling wine no longer sparkling, the cake-encrusted china plates, the knives and forks that had dropped to the floor or been left in odd corners. Then there were, of course, the silk-upholstered chairs, the samovars, the dying braziers, sodden torches, all to be done away with quickly, before the fragile, splitting ceiling came crashing down. Workmen stood on a ladder, detaching the heavy chandelier that had been borrowed from the music room. While all this was being done, there were the tables to set up for the midnight supper, the food overseen, and, when supper was over, the clearing and wiping of the tables to be supervised and the drunken men to be assisted up the stairs and into bed. It was nearly sunrise when the African began to make the last of his rounds, checking all the rooms for stray glasses and cups and smoldering cigars, extinguishing gas lamps and chandeliers and snuffing out the flames still burning atop the melting remnants of once long and elegant waxen tapers. In the enormous windows night was fading, dawn was coming, colorless. He opened another door.

Something was hanging in the window of the smaller drawing room. Something large that did not belong there. It revolved slowly, its separate limbs dangling. Ato drew nearer, held the burning candle up to see more clearly. Gorgeously dressed in oriental costume, the body was a woman's—face dark and mottled, tongue stiff between the teeth. Ato stepped back, staring. The gods had not let go of her easily, he thought, seeing in the distortion of her face the marks of the woman's struggle against their power, which was life itself. Her face showed that the gods had fought with all their might, but she had triumphed in the end, her tongue protruding in defiance. A great and powerful will had broken the vessel that contained it, escaping to a gentler realm.

Drawing up a nearby chair to stand on, Ato wondered if it was the chair she had used to climb to the top of the world and throw herself into the void. With careful respect he set his feet upon the same surface from which she had launched herself. He took a knife from his pocket and cut the cord that still anchored her to the earth. Released, she fell stiffly into his arms; her head rested cold against his cheek. He held her body for a moment, then laid it on the floor. Lowering himself to his knees, he spoke words in a language he had not heard for many years, words that had stayed in his head from childhood as if they had been carved there.

But there was much to be done now. The prince to be informed, the priest who would do honor to her spirit to be called for, the broken remnants of the vessel to be attended to with reverence. It would be hours before he would sleep.

Alexandra drove back to Petersburg alone that very afternoon, the death of Captain Mecklenburg-Ulyanov's young companion having brought the party prematurely to an end. Though the contingent of guests had been eager to take part in the solemn drama of the tragedy (for here was a disaster more enthralling even than the snowstorm), the prince had announced the betrothal celebrations at an end and sent them all back home. Too tired to think, Alexandra collapsed against the seat in the coach and did not watch the winter landscape flying by.

It was late in the evening when Alexandra was handed down from her own droshky by the solicitous Istvan, who had collected her from Andreyev palace in answer to a hasty message that the mistress was arriving days before she was expected. A smiling Matryona, standing in the open doorway at the top of the steps, received her exhausted mistress as she tottered from the helpful arms of Istvan and into the doorway of the darkened palace. Praskovia and Matryona both assisted their mistress up the endless flights of stairs into her bedroom, where, stripped quickly of her clothing, she was buttoned into her yellowed cotton nightdress, wrapped in a heavy blanket, and tucked inside her bed. She fell asleep upon the instant and slept a dreamless sleep.

Alexandra woke up thirsty in the morning and was desperate for a glass of hot black tea. She hoped there was some in the house, that Matryona and Istvan had not exhausted the precious store that she had meant, but forgotten, to replenish before she'd left. Alexandra called out for Praskovia, but she was still asleep, it seemed, for she did not answer from her pallet in the hallway

on the other side of Alexandra's bedroom door. She called for
Matryona, shouted loudly, but got no answer. Grumbling, cursing, complaining to herself of the lazy serf, she put her foot out
of bed to feel for her slippers on the floor. Her toes met cold,
hard wood. The slippers were not there. It was the same little
joke Matryona had pulled before, of which Alexandra was growing very, very weary now. She noticed with approval that her
clothes had been picked up from the floor and put away. At least
that Matryona was good for something, but perhaps it had been
Praskovia herself who had done it, which was far more likely.
Barefoot and shaking in the cold, Alexandra crossed the room
and opened her door.

Praskovia lay in her usual spot in the hallway by the door,
whistling rhythmically through her nose in the music of satisfied
sleep. Alexandra hated to wake her, but she had to have that cup
of tea, and Praskovia, after all, was more thickly dressed than
she, would have boots on, and, warm in her many layers of skirt
and blouse, could safely go downstairs into the kitchen with its
floor of icy stone. She prodded the sleeping body with her foot.

"Wake up," she said. "I want a cup of tea."

Praskovia grunted and burrowed deeper into sleep.

"Wake up," said Alexandra, prodding more forcefully.

Praskovia opened her eyes and glared at the one who dared
to interrupt the greatest pleasure of her life. But she rose, wiped
her eyes, gathered her skirts together, and crept unsteadily down
the stairs, still too sleepy to notice that her boots were gone and
she was walking in her stocking feet. Alexandra could hear her
slamming doors until she reached the kitchen, when there was
silence. Then more slamming of doors until Praskovia appeared
at the foot of the stairs.

"No tea, my lady countess," she shouted up, "no tea at all!"

"I'm coming down," said Alexandra. She went back inside her

bedroom and crossed the floor into her dressing room, where she expected to find the coat that she had worn last night, which was the only one she had and which would have to do for a dressing gown since she could not find her tattered robe. But when she opened the single wooden wardrobe that was left in the room that had once housed more than a hundred dresses, she found it empty. Odd, how very odd, she thought. And where was the traveling gown she'd worn last night? Her bonnet and her boots? Her sable muff? What about her other clothes, not the new ones (they were in the trunks downstairs), but last-year's fashions, the ones she could not wear without remaking them?

Alexandra swallowed hard, hoping to bring some moisture into her mouth, which was suddenly dry. A suspicion had begun to grow. Her heart began to beat with fear. Gathering up her skirts, she took off running through her bedroom and into the hall and down the stairs, pushed past Praskovia, ran barefoot through the endless series of rooms that echoed with the sound of her pounding feet—through the empty drawing room, the empty dining room, the empty sitting room, the empty library, the empty ballroom, the empty salon, the empty receiving room—and into the empty hallway, where she stopped. Empty like the others—where were the trunks that Istvan should have unloaded from the carriage and brought inside the hallway? Of course, she had only assumed that he brought them inside; she had been too tired to see. Clearly, he had not unloaded them at all, the lazy thing, but left them in the sledge. That had to be it. "Holy Mother, mother of God," she muttered, and turned and started at a run toward the back of the palace, down the endless hallway, past more of these enormous empty rooms and through the kitchen, "Holy Mother, mother of God," and out the door and into the courtyard and across the burning snow, where she slipped and fell and got slowly to her feet, and made her way more carefully to the carriage house, which was empty too. And the stable, empty of its two remaining horses.

"Get out of the snow!" Praskovia screamed across the court-yard from the doorway of the kitchen. "Get out of the snow before your little feet drop off and then you'll be a cripple with a crutch and make more work for me!" Alexandra stood gasping a moment in the shelter of the stable, a stitch in her side impeding her from drawing breath. Gone, all gone! Her clothes, her car-riage, her horses, what little that she had, was gone! All gone! And Istvan too—Matryona had taken him as well. That Matry-ona, damn her soul to hell! So this was her revenge.

And then another suspicion struck her, even worse, and she was off at a run more desperate than before. Back across the courtyard, past the screaming servant and into the hallway and through the endless echoing rooms and up the endless hard and icy stairs and into her dressing room, where she threw herself to her knees and snatched at the bottom drawer of a wooden chest. "Holy Mother, mother of God," she whispered, digging deep inside the empty drawer with beating heart, and finding what she sought—a leather purse where she'd kept the diamonds and rolls of paper rubles—she found that it was empty too, and the disaster was complete.

PART 2

The palace cracked with cold. Through the crevices that opened in its walls, frosty moisture seeped. The vine- and fruit-shaped moldings that spread over the ceilings strained, split, and chips of white plaster crumbled to the floor as if it were snowing inside the palace itself. The tremendous fireplace in the kitchen, once the red-hot heart of the house, was ashen, dead. Frost was forming on the great iron kettles.

Praskovia had not ventured into the kitchen at all these past few days. What for? Even if there had been tea, which there was not, fires could not be set to crackle under the kettles, so there could be no boiling water to steep the leaves. Whatever remnants of food had remained in the kitchen had been carried off as well, along with the money and the fuel. The only embers of life still to be found inside the palace were the single serf and her mistress. One of these, it seemed, would soon go out.

Although Praskovia had bundled the countess, whose teeth were chattering violently, tightly inside her bed, tied rags round the bluish feet, rubbed and chafed the brittle fingers and toes, the countess had only trembled more than ever. A fever had taken hold inside of her. Muffled voices mocked at her inside her head; she tossed her body back and forth to get away from them.

They began to starve. Even if there had been money for food, there was no way to buy it because not only had Matryona taken the last of the tea, the last of the hoard of bread, potatoes, fish, and pickled beets, the firewood and coal, but also every scrap of her mistress's clothing and her fellow-serf's as well. Praskovia's coats and skirts and scarves and shoes were gone, and although she still had the clothes in which she had slept, sometime during the night Matryona had untied the boots of her old enemy as she slept and pulled them off.

The first few days of her mistress's fever, Praskovia had warmed her by chopping up the chest of drawers and tables she found inside the little room and tossing them into the stove. When their heat had been exhausted, she lugged from the kitchen and up the stairs the table, the rickety chairs. The furniture that had occupied the one drawing room for "company," the silk-upholstered chairs and carved mahogany pieces, had already been removed by Matryona while the mistress had been away at Pandemonium. So when the last of the kitchen's furniture had been burned, Praskovia climbed inside the bed to warm her mistress with her body. What would they do for food? Her mistress must have food or she would die. A doctor! A doctor! Praskovia didn't know of any. And even if she had, how to send for him? No carriage, no Istvan, no boots for walking there herself.

Praskovia could think of only one thing to do. She slipped off one of her skirts, tore it into rags, and wrapped her feet in them. These rags she secured on her feet by ripping long sections off another skirt to bind them with. She tied her kerchief more tightly under her chin and slipped the top blanket off Alexandra's body, tugging it gently from the quivering, clutching fingers. More rags she tied around her hands. Wrapped in the blanket, she made her way out of the room, down the stairs, through the hallway, and out onto the front steps of the palace.

The cold landed on her like an avalanche. She felt herself collapsing under it, skin withering, drying, freezing. Her nose seemed to fill with liquid ice, which spilled out of her nostrils, necessitating a wipe from one of the dirty rags that served for gloves. Looking out at the street in front of her—the carriages skating by on the frozen street with their bundled passengers and coachmen huddled in their coats and the jingling harnesses that sounded merry in a way that raised her ire—Praskovia peered at the faces of the coachmen, hoping to find Platon Platonovich or Stepan Olegovich or old Matvey or Igor. Oh, why didn't they come? They would give her money. They knew her. But it was a different world, she thought, a world she did not know, one that did not know her.

She stepped down.

"In the name of God," she wailed, extending her rag-enveloped hands. "In the name of God, a kopeck, sir," she begged of a passing gentleman in high expensive hat and leather gloves and beaver coat, but he hurried past her, shaking his head. Tears were running down her face, but Praskovia did not feel them. Her face was numb with cold. For hours she stood and begged of the soldiers in their great warm duty coats, of the merchants in their warming furs and rich peasants in thick felt boots. For hours she watched them go by, ignoring her, and she cursed them under her breath and blew on her fingers, the bare tips of which were yellowing, becoming translucent as rotten green grapes, soon to whiten, then blacken, then crumble off the bone.

Her fingers in her mouth to protect them, she grew bolder, began to follow the men, pleading, plucking at their long black coats, and she felt as if she no longer belonged to the city, was no long Praskovia, stewardess of Korvin palace, but a stray cur to be beaten aside with a heavy, silver-topped walking stick as it begged a crumb for its starving belly from one who, comfortable and full, was set on more important business. However, like a skinny cat still confident in the beneficence of humanity, still approaching to rub itself against a woolen leg though it had already been kicked aside so many times, Praskovia stayed on the street, continued to accost each passerby, hands out, begging. One man, an old peasant in a dirty fur cap, turned and spat in her face. Another knocked her down. But another, dressed almost as a gentleman, stopped to listen.

His eyes were wet and red, and he peered at her from under his fur-trimmed cap.

"A ruble and fifty kopecks," he whispered, his eyes darting round, "if you have a place. Do you have a place?"

Praskovia lowered her eyes. She had not expected this. It would take some time to take it in. Why, she was over forty, with only enough teeth to bite her bread. Well, she supposed she was still a strapping woman. *That* he had seen. Still able to perform her God-given functions. So why not? He himself was not half bad in any case, this man, strong and firm and full in his warm wool coat. A host of possibilities suddenly presented themselves—not only money, but the coat she might talk him out of, the hat she might coax from his head.

"Oh yes, sir," she cooed, "I have a place warm and cozy and waiting just for you!"

Glancing over his shoulder from time to time, the man followed her down the alleyway toward the back of the palace where the courtyard was, and Praskovia glanced back at him to see if he still followed, which he did, face hidden in his collar, sunk inside his coat with shame. What shame? How silly they were, paying such a sum as a ruble and fifty kopecks for what so many gave for free, herself included. She wondered why she had never tried it before, and of course there had been those of her acquaintance who had urged her to, to earn a few kopecks here and there to buy a new hat or scarf—money of one's own that one did not have to ask the mistress for.

"Here, my sweetheart, in here," she said, beckoning to him from the doorway of the empty stable.

How sweet and shy he was, frightened and weak, in need of her special help. It had been years since she had held a man in her hand and felt his power grow in her expert care. "Oh that's good, you're doing very well," she cooed in his ear, "good boy, good boy, you're my good boy."

Afterward, when the man had buttoned himself and slunk away, Praskovia sat on the stable floor, her legs crossed under her. The fur-trimmed cap sat jauntily on her head, and she weighed the silver kopecks in her newly mittened palm, more kopecks than he'd offered her at first—so many more.

With the help of the tea and vodka that Praskovia spooned into her mistress's mouth, and the grace of God, the fever broke by morning.

Alexandra sat up against the pillows Praskovia had arranged to support her back and took into her mouth a spoonful of slippery boiled egg. Walking proud and warm in her new hat, Praskovia had made her way to the small market on Dunskaya Allee and there had bought a pair of tin cups, some spoons, a cracked plate or two, a worn and ragged coat, a pair of boots of bright red felt, a loaf of bread, a small bag of eggs, sugar, tea, and vodka. Then she'd gone out again for firewood: an armful, heavy. And still there was money left! She could feel the warm coins between her breasts, these earnings of her very own.

"Praskovia," said Alexandra from her pillow, "where did you get the money to buy this food?"

Praskovia, spooning up another bit of boiled egg, informed her mistress that she'd saved it on her own, had had it all along.

Alexandra, savoring the mild taste and soft texture of the egg—the first food she had had in days—was nonetheless skeptical.

"Saved it from what?" she said. "It's not as if you earn a salary, like Istvan. He's a free man. You're not, and don't get paid."

"My soul is my own," said Praskovia, taking a leap in logic, eager to avoid a proper answer, "that you cannot own."

To further distract the mistress, Praskovia began the long story of her Aunt Anfisa's visit to the Gypsies. It seemed that after her husband, Uncle Yurko, died, she had been plagued by visits from his ghost, which bent over her at night and breathed bitter vodka breath into her face until she couldn't stand it anymore.

"Praskovia, where did you get that money?"

Praskovia hung her head in a pantomime of shame. "I begged it, little countess, begged it in the street."

"A beggar in the street? You? Us?"

"Yes, little countess," said Praskovia, trying hard to force some tears but wanting to smile as she thought of the ease with which she had talked the poor man out of his hat and gloves and more than three times as much money as they'd agreed upon. "I begged."

"Impossible!" Alexandra threw back the covers, swung her body out of bed, and stood, a purposeful hand swinging out in Praskovia's direction. But the intended blow to her servant's ear was interrupted; the room began to tilt and slide. Alexandra clutched at the air and fell back onto the mattress, which sagged sadly under her. She put her head in her hands.

"Mistress," said Praskovia, bending over her, "you must not tire yourself. You must not get out of bed."

Alexandra pushed her away. Again she tried to stand, and this time felt the room settle down around her as her body adjusted to its new position, the floor flat and stable beneath her feet. Starved and sick as she was, she knew she could not remain in bed, but had to take command of the situation before Praskovia did something truly terrible, as she was beginning to suspect she already had, for she was far too pleased with herself for someone who had just suffered the abasement of beggary.

"I'm going out," she said. "Bring my clothes. I'm going to Trenyakov. He'll know what to do."

"Mistress, you haven't any clothes."

"Oh yes," said the countess, "quite right. That Matryona." She sat back down again and held her head. No clothes, no money, no horses, no carriage, no coachman, no Kolygin, no Rybynsky. And after all her hard work—the afternoon teas she had sat through listening to the dull chatter of the Petersburg elite, the tedious balls, the callow young men who stepped on her feet and coughed in her face and stared at the floor, their foreheads wrinkled with trying to remember the steps and think of something to say, the after-theater parties where too much champagne was drunk and the older women caressed the thighs of the fresh young footmen when they thought no one was looking, the tedious fittings, the hats and gloves to choose—after all of this, she had less than when she started. Not even any clothes. Nothing but the ragged and thin old nightdress, smelly with sickness, that covered her right now.

"I have to go to Trenyakov," the countess said, but before Praskovia, anticipating another lucrative encounter somewhere on the way to Trenyakov's, could open her mouth to suggest that it would be more fitting for her to go in her mistress's place, the countess fixed her with a look and told her, "*You're* not going anywhere."

Praskovia did not protest—until her mistress added, "Give me your clothes."

"I won't!" Praskovia cried. The lovely fur hat and gloves, the pretty red boots she'd earned herself? "What's wrong with begging in the streets? Better to do it honestly in the streets than beg from that old Trenyakov, the way he looks at you. If he gives you money, I know why!"

The countess lifted her hand and slapped her servant in the face. Praskovia began to cry, and Alexandra too. They were poor now, poor as anyone in Petersburg, and what was left of the pride of the Korvins but this empty palace and a ragged night-gown trimmed with yellowed lace?

Separately they cried, and then in each other's arms, until the countess admitted that perhaps begging was not so shameful after all, and the serf protested that she was sorry that she'd done it, but she'd only done it to save her mistress, and they both knew they weren't talking about begging, but about something else, and so they cried again.

"And now I must see Trenyakov," said Alexandra, disengaging herself from Praskovia's clinging arms.

Praskovia, though agreeing that Trenyakov was a fine man, a good and honorable one indeed, would still not give up the clothes.

"Then I'll be naked, little countess," she said, backing away.

"For heaven's sake," cried Alexandra, "I won't take *all* your clothes, just the outer ones, your skirt and blouse, your coat and your boots."

"Not my boots! I bought them with money that I earned myself, and you can't have them."

The countess suggested that Praskovia was being childish. To no avail.

"Mistress," said Praskovia, the clever thing, "you know you can't go out in these." She spread her hands to indicate her peasant clothes. "What if someone saw you? Then all of Petersburg would know your shame."

The serf was right. Nor could she send Praskovia with a note for Trenyakov asking him to come and see her. Even if she wished to take the risk of allowing Praskovia out on the street to ply her trade again, it would mean that Trenyakov would appear at the palace, and what would she wear to receive him? Her nightgown?

Praskovia was walking up and down the room, head bent to admire the vibrant color of her new red boots—the favorite color of the Russian peasantry, as satisfying to the eye as bread to the belly. She jingled as she walked, as she had always jingled, the keys that hung from her belt the emblem of her status as stewardess, as keeper of the house, guardian of its hearth. It had always been a comforting sound, this jingling. It had meant that Praskovia was coming, or going, but generally taking care of things, passing in and out of rooms and overseeing the household's affairs, though there were no rooms to lock anymore, no stores and larders to protect from thieving serfs, and so Matryona, always jealous of those keys, had not bothered to try to take them too.

Struck by a sudden thought, the countess cocked her head.

A young man pushed open the door of the offices of Oleg Trenyakov, Esquire, and entered the outer room.

"Yes?" The law clerk looked up from the fingernails he'd been picking with the nib of a pen. The purple stain it left on his fingers only added to the impression of personal disarray, and he could not, with his frayed cuffs and uncombed hair, have presented a greater contrast to the young man who stood before him in polished boots, black merino frock coat smooth as cream, and top hat set at a rakish angle on his head.

"My good man," said the youth, pointing his gold-topped walking stick in the clerk's direction, "get up, get up, and call your employer. I have important business to discuss with him." The young man leaned on his cane and stared at the clerk with an arrogance that made the clerk, himself a runaway serf, tremble in his scuffed and sour-smelling shoes, sure he'd been found out, that someone had come to claim him for his master.

"Come, come," the young man insisted, beginning to remove his gloves, "I haven't all day here." However, the effeminacy of his voice identified him quite clearly not as a detective but as one of the swellest of the city's young swells, and the clerk relaxed. He had seen many of this type coming to Trenyakov. The affectation of the high-pitched voice and decadent manner marked his membership in the city's most exclusive set of smart young men, it being this year's fashionable amusement to drive their fathers to the point of popped veins and raw shouts by affecting a lavender-tinted refinement suggestive, however erroneously, of the most commonplace but father-provoking of the vices they had to choose from at the city's banquet of sin, others of which (gambling, women, violent pranks) frequently landed them at Trenyakov's door for help in cleaning up the legal mess before their fathers found it out and cut them off without a cent.

"Your name, sir?" asked the clerk, ducking his head.

The young man, who had taken off his gloves but not his hat, suppressed a smile, as if the clerk had said something funny and he was trying not to laugh.

"I decline to give a name," he replied, "but I assure you, he will receive me when he finds out who I am."

The clerk would have liked to suggest that it was impossible to find out who he was if he did not give his name, but he was sufficiently intimidated by the voice and the manner of the fashionable young man—most of all by his arrogant refusal to remove his expensive hat—that he rose from his desk and disappeared behind the door to Trenyakov's office.

In another moment he was back, fortified by Trenyakov's absolute refusal to entertain the presence of the visitor without first being told his name.

"He won't see you."

The young man leaned forward on his polished walking stick.

"I think he will," he said. "Just tell him I have business with the executor of the late Count Korvin's estate." He straightened up and flicked listlessly at a spot on the sleeve of his coat with his flaccid leather gloves. Ostentatiously, he sniffed.

Having vanished again behind the door, the clerk returned with the news that Trenyakov would see him, and the young man swept past him and vanished behind the door himself.

Trenyakov peered over his spectacles at the visitor. This was no one he knew.

"Who are you?" he said, "I know every creditor and partner of the late Count Korvin's, but I don't know you. Your refusal to

give your name to my clerk suggests unsavory motives or crimi-
nal designs." This was perhaps a bit harsh, but Trenyakov did not
like to be disturbed at his work, which at this particular moment
consisted of examining with a magnifying glass the pitted marble
surface of one of the sculpture fragments he had recently purchased and for which he had paid through the nose.

The young man did not reply but simply leaned on his cane,
his eyes sunk in the shadow of his high silk hat.

"If you will not state your name," said Trenyakov, "then state
your business."

The young man cleared his throat. "Extortion," he said clearly.

Trenyakov began to rise from his seat in outrage when the
young man reached up and pulled off his hat. Hair spilled out
from beneath it and fell to the young man's waist, which he bent
from in a low, sweeping bow.

"I fooled you!" cried the countess, straightening up. "Admit
it! You didn't know that it was me."

Trenyakov threw himself down in his chair, pulled a large
handkerchief from his breast pocket, and mopped his forehead.

"No, Countess," he sighed, wanting to wipe his neck as well,
but deciding against it as a peasantlike gesture too crude to perform in the presence of a lady of high birth. He stuffed the
handkerchief back into his pocket, where it made a large lump
right over his heart. "I did not recognize you."

Alexandra sat down in one of the chairs in front of the
lawyer's desk and placed her top hat on her knees. "I'm sure you
are wondering why I am dressed this way," she said, more cheerful than the lawyer had ever seen her in his life.

"I certainly am."

"I'm sure you are wondering what has happened in my life to
bring this about."

"I certainly am."

"It's a long story," said Alexandra.

"Start it," said Trenyakov.

The countess requested a glass of water, mentioning that she had lately been ill and that she had walked all the way to his office on her own.

"Ill? And you walked all the way? Oh, my dear Countess," said Trenyakov, rising from his seat, and lumbering out on his short legs from behind his enormous desk, "I will do more than give you something to drink. With your permission, I will take you to lunch."

The countess, delighted, leaped to her feet. She had never been inside a restaurant, it being the practice of well-brought-up young girls and married women of social standing to avoid these vulgar establishments, most of which contained on their upper floors a number of rooms whose doors had only half the complement of doorknobs and could only be opened from inside, the proprietors mindful of the modesty of those who were dining privately within. Proper young ladies, on the other hand, were hothoused like flowers, displayed only at selected times, and never in public places where anyone could gawk.

"Dressed as you are," said Trenyakov, lifting his own silk hat and frock coat from a coat stand in the corner of the room, "we may go anywhere for lunch—that is, if it won't offend your modesty and provided that you keep your hat on."

They made an odd picture, the short man and the tall girl, identically dressed in black as they descended the stairs of the building side by side. However, stepping out into the street, they joined the flock of other gentlemen, also identically dressed, who strutted and picked their way along the boulevards like crows that had landed in a field of snow, each so absorbed in his journey that none of them noticed that the face under one of the hats was too finely molded to be masculine.

"Perhaps I ought to take you home instead," said Trenyakov, suddenly uneasy as he tossed up his hand to attract the eye of a passing cabby, who instantly thrust his feet down and sawed at the reins until he had pulled alongside the misproportioned pair.

"Oh no," said the countess, "this will probably be my only chance!"

Trenyakov decided instantly that only the most respectable restaurant would do, one that actresses and ladies of the demi-monde did not frequent, knowing that of course these were just the sort of people the countess was hoping to see. By her elbow he lifted her up into the cab and then, already out of breath, but with a last great surge of effort, swung himself up after her and landed with a chuffing of relief on the opposite seat, which promptly hissed and flattened. Unnerved by the sight of the masculine figure the countess presented to the world, and so successfully, Trenyakov found himself struck dumb, too shy to ask her for an explanation. He spent the short ride to the restaurant staring up at the ceiling of the cab, his lips occasionally moving as he sought to give her the impression that his mind was enmeshed in the tangles of various legal problems of vital importance to the state.

On entering the restaurant, Trenyakov had to urge the countess past the lady who was sitting behind the cashier's desk fiddling with her painted nails. Alexandra had never seen such a woman up so close before, longed to see her closer, and edged herself in the woman's direction, trying not to stare, but fascinated by the unnatural pinkness of the woman's cheeks and the lurid red of her lips, until Trenyakov managed to distract her by pointing out that the headwaiter was approaching them. This man, with enormous rounded hips over which the tails of his coat were widely spread, was rushing up with a widespread smile to greet the famous lawyer Trenyakov and the young gentleman who was his companion. The young gentleman perversely refused to surrender his hat but allowed his coat to be taken by a footman, and the headwaiter, assuming that this refusal to remove the hat was a new fashion among the gilded youth of Petersburg, did not insist but instead filed the small fact away in his head, where it was added to the bottom of a long list of fads and customs practiced by his aristocratic clients, which it was his duty to remember so that he could preserve his air of imperturbability in the face of the very oddest of their habits.

He conducted the two to a table under the central chandelier, where Alexandra seated herself, took the menu without opening it, and swiveled her head. There was not a woman to be seen, though men were everywhere, pairs of them, quartets, octets, all making the music of lunch with the scraping of silver against china, the chinking and clinking of glasses, and the spurts of laughter rising above the steady chattering hum of talk.

At the next table, a pair of men, one short and plump, the other tall and blondish with a beard, were conversing intensely. Alexandra wished that she could hear what they were saying. She wished she could hear what all of them were saying in their hidden world of men. While Trenyakov, lost in the contemplation of the menu, raised his eyes heavenward as if seeking divine guidance in his choice of lunch, Alexandra leaned back in her chair.

"Give me your advice," said one of them.

"What about?" said the other.

"About this. Suppose you're married and you love your wife, but you've fallen in love with another woman . . ."

This provocative statement was interrupted for Alexandra by the reappearance of the headwaiter, smiling broadly and proffering yet another menu, whose purpose Alexandra did not yet know, but which Trenyakov accepted while continuing to squint at the first.

"Have you decided, Count?" asked Trenyakov without looking up, while the headwaiter, hearing the word *count,* turned his face to Alexandra and beamed at her with an intensity so great that Alexandra feared for his mental health.

"Your excellency," he intoned at her, bowing as low as his heavy belly in its stretched white waistcoat would allow. Alexandra expected to see the buttons pop, but they did not. "May I recommend the Flensburg oysters? They are very fresh."

Shrugging, Alexandra looked at Trenyakov, who grunted in disapproval.

"Nothing from Ostend?"

"Unfortunately, no, your honor. But they're fresh. We got them in just yesterday."

"Count?" said Trenyakov, looking up at her at last, the corner of his mouth twitching in amusement, his eyes shining at her over the glasses that had slipped down his plump nose.

"You decide," said Alexandra, already turning her head in the direction of the tantalizing conversation droning on behind her. "Whatever you choose will be good, I'm sure."

"Another moment, then," said Trenyakov, and waved the waiter away. He went back to studying the menu with even greater concentration than before, which left Alexandra free to return her attention to the conversation of the two men.

"I'm sorry," the other voice was saying, "I think you know that so far as I am concerned there are only two kinds of women. Or rather, no... there are women and there are... I have never seen and I don't think I shall ever see any charming fallen creatures, but women like that painted Frenchwoman at the cashier's desk, the one with the ringlets, such women are vile creatures for me, and all fallen women are the same."

"And the woman in the New Testament?"

"Oh! For goodness' sake! Christ never would have spoken those words if he had known how they would be misused. Those words seem to me the only ones people remember in the whole Gospels. However, I am saying not what I think but what I feel. I have a horror of fallen women. You are afraid of spiders and I am afraid of those horrible creatures."

It was fascinating! To know what men talked about when they were alone, to hear their fresh, unguarded opinions, those that were normally hidden from females. Such a conversation was not fit for the ears of a respectable young lady—how delightful to be in a position to hear it. Of course, Alexandra had to admit to herself that she did know one man ill-bred enough to speak to her about such unsavory topics, but that had been only at the beginning of their acquaintance. He had then fallen boringly in love with her and, retreating into respectability, become as dull as the others.

She listened for more.

"What is to be done?" cried the first voice. "Your wife is getting old and you are full of life. Before you have time to turn around, you feel that you are no longer in love with your wife, however much you may respect her. Then all of a sudden you fall in love with someone else and you are lost! Lost!"

This was getting better and better.

"In my view, love," said the other man with great earnestness, "both kinds of love, which Plato defines in the *Symposium*—both kinds of love serve as a touchstone for men. Some men understand only one kind and others only the other. . . ."

What were these two kinds of love? she wanted to know.

But Alexandra's attention was torn away from the conversation by the reappearance of the headwaiter, who was now staring at Trenyakov with an expression of obsequious expectation. Trenyakov snapped his menu shut and looked up at Alexandra.

"Astrakhan melon and Parma ham to start?"

Alexandra shrugged.

"Imperial boullion?"

Alexandra nodded encouragement.

"Creamed lobster for the fish," he went on, gaining confidence, "grilled ptarmigan, tenderloin of beef with thick sauce, asparagus, peas, and a charlotte russe!"

"Magnificent, your honor," whispered the headwaiter, shaking his head as if in disbelief at the brilliance of his choice, the sophisticated juxtapositions of texture and taste. Alexandra herself clapped her hands. Trenyakov dropped his eyes in pleased embarrassment, his tender-looking, sparsely covered scalp reddening sweetly.

The second half of Trenyakov's performance—the ordering of the wines to correspond to each of the courses—left the headwaiter breathless.

"Perfection," he intoned, eyes heavenward. Alexandra noticed that the two men behind her had gotten up to leave and were walking out, which gave her the opportunity to study them more closely. The short man, the one who no longer loved his aging wife was, she saw now, fittingly fat with the indulgences of the table, the skin beneath his eyes purplish and pouchy as if infused with the residue of the rich dark port he probably drank too much of. The man was clearly a sensualist, an exponent of what she supposed was the "other kind of love" that the taller man had spoken of with disapproval in his voice. What was that kind of love? And the taller man, she saw now, was slender and strong, with a wheat-colored beard and eyes of a sun-infused clarity. He looked as if he spent a lot of time in the open air. And the love he had spoken of? What was it?

He was the sort of man that Alexandra thought she would like to know. Perhaps to fall in love with.

The waiter was already rushing back with a bottle in one hand and two plates of Parma ham dexterously fanned in the other.

"And now," said Trenyakov, leaning slightly back in his chair to give the waiter room to deliver the ham, "I must hear your story."

Alexandra had reached that point in her narrative where she discovers the perfidy of Madame Lavorine. Earlier, while they had eaten their oysters, Alexandra had set the stage for this betrayal, and Matryona's later one, and now, as they started on the tenderloin, swimming in thin natural juices that bled deliciously into the dense eggy sauce, Alexandra was explaining how the deceitful little woman had elbowed her aside during a rousing discussion with the handsome Count Kolygin of the chemical principles behind effective stain removal, how the little woman had pushed herself in between herself and the count and taken over completely, leaving Alexandra to hang about listlessly on the sidelines until she had had no choice but to withdraw. Of course the countess had been careful to omit her own perfidious pursuit of another woman's suitor, ill-fated as it was, and was prudently planning on omitting the fact of Ulyanov's proposal as well (fearing that Trenyakov, knowing of her desperate situation, would pressure her to accept him). She was building up to the astonishing announcement of Lavorine's engagement to the count when she was interrupted by the sounds of a commotion at the entrance to the dining room—slurred, angry shouts and measured, officious pleadings. This continued for a minute or so, until all of the diners had been alerted and all had opened their ears to try to catch the substance of the argument, which they could not. Then, much to Alexandra's amazement, Ulyanov himself staggered into the dining room with a lady on either arm. The orchestra, on seeing the entrance of an officer, instantly left off playing the luncheon music they'd been tinkling and strumming at in boredom, and struck up, as they always did at the appearance of a military man, the anthem of his regiment, in this case that of the 17th Hussars, Zamoyski regiment.

Obviously drunk, his tunic wrinkled, unbuttoned, and spotted with food, Ulyanov had each of his arms around one of the two ladies, who were clearly of questionable reputation. He pecked at each of their red-rouged cheeks and staggered from time to time as the orchestra piped him to his table, which was not far from where Alexandra and her companion sat. The assemblage of diners fell silent, hoping to witness an interesting, preferably scandalous diversion from the ongoing process of their respectable lunch. The orchestra fell silent too.

They were not disappointed.

"Vodka!" shouted Ulyanov, throwing up his arm so forcefully he staggered backward. "And not a silly glass, but a bottle big and cold!" Without waiting for a bottle to be brought to him, he jumped to the top of the empty table, scattering silverware and china, the linen napkins fluttering to the floor while the "ladies" screamed. Swaying, he stared aggressively round at the diners who were looking up at him, expectant. Ulyanov opened his mouth, about to make an announcement of some import to the crowd, when the diversion was unhappily cut short by the appearance of a cossack policeman in an enormous fur hat, with bandoliers across his chest and a rifle in his hand. With the help of the headwaiter and the two ladies, the cossack gently encouraged his captive to vacate the podium and come along home. In a few moments Ulyanov, followed by the two ladies, had been hustled away.

"Ah," said Trenyakov, turning back to his lunch, "young Mecklenburg-Ulyanov. Now there's a young man with heavy cares and great responsibilities ahead of him. It is good to see him enjoying himself."

Alexandra, who had sunk down in her chair for fear that Ulyanov might recognize her, straightened at the sound of the orchestra starting up again with another clash of martial music and swiveled her head round to see if that pitiful creature had returned—so sad to see him that way, though of course she had never liked him. The suicide of his mistress must have hit him hard, especially since it had surely been his fault in some way. It was, however, another officer who was being honored by the music, who was now being led with great ceremony and much craning of heads to the very best table in the house, where he was seated most obsequiously by the headwaiter along with his civilian companions.

"Who's that?" Alexandra put a hand to her chest to quiet the pounding of her heart. She still had not regained the breath that had escaped so violently from her lungs when she had seen Ulyanov, and she was grateful for this distraction from the confusion of her thoughts.

"Who?" said Trenyakov, turning his head.

"That officer. Why are they making such a fuss?"

Trenyakov turned back to her and smiled strangely. He shook his head. "How odd," he said softly, laughing to himself, "how very odd. Now there's a story."

"Start it," said Alexandra, with a smile.

"Oh, I am merely struck by the remarkable coincidence," Trenyakov explained, "that there should be two at this moment. Two right here."

"Two of what?" asked Alexandra.

More heads were craning, murmurs growing louder, and a few of the diners had gotten up to approach the officer's table to pay their respects. Why they should want to offer their respects to this undistinguished-looking middle-aged man in the worn-looking uniform of an officer of low rank was something Alexandra could not understand. Why, he was not even a colonel, much less a general. And how strange-looking he was—slight of figure, delicate of face. He resembled a boy grown old who had never been a man.

Trenyakov leaned across the table.

"Two women dressed as men," he said. "That officer is as much a female as you are."

The aged boy was instantly transformed in this change of context. What had merely been odd was now grotesque—the woman's sun-hardened skin, razor-chopped hair, and manly bearing rendered her appearance bizarre.

"It's Nadezhda Durova, of course," said Trenyakov to Alexandra, who gaped openly. "She has only just published her fantastic memoir and is being lionized by the literary set. The Cavalry Maiden, they call her. A lady of high birth, like yourself. She was bored with her life as a woman. She found it too restrictive. She wanted adventure and excitement, to escape the life that was planned for her. So she ran away from home. She disguised herself as a man and joined the hussars, where she served with distinction for many years. A remarkable woman. You should meet her."

"Heaven forbid," said Alexandra, "I think she's quite horrible."

"No more horrible than yourself, my dear countess," said Trenyakov, gesturing toward the top hat Alexandra wore to conceal her hair.

"Yes," said Alexandra, "but I dress as a man out of necessity, not volition. I simply had no other clothes, you see. I was lucky my father's fitted me so perfectly."

"Ah," said Trenyakov, "then the mystery is solved, but not the reason behind it."

Alexandra resumed her story, which she continued to tell as cheese and fruit were put before them, as the towering charlotka was carried with pomp across the dining room and set down on the table, as tiny cups of Turkish coffee were served with a sugar-powdered slice of rubbery candy on the side of the saucer.

"How terrible," said Trenyakov, setting down the slice of turkish delight that had a bite out of it, revealing a jellied interior that tasted of roses, but whose richness now excited more guilt than pleasure in light of the countess's plight. "An absolute disaster, I must agree," he said. "My poor Countess. What will you do?"

Under Trenyakov's sympathetic eyes Alexandra wilted visibly, collapsing under the weight of her recent troubles as if Trenyakov's assent to their enormity confirmed what she herself had tried hard to ignore. Tears came to her eyes, but luckily did not escape her lower lids to drip revealingly down her cheeks.

Trenyakov fell silent, allowing her the privacy of her emotion by averting his eyes to the surface of his slice of candy, where he made patterns with the tip of his finger in the thick powdered sugar, sweet as snow on roses, which might have been Alexandra's own cheek. The solution was simple. He might marry Alexandra himself. He had money, influence, even a kind of fame. He would not be so bad a choice for an impoverished noblewoman. He had noble blood himself, though the son of a serf. But . . .

Trenyakov shifted in his chair, feeling his shirt strain against his distended belly. He straightened up, sensed a slimming effect, but at that moment reached up unconsciously to pat his thinning hair into place. It was no use, of course.

"I will do all I can to help you," he said. "Perhaps your father's friend the princess might be applied to." He was too shy to offer her money himself.

"No!" said Alexandra. "That horrible woman. How she tortured me all my life."

"Ah well, then, no," said Trenyakov. He searched his mind for some solution to her trouble, and a horrendous thought appeared. The poor countess in her poverty might be forced to seek the typical solution of the indigent female—the despairing, the distressed, the truly down and out—to the problem of her self-support. Why, he himself had contributed to the disgrace of one of these defenseless women, with a tall blond girl very like the countess, of good family, but left without a penny. Selected from a fine display in the city's best bordello, she had given him much pleasure in his fantasies of reciprocated passion, and his heart, safely shielded, had played joyously at love, which he had paid for handsomely with money, extravagant gifts, and even more extravagant declarations of an affection not without authenticity, for the girl had been lovely and pitiful. However, feeling the warmth in his heart increasing at every successive meeting, he had resolved to avoid the girl and choose another less touching, a more practiced courtesan with a heart as hard as he wished his own to be, and when he had seen the lovely girl months later on the street, reduced to a common whore, he had turned away from her.

Breathing raggedly, Trenyakov fumbled in his pocket for his wallet. He insisted that the countess take the money, all he had, insisted so violently he was sure he frightened her. Every coin and bill he had upon his person was pressed into her hands, and after he had seen the countess home, he returned to his office.

The rooms were empty, dark. Trenyakov knelt on the floor

before his iron safe, cooling his head against the metal a moment, and then he opened it. Stacks of paper rubles, neatly tied in chunks with string, reached nearly to the top. He removed half the contents of the safe, filled a briefcase, and went out again.

Trenyakov wrapped his neck more tightly in the scarf and held his black top hat down on his head to keep it from blowing off in the lethal wind from the Gulf of Finland, from the darker colder north across the sea, the edge of the world. He started off across an empty square. He walked through many empty squares until he found one full of life. Arms beckoned him, breasts pimpled with cold were briefly exposed and covered up again when he did not agree to buy. But he was not buying tonight. Looking into each of the ravaged, rouged faces, he shook his head, but still pressed into the grasping hands a paper note, a coin. He did not find what he was looking for, and when the briefcase was empty, he went home again.

Tired as Alexandra was, she could not sleep. Since the series of disasters which had lately befallen her, she had had no time to think. Now, however, lying in bed, thoughts crowded into her mind, and she could not keep them out.

What was she to do?

Praskovia's feet were in her face and smelling bad, a phlegmy snore issuing from the serf's other end. At least she was warm, a living hot-water bottle, a soft and breathing stove.

What was she to do? The money Trenyakov had given her would last a few months if she was frugal. Then what? He had spoken of the old courtesan, the princess, but Alexandra's pride would not support another application for her help—the help she had already given had had strings of bitter malice attached, the cruel whim of an arid soul.

"A woman like that," her father had said once, "detaches her heart from her soul and lives on it like money until it is gone." And clearly, it was gone.

What else? Who else?

Ulyanov. He had wanted to marry her, but his disgraceful appearance in the restaurant suggested to her that his heart was tormented by the memory of another, by his guilt over the woman's death. Even if Alexandra were willing to marry him, which she was not, what sort of husband would he make her now? His reputation had been further sullied by the scandal of the suicide, and marriage to such a man would do nothing to restore her fortunes, would only be another step downward on her already downward path. In any case, even if she were willing, which she was not, how was she to go about it? Go to him and ask if the offer was still open? Tell him she was completely at his mercy now? He would most likely laugh in her face, or offer her less than marriage just for spite

The way he'd pawed at her! How she would love to challenge him for that insult, level a pistol at his heart, or press against it the razorlike tip of a rapier until she had deflated him completely. That letter declaring his love had clearly been an opening gambit to set her up for his proposal, itself a ruse, something to throw her off her guard. What had he really planned for her?

Seduction, abandonment, disgrace—to leave her with a sickly child whose milk and bread she would have to beg in the streets, or worse.

One hundred thousand souls. How had she let Count Kolygin slip away? What arrogance had there been in her to believe she could give him nothing and keep him coming back for more of it?

One hundred thousand souls. She would be lucky to have an

egg, a small one, to eat tomorrow. Perhaps a piece of sour bread. A pickle, a beet, half of a potato. What was she to do?

Get down on your knees and pray for guidance. Shivering, she emerged from the bed, walked across the room, and knelt in front of the icon, enjoying the pain of bony knee against hard floor, a punishment for her arrogance in letting Kolygin slip away. But behind her arrogance there was greed, and that was worse. A true Christian would be content to live on ashes, eat the air. Why couldn't she forget who she had been and be content with what she was becoming?

"Oh Holy Mother," she said, looking up at the icon, its silver dull in the darkness, and it occurred to her suddenly to wonder why she hadn't sold it yet. That silver frame clearly would increase its value, which already was fairly high, as it was the work of a famous artist and very old.

Another sin! She half rose from the floor and dropped to her knees again to feel the punishing pain.

And what part had she herself played in the death of that young girl, with her own involvement with the rake Ulyanov? She dared not look the Holy Mother in the face to ask, but laid herself out full length on the floor and spread her arms until her body formed a cross. She opened her mouth to taste the dust.

It occurred to her that this histrionic penitence would not put food on the table for herself and Praskovia. They could not, after all, eat dust and ashes and air. Trenyakov's money would soon run out, and she could not ask for more without compromising her respectability. If she took more money from him, he would be keeping her, and how long would it be before he might demand that such an arrangement render him his due?

Alexandra turned her head, pressing her ear against the floor and listening to the pounding of her blood as if she would hear

her heart that way, discern in the rhythm of its beating some
fundamental truth about herself, the complicated organ a small
planet she must discover, map. Who was she? Perhaps she was
not the Countess Korvin after all. Perhaps her impoverishment,
her loss of station, was only fate's righting of what had been
wrong to begin with, her destiny bending her toward poverty,
obscurity, her rightful path.

"Nonsense!" Alexandra picked herself up off the floor and
got back into bed, lying flat on her back, still thinking. Escape
was what she wished for. That woman in the restaurant, that
Durova, how wise she had been to evade a woman's dependent
lot. *She* had not had to worry about marrying for money but had
made her own way in the world of men, with distinction too.
Oh, if only she had the cash to buy herself an officer's commission, she might escape from her womanhood as well. The masculine skin had fitted her so comfortably, and not a head had
turned to scrutinize her face and figure, suspicious of her femininity.

Why had her father done this to her? How could he have
left her this way, in poverty and worry? She wanted to spit and
curse his name, and the impulse brought her upright in bed
again, ready to throw herself down before the icon to beg forgiveness for her sin against a daughter's love. But she was tired
and her knees hurt. Oh, she knew that her father had not
intended this. Trenyakov had explained it, tried to comfort her.
Her father had expected something to come along to restore the
fortune, but then he had always been a dreamer, one who lived
in the luminous landscape of his mind, where anything was possible.

How pleasant that must be, how nice, she thought, feeling
herself grow drowsy. She turned on her side, put her hands
beneath her head, and unclenched her tired mind to ready it for

sleep. Its hard structures, which molded thought into logical shape, began to soften, and all manner of irrationalities began to drift across the blank screen of her consciousness. She began to hear her father's voice again, calling out to her from a distance, but he had done this so many times before in odd moments that she paid it no attention and concentrated on her descent into unconsciousness. The voice, however, would not be ignored. It shouted more loudly, and for the first time she could hear it pronounce a syllable, a sibilant in fact, presumably the beginning of a word. A clear hissing s, followed by an unintelligible vowel and perhaps another consonant, indistinct, began to repeat in her ear, as if her father, shouting the sharp initial s over and over, was exulting in his success at penetrating the veil between two worlds with just this tiny point of sound. Or perhaps he was driven to pierce the veil in many places until he could shred its fabric, rip the barrier apart, and reach through it to beg forgiveness.

"Sorry" was what she supposed he was trying to say, "sorry, sorry, sorry."

In the morning, Alexandra went to her father's room to dress. It had not seemed right for her to keep his clothing in her own wardrobe, and so she had hung it back up in his the night before. While she was buttoning up her trousers, her eye fell on the few trinkets that were left on the table. Of course she could not sell his clothing—she needed it to wear—but the decorative lacquer boxes might be worth something after all, she thought, intricately painted as they were. They might fetch a few rubles to keep her and Praskovia eating a few days longer. The silver-plated razor could be taken to the bazaar—it might yield some kopecks. And the crystal egg? Surely someone would want the pretty thing. She picked it up, weighed it in her hand, imagining how it had felt in his, turning it over and over as he had used to do. She experienced the satisfaction he must have felt at rubbing fingertips over the smooth, separate planes of its faceted surface, and the sensation comforted her, brought her closer to him, as if she were inside her father's skin, inside his mind. . . . No, she could not sell it. She slipped the egg into her pocket, as her father had always done.

Suddenly she felt the sensation of her father's voice inside her ear again, that insistent shout from far away. It was louder, more urgent now than ever, hysterical in tone. "No need, no need," she said out loud, sympathetic to the anguished sound and wanting to comfort him, "you've said you're sorry. I heard you say it. I know you are. I know. You can go and rest now. You can rest." The voice would not rest. It circled round inside her mind until it shouted indistinctly in her other ear, and she felt a tugging or a nudging at her hand, the one that was rubbing at the surface of the crystal with her fingers.

The voice broke through, the words were clear: "Sell it."

It was, of course, a diamond—an enormous one. And of course her father would have kept a diamond in his pocket, left it lying about the house on random surfaces and old tables. It was just like him.

It netted her quite a tidy sum. There was not only enough to buy a carriage secondhand and a pair of horses, but money for a modest wardrobe and even a frugal living for herself and Praskovia, and perhaps another servant, for the next year or two. Certainly enough time for Alexandra to find herself a suitable, and suitably wealthy, mate.

And yet Alexandra, initially inspirited by her father's leap across the barrier to her aid, by this transcendent proof of love, until she felt, for a moment, as if she were floating above the world, came down quickly with a bump. Her fittings for the new complement of gowns were even more tiring, more irritating than she remembered, the parties, cotillions, balls, and teas more tedious, the men she encountered more respectably dull. She felt the restrictions of femininity as never before as, trussed in her corsets and tripping over her skirts, she went from her palace to the carriage, from the carriage to another palace, from that palace back to the carriage, and then home again, an endless, futile round inside the tiny social sphere, which was all that was allowed her as a woman, as if she were trapped inside a bauble made of glass and able only to stare with longing at the wider world outside.

Olga's marriage had taken place. On that day, Alexandra, begging off, claiming illness, had stayed in bed, smoking cigar after cigar and staring up at the ceiling, studying the water stains as if they were clouds, looking for shapes and meaning, finding none. On other days, and these days came more frequently, she refused all invitations and instead wandered aimlessly through the empty palace, thinking of nothing and smoking more of those cigars.

Spring came. With that, the thaw, when the city's giant heart seemed audibly to break as the solid veins of ice that were its rivers tore apart in the overwhelming warmth, thundered in the night, shrieked and moaned as if mourning the end of somnolent winter, with its slowing of time, its trapping and taming of the sun. Alexandra too felt the sadness of the year's turning, of time rushing on.

One evening, at Praskovia's irritable urging, her incessant prodding to "get out and find a man before your teeth fall out and your breasts fall down," Alexandra attended a musicale at the home of one of the city's most prominent citizens. In the palace, the music room looked like all the other music rooms, and the sight of more of those potted palms that forested the city's palaces made her feel as if she might do violence to someone, anyone, not least to the Armenian prince whose heart she had been cultivating halfheartedly these past few weeks, who stood beside her now as the music tinkled on and on and his voice droned on and on, talking of the homeland he had never seen, where the peasants, he was saying, had found the most ingenious uses for the country's especially fragrant apples, its large and luscious pears, making of them noodles, liquors, dolls.

"And the mountains of my country are magnificent," he was saying, his dark eyes shining as he tried to keep them from dropping down again toward the countess's revealing décolletage, where her breasts, he thought, were firm as pears themselves, but needed further ripening.

"No doubt," said Alexandra.

"They were made by the hand of God."

"Wasn't everything?"

"Made special by God. I will relate to you a story we tell in my country about ourselves. While God was working on creation, all the other peoples gathered round to watch his handiwork and choose for themselves where they would live. But we Armenians, we are independent, we are life-loving, we refused to leave our table where we drank and ate and talked. And so when God had finished, all the lands were given out and there was none for us! 'You have forgotten us!' we said to God. He thought and thought, and then he said, 'All right. I give to you the land that I was saving for myself. I call it Paradise.' "

Alexandra smacked her fan against the palm of one hand. She did it again, then set up a rhythm, the soft smacking of the fan against her hand somehow soothing her. She looked past the prince, over his shoulder, to see if there was anyone else in the room who might be more interesting, and rationalized her rudeness by insisting to herself that since she had already looked at him quite often as if he were the most wonderful man in the world, it was now time to make it clear that she didn't care if she never saw him again.

"Is that not a charming story?" the prince insisted. Sensing the sudden loss of her attention, he stepped closer, smelled the fresh scent of her hair, and felt the beginning tug of love. If only he could get her interested again, make her look at him that way again.

"It would seem to me that you've been had," said Alexandra suddenly.

"Oh?" said the prince, distending his dark nostrils to catch more of her delicious smell.

"More likely he gave you what the others didn't want, what was left over at the end, Prince."

"Oh no, Countess," he said, but softly, his full, round voice losing body as if deflated by the pin she had stuck in his national pride, "it is truly Paradise."

"If it's Paradise," she said, "then what are you doing here?"

Alexandra watched the prince walk away and asked herself, Why did I do that? He was a decent man and not bad-looking— golden-skinned and smelling suggestively of the smokiness of autumn, of fragrant, burning wood, as if he practiced the southern style of outdoor charcoal cooking at odd moments in his bedroom. However, the needling she had given him had relieved her sense of irritation, if only for the moment.

Alexandra backed up against the wall, retreating into the shadow of one of those palm trees. Resting against the cushion of her bustle, hands behind her back, she watched the guests as they moved around the room like marionettes with painted smiles and eyebrows frozen high on their foreheads in permanent expressions of delight. There was old Countess Protopopov fawning over her hated social rival Madame Renchenko, kissing and petting her, taking her hand. Other guests sat on stiff chairs with plates of too-rich cake on their knees, talking of nothing and waiting for the escape from one another that the music would provide.

They're all deadly tired of each other, Alexandra thought, and all dreaming of the moment they can go to their estates so they can invite there the people they are deadly tired of so they can be deadly tired of them in a whole new place.

Her feet hurt. She had tried to save money on her shoes, which were cheaply made and pressed uncomfortably against her toes. Her corset hurt her too; Praskovia, in an effort to make Alexandra's meager breasts pop out in invitation, had laced her far too tightly.

And now Anton Pavalinsky was making his way across the

room in her direction, his puppet face fixed in an expression of delight that she knew from experience had not been painted on. He had monopolized her for a period of one full hour the week before at Countess Bariatinsky's ball, batting aside her efforts to escape while he told her all about his latest interest, which was keeping lizards. The delights, the dangers, the delicacies of dealing with these small reptiles, what they ate, where they slept, how they (here he lowered his voice) mated, and the many variations in personality observable among the tiny population absorbed his every waking hour, he had informed her. It was a subject that might actually have interested her had her general mood been better, but a resumption of the topic at this particular point would be unbearable.

She knew she ought to hold her ground and speak to him. No suitor was, at this point, to be rejected out of hand. It was her duty, for the sake of the restoration of her name and fortune, to endure the pettiness, the boredom, the forced politeness, the fake delight in every detail of the social effort, and most of all the degrading evaluation of herself that constituted social life at the upper levels of Petersburg society. Any man who belonged to that society had the right to check out what she had on offer—in other words, herself—to see if he wanted to buy.

And what? What did they want to buy? The wealthy merchants boring their way through the ceiling of the class above them might want to buy her lineage, her blood and bones to mix with theirs, bore their way into her very body to plant the seed of their social rise in the person of a son half noble. The older ones would want her youth, of course. And the younger ones were seeking admiration, the yeast that would plump their flattened egos, beaten down as yet by the difficult process of becoming men only to rise again in the warmth of wifely comfort and support.

Alexandra at that moment had no interest in serving as yeast to expand anyone's ego; she was more interested in her own. Turning quickly, she slipped through a tall French window into the spring-soaked air outside. Standing on the balcony, she leaned her elbows on the parapet and began to wriggle and nudge herself free of her shoes, her large plump bustle rustling. The coldness of the stone was refreshing against the flaming bottoms of her bare feet. Oh, look at the city! Light shimmered on the moving water—the river and canals burned with stars. And inside each of the windows that decorated the tremendous sky, toylike figures moved in their faint yellow boxes of light. All over the city, other lives were happening. All the people out there—what were they doing? She would never know. For the rest of her life she would go from carriage to palace, palace to carriage. That is, if she were lucky enough to marry before her money ran out. Otherwise? She did not want to think of otherwise.

From the window behind her, Alexandra heard the sound of women's voices. Listening, she was surprised to hear her name.

"The Korvin girl," one of the women said, "poor thing."

"She thinks we don't know, and she goes on with it, pulling the wool over everyone's eyes," said the other. "I think it's outrageous."

"Oh, let her alone. The poor girl is doing the best she can with what she's got."

"Which isn't much," said the other.

"Oh really? I think she's rather pretty. She's certainly quite tall. There's a certain elegance she has."

"That's not the point. My brother had some interest, but when I found it out I put a stop to it, you can be sure of that. A fortune hunter? Not in my family! My brother's very foolish."

Alexandra knew the woman's voice from somewhere but did not stop to figure out from where. Stuffing her feet back inside those cheaply made shoes, she swept back into the room, and though her heart seemed to have grown enormous in her chest, crowding out her breath, she held her head up, walked majestically. Through the blurring of her tears it was difficult to find her hostess, but, narrowing her eyes, she brought the woman into focus and approached. A pretended sneeze allowed her to bring her fingers to her eyes to remove the accumulated tears as they threatened to spill, and she was ready to make her excuses.

"A headache! A bad one!" she claimed, pressing her fingertips to her temple to indicate the source of her distress.

"It must be," said her hostess, "you certainly look like you're in pain. Go home, dear girl!"

Alexandra called for her carriage, retrieved her cloak, and waited with tapping toe in the vestibule until the carriage came. She spoke to no one, though some departing guests, also waiting, tried to engage her in some sociability. On arriving at the palace, she pushed past Praskovia, who had opened her mouth to inquire what the mistress was doing home before her time, trotted up the stairs, and slammed her bedroom door behind her. Not bothering to undress, she sat in a chair, smoked cigar after cigar, got up and paced around the room, sat down again and smoked some more. From time to time she lay down on her cot to rest, but could not fall asleep, and soon she was up on her feet and wandering the floor again, smoking another cigar. It was many, many hours later when—throat shredded, eyes burning, and head genuinely aching—she opened the door again.

It was morning, and Praskovia was sleeping peacefully on her mat. Alexandra prodded her with her foot and asked that Praskovia get her a pair of scissors. When Praskovia came creaking up the stairs again, the scissors in her hand, Alexandra grabbed the instrument away and dashed into her room with it before Praskovia could stop her.

"You're mad! I'll call the doctor!" Praskovia cried, running in and snatching at the scissors, but her mistress had been too quick for her. She was standing in front of the cracked mirror with an expression of fanatic determination, and the first of the long blond swaths lay already on the floor. Round her head she went now, removing the hair chunk by chunk and throwing these discards to the ground, where they lay in a gleaming pile; the weeping Praskovia, on her knees, grieved over the mound as if over a freshly closed grave piled high with dirt.

"Get up and help me get these clothes off," said Alexandra, throwing the scissors to the floor. And when they were off—the confining dress, the lacy underthings, the squeezing corset—she walked naked through the room and retrieved from her wardrobe the bloomers, the undervest, the stiff white boiled shirt, the separate collar and cuffs and the studs that joined them to the shirt, the trousers, the cravat, and the coat that she'd been hiding there behind her dresses all along, and put them on.

She clapped the black top hat onto her chopped-looking head and called for her carriage. Praskovia shouted down the stairs for the newly hired coachman, just a boy. He jumped down from his sleeping spot on the stove beneath the stairs, buttoning his trousers as he ran.

"To the lawyer Trenyakov," said Alexandra while Praskovia wept at her side, and she went down the stairs prodding with her silver-topped walking stick, twirling it from time to time. Out into the street she went and waited, whistling, for the new coachman to emerge from the stables with the carriage.

A fine spring morning, she thought, smiling up at the sky, tapping impatiently at the ground with the tip of her walking-stick. And when the boy came with the carriage, she threw off his helping hand and sprang easily up and in. The ride to Trenyakov's was most pleasant—so many sights and sounds. She put her head out of the carriage to drink them in, distending her nostrils unattractively, as men were allowed to do. When she arrived at Trenyakov's building she went right in and up the stairs, pushed the door right open, stepped inside, and announced as her purpose in a loud and confident voice "to see the lawyer Trenyakov." And when Trenyakov opened his door, startled by the volume of the voice outside, she strode right past him into the room, where she swept off her hat to display her shorn head, settled herself in a chair before his desk, crossed her legs masculine-style ankle upon knee, lit a cigar, looked up at him, and announced that she wished to join the army.

Trenyakov's mouth dropped open. Then he closed his lips over his teeth in a sly smile, as if he had trapped something delicious inside his mouth and were savoring it.

"Any particular branch in mind?" he asked, scurrying behind his desk and seating himself quickly. Then he leaned back and folded his hands across his padded belly as if he'd just finished that delicious meal.

She hadn't considered this. She knew nothing of the army. She drew on her cigar a moment, blew out the smoke in concentric circles, then answered: 17th Hussars. Zamoyski regiment.

It was the only one she could think of at the moment.

lexandra would never know which strings Trenyakov had pulled at the Ministry of Defense and which palms he had greased with his own money for the delectable privilege of seeing this young woman transgress the social codes of her time, but Trenyakov arranged it all, and quickly. The road to an officer's commission led in two directions: a candidate graduated from one of the service academies and was immediately commissioned, or he served one year in the ranks, among the raw recruits of the peasant villages, and then took an officer's examination. Both requirements were waived. In deference to what Trenyakov had explained was the lofty social position of this officer candidate, Alexandra would be allowed to take the examination without first having served in the ranks. She could then purchase her commission.

And so Alexandra Korvin, countess, disappeared from Petersburg society. Notes had been sent to those few of Alexandra's friends and acquaintances who would care what had happened with the announcement that Countess Korvin had lately departed for abroad, some indeterminate destination among the spas and pleasure spots of Europe, and would be away indefinitely. The comings and goings from the Korvin palace of a young man with cropped hair were explained as the presence of a distant relative, one Count Anatol Karpatsky, who had come to Petersburg to join the cavalry and who, preparing for his officer's examination, was not to be disturbed by invitations to teas, dances, musicales, dinners, receptions, or balls. Thus, the newly christened, newborn "Count Karpatsky" sat alone at a newly purchased desk in a small empty study on the third floor of the palace and, fortified by an endless succession of cups of heavily sugared tea and plates of cucumbers (which Praskovia deemed especially healthful), surrounded by stacks of books and manuals, buried herself in the study of tactics, artillery, communications, engineering, sapping and bridge construction, administration of the regiment, the proper handling of firearms (rifles, pistols) and of cold arms (swords and lances), of service both garrison and interior, of scouting and fighting, and the schooling of horses for the ranks.

A riding master was hired to shout irritably at her daily as she bounced round and round the ring in the riding school behind the palace on one of the carriage horses, determined to master the sadistic "cavalry trot." A fencing master came three times a week, sweating elegantly behind his mask. And twice a week Alexandra left the palace and was driven to the apartments of one Colonel Spirkin, a retired officer of the Zamoyskis, who, as her special tutor, was in charge of overseeing the progress of her academic work and of inculcating in her the labyrinthine set of rules that governed the behavior of an officer of the Zamoyski regiment.

According to the colonel, an officer of the Zamoyskis was modest, did not brag or boast. His personal conveyances, owned or hired, were plain and unadorned; therefore he must, even when standing drunk on the street and calling for a hansom or a droshky-for-hire, be careful to avoid the ones with elaborate trim or garish colors. When overtaking the carriage of another officer of the regiment, one did not rudely pull ahead, but requested permission first even if a lady was waiting far across the city and one was late. When attending opera or theater, there were regimental rules dictating location of seat and conduct during intermission, all of these rules complicated, strict, and senseless.

Holding a delicate china cup of Turkish coffee on the palm of a large, rough hand, and sipping delicately at it from time to time, Colonal Spirkin paced back and forth on the worn carpet of his drawing room as he emphasized to Alexandra the importance of "keeping up."

"Keeping up what?" Alexandra would ask, knowing the answer, but enjoying it every time.

"The honor of the regiment! For tsar, church, and country!"

An officer of the Zamoyskis bragged only of his failures and never spoke of a success. He respected all but bent the knee to no one but the tsar. He was quick to share a drink, a plate of food, the hand of friendship. He was gay and free with liquor, and protective of all women, serf or free.

"The honor of the regiment," he said, turning to fix on Alexandra a rather menacing gaze, "even unto death."

"Even unto death?"

The colonel explained that the epaulets were literally guarded with one's life, "the symbol of all you are," and that all Zamoyski officers were required to carry upon their person at all times (here the colonel bent, grunting, and drew a small pistol from within his boot) a revolver with which to avenge any insult to the epaulet. A torn epaulet required challenge, and if one failed in the duel to kill the scoundrel who had insulted the honor of the shoulder board, then the gun was to be turned upon oneself.

Oh boy, thought Alexandra, sinking back into her chair, hoping to give herself time to take this in.

"Poland," said the colonel suddenly, intoning the word with a solemnity that freighted it with a mysterious significance.

"Poland?" she inquired, confused at the skip in the colonel's logic—he had just lately been discussing the necessity, nay, the duty of committing suicide if one found that one's uniform had sustained a rip.

"Christ of nations," the colonel said in a quick, low voice, looking over his shoulder as if expecting the imminent appearance of the secret police, "bitten in three and left to rot in the poisonous bellies of the triple Satan of the world."

Alexandra's forehead crumpled with the effort to make a reasonable connection between Poland and the tearing of the uniform. As for the triple Satan, she supposed he was referring to the partition of that once great nation among the three powers of Prussia, Austria, and Russia herself—but what had that to do with the epaulet? she inquired of the colonel.

"Everything."

"Oh," said Alexandra, still flummoxed, "and why is that?"

"Because we are a Polish regiment," he told her in a confident tone, as if the logical connection had now been made as clear as day.

"But there is no Poland anymore," said Alexandra.

"Polish in spirit we are," he said, "living heart of the Zamoyski, great magnates of Poland! Patriots! And heirs of the Polish horse we are, scions of the greatest cavalry that Europe has ever known."

"But we are Russian," insisted Alexandra, now hopelessly lost.

"Don't say that." Tears began to fill his eyes. "Polish in my heart. So are all of us hussars of the Zamoyski regiment."

Alexandra, confused as she was, was nevertheless offended at the suggestion she identify herself with the snotty Poles. The great snobs of Eastern Europe, the Poles never tired of reminding their more powerful neighbor to the east of Poland's superior culture and refinement and delighted in mentioning that period not so long ago in Russia's past when her books had had to be written in Polish, the Russian language still too crude and blunt to express any delicacy of thought, still rough and dry as a potato just pried from the ground, still grimy with peasant dirt. "Still eating your meat raw, I see," she had heard one of them say at a dinner party where steak tartare was served—thus the haughty Poles. Haughty too in their military code, which emphasized honor and daring before prudence, as if the Poles were too prideful to value ordinary, dull success. Not for the Poles Kutuzov's stealthy, cowardly, but brilliant withdrawal before the menace of Napoleon, which she had just been studying. In battle, they were lunatics, happily suicidal, not caring if they lost so long as they did it with panache. Suicide before dishonor. Aha! The epaulet and Poland—Alexandra closed the logical circle but was hardly reassured. A Polish regiment run by Polish standards?

"How grand it must have been to sweep across the plains of Poland on your horse with your wings screaming in the wind to face the Tatar menace! To annihilate the Turk before the gates of Vienna and save the continent of Europe from the infidel! To smash the rottenness of the Teutonic knights, to rub the filthy Swedish noses in the dirt!"

"But you are Russian," Alexandra insisted, "and, thankfully, so am I."

"I know," said the colonel, "I can dream, though—can't I, for myself? Even if you have not the imagination or the soul?"

When, after three months of daily training and strenuous study, Alexandra could shoe a horse, recite twenty pages of army regulations from memory, discourse knowledgeably on tactics, discipline, and drill, and, while galloping across a field, remove her saddle, hold it across her forearm, and jump three low fences without falling off her horse, she was allowed to take her examination. Which she passed. And so Alexandra, newly commissioned and fitted out in the opulent red and white uniform of the Zamoyski hussars, mounted her horse, an enormous black stallion named Hercules chosen for her by Colonel Spirkin, and rode out of the city in the company of her batman and her orderly, who had come into Petersburg to meet her and bring her back to join the regiment, which was on maneuvers some thirty miles beyond the city limits. Praskovia stood weeping noisily on the steps of the palace, waving a handkerchief and thinking of all the delicious things she would buy to eat now that the mistress was gone and could not stop her. First thing she would fire that new coachman and keep his salary for herself.

It was late afternoon when the three set out upon the road leading out of the city and toward the series of tiny villages where the regiment was quartered, but that did not matter since it wouldn't get truly dark again for another month at least, a phenomenon of the northern latitudes known famously as "white nights" or "midnight sun." Alexandra, too shy to speak to her new comrades, though they were under her command and at her beck and call—the orderly to care for her horse, the batman to care for her person—stared straight ahead as Hercules ambled along, the shifting of his hefty hindquarters rocking her in the saddle as gently as if he were rocking her to sleep.

The road softened from city stone to country dirt, narrowed, grew green with summer trees, and Alexandra occupied herself by staring at her horse's ears, each of which seemed to have a life of its own, alive to sounds that Alexandra could not hear. From time to time she looked at the sky above the branches of the leafy trees, tracking the progress of the coming on of a night that would never come.

"Your honor," said the orderly, whose name was Pavel, trotting briskly up to her, "permission to answer the call of nature."

Oh dear, thought Alexandra. What would she do herself if she should have to go before they reached the town? Come to think of it, she did! By God, she could hardly squat right there at the side of the road. What would they think of her if she went off in the bushes, like a woman?

She hadn't thought of this.

"Permission granted," she answered, her hands shaking slightly as she pulled on Hercules' reins. The orderly, Pavel, didn't even bother to turn his back, but pissed happily against the side of a tree, holding his weapon meatily in his hand. It was Alexandra's first clear sighting, and she could hardly bear to look and hardly bear to look away. When he had finished, he actually shook it, like a predator grasping an animal's neck between his teeth and shaking hard to break it.

As they moved off again, Pavel beginning to tell the batman, Nikifor, of his exploits with a certain maiden behind a haystack in an open field, Alexandra wondered why men always had to piss against a tree. She had seen the peasants do it. Why? Why couldn't they just let it run out onto the ground, like females? Pavel had actually watched his golden stream with pride, aiming it at the target of the tree, smiling with satisfaction when he hit the mark. Did everything have to be an achievement?

Before she saw the little village of Variochka (which hardly merited the title "village," much less any name at all), she smelled it as the smoke from the evening stoves in the peasant huts. Hercules, sensing supper was near, grew restless under the saddle and began to pull against the reins until she allowed him to break into an eager trot, which did nothing for her bladder, but which brought her closer every second to relief. Her relief, however, had to be postponed until she had dismounted, seen Pavel lead Hercules away, and gone with Nikifor into yet another hut, this one the designated "inn" of the village, to be presented to the regimental commander, who was holding court there surrounded by several of his staff, all of whom were eating and drinking silently as a young peasant girl with bare, dirt-encrusted feet plucked at a balalaika with a broken string.

A huge man, the colonel looked up suspiciously from his plate, accepted the salutes and introduction with indifference, and went back to his food. His enormous cheeks began to work again upon the chicken wing he held in his greasy fingers while Nikifor, distressed, waited until sufficient time had passed until he could interrupt the colonel's eating again. Alexandra, equally distressed, but standing stiffly at attention with her shako cradled in the crook of her arm, as she'd been taught, struggled to forget her aching bladder. They stood watching as the colonel ignored them and ripped into the chicken's breast, extracting the tender white heart of its meat. The balalaika plunked on. The colonel sucked the flavored fat from his fingers and tore another strip of chicken from the tiny rib cage.

"Your excellency, excuse my interruption," the batman said. The colonel, pausing, shot a hostile glance at the timid batman, his small eyes growing smaller until they seemed about to disappear inside the fatness of his cheeks. "Excuse me, sir, but you did not mention a squadron for Cornet Count Karpatsky. That is, to which squadron shall he be assigned?"

It seemed an eternity before the colonel answered. Alexandra crossed her legs.

"Ulyanov's," he replied, indicating with a wave of his hand that the interview was at an end. "They're in the field."

Relief. Blessed relief. Having at last achieved it, Alexandra continued sitting primly on the chamber pot in the bedroom of her new quarters, the bedroom being all of the quarters that there actually was, and thought about her coming meeting with Ulyanov. Could it really be he? The same Ulyanov that she knew? The one who had proposed to her? The one who'd pawed and poked at her? Of course it was. This was his very own regiment. Oh, why hadn't she been able to think of another? She could hear the impatient sound of Nikifor's boots as he paced on the gravel outside the hut. She ignored him and continued to sit. Of course she had known that she would encounter the hated Ulyanov in this regiment, but she had not anticipated actually having to serve under his command. It was most irritating. The thought of taking orders from him boiled her blood. What a bad idea this all had been!

And yet, she asked herself, planting her elbows on her knees and resting her chin on her balled-up fists, why did she feel perfectly happy? The miserable one-room shack she was to share with another officer as yet unmentioned and unmet (whose second pair of boots stood large and rigid on the packed-down dirt of the floor) seemed to her a most delightful domicile. Why, she would be sleeping on the floor! On a straw-stuffed pallet! What novelty! How glorious this was! The tiny window was filled with the spectral glow of the Russian summer night, and the air was light and fresh with the scent of grass.

Emerging from the hut, Alexandra breathed deeply of the fragrant air and mounted Hercules again. Pavel and Nikifor trotted behind her on their mounts, allowing her to lead, as befitted a commissioned officer, though she had no idea as yet of where to go. Onto the road, they told her, and then into the field.

Into the field! How dashing it sounded. The field of battle. Would she join it, taste first blood? Dash across the plains, wind screaming in her ears, just as Colonel Spirkin had described?

"Into the field," however, meant just that. Into the field beside the road, where Squadron Four was found to be picking mushrooms in a thin forest that stood on one side of the high grass. In the silvery evening light, she could see them moving through the trees, their bodies bent as they searched along the ground for a sight of fungus, their shakos upturned in their hands to collect whatever morsels they might find.

Pavel stood in his stirrups, looking out over the high grass toward the trees.

"I see him," he said, turning his horse.

Alexandra saw him too, not a minute later. As the three rode up, Ulyanov, who was lying on the ground, head pillowed on his folded-up pelisse, hands folded over his stomach, did not rise to greet them. His eyes were closed. He did not open them.

"Shh," said his cossack batman, who was standing over Ulyanov as if keeping watch, an expression of annoyance on his sun-ravaged face at the thought that his master might be wakened for so trivial a purpose as the introduction of a newly arriving officer, "he is resting. His labors among the womenfolk have been mighty. As we know it, all of us."

But the dutiful Nikifor, sweating with the anxiety of handling this introduction correctly, according to regimental protocol, stepped forward.

"Your excellency," he stated firmly, clicking his heels and snapping his head up and down, "I have the duty to present to your excellency his honor Cornet Count Anatol Karpatsky, who has just arrived from Petersburg to fill the vacancy left by the departure of Cornet Yuri Arkadyevich, who most regretfully was kicked out."

Alexandra stepped forward, but Ulyanov showed no signs of stirring. He seemed to be asleep.

"Your excellency, sir!" Nikifor shouted. "I present to you Cornet Count Anatol Karpatsky!"

Alexandra, not knowing what else to do, leaned over and peered into a face angelic in sleep. She noticed that Ulyanov had not shaved, perhaps for days, so his peaceful face was lightly stubbled. And his dolman was half unbuttoned. Such a breach of discipline! She suppressed the impulse to prod him with the sharp tip of her boot. It would feel even more wonderful to kick him. That would teach him to treat a fellow officer with such disrespect!

Nikifor shifted impatiently from foot to foot. The cossack batman stuck out his chin at the nervous Nikifor and gripped the handle of his sword.

Ulyanov opened his eyes, looked up into the face that wavered above him, stared for a very long moment, then closed his eyes again and turned on his side, head pillowed on his folded hands. "Such a pleasant dream," he said, "to see her face."

"Enough!" cried the cossack batman, brandishing his sword in Nikifor's face. Nikifor ignored him.

"What are your orders?" Nikifor asked the drowsing figure.

"Hey," cried a red-faced sergeant who was sitting on the ground tearing petals from a daisy, "that's my job! He gives the order to *me* and then I give the order to *him*!" He leaped to his feet and snapped his heels together. "What are your orders, sir?"

"Oh . . . tell him to go pick mushrooms" was the indolent reply.

The red-faced sergeant snapped to attention and turned to Alexandra.

"Captain Mecklenburg-Ulyanov orders Cornet Count What's-His-Name to go pick mushrooms!" He had forgotten the new one's name, but still discharged his office stylishly. He sat down again and picked another daisy.

And so she did, joining a hundred men, gorgeously dressed, creeping quietly and peering solemnly at the ground as their boots gathered the evening wetness from the grass.

Mushroom hunting, that great Russian pastime, appeals to something indefinite in the Russian soul. A thing unplanted, the mushroom grows out of the melancholy Russian air, affixing itself to the underside of that peculiar northern landscape of ashen birch and faded firs. How very Russian is the mushroom! Vague in its colors, or lack of them, the color of bone, the color of dust—ungreen, the perfect product of Europe's poorest soil—it tastes of thin smoke and empty roads, the bitterness of winter, the whiteness of the sky.

On their way back to the village, the tired soldiers carried their upturned shakos before them on their saddles, these improvised buckets mounded with their treasure. They sang in deep voices, joyful, announcing the arrival of the treat to the village families with whom they were quartered, while in those peasant huts, women in red kerchiefs and ragged skirts paced back and forth on dirty feet, ready with sizzling skillets, with butter and onions and sour cream.

But Alexandra would not eat here, among these men of the squadron, among these villagers. The officers of the squadron took their meals at the village inn.

Alexandra had just dismounted before her hut when Nikifor, who had gone on ahead, appeared with a bowl of steaming water and a bar of rough soap. He set it on the bench outside, watching with apprehension as she cupped the water and wetted her face, fearing that the water might have been too hot. He snapped a towel from his arm when she turned her wet face in his direction. This quality of service, with its compulsive attentiveness, was one that Praskovia had never even tried to achieve; the very idea of it would have brought from the old servant a mocking laugh, and it made Alexandra herself laugh, delighting to think of it, delighting in this lovely night, this extraordinary freedom from herself and her former life.

"Forgive me that I rush you sir," he said in a low voice as Alexandra scrubbed her face dry, "but the colonel eats with us tonight. He does not like to wait for his food. We cannot be late. They are surely already sitting down."

"But wasn't he eating dinner when we saw him last? When we met him at the inn?"

"Shh." Nikifor pressed his finger to his lips. "We do not speak of that."

"Why?"

Nikifor was silent. Alexandra could only conclude that the colonel was sensitive about his weight. Any affiliated topic was obviously taboo, especially, it seemed, such contributing factors as the number of his meals.

"Well, we can speak of it when he wishes us to admire it," Nikifor added, qualifying his earlier statement.

"Admire it?"

"Yes, often he will challenge himself. He will set the goal and work to achieve it. In such cases, he enjoys an audience."

"Why doesn't he challenge someone else?"

Nikifor shook his head, looked sad.

"There is no competition," he said.

Alexandra could not wait to see this man in action. In a nation of enormous eaters, his primacy was clearly a phenomenon. "Does he eat with us every night?" she asked with hope in her voice.

"Oh no, your honor. The regiment is spread among many towns, and he eats with each squadron's officers once a week. That is six nights' dinners."

Alexandra could not resist.

"And on the seventh day he rests?"

"Oh no, sir, then he starts again."

Nikifor had been transferring Alexandra's mushrooms from her gold-encrusted, red-plumed shako into a large kerchief; he tied knots around the bulging bundle, wiped the shako out with the damp towel, and handed the shako back. Alexandra settled it on her head, pushed the strap snugly beneath her chin, and adjusted the fur-trimmed pelisse, which hung dashingly from her shoulder, while Nikifor knelt on the ground to polish her boots, spitting on them carefully and wiping them clean with the towel. Alexandra had to admit that the uniform of the hussar— the gold-barred tunic sewn stiff with at least a pound of gold braid; the clinging breeches, decorated on the front of the thighs with intricate figures; the shining tasseled boots; the towering shako; the insouciant pelisse; the shining sword; the embroidered pouches and purses that hung from leather straps across her body—had to be the most magnificent outfit she had ever worn. There was a barbaric quality to its luxury, an oriental opulence, its elaborations utterly unfunctional, seemingly superfluous, but serving, she supposed, to mold the soul inside to the martial spirit, to move it to acts of valor that would justify the splendor of the outfit. Pity the man who would dare to disgrace its glory! Wearing it, she felt she could kill somebody. Easily.

Sword banging against her leg, spurs jingling, Alexandra strode across the village to the inn, Nikifor following respectfully a few paces behind with the bundle of mushrooms, but the valor Alexandra felt dissolved immediately upon opening the door to the inn and seeing turn toward her the eyes of all the officers at the table. In the nine faces that scrutinized her, Alexandra saw, in varying shapes and proportions, the bony bulge of brow and chin, the prominence of nose, and the roughness of texture of the oddly two-toned skin, all of which define the masculine face and distinguish it from the female's. She swallowed in fear. Would they know? *Did* they know? Did it occur to them that she was far more the outsider than they knew? Although the feminine fat had been stripped from beneath her skin first by the weight loss she had suffered in her illness and then by the rigor of her training, though her breasts had shrunk to near nothingness and her hips to near-masculine narrowness, and her shoulders had been widened by her epaulets and her hair shorn away in brutal masculine style, she could not coarsen and enlarge her delicacy of feature or fill the empty space in her breeches, at which she was certain they were staring right now, all nine of them.

Her hands began to sweat.

What would they do? Ridicule her? Throw things? Drive her out? Or strip her for confirmation, then hold her down and punish her presumption by filling that empty space, all nine of them waiting their turn?

One of the officers stood. He raised his glass.

"Cornet Count Anatol Karpatsky! Welcome to the regiment!"

With cries of "Hear! Hear!" and "Honor to the tsar!" and "Glory to the regiment!" nine glasses were raised to nine pairs of lips, nine throats received their contents, and nine glasses hit the floor with a glorious smash.

The junior officers jumped from their seats, landed with clattering boots upon the table as if exulting in their strength and youth, jumped down again and, in celebration of the arrival of a brother soldier, another male to bond with, assaulted her in welcome. She was squeezed at the shoulder, smacked on the back, hugged and triple-kissed in manly Russian style until her cheeks burned red with the roughness of their prickly faces, already sprouting whiskers though they'd shaved that morning. The senior officers watched in approval from their position at the head of the table.

"Vodka for our brother officer!" they cried.

A vodka was set before her. Nine pairs of eyes watched as she drank it off, employing the quick jerk her father had taught her in their secret lessons.

"Another vodka for our brother officer!" they cried again.

Alexandra dispatched the next, delighted that it was all so

easy, reveling in the acceptance of the group, and enjoying the warmth of male fellowship—how kind they were!

Ulyanov, who sat next to the colonel at the end of the table as was his privilege as squadron-commander, watched the newcomer with an odd, a puzzled expression on his face.

"Another vodka for our brother officer!"

The keeper of the inn, smiling slyly to himself (he had seen it all before), poured another stream of vodka into the glass, and Alexandra, about to ingest her third, remembered her father's admonition that the secret to holding one's liquor was to eat steadily all the while, ingesting as much stomach-coating fat and water-retaining salt as possible to combat both dehydration and irritation of the stomach lining. She reached for a plate of sliced sausage with one hand and a dish of salt with the other.

It was when the disapproving murmur rose from the crowd that Alexandra began to understand that these offerings of vodka were not a simple show of fellowship or a celebration of the arrival of a new and interesting friend to get to know.

"No fair!"

"That's cheating!"

"Get those sausages away from him!"

Alexandra's stomach, which had lain dormant all day long, its needs forgotten, now awakened and began to whine. Protesting her inattention, it clenched itself angrily inside her belly. Oh, why had she forgotten to eat at least the rolls and cheese that Praskovia had packed for her?

Eyes gleaming, the junior officers stared at her in sadistic challenge. The seniors watched with sympathetic interest, unwilling to intervene in this primal ritual, this initiatory rite, this test of manly fortitude—they had all endured it, so should the new boy. Ulyanov, seeing Alexandra's face above the stiffened collar of this young cornet, thought that he was surely going mad. The colonel continued plowing through his food and did not look up.

Alexandra's hand shot out; she seized the glass, and, smiling stiffly at each of the expectant faces, raised it to her lips. She drained it quickly, slammed it back on the table, and wiped her mouth with the back of her hand. But how much further could she go? Her stomach, dashed with the caustic vodka when it had been hoping for some food, threw a screaming fit. One more shot and she would certainly pass out. Then what would they think?

But this, it seemed, was exactly what they intended for the new arrival.

"More vodka for our brother officer!" The innkeeper poured another dose.

Alexandra stared down at the lethal liquid, the deadly elixir. A brief, feminine impulse to manipulative tears, to the seeking out of a masculine breast to fling herself upon for comfort and protection, was beaten back. She had entered this masculine milieu, where pointless daring was the point, and was now subject to its norms. That is, if she wished to remain. And she did not wish to let them get the better of her now.

She would play by their rules. But how? Surreptitiously she cast a glance in the direction of the colonel, who dominated the table silently as he ate, indifferent to the world around him but clearly in command of it.

She rose to her feet. "I challenge you," she said, staring at each in turn. "I challenge you all!"

A murmur of confusion rose from the gathering. Challenge them to what? A duel? There had been no provocation according to the standard rules. Why, they were simply showing fellowship, inviting a brother officer to drink.

"An eating contest!" Alexandra cried.

The colonel looked up from his plate. Success.

"No fair!" cried the junior officers. "It's a drinking bout! No eating allowed, not until you've drunk!"

The colonel did not say a word. The table fell silent. Knowing of the colonel's special skills and his eternal, thwarted quest to test them against a worthy adversary, the officers held their breath to see what he would do.

"A charming idea, young man," the colonel said suddenly with a smile, his brutal face softening at the prospect of displaying his talents. "I have not been challenged in many a year. The competition has been thin. But I am eager to see what you can do. Name your weapon!"

The junior officers sighed in one body, disappointed that their own challenge would go unmet tonight.

Oh my, Alexandra thought. The man had to weigh maybe three hundred pounds. She hadn't a chance. But at least it would distract her brother officers from the vodka and get some food inside her stomach before she fainted, or vomited, or died.

"Eggs," she said. They were nutritious and easy to digest.

"Boiled or fried?" asked the colonel, pushing his plate away.

"Boiled. And pickles."

"Fair enough," said the colonel. "Speed or volume?"

Eating boiled eggs at top speed and interspersing them with garlicky pickles would surely bring a swift and messy end to the contest and not in her favor, Alexandra thought, especially after all that vodka. She must at least acquit herself honorably. She sized up her competitor. Yes, he was big, but so was she. She could eat more than the average woman, and she had the advantage of an empty stomach, while he had been stuffing steadily all day long. No, it would not be too embarrassing.

"Volume," she answered, "I'd like to go for volume. And I'd like a snack first. I'd like my mushrooms cooked in sour cream.

And some bread while the eggs are boiling. And there's a bit of sausage here. If that would be permissible, sir."

The colonel peered at her. "Are you sure? You might place yourself at a disadvantage."

Of course, it was simply a ruse. Not only to get some food into her stomach as quickly as possible, but to make it impossible for the junior officers to make her drink more vodka on an empty stomach while the eggs were being cooked.

"It evens the field, sir," she said. "My stomach is empty, and I would not like to take advantage of the fact that you have had your dinner already." Twice, she wanted to add, but didn't.

"That's fair of you," he replied, "very fair. I appreciate that. Yes, I have had a little to eat. The playing field would not be even."

Alexandra reached out for a slice of sausage and conveyed it to her mouth. She chewed defiantly, looking into the eyes of the junior officers. There was not a thing they could do about it.

Nikifor, tossing the bundle of mushrooms at the innkeeper, dashed out into the streets of the village, shouting, "A contest! A contest! The new cornet has challenged our powerful colonel!" And so, buttoning their tunics, pulling up their pants, hopping along as they struggled to get their swollen feet back inside their boots, the hussars came running up to crowd around the inn, to peer in windows, to mill about at the open door. It was not long before the villagers got wind of it too, and, pushing and shoving, claimed their places at the windows, at the door. Children were placed on shoulders. The women, jostling, stood on tiptoe to try to see inside.

The headman of the village took upon himself the task of making book. His granddaughter squatted, stick in hand, recording the bets by scratching misspelled names and misshapen numbers in the dirt. Before long, the computations covered the area all around the inn and intruded into the road. The careless feet of the crowd, however, kicking up dirt and treading over numbers, had soon hopelessly confused the book, and another method was found involving an old piece of newspaper and a crushed fragment of pencil, the only writing implement the village owned, since none could read or write except the granddaughter, who had learned the skill imperfectly from the village priest, who was usually drunk.

Odds favored the colonel, but faith in God's protection of the underdog was strong.

"Just look at him! He's just a boy! A skinny boy," some villagers scoffed.

"And so was David when he met Goliath" was the answer, delivered with an elbow in the ribs and a smirk of superiority at this obvious evidence of superior knowledge of the Bible.

Bacon sandwiches were being hawked; someone had set up a grill. Bottles of vodka were uncorked. Beer spilled down backs, soaking clothing, evoking screams, provoking slaps. Children whined.

Inside the tiny inn, Alexandra had finished her fortifying snack of mushrooms and sour cream. She stood up, walked to the head of the table where the colonel sat, and dramatically unbuttoned one of the buttons of her tunic. She snatched up a napkin, ran it over her hands, and dashed the thing to the ground. Then she sat and faced the colonel. The first round of boiled eggs, steaming hot, appeared before them. Maintaining eye contact, each of the contestants grasped a boiled egg and held it in the air for all to see.

"It's begun!"

Plunging her teeth into the gelatinous surface of the egg, Alexandra felt a tremendous sense of well-being. She had always known she had talent as an eater, but never had these capacities been truly tested. True, she had acquitted herself as well as many men at certain dinner parties, but always she had been subject to the restraints and constraints of ladylike behavior, which dictated moderation in exercise of gustatory skill. Thus the opportunity to develop her potential had been denied her. Men, of course, could eat as much as they wanted—yet more evidence of the oppression of the female sex. Why should gluttony be tolerated in the male, even approved of? Why were women held to a higher standard of virtue?

If only Ulyanov weren't watching. She was suddenly not so sure she wanted him to see this. But this repressive feminine modesty must itself be repressed. The time for total realization of the self was now at hand. She allowed her teeth to meet inside the egg.

A bit dry, the egg, and the crumbly yolk was still hot. It was not going to go down easily. However, consumption of water must be limited. She needed all the room in her stomach she could find.

Since time was not a consideration, the colonel allowed her to finish her egg before he started on his next. Through the first dozen eggs, the entire contents of the bowl, they matched each other easily egg for egg, eating steadily at each other, eyes locked, jaws moving up and down.

The end of the first round was announced from the open door: "No advantage either side." A sigh went up from the crowd.

Now the second round began, with pickled cucumbers striped in shades of ivory and moss-green, pallid in their bath of greenish juice. Delectable as the pickles were, a burst of stark flavor on the tongue, Alexandra knew that their high water content could finish her quickly if she did not pace herself.

Saluting her adversary with the stiff-soft vegetable (*morituri te salutamus!*), Alexandra dug her teeth in and squirted herself in the chest. The colonel did the same. They smiled at each other, friendly competitors, dedicated to advancing the cause of their art. Six fat pickles were dispatched in the process, savored and slowly munched.

"End of round two. No advantage either side."

Waiting for the next installment of eggs, the colonel, whose tunic Alexandra noted was capacious in construction, leaving room for expansion without the unbuttoning of any buttons, lounged back in his chair and began to discourse on his philosophy of eating.

"It is my contention," he opined, "that although the repetitiveness of this meal, egg after egg, pickle after pickle, might seem to dull the appetite, the actual effect is quite the opposite. The truth is, we so seldom pay attention to the variety of flavor offered by different specimens within each category, in their pure and unadulterated form, that is. Let me clarify. One might say that an egg is an egg. That all eggs taste alike. But subtle variations in flavor are detectable if one pays sufficient attention. Just as a certain vintage may show infinitesimally fine variations in body and bouquet according to the location of the vine—how much sun that particular grouping of grapes may have received, how much damage from the wind, or nourishment of rain—the egg shows the same fluctuations dependent upon the identity of the hen, her diet that specific day, her mood perhaps."

"All eggs come from the hen Pelageya," said the innkeeper in a tone that indicated a certain amount of offense had been taken. "She eats the same always—not enough, she thinks—and is always in a very bad mood." He set the bowl of newly boiled eggs with a certain vehemence upon the table.

"Forgive me," said the colonel, bowing his head, "I did not mean to impugn the quality of Pelageya's eggs. I was simply making a point." He gently grasped an egg and held it up. "How often do we pause in our round of daily tasks to appreciate the beauty and complexity of the egg? To truly experience its subtle magic?"

Alexandra had to admit to him she had been, up to this point, neglectful in terms of her attention to the glories of the egg. Until now, she had simply eaten them and thought no more about it.

"Ah, but that is exactly my point! Observe the structural perfection of its form, how impeccably that shape expresses the smoothness of its emergence into the world, rounded as the head of a baby at the bottom and tapering to a point where the hen effortlessly pinches it off before beginning the extrusion of its twin in an endless chain of identical productions that perfectly represents—eternity."

Alexandra admitted that the egg was indeed profound.

"And inside the purity of its blinding whiteness"—the colonel took a bite—"a miniature sun."

Alexandra ventured the theory that the popularity of the egg in world cuisine was motivated as much by its symbolic significance as its nutritional value.

"Quite right," said the colonel, "quite right. Most particularly in northern climates such as ours, where the sun is of magical significance and the idea of ingestion of its valuable warmth takes on special power."

Hence the importance of the egg in Russian iconography, Alexandra stated, where the white of the egg might also be held to signify a certain spiritual aspect, a moral striving toward purity of soul, transcendental negation of the self in its union with the Almighty God. Russia had ever been a spiritual leader.

"Eat your eggs," said the innkeeper.

Another round began. Eating slowly, Alexandra indeed felt herself in communion with the meaning of the egg. If she did not concentrate hard upon this subject, she thought, she might easily throw up.

Pickles again. Alexandra was slowing down.

Eggs.

Pickles.

Eggs.

"Round seven is complete. Advantage—the colonel."

Now she rallied, drawing forth from the inner recesses of her soul a strength of will she had not known herself to possess. The truth was that the colonel was faltering too, his capacities limited by the two enormous dinners lying fallow in his belly. Alexandra began to pull ahead.

"Round eight. Advantage—the cornet."

But the colonel was not so easily defeated. Summoning up all the discipline of his many military years, of a spirit trained to exceed its own limits, to force its soul to its own conceit, the colonel with a final burst of gustatory energy inhaled such a number of eggs that they seemed to disappear like snowflakes in his mouth. He had eaten the last of them. The bowl was empty.

The colonel fixed his eye on Alexandra. The crowd held its breath. Would she call for more?

"I concede," she said.

The expense of spirit in a waste of shame. Alexandra felt no triumph at all, although she had held her own in the contest very well. There was no sense of potential developed, of limits overcome. She felt awful. What, indeed, had she accomplished? Her stomach stuck out as if she had swallowed a globe. Seduced by the masculine imperative to pointless physical daring, she was pregnant with pain. And what would Ulyanov think?

Not that she cared. It was simply that, having once been attractive to him, she wanted to go on being attractive. The fact that he could not possibly know that Cornet Count Karpatsky was indeed herself was immaterial at this moment. Her feminine nature pulled her one way. The dictates of her situation pushed her in another.

She wanted to be carried to her bed, limp and languishing in manly arms, laid tenderly upon it to be comforted, cosseted, kissed—to be watched over as she labored, digestive system churning, to give birth to her own relief in case she died before the morning. Instead, in accordance with draconian masculine standards of indifference to discomfort, of spartan fortitude, she was expected to walk.

And walk she did. Nikifor, pockets suspiciously plump with thick and squarish shapes suggesting wads of banknotes, hovered at her side but declined to offer a supporting arm. The jackal-like junior officers were watching. She must make it to her quarters on her own.

"Not a sound," he whispered, "not a sound. They will not respect you. They will not accept you. You must not vomit or fall down. Straighten up. Watch your feet. Keep watching your feet as they walk."

She might as well have drunk the vodka if this was where her clever ruse had landed her. But she supposed that had been the point. They had won after all.

Lying on the straw pallet in the small hut, Alexandra felt herself a living trophy to the final triumph of the junior officers, her mountain of a middle obscuring her feet, from which Nikifor was peeling her leather boots. The night air seeped soothingly between her toes. She wriggled them—about the only part of her she dared to move at all. Having placed the chamber pot considerately near his master's head, the batman withdrew and left her to it.

"Your honor, good night," he said with a bow, and went off to God knew where.

Through the open window flowed the pale air of the Russian summer night, touched with the stellar cold of the arctic waste not far away, its empty sun, its endless vastnesses of white. Siberia was in the air, and Finland, and the land of the aboriginal Lapps, who ate the tongues of reindeer, wore their skins. The cold deserts of Asia, continent-wide. A lucky thing, to be Russian in the summer. Where others soaked in their own sweat through a pillow-turning night, Russians slept snugly in their peaceful beds, their nostrils drawing gently at the steppe-cooled air. Alexandra was soon asleep.

Through the open window poured the sounds of continuing revelry. Laughing, singing, the rhythmic banging of pots, the squawking of startled chickens, squeals of pigs, the stamping feet of dancers, a scraping violin. It had been a big night in Variochka.

lexandra had been sleeping for several hours when something woke her. It was giggling. Feminine giggling. Whispering voices, raspy breathing, a moan. The peach-sucking sound of a ravenous kiss. A slap.

"Shh." Then the sound of more kisses, a hushed male voice. "Don't wake the poor fellow." This remark was followed by another giggle and then the sound of a female voice saying, in harsh peasant tones, "Let him listen, let him look. Salt on the loaf is what I say."

Silence, heavy breathing, the sound of a body smacking into the wall, a hard clunk as the bony skull hit the wood. More peach-sucking kisses.

"Oh!" said the woman's voice, "such a little loaf! What can I do to make it rise?" A dirty giggle.

"Not so hard," said the man in an angry whisper.

Alexandra lay still, taking her breath in tiny sips through her mouth, hoping to be as inconspicuous as possible. She had no interest in witnessing the coming event, much less in salting anyone's loaf that way, but even the attempt to cover her ears might attract their attention. Oh, why weren't ears like eyes, with lids that one could close?

"Tcha!" The woman made a sound of disgust. "You're no use! I could do better with a pickle!"

"Give me a minute. Just give me a minute," the man pleaded in a whisper.

"I know," said the woman, "I'll wake up that boy over there. Then he'll do your duty for you. I'll get my satisfaction from him!"

"No, wait, wait! That's it! It's him! It's hard. . . ."

"No it's not," the woman mocked. Another dirty giggle.

"I meant it's hard to concentrate with him there."

"You're no man!" the woman's voice accused. "I've been done by three at once and each watched the other to salt the loaf! Are you a shy little boy, afraid a big man will see your little pickle?"

The man seemed to take this question seriously. He did not answer for a moment, as if he were thinking.

If I were he, I'd belt her, thought Alexandra.

"No, no, it's not that," the man whispered in a voice Alexandra recognized as cultivated, surely one of the officers', but whose? "It's that he reminds me of someone. It's very strange."

Alexandra could not suppress a sudden intake of breath. Ulyanov!

"And who does he remind you of?"

"Nobody," said Ulyanov. "I've had too much to drink is all."

"You don't like me," said the woman.

"Oh I do, very much." His voice was softer now, melting into wordlessness, a murmuring slow and sweet as syrup, pouring honey over the girl. To trap her, Alexandra thought, imagining now that the girl's sticky limbs were stuck to the wall so that she was helpless, immobilized, as Alexandra once had been herself in the sticky web he spun with his voice, though she herself had quickly broken free.

Don't listen! Alexandra wanted to shout at the girl. We should stop up our ears with wax like those sailors with the Sirens! Too late, in any case—a startled squeak from the girl told Alexandra she'd been pinned to the wall in a single thrust like a butterfly spread and mounted on wood, and a rhythmic thumping and bumping began.

Alexandra covered her ears. The thumping and bumping, the grunts and soft cries were muffled and drowned in the sounds of her own body. She could hear nothing but herself, the emptiness inside her amplifying in its hollowness the lonely rasping of her breath, the monotonous beating of her heart. Her nose prickled. Tears were coming. She could not stop them. They gathered until they broke against her lids and slipped out beneath to flow down her cheeks.

And she hadn't any idea why those tears should be.

Ulyanov, as it turned out, was not her quartermate. The pair of extra boots that stood erect upon the floor next to the pallet belonged to one of the junior officers, who had stood patiently outside the hut, checking occasionally through the open window for signs of completion, until his superior officer, Captain Mecklenburg-Ulyanov, had finished his appointed task, and he and his companion had slipped away.

"Awake there, Karpatsky?" said the officer, throwing himself onto his pallet and pulling off his boots. "Don't see how you could avoid it, with that going on."

Alexandra murmured, pretending sleep.

"He does that every night. Drives me crazy, he does, always when I want to turn in. Is it too much trouble for him to find a barn? Oh, he wouldn't dare take the girls back to the merchant's house. Even if it weren't too far away, there are young daughters there, and he's after them too. Good luck to him with their father hanging around watching his every move."

Alexandra heard the sounds of rustling, a body wrestling with itself on the pallet. She had an awful feeling he was undressing. She hoped that this was not so.

It was. "We haven't actually met," said the officer, leaping from his pallet. She heard him cross the room, the hollow thump of bare feet. "I'm Lopukhin." Opening her eyes, Alexandra saw

him standing naked, his hand stuck out to shake, his manhood
dangling right above her.

Oh dear, she thought, trying not to look. She sat up, grabbed
the proffered hand, and shook it. Lopukhin padded back across
the room, threw himself down, and crossed his hands behind his
head. Alexandra could not help herself. She had to look. She had
never seen a naked man before.

Of course, she had seen little boys. Naked little peasant boys
with their tiny appendages splashing in a stream or being doused
under the village water spout. She had been under the impression that the appendages would increase their size in proportion
to the body's overall growth. Greek statues had confirmed this
supposition, but she found, in looking at the uninhibited young
man lazing on the bed across the room, that she had been seriously misled. The apparatus was enormous, way out of proportion so far as she could judge, an aesthetic mistake, as if God had
been distracted at the moment of creation, or joking, perhaps. It
was positively disorienting, genuinely unnerving, but she could
not tear her eyes away. Luckily, the weird illumination of the
northern summer night gave her eyes full access.

"You did well tonight, Karpatsky," said Lopukhin, whose eyes
were closed, so he did not know he was being stared at. "You've
definitely started off on the right foot. We thought you'd fold
much sooner, but you didn't. And you've found a friend in the
colonel. After you left, you were all he could talk about. I
wouldn't be surprised if he made you an adjutant."

Alexandra had turned on her side and was supporting her
head on her hand so that she might have her fill of looking at him.
His chest was marvelously flat, with faint muscular bulges tipped
by the tiniest of nipples. She had to wonder why men had nipples—what was the point? God's distraction again, she supposed.

"So," said Lopukhin, "what do you think of Ulyanov?"

Alexandra had not expected this question. Of course she could not tell the truth.

"He seems nice enough, I suppose. But I really can't say. I don't know him yet."

"You'll like him," said Lopukhin. "We couldn't have a better commander, and he's all man! He can't see a woman without going after her. It's a vow he's made, to sleep with every woman that he meets. Of course the men think he's God. Every few days, in the morning, they all gather round his batman, Babbish, and ask—how many? Babbish keeps the tally, just like Leporello in the opera."

"Well," said Alexandra, her voice loud with sudden irritation, "how many is it?"

"Who knows? Who knows?" he said sleepily, and began to sing in a soft, tuneless voice, "*Ma in Ispagna, son già mille e tre, son già mille e tre . . .*"

Alexandra recognized the fragment of the "catalogue aria" from *Don Giovanni*, where Don Juan's servant Leporello reads from a scroll the recorded tally of the women his master has seduced: this many women here, and this many women there, "but in Spain already a thousand and three." Could it really be that many?

"You mean he actually keeps score? Writes it down?" she asked.

But Lopukhin was already asleep. And soon, unable to fight any longer with the heaviness of her eyelids, she followed him.

Lopukhin's naked body, still sprawled in sleep across his pallet, was blinding white in the morning sun. All that naked skin, the tufts of coarse dark hair—Alexandra was shy of looking at him now. He was much too real, as was the coarseness and poverty of the hut that quartered them, so poorly put together that slices of sunlight showed in the cracks between the boards. The chamber pot, set in the middle of the tiny room, stank—Lopukhin must have used it in the night.

How odd, how very odd that I am here, thought Alexandra. So this is the life of men. But there was no time to lie in bed and think. Her bladder ached. She must be up and dressed before Lopukhin woke. She rose uneasily, unsteadily to her feet. Her bones were sore, as if someone had beaten her heartily with sticks. And amazingly, she felt a ferocious hunger, as if her stomach, having been stretched beyond its limits, was crying for more and more and more. But what was she to do? Her feminine fastidiousness prohibited the use of that brimming chamber pot. Besides, how was she to wash?

To her relief, Nikifor, who had been waiting outside the hut listening for sounds of wakefulness, called to her through the window that he was bringing water to wash, and tea. He hurried inside, took the chamber pot, and hurried out again, careful not to spill. She heard him dump it near the window.

"Now you take care of yourself, your honor, and I will be back with what you need," he said, depositing the now-empty vessel on the floor.

Oh, but how could she use it, with a man right there in the room? Not only that, a youthful, handsome man. Focusing her eyes on Lopukhin's face (careful not to see the rest of him), she saw that his face radiated the self-satisfaction of youth enjoying its rest, curls of hair plastered damply to his gleaming, muscular neck in the sweat of summer-morning sleep.

She stared with longing at the chamber pot. But no, she couldn't. She simply couldn't. She would have to wait till later, when Lopukhin was gone.

Nikifor, returning, set a basin of water, a bar of soap, and a ragged towel on the table between the beds. Beside these things he set a glass of steaming tea.

"Forgive me, your honor, I could not find your razor among your things," he said, standing erect in military fashion and snapping his heels together.

"I did not bring a razor, Nikifor," said Alexandra solemnly. "I do not shave yet, though I think I feel a whisker starting here." She pointed to her chin.

"Ah yes, you are very young," said Nikifor, bowing, but his eyes flicked up and peered for a moment at the spot she had indicated. He withdrew to wait for her outside.

It was really not so difficult, apart from the problem with the chamber pot. She splashed the water on her face, soaped it, rinsed it, dried it with the towel. The almond creams she would have used to smooth the dryness from her face and hands—well, she hadn't had them for the longest time in any case. No lavender-scented baths, no gardenia rinses, no clouds of rose-petal powder. Really, it was not so different from her recent life in this respect. As for modesty, it was simple to turn her back, unbutton her tunic, insert the moistened bar of coarse soap into her armpits, and vigorously rub, then to splash water to remove the suds and dry herself beneath the arms. Her tunic hung about her, forming a barrier to prying eyes. Yes, she could manage this with modesty.

But she still had to use the chamber pot.

No time for that. She had buttoned up her tunic, swung her pelisse onto her shoulder, buckled on her sword, and settled her feathered shako dashingly under her arm before she realized she was barefoot and, red-faced, sat down on her pallet to pull on her boots.

She met Nikifor outside.

"So," said Alexandra, striding along beside him, "what now?"

"Headquarters. We see the captain. Have breakfast. Get your orders for the day."

Headquarters was the very same village inn across the tiny dirt road where Alexandra had eaten herself sick the night before. Inside, she found Ulyanov sitting at the head of the large table, papers spread out before him along with an empty plate, an unused fork and knife, an unfolded napkin, though he held a glass of tea. Along the sides of the table were three of the junior officers, while three sergeants stood up behind Ulyanov. All looked up at her when she entered. Alexandra stared at the breakfasts that lay half finished on plates before the junior officers—cracklings of eggshells, rich yellow stains of yolk, crusts of bread and cheese smeared with country butter. A large loaf of chocolate-colored bread sat in the center of the table surrounded by pots of brightly colored jam. She was ravenous.

"Cornet Count Karpatsky reporting," said Nikifor.

"Yes, yes," said Ulyanov in irritation at the formality, waving it away with his hand and frowning at the new officer who had been placed under his command. Alexandra, able for the first time to look at him at her leisure and to see him clearly in this morning light, was surprised at the difference in his appearance. His loose, unbuttoned tunic showed his large collarbones, and it was clear from the sharp edges of his unshaven jaw, the architectural protusion of his cheekbones and nose, that he had grown thinner since she had seen him last. His tired, glittering eyes were underlined with darkness

This was a different Ulyanov, thought Alexandra, one she had never seen before. He seemed much older now, and though he carried the nub of a cigar clamped jauntily between his molars, the cigar casting elaborate curls of smoke into the air around his head, the aspect he presented to the world was some-how faded, inner-looking, as if he was preoccupied with some-thing deep inside his mind of greater importance than the world outside, and it was this inner worrying that had sucked the flesh from his bones, sapped the color from the hair at his temples.

As Alexandra stood to attention before him, her shako posed in the crook of her arm, he fixed on her the same questioning gaze he had directed at her the day before and narrowed his eyes as if trying to look harder, see more thoroughly. One of the ser-geants standing behind him—a heavyset older man with curly gray hair—leaned over and said something in his ear.

"Karpatsky," said Ulyanov, lowering his eyes to the papers spread before him on the table and making some marks with a pencil, "would you like to take command of your platoon today? Or are you tired from your exertions of last night?"

You're the one, she wanted to say. Instead, she set her mouth and said nothing.

Seeing her refusal to answer him, he looked up at her again. The junior officers left off their conversations and stared.

"I see you do not wish to command a platoon," he said offi-ciously. "You are clearly tired. Perhaps you'd like to stay in bed today. To recover from your mighty battle with the colonel."

"I would not!" she stated emphatically, though this was exactly what she wished to do, and added, "Sir!" though it galled her no end to say it. His hostility toward her was clear. But was it directed at Karpatsky or at Alexandra? She did not know. She was aware only that the balance of power had shifted horribly in his direction. But then, what had she expected? It was the price she had to pay to escape St. Petersburg.

"Oh, so you *do* wish to take command of your platoon today. Sit down, sit down, fortify yourself with food. Again. And again.

And again." His voice was so sharp that the junior officers felt they had leave to laugh at the ridicule. Why was he being so cruel?

She sat and ate in silence, the innkeeper solicitous (he had won a tidy sum the night before), considerately omitting eggs but bringing her cheese and cold meats. Lopukhin appeared, dashing through the door and throwing himself down in the seat across from her, reaching for her food with an air of propriety, as if his position as her quartermate permitted him this intimacy. Alexandra, seizing her chance to escape for a moment to return to her quarters to use the chamberpot, rose from the table.

"Karpatsky," said Ulyanov, "where are you going? Are you tired of our company already? Or are you simply unaware that you have not been dismissed?"

She sat down.

Lopukhin looked at Ulyanov with amazement, then looked at Alexandra.

Leaning across at her, he whispered, "Don't pay any attention. He is usually extremely kind, especially to newcomers. And he's pretty lax about formalities. I don't know what's come over him. But he has not been himself for quite some time. I suppose he is still recovering."

"From what?" whispered Alexandra.

"From the tragedy for which he blames himself."

Alexandra dropped her eyes and began to toy with the food on her plate. Whatever part she herself might have played in this tragedy was something she did not wish to think about, but think it about it she did at this moment. She had played with his heart, snatched it away from another who had truly loved him, slave though the girl had been, and used this tender organ to satisfy her vanity and to improve her skills on the field of amatory battle, to practice the manipulations of male emotion, which, though a necessary survival tactic in the circumscribed world of womanhood, were no less shameful for that. The thought of this dampened her spirits, which had been radiant with excitement at the idea of taking command of an actual platoon, of exercising her hard-won knowledge on a living body of soldiers.

To her relief, the entire company of officers soon rose and, talking excitedly to each other, began to file out. She followed them, feeling Ulyanov's narrowed gaze upon her back as she went out the door and then broke into a run. She was able to use the chamber pot in privacy and, when she had buttoned herself up again, adjusted her pelisse and shako, and returned to the inn, she found the curly-haired old sergeant was waiting for her outside, and Ulyanov himself was nowhere to be seen. Pavel had appeared, leading Hercules, and the enormous stallion, impatient for his exercise, was giving the orderly a hard time, snorting and shifting his hindquarters first this way and then that way, seeming to dance with Pavel, though clearly Pavel did not see it quite this way, for he punched the horse in the center of his broad, leather-colored nose. Seeing Alexandra making her way quickly toward him with a look of disapproval on her face, he hung his head guiltily, grunting his regret.

Alexandra soothed the snuffling muzzle, which searched her hand for treats, its surface velvety as a mushroom spiced with whiskers that tickled her palm. He was clearly no worse for wear and had probably barely felt the blow of the puny human, but the horse was milking it for all it was worth, making soft little sounds that could have been interpreted as tiny sobs.

"Your honor," said the sergeant, "you wish to set a punishment."

"A punishment?"

"A lashing with the whip before the men."

"I didn't say that," said Alexandra, watching Pavel drop his head and kick at the dirt, ashamed and apprehensive.

"You should give him twenty lashes and take away his ration of bread for seven days."

"Is that the customary penalty for this?"

"It is, sir."

Alexandra thought. It was her first decision as an officer. Her inclination was to mercy, but perhaps that would undermine the unit's discipline. She looked around for Nikifor, but he was nowhere to be seen. She wanted to fit in and be accepted, do what the other officers would do, but how could she betray her own morality, her sense of reasoned judgment and proportion? The customary penalty was too harsh.

"I will deal with him later," she said, inserting her foot into the stirrup and swinging herself up and onto the saddle, where she landed lightly with a satisfying creak, Hercules' barreled belly warm against her clinging legs. In the saddle, joined to her massive mount, she was secure, looking down upon the smallness of the world.

But the sergeant would not let it go so easily. He walked up to her and raised his face.

"Your honor," he said, "I did not hear you properly. What punishment did you set?"

Oh, for heaven's sake, thought Alexandra. But if she must, she supposed she must. She had set herself beneath the yoke of military discipline and she must conform. It was fascinating to her, this emphasis on the mortification of the body—their own and others'—as it seemed to suggest an attempt to transcend the flesh, as if the body were only to be used in the service of something higher, its limitations flogged and whipped away, its weaknesses punished brutally. Nature was to be not cherished but twisted, broken, conquered. What Pavel had done was only something natural, a reflex of frustration, but apparently this was not to be allowed.

"No lunch," said Alexandra from the height of her authority.

"Excuse me, sir, I did not hear you properly."

Alexandra stared at him. He clearly wished her to set a harsher punishment. "All right," she said finally, "loss of ration for one day." Disgusted at the lightness of the penalty, the sergeant turned and delivered her words to Pavel, who had been expecting corporal punishment. He nodded tearfully at Alexandra, relieved.

"Loss of ration for one day," said the sergeant, shaking his head as he walked away toward his horse.

Now she faced the platoon itself. Thirty men on horses in a jumble in a field. All thirty pairs of eyes were trained on her expectantly. What was she supposed to do with all these men? She had no idea. Thirty shakos glittered in the sun and thirty swords. Thirty horses snorted, their heads pulled up from the grass they'd been straining toward with lips drawn back from scummy teeth in anticipation of a snack. Alexandra chewed her lip. She searched her mind, but it was empty. All that she had learned was gone. She tightened her fingers on the reins to stop the shaking of her hands, which failed to stop. Her throat was dry. She swallowed. It felt drier.

"Your honor," said the sergeant gently, leaning toward her from his saddle, "I did not hear you properly. I believe you said you wished the men to practice wheeling."

Alexandra closed her eyes. She opened them again and smiled with relief. "That is exactly what I said," said Alexandra.

"You wish the men to practice wheeling, sir?"

"I do indeed."

"An excellent place to begin." He nodded solemnly. "A most wise choice."

The sergeant shouted the order to the trumpeter, who, also seated on a horse nearby, raised his glinting instrument to his lips and called the corresponding signal in soft and mellow notes. All at once the thirty horses formed a line and began to trot, a wall of horses moving toward her. It was thrilling. All this at her behest?

"Wheel right!" the sergeant shouted, and the trumpet blew the proper sequence of mellow notes, a different tune. The horses at once began to turn, all in one motion, a curling wave of black sweeping sideways through the golden grass.

"Hold the center! Close that space! You're messing up the line! It's wrong, all wrong!" the sergeant screamed. "We start again! You sloppy pigs!"

And there was really nothing else for her to do.

The shouts of the sergeant and the call of the trumpet were drowned in the milky morning air, which was beginning to curdle with the heat as the sun moved upward in the shimmering sky. The softened sounds of pounding hooves and swearing men were interspersed with the sharp and silvery cries of the birds, and she could hear the papery sound of leaves blown about by a heat-thickened breeze. As she sat quietly on her horse, watching the exercises with a fierce attention that suggested skilled evaluation (it was not), sweat ran down from her scalp and slipped under her stiff, high, gold-embroidered collar. Why couldn't she remove her hat, allow her scalp to breathe? Why didn't they all? And was there anything worse than the raw and dampish feel of wool on sweaty skin? Why not remove the tunics too? There was no one to see.

Feeling powerful in her righteousness, her concern for her

men, Alexandra suggested as much to the sergeant, whose discipline was so fierce he had not yet even raised a hand to wipe the streams of sweat from his livid face, not even once.

"What?"

She repeated her suggestion. "At least the shakos, sergeant." As if she were asking his permission. She must watch that tendency. It was she who was in command.

Keeping his eyes on the men, who were now jumping two by two over rotting logs, the sergeant scratched his nose as if he were puzzled.

"The shakos are regulation issue," he said, as if this would settle the matter once and for all.

"But why do they have to wear them in the heat?"

"Why? Because the hats protect their scalps from sunburn and the visors protect their eyes and shield them from the sun so the men can see what they are doing."

"Oh," said Alexandra, feeling foolish.

The sergeant's eyes went blank. "Is that your order, sir? Do you wish the men to remove their shakos?"

"No," said Alexandra, "I do not."

"And their tunics, sir, whose heaviness impresses on their minds the gravity of their task in defending their country, the discomfort of wearing them in the heat toughening their hides and preparing them for the greater privations they will suffer in time of war, do you wish the men to remove them, sir?"

"No," said Alexandra, dropping her chin-strapped chin, "I do not."

The sergeant paused a moment, thinking. A smile appeared at the corner of his lips, or at least so Alexandra thought.

"This sergeant is most pleased to see an officer's concern for the comfort of his men," he said in his harsh and brutal voice.

"This sergeant is pleased to see an officer's initiative in this direction. This sergeant will speak most highly of this officer in the future."

Together they watched the men.

And when the soldiers had been drilling for more than three hours, the sergeant suddenly leaned in Alexandra's direction and cupped his ear as if to catch words she had not spoken.

"Did your honor suggest that the men and mounts might benefit from a refreshing swim before their lunch?" said the sergeant, though of course she had suggested nothing of the sort, having been at that moment occupied in experiencing the infinitesimal cooling sensation of a drop of sweat that was tracing its way along the side of her nose.

So a swim it was to be, as Alexandra ordered it, and the men, with yells of wild approval, threw their shakos in the air and wheeled their rearing horses toward the distant river that glittered through the trees. In an impressive display of dexterity at the gallop that would have done a cossack proud, they shed tunics, swords, boots, and even breeches as they rode so that before they disappeared on the other side of the wood and into the river, Alexandra had been treated to the sight of some thirty naked bottoms bouncing lightly in the saddle, soft and white as boiled eggs.

Alexandra let go of her reins, dismounted with a creaking of the saddle, and pressed her face against the glossy black barrel of Hercules' side as he dropped his giant head to the ground in search of grass. The sergeant and the trumpeter had gone to join the swimmers, their horses ambling at a dignified walk but tossing their heads, their jaws straining wide in protest at the mouthful of metal that ruled their big bodies, forcing them to walk when they wanted to gallop with the others. She stood alone in the middle of the meadow listening to the rip and munch of Hercules' gigantic teeth browsing the grass.

It was time for officers' mess, she knew, luncheon at the tavern in the village. They would all be there now, Lopukhin, the junior officers, Ulyanov himself. But the meadow was warm and quiet, the grass was fresh. There were no officers here to test her, tease her, possibly unmask her. She threw her shako on the ground, and, looking round to see if anyone could see, unbuttoned her tunic to show a linen undervest soaked through with the sweat of the morning and sticking to the small soft mounds on her chest. She threw herself on the ground and lay on her back, opening her face to the sun in the hope that the incisive light of the early afternoon would quickly scar and coarsen her tender female skin. If only the rays of the sun would draw the beard from beneath her skin as well, make it sprout the way it drew the flowers and grass from the ground. But there were no seeds there.

Not that she wanted a beard. But oh how she envied the energy of maleness, the daring they were allowed to exercise, the dangers which tested them, the freedom they had to move about where and when they pleased—the many, many privileges to which men were solely entitled.

The warmth of the sun on her face and body was soporific, and Alexandra's mind began to loosen its grip on consciousness. Odd thoughts appeared, strange juxtapositions forming as the mind's logical structures melted in impending sleep. She heard the soft wordless murmurings of Ulyanov's voice as she had heard it the night before while she lay on her pallet in the hut, but she was the woman now, or rather she was both herself and the peasant girl, and the voice was across the room, but also in her ear and his hands were roaming over her body, the edges of her tunic lifted away from her breasts to expose them in their casing of linen, a soft finger tracing their shape, and then the hand slid down between her legs to cup her there, but it might have been the air, so soft was the touch. It was pleasant, lulling. Deeper she went into sleep.

A loud clearing of the throat brought her back to consciousness. Opening her eyes, she saw that Ulyanov himself was standing over her.

"Karpatsky," he said, "you are lying here asleep when your horse might have wandered off God knows where. Get up, get up. Up, up, up. See to your mount. I am beginning to question your fitness as an officer, at least for the Zamoyskis. And you are expected at the mess. The others cannot start their meal without you. Have you no consideration?" He prodded her with the toe of his boot.

Alexandra would have liked to reply that he had been in much a similar position the day before, when she had first come upon him sleeping on the ground surrounded by his officers, one of whom was picking flowers. And that the Zamoyskis themselves, notwithstanding their reputation for ferocity, had been creeping through the forest not exactly in search of the enemy. Mushrooms had been their quarry. But obediently she mounted Hercules and started back to the village, Ulyanov riding arrogantly ahead.

If Alexandra had hoped that the junior officers had forgotten her evasion of the drinking challenge of the night before, she was dead wrong. When she entered the tavern they were ranged around the table looking maliciously expectant, and in front of the one empty place at the table there stood a row of glasses full of clear liquid that Alexandra suspected strongly was not water. She knew she would be expected to drink all ten of these glasses of liquid.

Ulyanov took his place at the head of the table, looking far more cheerful than she had seen him this morning—the dark clouds in his face had been dispelled, replaced by radiance. Or perhaps it was only that the angle of the sun where it came in through the window had changed.

"A toast to our new officer!" he cried, lifting his own glass of clear liquid.

All raised their glasses but Alexandra.

"Karpatsky, you're not drinking," said Ulyanov, who, having dropped the formal air he had had with her in the meadow, was struggling with his lips as if suppressing laughter.

"Captain Mecklenburg-Ulyanov," said Alexandra, though she knew this would delay the inevitable for but a moment, "far be it from me to correct your manners, but you seem to have forgotten that one does not drink to oneself."

A murmur went up from the junior officers. It was true. Ulyanov had forgotten. One toast had thus been wasted, and Alexandra watched with satisfaction as they drained their glasses. The innkeeper poured another round. Ulyanov gazed at her with what seemed to be a sparkle in his eye. The junior officers looked expectant.

"Cornet Count Karpatsky," he said, "far be it from me to correct your manners, but one does not correct the manners of one's commanding officer."

The heads of the junior officers swiveled in Alexandra's direction.

"Captain Mecklenburg-Ulyanov, far be it from me to challenge your authority. I meant only to challenge your memory."

"Hear. Hear," murmured the junior officers. Their heads swiveled back to Ulyanov. Alexandra eyed the plates of cucumbers and sausages with longing. But more than that, she would have wished to change the wine before her into water. She had been out in the sun for hours, and not only was her throat as dry as sand, she could feel the tightening effect of sunburn on her face, the hot tenderness. Her uniform itched. Surreptitiously, she laid a casual hand upon the table, intending to inch it forward to snatch a cucumber, which looked refreshingly like glistening cold white solid ice within its band of cooling green.

"Well said, young Karpatsky." Ulyanov nodded, still looking as if he were fighting to suppress a laugh. In fact, he seemed to be struggling with an entire bellyful of tremendous glee. Unable to contain it any longer, he burst out in a guffaw that brought nudges and sidelong glances from the junior officers, who had not seen their commander do anything but mope and drink for several months.

"Nevertheless," Ulyanov said, serious again, "I didn't like your tone. And it is thus my unhappy duty to place you under arrest."

"Arrest!" cried Alexandra, leaping to her feet. "Why?"

"For insubordination, of course," he said, punctuating his explanation with a smile, his glee suppressed, but clearly still in force.

"Oh," said Alexandra, forgetting herself, and speaking to him as she might have several months ago, "just because I criticized you."

"That's right," said Ulyanov.

Back and forth went the heads of the junior officers, stunned at the disrespect, the breakdown of discipline and civility on either side. They hoped it would go on and on.

"And," Ulyanov continued, "I'm doing it because I can. Lopukhin, get Bobrinsky. Direct him to escort Cornet Karpatsky—"

"That's Cornet *Count* Karpatsky to you," said Alexandra.

"Excuse me, direct him to escort Cornet *Count* Karpatsky to the guardhouse. And that's an extra twelve hours of confinement for your display of pride, your *honor.*"

Alexandra stared at Ulyanov a moment, but he did not look back at her. Instead, he seated himself and popped a round of sausage into his mouth, which he began to chew with a relish that the regiment had not seen in a very long time, his food having been something he merely picked at or, when reminded by his worried batman that he must eat, had placed with reluctance inside his mouth and masticated mechanically. Having finished the bite of sausage, Ulyanov was now rubbing his hands as he surveyed the selection of delicacies arrayed on the table, and, taking up his fork and knife, he began to fill his empty plate with pickles, cheese, ham, eggs, and bread. As the junior officers watched in astonishment, Ulyanov tucked into his meal with vigor, sharply slicing a piece of ham and smiling at it in appreciation before he deposited the morsel in his mouth.

"That's all, Cornet," he said, looking up suddenly from his plate, cheek bulging, "Bread and water for thirty-two hours."

Sergeant Bobrinsky, clasping her by her arm, marched her out of the tavern, across the dusty street, and into a dilapidated barn, which was the temporary guardhouse. Nikifor came rushing in with a large tray containing two glasses of water, which she drank off instantly, wiping her chin with the back of her hand, and several slices of bread with butter and cheese, which she ate standing up. Nikifor saluted her and withdrew, leaving her alone inside the darkened barn. The angle of the sun coming through the slits between the boards told her it was past noon— the deep part of the afternoon, a time of day that had always made her melancholy, the quality of light depressing in its staleness, its emptiness. What was she to do in these hours before Nikifor would come again? She sat down in the straw and rested her chin on her knee, trailing her fingertips meditatively over the slick surface of her boot.

She began to ask herself if Ulyanov had recognized her. He had certainly stared at her with an expression of puzzlement often enough, shaken his head as if to clear it of obstructing shadows. His hostility to her this morning, his sternness when he'd caught her napping in the field, would certainly be appropriate to a man whose heart she had hurt. If so, then why had he arrested her? Surely a gentleman would treat a lady of his acquaintance with more tenderness, especially when he had once professed himself to be in love with her. But then, of course, he was not really a gentleman.

She wondered again if he had ever really been in love with her at all. Whether his love had been sincere or whether his declaration by letter and his proposal of marriage had merely been strategies, tactics, part of the artillery in his arsenal of seduction, another arrow in the quiver he carried to aim at the hearts of the fair sex—she had gone over the question many times in her mind these past few months. She still did not know what his intentions toward her had really been, but from what she had heard of his deep distress at the death of his mistress and what she had seen herself of the residue of pain in his eyes, she was more likely to suspect he had been insincere all along. Yes, of course. After all, despite what Praskovia had told her, she did not believe it was possible for anyone to be in love with two people at once.

Still, he had saved her, in a way, whether he had done it by design or not. The junior officers had been bent on forcing her to drink. There being no drunk like a vodka drunk and no hangover like a vodka hangover (the tortured brain pounding the bony walls of the skull screaming for someone to let it out), Ulyanov, by arresting her, had clearly rescued her from a fate worse than death, or even, had she poured enough vodka down her throat, from death itself—it had happened before and had

been reported in the newspaper when this or that young gentleman, playing drinking games, had poisoned his system and
passed away.

Alexandra heard the crunching sound of footsteps. The footsteps did not die away, though, nor did they make their way up
to the door of the barn. They simply went back and forth with a
creaking of boots, a rattling of metal. She turned her head and
saw the slices of light between the boards darken and lighten, as
if someone were walking back and forth outside. A sentry had
been posted—why? Must the village be protected from her
depredations? Was she a ferocious renegade? No, the prisoner
had criticized someone's manners at luncheon. She would never
understand the nutty hearts of men.

"Halt!" Alexandra heard the sentry shout, snapping his rifle.
"Who goes there?"

"Cornet Lopukhin!"

Oh, for heaven's sake, she thought, it's broad daylight. The
sentry can see perfectly well who goes there.

"State your business."

"To speak with the prisoner, Cornet Count Karpatsky."

Was there no end to this masculine love of rules and regulations? Of military display? This dressing up in special outfits and
pinning decorations on each other? Playing with their swords
and guns?

"Carry on, your honor."

Lopukhin knocked on the wall of the hut. "Karpatsky!"

"Yes?" Alexandra put her ear to the wall.

"I've come to tell you how much we all admire what you did."

"You do?"

"Oh yes," said Lopukhin, "it isn't often we see such bravery!
To stand up to a senior officer that way, with such panache, such
style! We've all been trying to get Ulyanov to arrest us for

months, but he just won't do it! And you managed it right away your first day here!"

Hoping to penetrate deeper into the incomprehensible masculine mind, Alexandra could not resist asking why the junior officers would seek to bring upon themselves the disgrace of incarceration.

"Of course everyone wants to be arrested," said Lopukhin, sounding puzzled. "Ulyanov himself has been arrested more times than I can count. I don't think any of us will ever beat him. Maybe you."

Looking round the hut—at the floor, which was littered with dry pellets of old chicken droppings and fresh curds of dog shit, at the rotting straw and broken glass—Alexandra decided this was a distinction she did not care to pursue.

"But why do they want to be arrested?" she persisted.

"How can you ask? It's the only way to prove our daring and insouciance."

Alexandra couldn't believe that someone would actually use the term *insouciance* in application to himself. But her question, at least, had been answered, though she wondered if she had raised some suspicions in Lopukhin by her stubborn incomprehension of what was obviously a foundation value of masculinity.

"Come round to the door," said Lopukhin, "I've got something to give you."

"Halt!" cried the sentry with another snapping of his rifle.

"It's just a bottle of vodka, Grishka."

Lopukhin's disembodied hand pushed its way through the partly opened door, the bottle in its fist. Alexandra took it.

"It's from all of us," he whispered.

Alexandra supposed she might as well drink it—it would be useful practice in holding her liquor, practice that could be per-

formed in complete privacy, away from the taunts of the junior
officers. Every hour upon the hour, she took a few swigs of
vodka and carefully noted all physical effects so that she might
learn to adjust herself to them. By the time the white slices of
light between the boards of the barn had darkened, she was
drunk. She practiced walking round the hut in this state. She
practiced sitting without losing her balance. Whenever the
drunkenness began to abate, she took another slug of vodka. The
dinner of bread and butter and tea brought by Nikifor was used
to test the effects of food plus vodka. When the challenge came
again, she intended to be ready.

She was still practicing an hour or two after her dinner (the
bottle of vodka was not yet empty) when she heard the crunching of feet on stones again and heard the sentry shout, "The captain!"

Ulyanov came into the hut carrying a blanket under his arm
and shut the door behind him. Leaning against the boards, his
legs crossed in front of him, his arms crossed over his chest, a
stub of cigar clamped between his teeth, he stared down at Alexandra, the orange tip of his cigar glowing in the semidarkness.
Alexandra, who had been sitting in the dirt in the middle of the
hut, knew it was her duty to stand in the presence of her commanding officer, and she tried to struggle to her feet, her arms
stretched out on either side of herself for ballast, but she did not
succeed and sat carefully back onto her bottom, lowering herself
as gently as she could.

"Are you ready to go home now?" he asked.

Alexandra raised her head and stared up at him, her mouth
open in an O.

"How . . . ?" she asked, slightly shaking her head, but not too
hard.

"I'd rather not answer that," he said, "except to say that there was no other way to be sure. I apologize to you for that."

Alexandra's face was instantly red. So the hand between her legs had been no dream. She hid her face by dropping it into her lap. It felt better that way anyway.

"I don't know what you think you're doing here," Ulyanov said quickly, eager to get past a distasteful subject, "but it has to stop right now. You could get yourself hurt. As you very nearly did this afternoon before I put a stop to it by arresting you."

"Don't know what you're talking about," said Alexandra drunkenly, chin now resting on her knees. She must remember in future to add the personal pronoun "I" to all the sentences that required them.

"I think you do know what I'm talking about, Countess," he said.

Alexandra was too drunk to argue with him. She wanted him to go away so that she could lie down in the straw, something that propriety prevented her doing in front of him now that she was in the presence of a man who knew she was a woman.

Ulyanov walked toward her and squatted at her side. "What's this?" he said, pulling the bottle of vodka out from under the straw. He looked at it, opened it, and smelled it. "I see they got to you after all."

"A present," she said sullenly, "because they're proud of me. They admire me."

"They don't admire you," said Ulyanov, "they simply wanted to win. And they have. Obviously. You are clearly very drunk, Countess Korvin."

Ulyanov knelt, took a handkerchief from his pocket, spat on it, and wiped at the dirt she had transferred from her boot to her face. Alexandra was too drunk to try to push his hand away. However, even the slight pressure exerted on her face by his fingers, the way he moved her flesh about on its bones as he wiped it, was enough to set her brain and stomach churning. "This dirty place," he said with a tsk of his tongue. "But I'm afraid I have to keep you here all night under the protection of the sentry so the junior officers can't get to you again. Tomorrow I'll send you home and no one will ever know of your . . . adventure." He tucked the bottle of vodka under his arm and stood up.

"Only thing I need protection from is you." Alexandra felt her stomach begin to clench, protesting the vodka. She fell forward onto her hands and knees and vomit spurted from her throat, splashing against Ulyanov's boots.

"I couldn't agree more, just what I deserve," said Ulyanov as Alexandra began to cry. "Many, many women have told me that the sight of me made them sick. You're the first one to follow through. Oops! Go ahead, get it out. Get all of it out. It's the very best thing. At least that's one thing that I'm good for."

Alexandra did not protest when Ulyanov covered her in the blanket he had brought and positioned her on her side. Before she had time to insult him again, she was asleep.

When Alexandra woke up with a head that felt two feet wide, she found that someone had removed her boots and unbuttoned her tunic. The hut had been cleaned—its rotting straw replaced with fresh, its dirt floor swept of debris—and Nikifor was sitting in the straw beside her, ready with a mug of beer. In a voice of practiced softness—practiced in the many years he had nursed the heads and stomachs of young officers through the punishment of the morning after—Nikifor explained the theory behind his treatment.

"Egg is for coating the stomach because its lining is burned away. The beer is to fool your brain. It wants more vodka, it's angry and complaining and tormenting you until you give it more. So we give it beer. At first your brain will still be angry, but then it will settle for what it can get. The beer will make it happy, and it will leave you alone."

It took a few hours, but Alexandra found that the remedy worked. By noon she was able to take some bread. By four she was ready for tea and jam. By seven she was ravenous, pacing back and forth in the hut and listening for the approach of Nikifor with dinner. She sat down on the floor to wait.

But Ulyanov came in, a napkin-covered tray in one hand, an oil lamp in the other.

"I've brought your bread and water," he said, setting down the lamp and tray.

Alexandra looked at him imperiously and remained silent. She had not forgotten the insult he had delivered while she had lain asleep in the field, his touching of her most private place.

Ulyanov, having seated himself across from her and set down the tray between them, lifted the napkin. On the tray were a small glass of water and a large mound of bread. "Drink," he said, nodding.

Alexandra, expecting water, spluttered as the vodka met her lips, but drank it down. This hair of the dog was apparently just what she needed to complete the cure—within a few seconds of drinking it, she felt entirely restored.

"Things are not always what they seem," said Ulyanov. "A thing may look exactly like another but be entirely different in its substance. As may human beings. Now eat the bread."

Alexandra lifted a slice from the mound and discovered a roast chicken. She tore a leg from the bird, rolled it in the loose salt at the edge of the plate, and looked at Ulyanov through narrowed eyes, tearing at the meat with her small teeth in a way that Ulyanov found enchanting in its peculiarly feminine voraciousness.

"It is sometimes necessary to remove an impediment, an obscuring layer, to discover the truth beneath," said Ulyanov. "Do you forgive me?"

"I'm not talking to you," said Alexandra.

"Oh please, dear Countess, if you do not forgive me, then I must challenge myself to a duel to restore your honor. And since I will be my own opponent, I will have to shoot myself." Alexandra did not find this amusing.

"Laugh, Countess," said Ulyanov, "it was meant to be funny."

"Ha," said Alexandra tonelessly, and went on eating.

"Ah, but perhaps you are not the Countess Korvin, and if you are not she, but in fact a he, no dishonor has been done you. And you have no reason not to talk to me. And I have no reason to shoot myself."

Alexandra had to admit that he had her there. Either she admitted who she was and was therefore allowed to maintain her rather enjoyable pose of outrage, or she did not, in which case she was simply Cornet Count Anatol Karpatsky, who had been disrespectful to his commander and was being properly punished by this confinement.

"I think shooting yourself would be an excellent idea," she said, deciding on the former as far too interesting a path to turn away from.

"Please accept my apologies," he said. "I know I committed a violation of your person, but I had to find out if what I suspected was true. Otherwise, who knows how long you might have gone on with this."

"Oh, I intend going on," said Alexandra.

"You can't be serious."

"I am absolutely serious."

"We'll see about that," said Ulyanov. "You know I have only to go to the colonel."

Alexandra had not thought it out this far. Of course he could stop her very easily.

"I have to think about that," she said. "Perhaps I will find a way to foil your plan."

Ulyanov opened the sabretache that hung from his belt and removed a cheroot. He held it up and waited for her to grant a lady's permission, which she did with a nod, and then he struck a match on the sole of his boot and applied the sputtering flame to the end of the long black tube.

"Explain to me something, though," he said, frowning, shaking the fire from the end of the match. "Why exactly are you here?"

"I'll explain if you'll give me one of those. I'm dying for a smoke."

Ulyanov's eyebrows jumped. He laughed. "My dear Countess," he said, "you don't smoke, do you? A refined young lady like yourself?" He lit one for her and passed it over the plate, watching with surprise and then pleasure as she smoked the cheroot as if she was long accustomed to the practice, which she was. They sat facing each other, identically dressed, identically smoking.

"I'm not so refined," said Alexandra, relaxing backward and supporting herself on her elbow, resting her boot on her knee. "I've been smoking for years. My father got me started."

"But answer the question, Countess. Why are you here?"

"It's a long story," said Alexandra, "and I am not certain I can tell you all the truth." Embarrassed to acknowledge to herself Ulyanov's own part in the story, Alexandra looked away from him and began to examine what looked to be a spot of grease on the wall.

"The truth," said Ulyanov, "is something women aren't good at. If you are here because you want to be a man, you must start there. You must tell the truth to me."

"I wasn't aware that men held a monopoly on the truth. I'd always thought it was the other way around."

"An interesting observation," said Ulyanov. "Perhaps we're not so different after all. But come now, the truth. Tell me why you're here."

"Why," said Alexandra, drawing the bitter smoke into her mouth and rolling it around on her tongue as if tasting the finest vintage of wine, "are you?"

"Why am I? You mean why am I here? I never thought about it. I suppose it was expected of me. All young men my age go into the army, at least for a year or two. I simply stayed on."

"But why? Why not something else? Why not the university?"

"I hadn't considered university. I always wanted the army. For the adventure, I suppose. A certain glamour in it, the uniforms, the color. A certain dash. And a kind of testing of oneself. One's daring, or courage, or ingenuity."

"Aha!" said Alexandra. "It is no different with me."

"But why should a woman want to test her courage?"

"Why shouldn't she? Do you think women are any less than men? That we don't seek to prove the same virtues in ourselves?"

"No," said Ulyanov, "I didn't think you did. As for being less than men, of course you're not. You're more."

"I don't believe you think that," said Alexandra. "The truth, Captain."

"The truth?" Ulyanov tapped his finger on the cheroot, dislodging a bit of ash. "You're less and more at once. Both more and less."

"But not the same amount. Not equal, that is."

"It's apples and oranges," he said. "The two cannot be compared. There's no common denominator."

"There is," said Alexandra.

"And what is that?"

"Our substance, our souls. We may look different on the outside, but be the same on the inside. A reversal of what you demonstrated with the glass of vodka."

Ulyanov fell silent. After a moment, he said, "I'd never thought of women having souls the same as ours. Some religions don't, you know."

"Don't what?"

"Think women have souls. But most of us are more concerned with women's hearts and whether they have them. The soul I'm willing to give you. It's the heart we worry about."

"Do we women appear so heartless?"

Ulyanov did not look at her and spoke quickly. "Some of you, yes," he said, and Alexandra was polite enough to look away, knowing to whom he referred, "others not. Others have more heart than they can bear, as I found out not long ago. I have been heartless myself at times. In fact, quite often. I suppose my belief in women's heartlessness, common among men, led me at times to treat them as if they really had no hearts themselves. And that, of course, is how it happened. Entirely my fault, the destruction of another human being." He fell silent a moment, then hurried past the subject. "But that is neither here nor there and no business of yours. *You* did nothing wrong." He rose to go.

Alexandra was relieved to hear him absolve her of any responsibility for the tragedy, but she was not certain she deserved it. And she was taken aback to hear him refer, even obliquely, to their former intimacy, one she did not wish to resume or be reminded of. Nevertheless, she did not wish to see him go. His was the only familiar face here, so far from home. And his company was actually quite pleasant.

"Please stay, Captain," she said, turning her face up past his boots to meet his eyes.

Ulyanov shook his head, threw his cheroot down, and crushed it under his heel. "Oh no, Countess, no need to be polite. I'm sure you will be pleased to see the last of me in any case, which you will, and soon. Tomorrow I will arrange to send you home." And he was gone. Alexandra heard the sentry outside snap his arms as Ulyanov passed.

Lying down in the straw with her cheroot, Alexandra thought of how interesting the conversation had been, how different he had seemed, and how fascinating all of this was, and wondered how she could talk him out of sending her home.

Outside was a summer evening, and through the thin boards of the barn Alexandra heard the sounds of a rawer life than she had ever known before—the cheerful whistling of a man as he pissed against the wall of the barn, his urine splashing like a fountain; a couple's quarrel punctuated by a ringing slap and a tiny smacking kiss; the snuffling of a pig as it wandered by, its snout appearing briefly under the wall as it nosed beneath the boards in search of food; the bright percussive sounds of children's voices; and all of it very far away from the thick high walls of her ruined palace on the Neva.

As it turned out, Alexandra needn't have worried. Her opportunity to foil Ulyanov's plan to send her home came the very next day. The colonel had come to lunch and, seeing her missing from the table and being told of her arrest, had ordered her sentence suspended, though she had only another hour to serve.

"Sit down here by me, Cornet," said the colonel, patting the empty chair at his side, "and tell me all about yourself. A trencherman of your ability is a valuable asset to the regiment, no doubt about it."

Sparkling as much as it was possible for so large a man, bending his head to the sound of her voice and laughing too loudly, the colonel gave unmistakable evidence of a partiality to Alexandra's person. The officers of the company exchanged glances while Ulyanov, seated at the colonel's other side, chewed his lip with a certain anxiety, eager for his chance to tell the colonel of the new cornet's impending departure, which, seeing the colonel's enthusiasm, seemed to him more urgent than ever, considering the colonel's reputed taste for handsome, slightly effeminate young men.

"Your excellency," he kept saying, trying to insert himself into the small chinks in the steady conversation, between Alexandra's tales of her background and education, which she was making up as she went along, and the colonel's loud guffaws and eager questions.

"And then," said Alexandra, casting a sidelong glance at Ulyanov across the table, "after my expedition to the wilds of Borneo, where I collected the feathers of birds of species never seen before—"

"I'd love to see them," the colonel interjected, breathing hard.

"—and the eggs of giant lizards who carry their young in pockets of flesh that hang on either side of their heads, I returned to St. Petersburg, where I found myself utterly at loose ends until my friend here, Captain Mecklenburg-Ulyanov—"

"Good man," said the colonel, laying a heavy hand on Ulyanov's shoulder.

"—persuaded me to join the regiment. I was reluctant at first. I wasn't sure I'd fit in with this manly company, myself a scholar, a poet, a scientist untrained in the manly arts. But Captain Ulyanov, whom I have known for many, many years, assured me that that could not be the case, that there was room for all sorts in the service of the tsar."

"Hear! Hear!" cried the colonel, "good man! Good man!" and turned his heavy, beaming face to Ulyanov, who was staring at Alexandra with an expression of such irritation, she rolled her tongue around on the inside of her cheek in delight at having outfoxed him so thoroughly, while Ulyanov himself, suddenly aware that Alexandra's protestations of unmanliness would only incite the colonel further, inserted his own tongue firmly into his cheek at the thought that she had only outfoxed herself, as she would discover when the colonel made advances toward her person. And how would the clever countess handle *that*? Such a large man, he was. And strong.

"So it was you who brought this delightful boy to the service of our little father, our great and glorious ruler! Good man!" the colonel said again, now clearly viewing Ulyanov as his benefactor, the agent of the delivery of this delectable young cornet, just as Alexandra had intended—an interesting irony.

"The tsar!" cried one of the junior officers, leaping to his feet and thrusting his glass of champagne so forcefully into the air that it spilled nearly half its contents on the table.

The cry "The tsar!" was instantly taken up by every officer at the table, all of them leaping to their feet and thrusting their foaming glasses in the air. In one movement the glasses were drained and in one movement smashed to the floor while the innkeeper's daughter, who'd been watching from the doorway, rushed in with her broom to gather the broken bits of glass. She'd been expecting this. They did it every day, at some point. She only had to wait.

They sat down again and went on with their lunch.

"In honor of *you*, my dear Karpatsky," said the colonel, "I have had my chef, my personal chef, prepare a small surprise, a little trifle to show my admiration of your capabilities." He snapped his fingers, and Alexandra looked up from her plate to see being carried toward her a monstrous cake.

"Go on," said Ulyanov as the deadly white construction—two feet high and decorated with furbelows of pure glistening sugared lard—was set before her. "Go on, dig in, Karpatsky, it's all for you."

"Indeed it is," said the colonel, gazing at Alexandra with an expression of greed. "I want to see you eat it all."

Nevertheless, it was with a feeling of triumph that Alexandra rode out with the regiment the next morning on the sixty-mile march to the next village, safe now from deportation from the regiment, secure in her position as apple of the colonel's eye. Sunlight dropped through the trees as men on horses streamed down the road as far as the eye could see. Squadron by squadron they rode, singing, three abreast, captain by captain, trumpets blaring, carried along on their sea of song, the bullfrog sounds of basses croaking darkly beneath the brightness of the tenors on this Russian summer morning.

Ahead of her Alexandra saw Ulyanov's back, which seemed stiff and disapprovingly straight as he bounced in his saddle. Beside her rode Lopukhin. From time to time peasant girls, pausing at their work in the fields along the road, shouted to the soldiers or raised their hands in greeting, or their skirts, at which Alexandra blushed and hoped that Lopukhin, who was laughing, didn't see.

"Nice fat thighs on that one," said Lopukhin, "I'd like to get my teeth in there. And something else."

"Of course," said Alexandra.

Sometimes children came running out to trot beside the horses, beg for treats. Alexandra saw all the squalor of rural Russia in these pathetic beings, their pallid faces smeared with mucus, legs rickety, eyes milky with disease, stomachs big with emptiness. The soldiers tossed coins at them, or crusts of bread. The children who missed the treats spat at the soldiers or called out dirty words. They were, in fact, barely children at all, but more like small, misshapen adults, toughened and coarsened early by the efforts to survive the poverty and sickness and deprivation of Russia's gigantic poverty.

But this is not the Russia of the mind. This is the real. So. Imagine instead these children as golden-haired, rosy-cheeked, plump—happy peasant cherubs casting admiring glances at the soldiers, shyly waving.

On that long march north along the rutted country roads, Alexandra was tossed back and forth and up and down in the saddle by the changing of gaits until she felt beaten and bruised. She had ridden before, of course, and considered herself a competent horsewoman, but this was different. Her legs were losing strength. Her arms ached. And as the sun rose higher in the sky, her tongue turned to cotton.

They stopped to rest. The trumpet called out the signal to halt, dismount, and fifteen hundred men led their horses from the road and settled in the grass, swigging from their canteens so that water ran down their chins. Some of the men collapsed into snores under the trees, their reins hooked round their wrists while their horses crunched at the grass. Some of the men built fires and boiled water for tea, which they drank from tin cups with a chunk of yellow sugar between their teeth. They discussed the thighs of the peasant girls, guessed at the weight of their breasts. They played cards and told stories, peasant legends in which the master was cleverly duped out of something—wife, or horse, or hay.

The trumpet sounded again, and fifteen hundred men swore and scrambled at the buttons of their tunics. Mounting up onto groaning saddles, they formed again in ranks, and they were off, rocking and bouncing down the road.

Ten hours in the saddle. By the time they reached the town, Alexandra's limbs had turned to water. She was flopping like a rag doll and Lopukhin, chuckling, reached over and grabbed the back of her tunic to hold her to the saddle.

"How do you like the cavalry, my boy?"

Alexandra leaned forward across Hercules' neck and vomited.

"Just fine," she said, wiping her mouth with the back of her hand.

"You did that well, Karpatsky," said Lopukhin, "you vomit like a cavalryman. No nonsense."

Alexandra vomited again.

They made their way to a large and elegant house, Lopukhin still holding Alexandra upright by the back of her tunic. He shouted for Karpatsky's batman.

"No shame," said Nikifor, who instantly appeared, "no shame." Lopukhin released her. She flopped off Hercules' back and fell into Nikifor's arms. Ulyanov, who was standing nearby slapping his hand irritably against his thigh, watched as Alexandra was half dragged inside the house. Once inside Nikifor lifted her body into his arms and carried her upstairs while the lady of the house—a plump widow in ruffled cap who had her eye on one of the hussars already—protested that anything that was needed would be there, "just ask." The entire contingent of junior officers clattered up the stairs behind Nikifor and his burden and stood chuckling and heckling in the doorway as Alexandra was dropped gently onto the bed.

"Hey, Karpatsky! What are you, a girl?"

"Hey, Karpatsky! We should call you Karpatskaya!"

"Hey, Karpatsky! Maybe you want to go home and play with your dolls!"

Nikifor got up and shut the door. He removed her boots and tunic, washed her feet in the basin of cold water a maid had brought, tucked her beneath the blankets, and crept out of the room, leaving Alexandra already asleep.

When she woke up several hours later, Ulyanov was standing over her. He looked very tall and very masculine, with his broad shoulders and leather straps and gleaming metal, and it occurred to Alexandra that perhaps this was all a very big mistake. She would never be a man—why was she trying? This ordeal of manhood was not meant for women, it occurred to her. In the past forty eight-hours or so, she had eaten herself sick, drunk herself nearly dead, driven her body until it broke, and all for what? To prove she was a man?

"Are you ready to go home?" said Ulyanov.

"No," said Alexandra.

"Fine," said Ulyanov. Turning on his heel, he went clattering out with his leather straps and his gleaming metal and his broad shoulders, looking more manly than ever from behind.

And now she would have to dance. She would have to dance like a man.

Like magnificent birds of prey in their scarlet and gold dress uniforms, sharp spurs on their shining boots, Alexandra and the junior officers slumped elegantly against the wall of the provincial ballroom, watching with boredom the provincial belles as they danced to the local orchestra. Knowing there would be no sexual payoff from these respectable maidens, that marriage to a Petersburg officer was the goal of these girls, and that thus the officers themselves were the prey here, the men tapped their toes in irritation and smiled politely while eager to fly to the holy festival of the Righteous Procopius of Vologda, Fool-for-Christ and Wonder-worker, a rival revel set to begin at moonrise in the field behind the local mill where vodka would flow and peasant skirts would rise. Out of politeness, they refrained from checking their pocket watches, and could only watch the window for minor changes in the light that told them time was passing.

A lone potted palm decorated the scarred floor of the room, whose large rug, rolled up, was visible as a long tube thrust up against the wall.

Alexandra herself was observing with disdain the extraordinary outfits of the local girls—grotesque approximations of Paris fashion, overdecorated and poorly cut. And their hair! What had they done to their hair? Alexandra noted with satisfaction that she was still the most attractive woman in the room, even if she *was* a man. The girls glanced shyly at the officers with reddened faces and trembling hands, turning their heads sharply to make their curls flip enticingly round their heads and laughing much too loudly.

"Aren't we going to dance?" she hissed at Lopukhin.

"We have to, I know," said Lopukhin, "they're expecting it, so we might as well get it over with. The sooner we dance the sooner we can leave. Good meal, though."

"Right," said Alexandra, moving away from the wall, about to experience the famous "walk across the floor." The masculine duty to make the first move in all romantic endeavors and the attendant vulnerability to rejection was something Alexandra had never thought about before. She found herself thinking— like any young man—suppose she refuses? Suppose she turns me down? In front of everyone?

The girl she chose to approach first was the most attractive in the room. If Alexandra had already tested her feminine attractiveness on men, she might as well test her masculine attractiveness on women. Surely women would be the true arbiters of her authenticity, of the success of her disguise.

The young woman fluttered her fan and blushed, leaving Alexandra to wonder if she herself had been so silly (she had, with Rybynsky especially). The girl, passing off the cup of coffee she'd been drinking to her hovering mother, swept out onto the floor at the end of Alexandra's hand and allowed Alexandra to encircle her waist and draw her close, as men had done to Alexandra.

Waiting a beat or two to catch the wave of the music before entering the stream of dancers, Alexandra noted the oddly fragile feel of the girl's rib cage, which moved and breathed beneath her hand like a living creature. Having danced only with men and so felt under her hand the solidity of the male shoulder—a steady anchor in the whirlpool of the waltz, a rock to cling to—Alexandra was unnerved. It was she who must guide this delicate object through the dance, instead of being guided. It was she who would be clung to, rather than clinging.

And she would have to do it frontward and in boots instead of backward in high heels. Oh, why hadn't she thought to practice this before?

Overshooting the mark in her effort to move forward rather than backward, Alexandra smashed against the girl's breasts. A repulsive sensation, rather like stepping unexpectedly on something soft. How can men like that? she wondered.

Now gathering the woman back inside the circle of her arms, Alexandra started in again and awkwardly succeeded in pushing the woman backward in approximate time to the music. Unfortunately, she had not taken into account the length of her spurs, and a scream and the sound of ripping cloth alerted Alexandra to the fact that she had miscalculated her distances and caught her spur in the skirt of another dancer.

With a bow of apology, ignoring a hostile stare from the

woman's partner, Alexandra set her jaw and started in again. She was sweating inside her uniform, and the effort to direct her partner's movements while doing everything she was used to in reverse was making her head feel tiny and constricted. The girl herself was pliant and uncomplaining. She endured a stepped-on foot, an aching rib cage, and crushed fingers on the hand that Alexandra gripped too tightly, but she only smiled. So why was it not working?

How much easier it was, thought Alexandra, to be a woman. The responsibility for this botch is mine. But so would be the credit if I did it right.

Then Ulyanov and his partner whistled past her, their movements perfectly melded, mirrors of each other. While pushing her partner round the floor, she watched them, and it occurred to her that it was this responsiveness to his partner—not masterful force, as she had understood it—that created grace, that this was how one danced, male or female, both following, neither leading, but always mirroring, always adjusting to the other. She had always done this as the woman in the dance. It had never occurred to her before that the man would have to do this too, that all of them who danced well had done it just this way.

Then putting her revelation into practice, concentrating on her partner's movements, Alexandra found the nub of grace, and though she lost it again from time to time, she was sorry when the music ended. The joy of this new accomplishment was indescribable—to cleave so closely to another human being, to breathe at one with him (or her), feeling no division in between, no separateness of will.

It occurred to her that she had never danced with him.

• • •

And the women at the ball? What did they think of Alexandra? How convincing was her masculine disguise? What were they saying behind their fans?

"Too boyish, that cornet. No muscle there, no heft. A fish. Throw him back."

"Poetic."

"Weak."

"An angel."

"Just as sexless."

There was one at the ball who saw Cornet Count Karpatsky quite differently. When Alexandra left the floor and stepped out into the garden to catch her breath, the colonel followed her. He had been watching her all evening with rapt attention, exquisite appreciation. An angel? Absolutely! Sexless? Not as far as *he* was concerned.

"Cornet," said the colonel, appearing from behind the screen of leaves, two glasses of champagne in his massive fists, "may I offer you some refreshment? You've been exerting yourself so dutifully in service to the local girls, I thought you must be thirsty."

"No duty," said the breathless Alexandra, taking a glass, "a pleasure, absolutely. I thought the girls were charming." She seated herself on a stone wall. The colonel seated himself beside her.

"I dearly hope," the colonel whispered boldly, "that that is not the case."

Alexandra gulped at her drink. What had he meant? She hoped it wasn't what she thought he meant.

"Oh, I perfectly agree," she said, deliberately misunderstanding him, "that they are not so elegant as our ladies of Petersburg, but they are certainly pleasant and pretty enough. And one's standards of feminine attractiveness must adjust themselves to what we find."

"Certainly," said the colonel, "and was there one who caught your fancy? Someone you might be dreaming of tonight?"

"Oh no," said Alexandra, careful now, "I liked them all."

"Tell me, Cornet," said the colonel, shifting his bulk closer to her, "have you ever had a woman?"

Having become accustomed to the freedom with which her fellow officers discussed their sexual exploits, Alexandra was not at all shocked by this question, and in fact was rather amused. How should she answer?

"Yes," she said, reasoning that since she was herself a woman, and certainly in possession of said self, she could reasonably conclude that she had indeed "had a woman."

"And what did you think? Did you like it?"

Thinking of her collision with the woman on the dance floor, and of her own natural feminine distaste for her own body, Alexandra could not resist an answer in the negative. A mischievous answer, sure to bring an interesting response.

"Ah," said the colonel, shifting his massiveness even closer, "then perhaps you number yourself among the select group who reject the conventions of society in appreciating the beauty of strength rather than weakness, those who resist the sapping of their own strength through the mundane duties of family life, those who, if you will, resist death itself."

Alexandra thought she was certainly all for that, but did not know how the colonel's program would manifest itself in daily life. She asked for clarification.

"Never grow up," said the colonel with sudden passion, "never grow old, be boys forever. Never die."

"I think," said Alexandra, "that that would be marvelous. But impossible. Time goes on, our bodies grow old."

"But not our minds, not our souls," said the colonel, "dear Cornet. I know that although this great carcass I carry around with me has grown flaccid and wrinkled and weary, my mind is as fresh and my heart as true as a boy's."

"But our minds and souls," said Alexandra, "must keep pace with our bodies. If not, there is then a disparity that is grotesque." She was thinking of Nadezhda Durova, the Cavalry Maiden—the boy grown old who had never been a man, the girl grown old who had never been a woman. Durova had sought, perhaps, to arrest the passage of time by remaining as sexless, as neuter as a child, a being not truly male or female but in between, always on the verge of becoming, always separate from the tide of life. However, Durova's body had relentlessly grown old, and the soul that shone out from the wrinkled face seemed itself to reflect the disparity, creating around her an aura of something thwarted, something stunted.

"No," she went on, suddenly disquieted in her mind, "we cannot resist nature. We must give in to it."

"But all that is great in our world is the result of resistance to nature," said the colonel, "of not giving in. What else is science, invention, art? Man's triumph over the dictates of nature, a force of pure mind matched against it and conquering it, twisting it to our will."

"True," said Alexandra, "quite true, Colonel." Her disquiet dissolved, and she looked at her shiny boots again with satisfaction. "And too," she said, pointing up at the northern summer sky, which glowed with a dawn that was always on the verge of coming but never came, suffused with the light of a sun which had never truly set, the sky locked in a state of in-between, "nature itself behaves unnaturally at times, as if it too resists the passage of time and the coming of death."

"And so," said the colonel, gazing at her ardently, "what

seems unnatural is not so unnatural after all. It could be the most natural thing in the world."

"Yes," said Alexandra, shifting her seat to move away from him, "it could be."

"I've never met anyone like you," said the colonel suddenly, quickly. "You're unlike any other man I've ever met."

Small wonder, she thought. Because I am a woman.

"I can talk to you as I've never talked to any other man. How is it you are so wise?"

Because ... I am a woman?

"I have never ..." The colonel seemed overcome by emotion. His voice caught in his throat, and, turning away from her, he gripped his knees as if struggling with himself. "I am a lonely man," he said finally, and then looking up at the sky, "despised and rejected of men."

"No one despises you, Colonel," said Alexandra. "You are greatly loved by the men."

"But not," he said bitterly, shaking his head, "by—"

Someone was coming through the door. Alexandra turned her head at the sound of creaking boots and jangling spurs. Ulyanov appeared, standing in the doorway looking very tall. He gestured to Alexandra.

"Excuse me, Colonel," he said, "I must borrow our cornet from you a moment."

Ulyanov, walking quickly ahead of her, led Alexandra round the side of the house, out of the colonel's earshot. He spoke to her sharply, fixing his eyes on her face and warning her to be careful of the colonel.

"And why is that?" she asked—a rather flippant question. She already knew quite well.

"His tastes are ... unusual."

"You may say it in plain words," said Alexandra, impatient to get back to her interesting conversation with the colonel and irritated that Ulyanov would question her judgment or her knowledge of the wider world and its many strange permutations. "I'm not a child."

"He likes boys," Ulyanov said in a low voice, looking quickly round to see if anyone might be coming, anyone who might hear. Alexandra could see the outline of Ulyanov's face in the half-darkness, its thinness. It gave her an odd feeling.

"Well then, since I am not a boy, he poses no danger to me." She turned to walk away from him, but Ulyanov caught her by the arm.

"He doesn't know that, Countess. And the danger is not to you. It's to him. Don't encourage his attentions. It isn't kind."

Alexandra, further angered by this criticism of her manners, tried to pull away, but Ulyanov held on tighter, and when she had wrenched her arm free and begun to walk away, he reached out and caught her by the wrist, which he circled easily with his fingers, remaining expressionless as she struggled, her boots twisting in the dirt.

"We both know you're not a kind woman, Alexandra," he said as she sweated and kicked, missing him each time, her wrist, trapped inside the iron circle of his fingers, feeling scraped and sore, as if she were manacled, "but you will treat the colonel kindly if I have anything to say about it."

"You haven't," said Alexandra, panting, "anything to say about it."

"Haven't I?" Ulyanov said, releasing her so suddenly she thought she would fall, but she managed to stay on her feet. "As your superior officer, I have charge of your deportment. It is up to me to see that you behave properly while you are under my command and don't make a fool of yourself, or anyone else. Otherwise," he said, "it's court-martial and execution. You see"—

he leaned closer, his face approaching hers—"you have put yourself entirely in my power." He smiled.

Alexandra stared up at him, her mouth and cheeks moving as she gathered saliva behind her teeth. She spat at him and missed.

Ulyanov only laughed at her. "My dear Cornet Count Karpatsky, that is clearly an offense against the military code, to spit at one's superior officer."

"Is it," she said, still breathing quickly, "listed in the regulations that one can exercise physical force against an inferior, against a junior officer in one's care?"

"Oh, absolutely," said Ulyanov. "I could have you whipped."

Alexandra, not knowing that this was not true—that only enlisted men were whipped, never officers—fell silent for a moment. However, she knew she was not in the slightest danger, and even if it had been true, she knew that Ulyanov, knowing she was female, would never give the order.

"But you won't, will you, Captain?" she said, dropping her head and looking up at him from under her eyelashes. As difficult as it was for her to admit, she had actually enjoyed the tussle, the feeling of being trapped by him, not able to get away, in the grip of superior strength.

"Cornet, don't go womanly on me now," said Ulyanov. "I thought you wanted to be a soldier. Aren't you trying to become a man? Do not try to claim the privileges of womanhood *here*."

"The privileges?" said Alexandra. "What privileges?"

"Oh!" said Ulyanov. "Why, the privilege of deference, of being above the rules."

"Since we are not even allowed in the game," said Alexandra, relaxing, now on familiar ground and beginning to enjoy herself, "the rules could hardly apply to us in any case. What you call a privilege is merely the fact of being left out of things."

"Excellent point," said Ulyanov, "and when you show us you can play, we will let you in the game."

"But if we are not allowed in the game in the first place," said Alexandra, hands clasped behind her back as she rocked back and forth on her boots, "how will you know we can play it?"

"You have me there, Countess," said Ulyanov, "but I suppose the question is, why do you want to?"

"Because it's everything. The game is life in the wider world."

"So you don't like the smaller, safer one of women?" he said.

"Not at all."

"Fair enough," said Ulyanov, "but you still have to show me you can play."

"I intend to," said Alexandra, and, deciding this firm statement would put a shapely period to the discussion, ending it on a forceful, dramatic note, she walked away.

To prove that she meant what she had said, Alexandra did not go to the festival in the fields. She did not, like the junior officers, sneak away from the provincial ballroom—from the ill-dressed, ill-at-ease local belles and their eager mothers—to get drunk with the peasant men, to take advantage of the looseness of the women. She did not witness the groans and giggles of the couplings in the haystacks under the moon, the scraping whine of the fiddles, the pounding of bare feet on the ground, the long thick braids of the unmarried girls whipping round their heads in their frenzied dance, or the eating of the dirt that revealed the pagan underpinnings of this celebration of the earth, hidden as they were within the cloak of the Christian festival.

Instead, Alexandra went straight home to bed. Tomorrow she was going into battle. She wanted to be ready.

A mock battle only, of course, but things would really be

exploding, and horses would really be charging. The grand manuevers outside St. Petersburg had brought regiments of infantry, artillery, and cavalry all together to test their training. It was the ultimate in masculine toys as the generals played against each other with real soldiers.

She rose early, Lopukhin snoring in the bed across the room (he had only just got in). She washed her body carefully, cursing the softness of her breasts before she bound them tightly in strips of cloth. She bound her feet, too, in strips of cloth (the cavalry did not wear socks) and pulled on her boots with metal hooks that caught at the little loops of cloth sewn inside the leather for just this purpose. She buttoned the metal buttons of her tunic and ran her hands with satisfaction over the heavy gold braid on her flattened chest. She buckled on her sword and sabretache, stuffed her sidearm in her belt, and, with her stiff upstanding shako cradled in her arm, she paced round and round the room listening to the snap of her boots against the floor, enjoying the swing of the sword. Then, carried away, she took Lopukhin's razor from his toilet case and, just to feel what it was like, shaved at the near-invisible downiness, hairs fine as spider-webs, that covered her face.

This brutal scraping of the face, she thought, must increase their ferocity, especially since they have to do it every day. No wonder they feel like killing.

Gathered with the officers after breakfast in the hot morning sun at the meeting point from which they were to ride out to the battlefield, Alexandra found out she was not to be allowed to lead her platoon in the charge. It had been decided (by whom, she wondered? She bet she knew) that her inexperience would undermine the success of the maneuver. But she took the news like a man, saluted sharply, turned, and tossed herself up into the saddle.

Ulyanov rode up to her, reached out with his hand, and gently tipped her shako back, peeking under it to see her eyes. She stared at him stone-faced. He smiled and pushed her shako back into position.

A shout, the blare of a trumpet, and they were off, trotting down the road, some thousand men silent, solemn in excitement, the only sounds the creaking of saddles, the pounding of hooves. In the distance were deep rumbles and boomings of cannon-fire, spurts of white smoke rising above the trees to form a fog that hung, moving and melting, high in the air.

The hussars massed at the edge of a field a few miles away, squadron by squadron, platoon by platoon, captains to the front, junior officers behind. The colonel, enormous on his heavy warhorse, was deep inside the whole formation, protected by a bodyguard of officers that formed a living wall around him. At the sound of the colonel's shout, the trumpet behind him blew a signal and the mass of men spread out in a wave, three ranks deep, poised to roll crashing into shore. The pennons on the lances flapped in the wind, and across the field the infantry—their purported enemy—crawled like ants in the smoky distance.

The horses snorted in excitement and smacked at the ground with oiled hooves, impatient to be off.

Staring straight ahead, Alexandra, who (much to her annoyance) had been placed directly behind Ulyanov, swallowed, her mouth dry. Hercules blew a blast of mucus from his nose and sighed so deeply that Alexandra felt his barrel ribs expand beneath her calves.

"Swords up. Lances up," said the colonel. An officer relayed the order to the trumpeter who sat beside him on his horse, and the trumpeter blew these words in sound. A thousand swords and lances shot straight up, as if a sudden forest had appeared. The officers, who carried only swords, unsheathed theirs easily, but Alexandra had some difficulty getting her saber out of its casing, her hands were trembling so; however, she managed it and held the saber upright, resting it on her thigh.

"Zamoyski hussars, forward, walk, march." The trumpet blared again, and it began.

Walk, walk, walk. Standing in her stirrups, Alexandra dragged at impatient Hercules' mouth with all her strength, Hercules snorting and chewing at the bit in irritation. Ahead of her Ulyanov's horse was sauntering, and isn't that just like him, Alexandra thought.

"Trot, march, march!" She had only to release an ounce of pressure on the reins to bring this about, Hercules breaking joyfully into the quicker pace, shaking his head because it was not quick enough. Sit, sit, sit, she told herself as she bounced about in the saddle, sit to the trot, she who had been trained to rise to it, but the cavalry trot was different and seemingly designed for maximum discomfort to the rider. She felt her shako slipping down to cover her eyes, and, saber in fist, brought her hand up to her head to tighten the chin strap, but Hercules, well trained, heard the trumpet call to gallop and suddenly rose like a wave beneath her and crashed down in the three-beat roll of a well-collected canter. Sweat dripped into her eyes. She had lost a stirrup.

The ground thundered softly with the sound of thousands of hooves, and the bristling forest of steel glittered in the sun and in spite of her dripping face, her slipping hat, Alexandra had never felt such excitement in her life, a kind of self-transcendence too, her heart pounding loudly as a military drum in rhythm with a thousand other hearts.

"Swords out, lances for the fight. Gallop, march, march. *Charge*," and the trumpet blew the call, and the horses stretched out in a wind of their own making, and their hooves flung dirt sky-high as the dust swirled and eddied in the heat. The forest of upright steel went flat; swords and lances lowered toward their targets—the infantry for whose benefit this exercise had been designed. However, though the infantry officers shouted, smacked, and swore at their men, the sight of a thousand points of disembodied steel rushing at them through the dust was quite enough to make them wet their pants. They ran, dropping rifles and carbines and muskets and whatever weight might impede their quick escape.

"Hold your ground, men, hold your ground!" the infantry officers were shouting.

"The hell we will!" the infantry shouted back, at least the ones who bothered to make a sound at all, most of them scrambling over each other, crawling under the legs of squealing, wheeling horses and across the caissons and the cannon and smacking and punching whoever might get in their way. The officers sighed. Behold the Russian soldier, they said. But these were new recruits.

It had been so exhilarating that Alexandra couldn't wait to do it again; she would have that opportunity right away. The umpires of the exercise concluded that they had not achieved success in their objective; the men had run. They were supposed to become desensitized to the sight of the charging cavalry. It was the whole purpose of the exercise. It would have to be done again.

The hussars wheeled and began to trot back to their starting place. Alexandra, having fixed her hat and adjusted her straps and regained her stirrup, was feeling marvelous. Without quite intending it, she threw an exuberant smile over her shoulder at Ulyanov as she passed, and it occurred to him that he had never seen a woman look quite so enchanting as this. Her face was streaked with dirt, but her teeth were white as peeled almonds against this dark background, and her eyes shone out like stars.

Relieved that she hadn't smashed one of those lovely limbs or cracked her pretty head, Ulyanov trotted happily after her, but in passing her he arranged his face in an expression of indifference.

He needn't have bothered. Alexandra, determined to prove her point, would not speak to him except officially, in proper military context. Over the next few weeks she took his orders, and she saluted snappily, but there were no tête-à-têtes, no encounters behind the barn, no battles of wit of the sort that would fill his head at night as he imagined conversations with her in which he always came out on top. There was no opportunity to grab her by the arm again. Or to progress to something even better.

She ignored him.

Every day he watched her growing stronger and straighter in the saddle, gaining confidence in command of her platoon, grace in her handling of cold weapons at the gallop, and accuracy with her pistol. She drank lustily with the junior officers and joined in their conversations but looked past Ulyanov when he tried to speak to her, as if she had not heard him. She skirmished, she scouted, she rode the flank in mock charges. As a result her face, ripened by the sun, darkened to the pink and golden color of a peach. Her eyes were bluer and brighter, her teeth more brilliant, her hair bleached to the color of sweet corn. Just looking at her made his stomach hurt, his heart.

It appeared that, despite her lackluster start at the dance, she had hurt the hearts of the local ladies too—serf or free. She seemed to drive them mad for reasons he could not comprehend, old hand with women that he was. A peasant girl approached him shyly with a bulging kerchief stained with the juice of the blackberries tied up inside it "for Count Karpatsky," and just why this should make him jealous he couldn't quite fathom at all. On evenings when Alexandra was drinking with the junior officers, Ulyanov, invited to dinner by a local merchant, would find himself accosted at the appetizer-table by a bright-eyed mother inquiring after the health of Count Karpatsky while her daughter flushed and fluttered right behind her.

Who could resist the tall and handsome youth standing at the edge of manhood with the something delicate, the something faintly fragile about him lighting maternal fires in all those feminine breasts?

Not me, Ulyanov thought.

And not the colonel, who sighed and blushed whenever she was near.

But what about Lopukhin? They always had their heads together, sharing a private joke, betting on who could eat more, drink faster, jump higher, or succeed at any number of those pointless, complicated tests young men like to set themselves for no other reason than to revel in their youth and strength. It raised Ulyanov's gorge to see her prancing off on her horse with Lopukhin at her side for an evening's gallop through the forest, see her bend her head to Lopukhin's words as they strolled the streets of the town after morning drill in search of their afternoon's amusement, listen to her laugh at Lopukhin's witless jokes.

Alexandra and Lopukhin ate together, rode together, slept together.

He watched Lopukhin for signs of those tender attentions of the sort a lover pays to his beloved. There was no question of Lopukhin's preferences—he was manly through and through. But did he know what his quartermate really was? Had he, at some point during the night while the countess slept snugly in her bed, crept across the floor to lift the blanket to uncover what was underneath? Had Lopukhin indeed discovered her woman-hood and profited from his proximity and her naivete? Had he plucked her tender flower for himself?

I'll die, I'll die, Ulyanov thought. And then I'll kill him!

Lopukhin himself, enjoying Alexandra's company more than that of any other friend he'd ever had, was puzzled by Ulyanov's seeming hostility toward him. Since the tragedy, the captain had not joined in the drinking games and filthy songs at evening mess, but at least he had been civil, mildly pleasant if distracted, and—though silent and locked inside himself—amiable in his way. Now, the captain sat brooding, glowering, radiating disapproval from his position at the table's head and aiming it directly at Lopukhin. What had he done to attract the captain's enmity?

"It's the most peculiar thing," Lopukhin said to Alexandra as he undressed for bed one evening in their little room at the top of the widow's house, while Alexandra, fully dressed, fiddled with something in her sabretache while lying on her bed. Naked, he threw himself on his bed, and one-handed, stuffed his pillow under his head with that masculine dexterity that still fascinated Alexandra and which she worked at trying to duplicate herself. "Ulyanov has changed. We used to worship him. Not only was he in on everything, he was the leader. That vow he made after the tragedy, saying he'd sleep with every woman that he met— how we admired him for that! That's the way a man should be! Not letting women slow him down, or frighten him with their emotions, or manipulate him into giving up his freedom. That a woman would go so far as to kill herself to punish him for not giving her what she wanted! How foolish of her! What did she accomplish? Killing *him* would have been so much better, but women never think of that—though, come to think of it, I think a few have tried. Anyway, he got right back on the horse again, and he was really going strong. The servant girls, the peas-

ant girls, the married women in every town. You should have
seen him in action. You could have learned. I forget what the
tally was, but Babbish kept chalking it up on the wall at the
mess, and let me tell you, when we saw those numbers change—
it was inspirational. A great way to start the day. And
now . . . you see for yourself. It's been months since the tragedy,
and he's not getting any better. He's going in the wrong direction, getting worse. I'm worried about him."

Alexandra, amused, wasn't sure which was the more humor-
ous—the fact that Ulyanov was reacting so beautifully to her
small revenge at his presumption, to her utter indifference to
him and her clearly demonstrated preference for the company of
Lopukhin, or the fact that Lopukhin still hadn't noticed what
stared him in the face every morning and every night. Hadn't it
occurred to him that his quartermate never undressed in front of
him? Lopukhin himself paraded his nakedness shamelessly before
her, pissed happily into the chamber pot while talking, and never
even removed the cheroot from his mouth. This was masculine
behavior, aggressively immodest, and, from the way he'd talked
about the suicide of that poor peasant girl, tough-minded, rough
in feeling. It must be this roughness of sensibility and this self-
centeredness, along with the aggression of which they were so
proud, that had led to the success of their sex. Their selfishness
was lordly, magnificent, the engine of their power, she supposed.
Egotism was their secret, exaltation of the self. No wonder
women had achieved so little—not valuing themselves, they were
always sacrificing themselves for others, deferring, standing in
the background.

She turned on her side, supporting her head on her hand,
and enjoyed the sight of Lopukhin's splendid nakedness, the
rawness of masculine power displayed so carelessly on the other
bed in the form of thick, long bone and muscle.

Lopukhin had lit a cigarette and was smoking thoughtfully. His marvelous chest went up and down.

"There's something else. I don't know if I'm imagining it, but he seems to be directing some ill will in my direction. I don't know what I've done."

Oh, it was working very well. But she really oughtn't to have used Lopukhin in this way. He was really a rather sweet fellow in his way, if not terribly perceptive, and she hadn't intended to harm the friendship of the lieutenant with his captain, warm relationships between officers being so necessary to the cohesion of the squadron. She felt it was her duty as an officer to try to put this right.

However, Alexandra had little opportunity to do so. Over the next few weeks, she saw little of Ulyanov as she went about her duties, learning more, growing stronger, imbibing more deeply the manly ethos, becoming more manly herself. With her platoon, she practiced rifle shooting at the gallop—a straw-stuffed target was set up for the men to try to puncture with their bullets on approach or slice at with their swords as they went flying past it on their horses. She went scouting after the enemy (a platoon of Russian infantry) as she and her men, their horses concealed in a culvert, hung in the branches of trees watching breathless and trying not to laugh as the infantry trudged beneath them and didn't notice she had used the very oldest trick of all—placing broken branches in the path underneath the trees so that the infantry in passing beneath would bend over to break apart the web of roots and grass and branches, or, swearing, kick the obstructing tangle apart, too distracted to look up to see the eyes that stared down at them from a perch not far above.

There was picket duty as well—a system of sentinels spread out across the landscape, small detachments of men clumped near the bottom of rising breasts of land to watch for spies, enemy scouts, and surreptitious movements of opposing troops under cover of dark, for black silhouettes against the lighter dark of night. Alexandra, sitting on the ground near her pacing sentries, pulled tufts of grass and chewed them, savoring their bitter green flavor, and, throwing herself back on the ground, stared up at the stars. She wondered what she could do to repair relations between Ulyanov and her quartermate. Clearly Ulyanov was jealous, but why? Was he really still in love with her? Or did he simply envy Lopukhin the company of the only female in the troop, womanizer that Ulyanov was, addicted to the scent of feminine flesh, gatherer of unwanted hearts? Whatever the reason for the captain's jealousy, Alexandra enjoyed tormenting him with her intimacy with the handsome Lopukhin. In the distance, wolves howled. In winter they would come closer, but not now.

The regiment was moving out again, back toward the city. On the way home, the men would camp in the countryside, learning to live off the land. Alexandra clung easily now to Hercules' back as they marched, and, while the chorus sang, she found that she could shut her ears and drowse in the morning air beneath the trees, the saddle rocking her to sleep and the sounds of the horses and men, creaking saddles, jangling bits of metal fading. Around her many other men were sleeping on the march, their chins bouncing softly on their breasts.

When the trumpet blew a halt she opened her eyes. The sun was directly overhead, its heat pressing on her head like a weight. She removed the shako and wiped at her forehead with her arm, scraping her wet hair. "Right turn, walk, march." Her squadron began to make its way across a field, and in the distance bits of white glitter showed where water was. They were stopping to water the horses, to feed the men. Insects chattered in the dry September grass.

Under the overhanging trees at the edge of the river it was cool. She rode through the shadows and into the water, where she felt between her legs Hercules' belly grow plumper with the water from the stream. Her legs wet to the thigh, she rode him up onto the bank and dismounted, leaving him to his meal of grass. But Hercules, seeking horsy company, wandered over to another large black horse whose giant head, his muscular neck stretched to its limit, was straining at the grass near a hussar who was sitting by himself in the shadows. It was Ulyanov.

There was no one about—the others had chosen a spot farther down the river for their horses, and Alexandra hesitated, watching him. He was tearing clumps of grass from the ground and throwing them with a fierce jerk of the arm into the river before him. Alexandra crept closer, making her way quietly through the grass. Although she was nearly upon him, Ulyanov had not seemed to notice her and went on throwing those clumps of grass into the water. She cleared her throat to announce her presence, but Ulyanov did not look up.

Alexandra squatted down beside him, her boots creaking.

"It's a good day, Captain," she said, "not too hot for the men."

Ulyanov did not answer her. He sighed deeply, as if irritated at the interruption of his summer's idyll at the river. He dropped his chin and rested his arms on the tops of his knees, his hands hanging loosely, relaxed, from his wrists. Alexandra had never noticed the size of his hands before, though she remembered the grip of his fingers around her wrist. She envied him his hands, with their prominent bones, bunchings of muscle, light dusting of hair, massive spread of palm. Her own were pale and thin and narrow, and she wondered if even after many years of exercise in the gripping of reins against the straining heads of horses, in the handling of heavy rifles, in the wielding of the weighty saber, they wouldn't look just the same as always—weak and undeveloped.

Alexandra, still squatting, moved herself closer to him and sat down, imitating his elegant posture, the casual posing of arm upon the knee, the loose hanging of the hands.

"Do you think the men will do well tonight in the exercise at foraging?" she said. "I think they will. They're fine men, all of them, and unit cohesion is excellent, don't you think? Don't you think unit cohesion the most important thing, Captain? The men's ability to cooperate with one another, to move and think in one body? It's the same with the officers, though, don't you think?" Alexandra was heading toward the topic of Lopukhin, determined to put things right. As much as she was enjoying her game, she had resolved to stop this childishness and leave Lopukhin alone. It was not military, not manly at all to use a fellow officer that way. She was just considering her next move in the conversation she was having by herself, Ulyanov not even grunting in acknowledgment at her words, when—she would never know how he had done it so quickly, so unexpectedly, a secret of that masculine dexterity to rank with the ability to build bridges and disengage a bra-clasp with the fingers of one hand—she suddenly found herself lying on her back in Ulyanov's arms, her head gently held away from the hard ground in the palm of that giant hand, the captain looking down at her. She was too startled to speak. His breath was warm on her face, and the rich masculine scent of him, with its spicy undertone of hormones, penetrated her nose, soothing her as if it were a soporific, making her eyelids heavy. She closed them.

Her lips had opened softly in surprise—just what Ulyanov was hoping for. He kissed her hard and smiled against her mouth when he felt her arms creep shyly round his neck. Breaking away, he looked down at her with an impudent smile, and dumped her in the dirt.

Mouth still open and wet with what he had left there, Alexandra, from her position on the ground, turned her head to watch him as he strode to his mount in his long shiny boots, inserted his foot into the stirrup, and swung himself into the saddle.

"Break's over, Cornet," he said. "Mount and ride on." Digging his spurs into his horse's rotund belly (the animal reared up dashingly at the sudden discomfort), he galloped off with the empty arms of his pelisse flying out behind him.

The regiment rode on until dark. Autumn was in the air, the white nights turning black so the stars were visible again, a dusting of brilliant snow across the sky portending the real snow soon to come. Alexandra, mounted on Hercules and picking her way across the broad field of the encampment, looked up at the stars and noted a sudden mysterious significance in them. She rode past hussars who already lay snoring by the shifting flames of their cooking fires, their faces glowing, asleep with chunks of bread, uneaten, in their sleep-loosened fists, while others, gathered round charred tin pots, five or six to the pot in that communal style of the Russian peasant, were eating boiled buckwheat with rough tin spoons. Some didn't bother with the spoons but reached in with their hands to coat their fingers with the sticky kernels and stuff them in their mouths. Gusts of laughter came from the gatherings of men, from the wordless streams of talk that flowed along the ground where they sat. Alexandra chose a spot as far away from Ulyanov as she could, dismounted from Hercules, lay down on the ground, and wrapped herself in her greatcoat to await a restless, troubled sleep.

It was the custom for a batman to live with the officer he attended in order to serve him most efficiently. How else was he to care properly for the boots, to clean and polish the leather progressively more scarred? To detach the crusts of mud from heel and spur? To see that his officer's uniforms were properly cleaned and pressed, though not too much, therefore preserving a dashing carelessness? To keep track of gloves and linen handkerchiefs and brushes, razors and combs and hair pomade? And accomplish a thousand other tasks to keep his officer up and running, up to speed?

However, it had not occurred to Alexandra that Nikifor would expect to live with her. So, on arriving back in Petersburg after the long march down from the northern roads above the capital and climbing up the steps of her palace on the Neva, she was disturbed, embarrassed, to find that Nikifor was right behind her, carrying in her things and *his* from the cab they had taken from the barracks in the center of the city where they had left their horses.

While knocking at her own tremendous front door, she wondered how she would feed him, where she would put him to sleep, and how she would keep Praskovia from opening her big mouth in front of the batman and letting the secret slip.

Praskovia, opening both the door and her big mouth all at once, gave Alexandra not a moment for a greeting before she blurted out with anger-reddened face, "She's back and she's pregnant!"

"Who?" asked Alexandra, too distracted at that moment to make the obvious connection.

"That Matryona thing, that's who!"

"Oh God," said Alexandra, forgetting that Nikifor was right behind her with the bags. "Where is she?"

"In the kitchen, stuffing herself!"

Alexandra pushed past Praskovia, leaving her to deal with Nikifor, who was stepping meekly now inside the hallway. She ran to the back of the palace, to the kitchen where she found Matryona, no mistake, seated in splendid state in the one comfortable, padded chair the palace still possessed. Spread out around her on the table was an assortment of delicacies—pickled fish, a cold roast chicken already missing its legs, dishes of pancakes and sour cream, sugary fruit preserves—from which Matryona was helping herself with such gusto that she did not even bother to acknowledge the arrival of her mistress. She sat fatly in her chair, popping a pancake into her mouth.

"Where's my money," Alexandra said, "and what have you done with my things?"

"Eaten," said Matryona cheerfully, licking her chubby fingers to emphasize her point. "We ate it up, all of it. We had a good time."

"I can see that," said Alexandra, eyeing the bulge in Matryona's middle, which prevented her from thrashing the servant thoroughly. "And where is Istvan? Is he back too?"

"Who knows? Gone back to Budapest, I think. When we ran out of money, he left me. So I came home."

Crowding up behind her mistress in the doorway of the kitchen, Praskovia put her two cents in. "A thief! A thief! I always knew it! I always said it, little countess! Look at how she stuffs her mouth!"

"Shush!" said Alexandra, turning on Praskovia. "And where did she get it, then? Who gave her all this food? Expensive food? I ought to beat you too!"

Praskovia threw her apron over her face and wailed through the cloth, "It's for the little one! It's for the little one, not her!"

Matryona, unassailable behind her bulge, smiled with satisfaction. In her war with Praskovia, she had triumphed once again. She looked up slyly at her mistress. "So what's with the getup?" she said. "And another thing. When are you going to sell this place so we can all live a little better? Giving yourself airs. You're not the Countess Korvin anymore the way you used to be!"

Alexandra went toward her, making threatening noises with her boots against the kitchen floor, with the rattling of her saber as she walked. Desperate to strike the woman, she satisfied herself by snatching the new embroidered kerchief from her head. "You shut your mouth," she said, "or you'll find yourself out in the street where you belong, with all the others walking it."

Praskovia rushed to Matryona's side. "How dare you say such things to her!" she screamed, stroking reverently the swollen belly while glaring in Alexandra's direction. "This is her home. She has a right to be here. She has a right to our help, and especially our food, as much as we can give her. And she's right. You ought to sell this place. How long can we go on scraping up a living from the street now that we've got another mouth to feed? Two!"

"For that?" cried Alexandra, pointing at the pregnancy. "I ought to sell this place for that? And who are you to tell me what to do? Just who are you? I own you!"

"That's right, you do," said Praskovia, sticking out her chin as if it were a weapon, "and just for that reason you should sell it. You owe it to us. It's your duty to provide for us."

"Never!" cried Alexandra, unexpectedly wounded by this point, which landed on her conscience like a cannonball, blowing a hole in her resolve.

"Then stop parading around pretending you're a man and get us a real one, one with money," Praskovia sensibly replied. "One or the other."

"Neither," said Alexandra. "I will do what I want."

"Selfish!" Praskovia hurled the stinging word.

"Impertinent. Presumptuous," hissed Alexandra.

"Perhaps," said Nikifor mildly from the doorway, from which he had witnessed the entire scene, "your honor would like to check his mail. You've been away for weeks. I am sure you must have received some important communications, perhaps from abroad, or something urgent needing your immediate attention."

It was clear to Alexandra now that Praskovia and Matryona had allied against her and cooked up this argument for selling off her birthright. No, no, no! She would not. She was still the Countess Korvin, and she would not lower herself in her own eyes or the eyes of others to climb down onto a lower rung of status to join those impoverished nobles who lived just barely, frugally, scraping a living from the land of some obscure provincial farm. She would find another way, but what? To go back to the marriage market was unthinkable. To corset herself again in womanly subservience, the constraints of femininity? Never!

I am a soldier, she protested to herself. But then again, unlikely to remain one (the thought landing on her like another cannonball) if Nikifor, who surely guessed by now her secret, her entire predicament spread out before him in this kitchen, a banquet of delicious gossip fodder, were to go and tell. And how indeed to stop him?

But Nikifor, standing impassive in the doorway, behaved as if he had noticed nothing.

"Your honor," he said, still insistent upon his former point, "surely you would like to see your mail. And if I myself were aware of where it was, I would fetch it for you myself. Failing this, of course," he went on, gesturing in Praskovia's direction, "perhaps your honor's . . ." He searched for the perfect word and, politically-minded as he was, located it. "Perhaps your aunt would indicate to me . . ."

It worked. Praskovia, delighted at her social promotion, which vaulted her way past her rival Matryona (aunt to the countess!), scurried out of the kitchen to find the mail while Alexandra, suddenly relieved of all her tension and ready to forgive, called after her, "We'll manage somehow, Praskovia, and Matryona can have all she wants to eat."

Nikifor now settled everything. Having first so skillfully intervened to halt the escalating quarrel between the mistress and her servants (and of course he had known it all along, that his master was a mistress), he accompanied Alexandra to her study up the stairs, declining diplomatically to comment on the depredation of what he recognized had once been a palace of magnificence and, once there, knelt to remove her boots, stood to unstrap the saber and sabretache from beneath her lifted arms, and settled her into a chair. Then he proceeded downstairs again, where he collected from the now flustered and flirty Praskovia both tea and mail and delivered both promptly to his officer, who, relaxing gratefully in her chair, accepted them with eagerness.

"But Nikifor," she said, "I must explain—"

"No explanation, sir," he said, snapping his heels together in salute. "I serve my officer in whatever way that officer might need."

"And your discretion . . ."

"My discretion has never been questioned," he said, "or my loyalty."

"Dismissed," said Alexandra, smiling, "and see if Praskovia can't find you something to eat before that Matryona eats it all herself. I know Praskovia won't stop her."

So that was settled, at least for now, she thought. Nikifor was no danger to her secret, and anyway, it was good to have him. She turned to her mail, of which there was a thick pile. Sipping at her tea, she began to open it.

Invitations. Invitations from those who had never been informed of her "departure for the west of Europe" or who had forgotten. Invitations to balls and teas and afternoon receptions, to weekends at country houses and evenings at the theater. Invitations from people she was certain she had never even met, representing the impersonal quality of social life in Petersburg among the aristocracy. And these social events had taken place in a world she had stepped out of, as if she had stepped off the earth itself and were now inhabiting another planet entirely, the life on earth going on without her.

She opened another envelope. But this was not an invitation.

My dear Countess Korvin, it began, *we have met only briefly, but that meeting has remained in my mind and grown these many months since.*

Alexandra's eyes skipped to the signature. A disappointment there. It was signed *From one who loves you more than life itself.* The hand was not one she recognized, and certainly not Ulyanov's. In any case, Ulyanov's effort in this direction (*I love you,* signed Ulyanov) had been pathetically short and woefully unimaginative and, she now knew for certain after the insulting incident on the riverbank, utterly insincere, which was clearly why he had taken so little trouble with it. This one, dripping with maudlin sincerity, contained an entire paragraph.

But wait! Could it be? Could Rybynsky be declaring himself at last? So often she had tried to tell herself she had forgotten him, but he still lived on in a corner of her mind, impossibly cool and perfect, an avatar of happiness, success, transcendence of the ordinary world. With suddenly trembling fingers she turned the folded letter over, looking for an address. There was none. However, the paper on which this missive had been written was thick and fine, a soft eggshell color, exactly the sort of paper her father had used, exactly the sort a man of Rybynsky's discrimination might choose as well.

Heart soaring, she unfolded the letter again and smoothed it tenderly with her palm.

My dear, she read again, then skipped down the letter to where she'd left off. *You tower like a proud and powerful oak tree in the forest of my thoughts.* Oh dear. Not like Rybynsky at all. Herself an oak tree? Wouldn't a graceful birch have been better, cliché that it was? The man was clearly no poet. *Please forgive my presumption in addressing you directly, but my heart and mind are so full of you that the festering boil of these emotions must be drained onto the page. This letter is my lancet! I have been told that you are presently residing in the west of Europe, and I can only hope that my letter will reach you there so that the soil of your heart might begin to prepare itself to receive the seeds of my love on your return and create a beautiful flower that will blossom to the sun of my heart.*

"Ick" said Alexandra. Rybynsky would certainly not be guilty of this vulgar sentiment, this outrageous lack of taste, this clumsiness of style. No, this was not from Rybynsky, but most likely written by some anonymity she had encountered at one of the tea dances, receptions, balls, cotillions, card parties, or evenings after the theater to which she had been sentenced during that last Petersburg season, which now seemed so far away.

She tossed the letter onto the pile of other opened letters. Then she picked it up and read it again. Then tossed it aside again and returned to the unopened pile.

More invitations. And then one letter whose handwriting she recognized. Having peeled it open, she read the following message:

Darling Alyusha, I am so unhappy. When do you return from abroad? What I must tell you I cannot set to paper. Your Olga.

Oh, the vicious irony of it!

Unhappy? Why? So far as Alexandra was concerned, Olga should be the most satisfied, most contented of women. Safe in the glitter of her palace, married to Rybynsky, in a position to bask in the glory of his magnificent intellect and figure, to be in his presence constantly, and in his bed! How dare she be unhappy! Alexandra jumped up and began to pace about the room. Her eye fell on the teacup she had been drinking from. The rim of the cup had a chip out of it, as if some tiny creature had taken a bite, some rodent perhaps, one of those vermin who creep in through forgotten crevices to escape the cold and settle in as companion animals to destitution, as familiars of the poor. How long before the rats had gnawed her palace to a pile of dust? Its entrails had been eaten out of it already; how long before it crumbled to the ground? She stormed toward the teacup, wanting to smash it, but her anger made her clumsy, and the sharp corner of a small and rickety table, too old, too worn to sell, dug at her thigh. She kicked it, sent it crashing into the wall. The teacup followed, shattering in shards upon the floor.

The letter from her secret lover. He must be rich if he had known her from before. She snatched it from the desk and looked at it again.

From one who loves you more than life itself.

It was not long before Alexandra discovered the identity of this secret lover as Countess Belkin's brother, the one who had been warned against her, as she'd heard in eavesdropping that very night she'd cut her hair. Alexandra ran into him one evening standing in front of the palace looking up at it just as she, having finished with her regimental duties and returned to the palace for her nap, was leaving again for an evening of carousing with Lopukhin. They were to meet at Szekely's, a Gypsy place, and she was late. Pulling on her gloves, she had reached the bottom of the steps when a gentleman standing near her coughed politely.

"Excuse me, Lieutenant," he said, failing to remove his hat, as men did always now when greeting her, "but are you acquainted with the Korvin family? I see you coming from the Korvin palace. Are you perhaps acquainted with the countess?" No wonder she'd had trouble remembering who he was. He was below average in every way—diminutive in height, deficient in good looks, too deferential in deportment. The sort of man she would never have taken notice of. "Forgive me for accosting you so boldly, but I simply must know. I have seen you come and go from here quite frequently, so forgive my presumption in asking so personal a question on such short acquaintance, but are you by any chance the countess's fiancé?"

Alexandra wanted to laugh both at his stilted speech and the idea that she might be her own fiancé, but she stifled the impulse and answered him decidedly in the negative. "Not likely," she said, catching at a bright idea she was sure would answer any suspicions he might have about the resemblance between the countess and herself, "since I am her first cousin."

The little man, who had been twisting his hands in anxiety, laughed and, much to her relief, thrust his hands into his pockets. Nervous men made Alexandra nervous.

"Aha," he cried, "just come to join your regiment, I see!" He was instantly cheerful, eager to make friends. He grabbed her hand and shook it violently. "My name is Durinov. Might I invite you to dine with me sometime?"

Insignificant as he seemed, and disappointed as she was to find her secret lover unattractive, he was definitely rich. He had that in his favor at least. And how better to evaluate a future husband than to see him when he does not know that he is being seen? "No time like the present," said Alexandra. "Are you engaged tonight? I am dining with a fellow officer. I am sure he would be pleased to meet you."

"Gladly," said Durinov.

They hailed a cab, one not too ostentatious (Alexandra had learned old Colonel Spirkin's rules of conduct well), and on the way to the restaurant Durinov could not stop himself from raising the subject of the countess.

"You live inside her palace," said Durinov, looking intently at Alexandra, "it must smell of her."

"Too big," said Alexandra, taking out a case of cigars and offering one to her new acquaintance, who, sunk so deep in his love for his companion, did not even respond to the offer of a smoke from her.

"You can see her things, though. The nightgown that she wears."

"I would never enter the room of a lady uninvited, especially when she is not at home."

"Ah," said Durinov, "I forget you are her cousin. You would be immune to her attractions."

"Most definitely," said Alexandra, striking a match on the bottom of her boot and hearing the delightful snap and sizzle as the sulfur-treated head took flame. She had practiced this a lot when alone in her room and was satisfied she did it rather skilfully.

"But tell me, is it me, or is she not the most beautiful creature walking on the earth?"

"I never thought of her as beautiful," answered Alexandra,

puffing on her rather cheap cigar, but pleased. It was quite true. She never had. Like many women, she saw only her faults and flaws and, furthermore, could not see what any man could see in any women—all bumps and bulges, they were. "Tell me, "she said, eager to acquaint herself with this aspect of masculine taste, "what is it you find so beautiful? I've always thought she was too tall, a bit awkward, gawky. Haven't you noticed the way she's always bending down to hide her height?"

"Blasphemy!" said Durinov. "She is a goddess! If you were not her cousin and therefore entitled to be critical, I would challenge you!"

Oh my, thought Alexandra, was he serious? Would he really fight a duel over this? Though she had lived intimately with males for the past six weeks, studied them as specimens in order to better imitate their ways, their minds were definitely still a mystery to her.

"And there's her hair," she continued, enjoying baiting him. "It's too straight."

"A skein of raw and undyed silk."

Alexandra grimaced at the ungainly simile and went on teasing. "Her skin could be a little clearer. She eats too many sweets."

"It's alabaster."

"Don't you think her . . . perhaps not well-endowed enough?"

"They're small, I agree, but quite perfect. I would die to worship them with my lips."

By God, she thought, did men really think of women in this way? *Worship them with his lips?* She herself could not imagine worshiping anyone, except perhaps for Rybynsky, and certainly not with her lips. However, she had to admit she found it rather sweet—if only his metaphors were more original.

"I think *alabaster* is too common a term to describe her skin," she said, hoping to urge him into further testimonials with the greed for compliments that would have betrayed her femininity had Durinov been quicker on the uptake. "Everyone uses that. I think you can do better."

Durinov wrinkled his forehead. "Ivory."

"I've heard that one before."

"Milk."

"That's better," said Alexandra, "but isn't it a bit pedestrian, mundane?"

Durinov, however, who was not so foolish as she'd thought, now stared at her as if understanding were breaking in his brain like day. Abandoning his inadequate attempts to describe Alexandra's beauty, he gazed at the countess herself with a rapt concentration that made her uncomfortable to say the least.

"Karpatsky," he said slowly as if hypnotized, "you bear a remarkable resemblance to the countess. Although of course there is that masculine roughness of feature, there still remains a certain purity, a delicacy . . ."

"Our mothers were twins," said Alexandra without missing a beat, and wanted to add that their fathers had been twins as well so that she might make the remarkable resemblance all the more convincing, but she decided that even Durinov was bright enough not to believe it and closed her mouth with a snap before she went too far and ruined everything.

"Aha! That explains it," said Durinov, nodding. However, as if unsatisfied by this explanation, or rather further intrigued, he leaned forward and squinted, peering at his companion through narrowed eyes as if hoping to remold Alexandra's actual features into the idealized perfection that existed only in his mind.

"By looking at you, I feel I can almost see her," he said, eyes squeezed to slits and the straining of the muscles lifting his upper lip to uncover glistening gums in which were embedded the tops of tartar-encrusted teeth. He looked rather like a small and curious rat, which did not improve his suit.

But perhaps, thought Alexandra, thinking of his money, I should learn to be more flexible in my judgments. The countess's further ruminations on the subject of love and its remarkable blindness were interrupted by their arrival at the restaurant. Lopukhin was waiting out in front, pacing back and forth while smoking a fashionable gold-tipped cigarette imported from France and costing the earth—Alexandra knew because her father had smoked them. On seeing Alexandra jump down from the cab, Lopukhin threw the cigarette on the ground in a sputter of orange sparks and came toward her smiling.

"Who's your friend?" he asked, all warmth. Introductions made, they proceeded into the building, where Alexandra, expecting the luxury and chic of the England, the only restaurant in Petersburg she knew, encountered a hazy curtain of smoke inside the vestibule so thick she had to clear it with her hands in order to find her way.

What is this place, she wanted to ask, but did not, unwilling to reveal her ignorance of this seemingly seamier side of life. Eerie, melancholic music wailed, vaguely Asiatic in its origins, it seemed, as was the smoke itself, for, drinking deeply of its fragrance, she began to feel that her brain was swelling deliciously, puffing up like a cake that was rising in the oven, but lopsidedly, so that she walked that way too.

"Steady there, Karpatsky," said Lopukhin, reaching out to grab her elbow.

"What is that wonderful smell?" she asked when she was seated at the table, whose dirty cloth she failed to notice.

"Opium. But none for you, young fellow," said Lopukhin, and called for the menu, while Durinov eagerly continued his perorations on the attractions of Countess Alexandra Korvin.

"Ah yes," said Lopukhin, studying the greasy card, "I know her well."

"You do?" said Alexandra, suddenly snapping to attention, righting herself in her chair. Had he known it all along? Uncovered her secret? Just what had he been doing while she was sleeping across the room from him?

"Three szekely goulash, three roasted liver of goose and salads of preserved vegetables on the side, Tokay and champagne, but not in that order," said Lopukhin to the grinning waiter, who was missing two teeth. Lopukhin had rightly decided that his companions were in no condition to think for themselves at this moment, but he himself, well accustomed to the fumes of opium, which he and Ulyanov had used to smoke together, though that seemed very long ago, had kept his head nicely. He returned to the subject of the countess. "I shouldn't say I know her well. That was presumptuous of me, an exaggeration. I saw her here and there last season, was briefly introduced, but I never had the courage to speak to her again. She had looked at me like I was some kind of . . . insect. And turned her back on me. I don't know what I did. Except be me."

"I recently had the courage to declare my love to her," said Durinov, raising his chin with self-importance.

"I wish I had," said Lopukhin. "I thought she was rather beautiful, but unapproachable, untouchable, like a statue. You're a better man than I am, Durinov. What did she say?"

"No answer yet," said Durinov, "but I doubt my declaration has reached her. She is abroad, you know."

"I know," said Lopukhin, peeling a shred of tobacco from his tongue. "I called on her once at the palace. They told me that she had gone away. But of course I was foolish even to try. She's very rich, you know. I didn't stand a chance. I'm such a nobody. I could only love her from afar. Just being me was not enough."

Alexandra might have been incapable of clear thought, but not of feeling. Had she really treated this sweet young man so cruelly, disdainfully? She dropped her face into her hands, rubbing at it as if to restore the circulation in her skin, which seemed to have thickened, gone soft and numb. The opium had seeped into her stomach, and she felt she was going to vomit. The kindly Lopukhin, aware of her discomfort, whispered something to Durinov, called for the waiter, paid the bill though they had eaten nothing yet, and gently helped to raise the tottering figure from her chair.

Outside, the fresh night air rushed into her lungs and quickly reached her brain, clearing it somewhat of the addling, disorienting fumes. Lopukhin, still supporting her by the elbow, was encouraging her to walk it off, walk it off, not to be embarrassed, walk it off. But her face was white as much with distress at the pain she'd caused her friend as with the discomfort of intoxication.

"I'm so sorry, I'm so sorry," she repeated to Lopukhin, while Durinov hovered in the background, looking on with concern on his small, pallid face. She plucked at Lopukhin's sleeve repeatedly, trying to force him to comprehend her terrible regret. "Do you forgive me? Say it, please!"

"No need to apologize," said Lopukhin. "It could happen to any of us. You're just not used to it. I know the first time I tasted the opium it happened to me, but luckily the captain was there to help me walk it off. And now I'm doing the same for you, my brother officer. We help each other, see? And there's no judgment, none at all, no shame. Now let's get a carriage and go somewhere else, somewhere not so . . . difficult for you."

Alexandra sat down on the sidewalk.

"I won't move until you say you forgive me," she said, looking up at Lopukhin with tearstained cheeks. She hid her face against her knees.

Lopukhin, knowing that intoxication exaggerated the emotions, was not particularly surprised to see this outrageous display of penitence for transgressing the manly code by showing weakness. However, the boy was being difficult, intractable. With a squeaking of boots he squatted and spoke gently. "Karpatsky, get hold of yourself. You can't stay here. Get up. I'll help you."

Alexandra shrugged off the hand he had placed on her shoulder and, pushing out her lips sullenly, buried her face more deeply in her knees, her arms around her head.

"I know what," said Lopukhin, still squatting at her side, a hand on her back, stroking it. "I know where we'll go. It's time you became a man, my man."

It was not one of the better-class bordellos of St. Petersburg that Lopukhin, considerate of his companions' purses, led them to, but rather a third-rate whorehouse that catered to seedy government clerks and prosperous peasants who, visiting the capital for the first time in their lives, shied away from the more glittering establishments—with Russian humility, they declined to share a girl with a member of the classes above them, though they might have had just as many rubles in their purse, or more. Her head entirely clear now, Alexandra sat stiffly in a worn-out chair in the parlor of the brothel, her feet resting together on the floor as she stared at the shiny tops of her boots, adjusting and readjusting their position so that her toes were perfectly aligned, for she was too embarrassed to imitate the postures of the relaxed Lopukhin (a leg hanging over his chair), the eager Durinov (sitting up very straight, neck straining to get his eyes even closer), both of whom were eying with enthusiasm the selection of females that were ranged in front of them.

Afraid that the very sight of these pathetic women would

contaminate her virginal purity or turn her to stone as if they were monstrous Gorgons, Alexandra hesitated to raise her eyes and look at them. Certainly she had been aware of their existence in the world. Their presence was ubiquitous in the city, where they could be seen crossing the bridges over the canals in their flamboyant clothing—a deliberate assault on the eye—or walking on a gloomy winter's day carrying frilled parasols against the frozen sun, or warming their hands inside furry muffs in the wet heat of the city summer while raising their skirts far too high when crossing a puddle. With these unseasonable accessories, which were designed, along with their clothing's shouts of color, to draw attention to themselves, and their open lewdness in displaying legs and breasts, these creatures had always represented to her a reversal of the natural order, in which the female protected herself from the harassments of the predatory male by maintaining her modesty, not calling attention to herself at all.

The whores displayed themselves now in the parlor of the brothel more lewdly than Alexandra could have imagined. Fat breasts were bare, swelling out over the rim of their corsets like rising dough, and a few of the women, aggressively seeking custom, bent over to display the plumpness of their posteriors, which strained against their dirty linen, as did the faint dark outline of their genitals, swollen as if these creatures were monkeys in a zoo. One woman spread her legs and touched herself between them. Alexandra tried to breathe as shallowly as possible, reluctant to draw into the bottom of her lungs the air that had shortly before been in theirs.

"Come, come now," said Durinov, patting her thigh, "make your choice. I see a lovely mademoiselle right there who seems to like you." Breathing oddly in his excitement, he pointed at a girl who sat, skirts hiked over her skinny thighs, at a small table,

leaning her elbow on it, resting her cheek on her hand and gazing at Alexandra with an expression of curiosity. Her hair was a
faded blond, as if she'd never had enough to eat to bring the
color out. "I myself will take that luscious fat brunette. How her
thighs must squeeze! I'll bet she could break me right in two."

"Shut up," said Lopukhin to Durinov, "you'll frighten him.
It's practice in love, Karpatsky," he said, turning to Alexandra,
hoping to reassure his friend, "nothing to be frightened of.
Someday you'll fall in love and marry. You need to know what
you're supposed to do. To show your love."

Alexandra was too distressed to reply to Lopukhin, who had
already rated the young Karpatsky, who seemed affronted by
this display of female flesh, as a prude. He so hoped he was not
the other. Not that there was anything wrong with that (the
Russian upper classes were extremely tolerant of all forms of
erotic irregularity), but Lopukhin knew that unusual tastes—if
Karpatsky had them—would form a barrier between himself and
his friend, inhibit their companionship, so much of which was
based, in young men, on the swapping of stories of amorous
exploits. Or perhaps Karpatsky was a religious boy, or one who
took his ideals of love too seriously. Perhaps he was just afraid.
In any case, Lopukhin did not care to pursue these complicated
speculations. The breasts on display, plump pillows he wished to
burrow into, were far too distracting. He was eager to get on.

"Nothing to be frightened of," he whispered to Alexandra,
leaning closer. "They're really very nice. And no matter what
happens, remember, they won't laugh at you. They'll understand.
Women are so good that way. They always understand."

"If you pay them," said Alexandra.

But Lopukhin merely laughed and said, "Of course!"

"We're wasting time. Let's get to them," said Durinov, revealing an unattractive sensual greed that virtually finished off his

suit so far as Alexandra was concerned. She was deeply, deeply disappointed in her friends, in men in general. It seemed to her that their vaunted courtliness, their tender solicitousness toward ladies, were sham, and the thousands of years' worth of sonnets and odes in adoration of women's purity, in exaltation of love, were nothing but a hypocritical shield for rutting crudeness and raw lust.

"Durinov's right," said Lopukhin, getting to his feet, "we're wasting time. We haven't even eaten yet, and once we get this over with, I know a Viennese place where the schnitzel is good."

Ah, thought Alexandra, no more talk of "love," but only of "getting it over with," as if this were some physical function like brushing one's teeth or eliminating bodily waste. But of course there was nothing Lopukhin or Durinov could have said to assuage her anger now, seeing as she did from the other side the realities of certain aspects of the male. She watched as first Durinov, then Lopukhin left the room, not even holding hands with the prostitutes they had chosen, but herding them like sheep, with hands upon their backs.

Seeing that she had no intention of selecting one of them, the other prostitutes, unchosen and therefore off duty now, dropped their petticoats over their knees, buttoned up their chemises to conceal their breasts, and began to chatter amongst themselves as eagerly as schoolgirls whose teacher has just left the room. Alexandra was astonished at their resemblance to ordinary human beings, and she stared at them openly. She saw that they were not naturally lewd and immodest. Clearly, they degraded themselves only in order to attract their customers. Why? What was there in this degradation that men found so alluring? Alexandra supposed there must be something deep in the male psyche that required the desecration and disrespect of womanhood in order to "salt the loaf." Perhaps she had the answer, it occurred to her. Remembering the savagery with which marauding wolves were mutilated when the peasants were able to capture them, how the serfs took pleasure in crushing the pointed heads and slashing open the starving bellies to drag out entrails and arrange them in comical shapes, Alexandra wondered if this impulse toward degradation might have something to do with fear. What is feared must be humbled, its power to alarm neutralized, destroyed, ridiculed. Perhaps this was why men enjoyed women's degradation. But what was woman's power to alarm them? Why would they fear women so much, if they did? We're all quite harmless, she thought. Certainly not so savage and dangerous as they are themselves. Gentle creatures, all of us.

Alexandra was so absorbed in these thoughts that she did not notice that the young blond girl had risen from her seat and was heading toward her.

"Come," said the girl, "they've paid. You needn't do anything you don't want to, but if you don't come with me, I'll have to give the money back." There was such pleading in her voice that Alexandra could not refuse. She rose from her seat and followed the girl up a set of squeaking stairs to a hallway lined with rooms from behind whose doors she heard the creaking of bedsprings, and muffled murmurings, an occasional shriek or loud grunt. Opening the door to one of the rooms, the prostitute ushered Alexandra inside and closed the door behind them.

A chair—once richly upholstered in silk, now shredded and stained with age—and a bed were the only furniture in the room. Alexandra watched the girl lift a large towel that had lain folded on the end of the bed and spread it out across the middle of the mattress.

"What's that for?" said Alexandra, hoping it was not for what she thought.

"Oh, to keep it clean," said the girl, sitting down on the bed, which creaked obscenely under even her minimal weight. Alexandra wondered if the bedsprings had been weakened by vigorous use or whether the bed had been made that way deliberately, for reasons she did not wish to think about. "We can't go changing sheets throughout the day. It would cost the earth!" said the girl, laughing nervously as if to mask her obvious embarrassment. This girl was clearly no embodiment of evil, only beaten and poor. Her half-exposed breasts, no luscious offering, were shrunken, and her bared clavicles showed the gougings of starvation.

Alexandra, not knowing what else to do, carefully took a seat in the battered old chair, wanting to wipe it first, but not wishing to embarrass the girl further.

"May I ask you a question?" said Alexandra.

"Certainly," said the girl, still sitting on the bed but grasping at the bedpost and raising her shoulders apprehensively, as if expecting a demand for some particularly eccentric form of pleasure which might involve some pain to herself, but still submissive to the possibility. Her eyes were mild.

"Why do you do this? You seem . . ." Alexandra did not know how to express it. She did not wish to insult the girl, but truly wanted to know. "You seem better than this. Why?"

"To help my family," said the girl quickly, as if desiring Alexandra's good opinion.

"Aren't there other ways?" asked Alexandra, suspecting that there weren't.

"There are, but they pay no more than fifteen kopecks a day, you know, and that wouldn't be enough. I tried it for a while. I made some linen shirts. I made six of them. But Klopstock, the civil councilor, never paid me anyway. He said I did the collars wrong. And the children were hungry. But it's not so bad, please don't think I'm bad."

"I don't think you're bad," said Alexandra as kindly as she

could, and this kindness seemed to break some barrier inside the girl, who now began to babble, pouring out her story.

"I didn't want to. I tried so hard not to. You mustn't think I'm bad. Darya Frantsova tried to get at me for months, to get me to do it, but I resisted, I resisted her so hard. And then one night my stepmother went at me too. My mother died, you know, and then my father married her. She's a lady, a fine lady, and made for better things, but my father drinks too much, and he can't keep a job, and I know my stepmother meant no harm, but she couldn't bear it any longer to hear the children crying for something to eat, and one night she said to me, 'Here you live with us, you eat and drink and are kept warm, and you do nothing to help!' and I said to her, 'Katerina Ivanovna, am I really to do a thing like that?' and she said, 'And why not? Are you something mighty precious to be careful of?' and I realized she was right. The children, there are three of them, they were so hungry and I thought, what is so precious about my body that I could let these children starve? It's only what you do when you are married. And don't we women marry to get money in the first place? So what's the difference? See, it isn't bad!"

Alexandra could not help but concede the legitimacy of this position. She herself had some doubts about the efficacies of marrying for money, but she had never seen the case for the link between the two stated quite so baldly. We are not so very different after all, thought Alexandra—wasn't Praskovia getting after her for much the very same reason after all? Asking her to sell her body in marriage to a man with money? At the sight of the dirty bed with the towel over it, designed to catch what she didn't want to think about, Alexandra shivered, thought: how long before she herself was reduced to such as this?

"But how do you stand it? How do you stand to be touched by them?"

"It's not so bad," said the girl. "Most of them try to be kind. They try very hard. They are ordinary men, no better or worse than any other, not evil, not bad. But they can't help themselves. They seem to need it in a way that we don't. To find some relief in it. It's hard for us women to understand."

It occurred to Alexandra suddenly that this girl was speaking to her as a woman. "Us women," she had said, as if she knew the truth.

"Tell me, do you know . . . ?"

"Oh, I knew it right away!" The girl laughed at her own cleverness. "If there's one thing I've gotten to know, it's men. And I knew right away that you weren't one of them. It was in your face, you know, the way you looked at us, as if you wanted nothing from us, and they're always wanting something. Not you, though."

"What is it that they want?" asked Alexandra, suddenly delighted to have made this friend, who could tell her so many things she wanted to know.

"I don't think it's what they think they want," said the girl, who had gathered herself up on the bed and was hugging her ragged knees, excited at this chance to talk, "They think they come for pleasure, but they really come to us for love."

"Love!" said Alexandra, leaping from her chair in a rattling of spurs and saber and other metallic devices hanging from her belt. "What's this got to do with love? It's animal!"

"But aren't we animals anyway after all?" said the girl, climbing down off the bed and approaching Alexandra, who towered over her, her very height the result of generations' worth of opulent nutrition, the girl's tiny size a legacy of poverty. "Don't be upset. You have to try to understand. Sometimes I feel them trying to bury themselves in me, to escape their griefs and disappointments. I try to comfort them with closeness. The world is hard and cold, but a woman's flesh is soft. I give them love the best I can. It's the only thing that makes it bearable for me, to think of it this way." She took Alexandra by the hand and led her back to the chair and made her sit. "I can tell you are a lady," she said. "You must sit and I must stand. But may I ask you why you're dressed like that?"

Alexandra, warmed by this luminous soul, began to pour out her own story. She told everything—her father's death, her poverty, the humiliation of Kolygin's defection, Rybynsky's rejection, the theft of her property, and her subsequent discovery of the freedom to be had in the guise of a man. It was good to have a woman to talk to. She thought of Olga suddenly. However, in the telling of her troubles, they dwindled as she compared them with the girl's, and what she had felt as the grandeur of her aspirations to worldly wealth and personal freedom dwindled too, into something quite trivial and small when held against the little prostitute's attempt to find some decency, some redeeming human warmth and worth in her degraded life. Paradoxically, the prostitute seemed entirely of spirit, nothing of flesh, someone who had sacrificed all of herself and found a greater freedom, a wealth more genuine.

"But you must marry for love," said the girl.

"You still believe in love?"

"Of course," said the girl, "and I dream that someday I will find a man to love me back. A man who could forget what it is that I am."

Alexandra was about to ask the little prostitute another question when there was a pounding on the door and she heard the voice of Lopukhin outside, asking Karpatsky if he had finished. Alexandra rose. "What you are is very fine," she said, feeling the words inadequate. "I'm a lady, it is true, but you are something better, better than I will ever be. I can only hope that there exists in the world a man who is worthy of you." And not knowing how else to express what was in her heart, Alexandra clicked her heels and snapped her head down in salute, as an officer does on greeting, or taking leave of, a lady.

The revelation of her cruelty to Lopukhin and the moral example of the little prostitute burned in Alexandra's mind, illuminating areas of herself she did not wish to see, but saw in spite of that. The memory of each ungracious act she had performed, each instance of cruelty or greed, fell like hot drops of liquid wax on tender skin, scarring her formerly high opinion of herself.

This examination of her faults did not, however, immediately translate into any alteration in Alexandra's behavior. In fact, it was the very opposite. Alexandra began to insist to herself on the rightness of her ways, shouting this loudly in her mind to drown out the whisperings of conscience, to distract herself from the discomfort of self-reproach, to aid in her escape from the bonds of guilt, to justify her failings.

Nevertheless, Alexandra did begin, from time to time, to slip Praskovia an extra coin from her frugal purse to buy fresh milk for Matryona, whom she erroneously imagined to be looking peaked and ill-fed, though the woman was in fact as plump and healthy as anyone who daily consumed two entire roasted chickens, a loaf of rich brown bread, assorted eggs and tidbits, blackberry jam and pickled beets and boiled marrow, great salads of vinegared cabbage and pots of buttered groats, all of which Praskovia provided the expectant mother by skimping on her own food and other household expenses, including Alexandra's cigars, cheaper brands of which she placed in the leftover empty boxes of the costlier.

The new coachman, whom Alexandra had hired just before going away on maneuvers, became another occasional victim of her studied kindness. So shy that he could not bear to tell his name (he was referred to within the household merely as "he" or "him," depending on the grammatical situation), this tall and thin young man, disfigured by a harelip and burdened by a mass of wild hair he used whenever possible to hide his face, insisted on sleeping in the stable with the horses, though Praskovia had fixed up a spot for him in the kitchen, complete with mats of hay to make him feel at home. On arriving back from the regimental offices in the late afternoon, her duties done, Alexandra would insist he accompany her to the kitchen for a glass of tea and a slice of buttered bread, and he would stand awkwardly in the back doorway, sipping shyly at his drink, nibbling at his bread and staring out toward the stable across the courtyard until Praskovia, exasperated, told him he could go, as she was eager to turn her attention to the courtly Nikifor, whose time in the kitchen had come to constitute the very center around which her day revolved, the sun to Matryona's moonlike belly.

Sometimes, on her way to the barracks in the morning with Nikifor, Alexandra might spot a pile of ragged filth resting quietly on the sidewalk, jostled by passersby until a hand emerged from the pile to rub its head, indicating the existence of the poor soul within. Alexandra would then call for the coachman to stop, and, leaping from the carriage, she would bend over the pile of rags and press a kopeck or two into the gnarled, dirty hand that crept out, palm up, to collect the alms. Often, she would arrive at the barracks with no cash in her purse at all—a matter of little import, however. The lunches and drinks she consumed at the Officers' Assembly were carefully tallied, slice of ham by slice of ham, apple by apple, glass of champagne by glass of champagne, and billed to her at the end of every month.

As for Ulyanov, she avoided his company, as he did hers. Embarrassed by the ease with which she had let him put her on

her back and the welcome she had given to his lips—the memory
of which angered her no end—she treated him with diffidence,
behaved distantly whenever she was forced to interact with him.
She had already gone too far, allowed too many liberties in her
eagerness to find out what it was like to be kissed by a man, and
she wanted to be certain that Ulyanov understood this clearly,
which he seemed to, for he was equally distant and polite when
giving her her orders for the day or asking her to pass the bread
at mess. She redoubled her kindness to Lopukhin, spending late
hours with him, after others had left the table rolling their eyes,
listening to repeated tales of his childhood in the Caucasus,
where his family had estates, where tribes of savage Turks and
Tartars roamed and the mountains towered, majestic, to the
skies.

How she loved the cavalry! On entering the regimental com-
plex each morning in the early light, she would look up at the
large façade of the main building to see how well it matched
with the buildings around it, another element of empire, another
bone fitting tightly into the skeletal structure of the body
politic. Stepping inside onto the polished marble floor, she listened with satisfaction to the loud, important sound she made
with the soles of her boots.

She loved the sweet smell of hay in the classical riding school,
where she and the other officers put their horses through the
most intricate of paces, forcing the animals' movements into
graceful forms, the warmth of Hercules' solid body between her
thighs as she watched herself in the mirror, unable to believe
that this was really she, for she rode with a precision she had
never imagined herself to be capable of, her mastery due to the
discipline of cavalry training, itself pointed toward something
more profound than the refreshing gallops, merry hunts, and
leisurely strolls on horseback through the park that had com-

posed her entire experience as a horsewoman in her life before she'd entered the army.

She liked most particularly the faces of the new recruits, another supply of which had recently arrived—delivery scheduled yearly for October. These were straw-haired country boys from Poland and Ukraine, who understood only vaguely what was said to them, that is, what they could sift from Russian into their related but quite different languages. The perpetual straining after meaning lent their faces an expression of sweet uncertainty. Far from home, so ignorant they couldn't even calculate the distance properly ("many, many days away"), herded by sniping, shouting sergeants who slashed at them with riding crops, they shuffled along in groups with drooping heads. Sometimes they were forced to trot and gallop like horses as they moved from building to building, but Alexandra's expressed objections were overruled with the explanation that they were getting ready to ride and needed to learn the gaits.

Serving as duty officer one night, she walked the halls of the barracks, standing in the doorway of each successive room in the endless hall, each room containing its complement of men bundled and curled in their beds, the bodies packed as tightly in the room as individual kernels of corn with their corn-colored hair. She watched them sleeping as profoundly as children do, and, understanding that they were in her care, thought of them as children. Going up to one of them, who, agitated by what seemed to be a bad dream, clenched his face and called out in his odd language, she bent over him and murmured words of comfort. He took her hand and held it until she tugged it away and continued on her rounds, appearing in each of the doorways of the rooms of the new recruits and straining in her mind to cast over them all a shield of benevolence and protection, which she hoped they might perceive through the mists of sleep.

The older, experienced hussars slept differently, sprawled confidently naked across their cots. These were men, not boys, seasoned fighters, many of whom had been on campaign and wounded, and Alexandra was astonished at what their nakedness revealed. During the day, clothed in their uniforms, they gave the appearance of normal men, civilized beings, if soldiers. But now she saw the matted hair that covered their bodies like the fur of foxes and bears; the charrings of puckered flesh on the surface of their skin were rivers and whirlpools of scarred tissue in those forests of fur, badges of success in the most unnatural and therefore most prestigious of male endeavors—the defiance of the most basic instinct of all, self-preservation. Their livid genitals, the dull red of specialized tissue, seemed further proof of their extraordinary status, extrusions of an inner savagery.

She crossed the yard into the courtyard leading to the stables.

"All is well in the stables of the first squadron, your honor!" shouted the sentry when he saw her, quickly buttoning his tunic and rising from the seat at the little table where he'd been drinking tea and playing solitaire. Alexandra put him at ease and passed down the corridor that ran between the boxes of the horses, who slept so lightly standing on their feet that the sound of her footsteps made them stamp, annoyed to have their peace disturbed. She passed out of this building and into the next.

"All is well in the stables of the second squadron, your honor!"

And into the next.

"All is well in the stables of the third squadron, your honor!"

She walked the halls of the stables of all six squadrons and then crossed the courtyard again to enter the administration building, which, entirely dark, contained the Officers' Assembly, the library, the regimental offices, assorted other spaces, and the regiment's museum, which was the room assigned to the duty officer and thus her headquarters for her rotation. There was no bed; only a cot with no blanket or pillow, for its use was frowned on. She was expected to sit up the whole night in a state of wariness and not even remove her boots. She would not be relieved until eight in the morning. And so, barring some distracting emergency—the sickness of a soldier, the invasion of the city—she had the building, and the night, to herself.

Coming into the museum, Alexandra lit the candelabras that sat on tables throughout the room and, taking up a small candlestick, went round inspecting the exhibits. On the walls were portraits of commanding officers stretching back a century or more into the past, paintings of battles famous in the regiment (mad dashes of color, tangled legs of stallions, streaming pennons, blood), glass cases filled with crosses and stars suspended from shiny ribbons, and here and there odd relics—the mummified finger of a famous general, shriveled and brown; an enormous glove of Peter the Great; the dried and empty bones of one of Napoleon's chicken dinners, eaten during the Moscow occupation. A faded Polish flag hung in one corner beneath a portrait of one Count Zamoyski, and next to it, fitted onto a dummy, was displayed the uniform of one of ancient Poland's winged hussars. The tunic was of chain mail finely linked, the helmet of iron barbarically pointed at the top; there was a wooden structure that formed the wings, and attached to that a harness of leather straps going under the arms. The faded feathers that studded the curved bones suggested that the one who bore them on his back was no ordinary man, but an avenging angel from on high, fallen to earth to punish the unrighteous. It was reported that the wings had produced, when the wind whipped through them during the charge, a terrifying sound, an hysterical keening—supernatural, mournful, portending death, as if the horseman were death himself, mounted on a pale Polish horse. Alexandra wondered at the imagination that had conceived of such a costume. The masculine gift for representing the martial spirit in wool and leather, manifesting such abstractions as daring, honor, dignity, and righteous rage in clothing form, was something she could not help but admire.

She went and sat down at a desk across the room. The deep part of the night was still ahead of her, and there was nothing to do. Would it be so wrong, she wondered, to put her head down? Just for a moment. If something were to happen, the sentries would wake her with a knock and never see that she had fallen asleep—they were not allowed to open the door without permission. The wood of the desk felt soft and smooth against her cheek. Her hands curled round her head, and soon she was asleep.

How long she slept she didn't know, but she was startled awake by the feeling of a hand upon her shoulder, shaking her, and her lids slowly opened to reveal to her Ulyanov's eyes looking directly into hers. Reddening, she leaped from her seat, clicked her heels clumsily, and saluted him, but could not suppress a waking yawn. He laughed at her.

"Have no fear, Karpatsky! As your commanding officer, I assure you I will not tell myself I found you sleeping at your post."

Alexandra smiled weakly, unamused. Ulyanov motioned her into her chair. "At ease," he said. "Please be at ease with me."

Unable to sustain his bravado, Ulyanov continued to stand in the middle of the room as if not knowing what to do next. She saw him swallow. His own face was red, and he shook his head as if irritated with himself, blinked his eyes, opened his mouth, about to speak, but then remained silent. He seemed to be trembling. His obvious discomfort increased her own. It was the first time they had been alone together since the kiss on the river-bank, and the memory of that meeting of their mouths loomed larger and larger in their minds by the moment until it had grown to an obstacle so enormous they were unable to find any way around it. Both remained silent, Alexandra sitting at her desk, Ulyanov standing awkwardly, until the captain, startled by the realization that he carried a large package in his arms, was able to retreat from the obstacle, circle around behind it.

"Oh!" he cried. "I have brought you something. It is a long night, and I thought you might need some . . . sustenance to get you through."

The package he had carried under his arm, and which she had been too disconcerted to notice, was merrily unpacked, both of them relieved to have found something to talk about other than that troubling kiss. Alexandra was able to look at Ulyanov and speak to him of her delight as he revealed within the layers of papers jam tarts, slices of sugared ham, a block of yellow cheese, and a small loaf, all of it warmed through by the metal canister of hot tea around which these delicacies had been packed—a huntsman's trick. Alexandra began to eat, the paper serving as her plate. She drank directly from the canister, as any hussar would.

Ulyanov pulled up a chair and sat directly across from her to give himself the pleasure of watching her eat the food he had brought to her. But it was not many minutes before the memory of the kiss loomed between them again, both of them falling silent as Alexandra was overcome by a terrible indecision over whether to choose a jam tart or a slice of ham as the next morsel she would eat, the resolution of this problem requiring a great deal of thought, and Ulyanov himself found that he was fasci-nated by the peculiar shape and size of the mustache that decorated the face of the general whose portrait hung on the wall behind the desk.

Ulyanov, however, began to grow impatient at the impediment posed by the kiss to the good relations between brother officers so necessary to unit cohesion, and decided to confront the issue directly. He cleared his throat to attract Alexandra's attention away from her food.

"I must apologize to you, Cornet," he said, wincing and turning red again, "I behaved in an ungentlemanly manner several weeks ago, conduct most definitely unbecoming, and I beg your forgiveness."

Alexandra swallowed the ham she had been chewing and stared at her lap.

"*You* did nothing wrong," he went on, gallantly absolving her of any part in it—though the absolution was not entirely justified considering the way she had teased him so mercilessly, tormenting him with Lopukhin. "I suppose I was angry in some way with you, not that I had any right to be, and in the most ungracious manner I was driven to demonstrate to you my strength and your own weakness. It was unconscionable."

"I probably deserved it in some way," Alexandra admitted, heart softened by the food, just as he'd intended. "Think no more about it, Captain."

"Deserved it? How could you deserve to be handled so roughly?"

"Well," said Alexandra, still staring at her lap, "I must confess to you I was deliberately trying to provoke you, to annoy you or punish you. I was angry too, at *you,* after you questioned my judgment and criticized my manners. And also for not taking me seriously as a soldier." The sudden honesty of this admission amazed even Alexandra, well trained in the womanly art of subterfuge. The sensation of candor was so pleasant, however, she could not help but look on the person who'd evoked it with benevolence. She raised her head and smiled, shrugged.

"I was only puzzled," he protested, resting his arm on the desk and leaning toward her. "You must admit it was rather an eccentric act to disguise yourself as a man and join the regiment."

"True," said Alexandra, nodding, "true. But I thank you for not giving me away or forcing me out."

"I can't say that I deserve thanks for *that*," said Ulyanov. "I am not so certain I am right to do it, to allow you to continue with this charade. I am so afraid you might be hurt. Though I admit you have done well."

"Have I?" said Alexandra, suddenly pink with pleasure.

Ulyanov smiled at her wryly, as if reluctant to admit to it, and nodded, shrugged.

"However," he said, growing serious again, "I do worry about you. I don't know how long you intend to keep this up."

"Oh," said Alexandra, "as long as I want, of course. I'm enjoying myself. In fact, I've never been so happy in my life."

"But how long can you continue? It may be impertinent of me to raise this subject, but an officer's life is expensive, and I was under the impression—perhaps I'm wrong about this—that you have been living under somewhat reduced circumstances. Aren't you worried about that?"

"Actually," said Alexandra, not offended at all that he had brought up finances, proud of the way she was handling it all, "I'm managing quite well. The upkeep of my horse does not cost so much, and I find the mess bills are not high at all. I could not eat at home for that amount of money."

"Your mess bills are not high because I pay them," said Ulyanov impulsively. Suddenly uncertain of whether he ought to have admitted to this act of charity, he shook his head, sat back in his chair, and raked his hair with his fingers. "It was my way of making amends for my insult to your person on the river-bank," he insisted, "but I am not certain it has been such a good idea. It only makes it easier for you to remain."

Alexandra, mouth open in astonishment, simply stared at him.

"I strongly encourage you, Countess, to abandon this folly. I cannot bear to think you might be hurt. I have done enough damage to women, one in particular, for which I cannot for-give myself. I cannot bear to think it is within my power to pro-tect a different woman from harm and that I shirked this duty. You must understand this, Countess." Ulyanov looked at her earnestly, the seriousness with which he took the issue standing out clearly on his face.

"Were you very much in love with her?" asked Alexandra, eager to have the answer to a question which had long puzzled her.

"In love with her!" Ulyanov cried, leaping from his seat and beginning to pace. "Why, she wasn't even human to me!" He covered his face with his hands a moment, then dropped them and began to pace again. "I treated her like a dog, a loving dog who licked my hand and came when I called, and when I had no more use for her, I kicked her away the way you would a dog." Ulyanov gripped the back of his empty chair and stared at Alex-andra. "I will never forget the way she looked at me, her eyes uncomprehending as a dog's, when I told her I was sending her away." He lowered his head. Alexandra thought she saw the shine of wetness on his cheeks, though the light was dim and she might have been mistaken.

"But Captain," she said, "it's not your fault. You did not kill her. She killed herself."

"Oh, didn't I?" he said, raising his head and gazing at Alexandra, "I took advantage of her presence in my household to ... She was in my care. I owned her. I am utterly responsible."

Alexandra, distressed at the sight of his pain, wondered about what to say to lighten his burden. "You may have owned the woman's body," she said after a few moments, "but you did not own her soul or her will."

"But isn't it the same?"

"Oh no," she said, "no human being can own another's will. To think you can is arrogance. You did not make her kill herself—she chose that path of her own free will, and in that way she punished you forever."

"Punished me forever," he repeated to himself, not taking his eyes from Alexandra's face, begging reassurance there, an explanation.

"Yes, Captain," said Alexandra, "it was *you* she punished, not herself. Her will to hurt you was stronger than her will to live, or even her love. I am not so certain she was such a pitiful, humble soul. There was tyranny in that act of suicide, the desire to impose her will on you, control your life and thoughts. Of course she knew it would torment you. In this way, she would be with you all your life, force herself on you. There are other kinds of force than the merely physical, you know. Other ways to violate another human being. I am not so certain now that she loved you. How could she have and hurt you so?"

"Oh," said Ulyanov, dropping his chin, "we often hurt the ones we love the most. Because it matters more." He seemed, however, more relaxed; he breathed a long sigh. "In any case, perhaps you're right. The memory of her will be with me all my life. I knew she would get her way, somehow. She always did." He came out from behind the chair and sat down in it, crossed his arms, crossed his legs.

Alexandra had no idea whether anything she had said was

true at all. She had known the woman only by sight and briefly. Her harsh analysis of the woman's character had been prompted by the desire to comfort him, and perhaps by a certain jealousy, too. However, even if there had been only a grain of truth in what she had said, she sensed she had succeeded in relieving Ulyanov's pain in some small way. This pleased her deeply. In fact, she was astonished to discover that she almost liked him.

Ulyanov slapped his palms on his thighs and rose. "I think it is time for me to go," he said. "I've taken up so much of your time. It could have been devoted to more important things than listening to my troubles."

"Oh no! Don't go!" The night was long and the building was so empty.

He sat again. They sat together some minutes in silence, both listening to the ticking of the clock, which had just struck three. Unable to bear the silence any longer, Alexandra finally said, "Five hours to go before I am relieved. You wouldn't by any chance know how to get hold of a pack of cards?"

He did indeed. Jumping up, he ran from the room, and while Alexandra cleared the table of the food but left the tea, Ulyanov searched the drawers in the dining room, found what he looked for, and returned to Alexandra at a trot.

"We will play piquet," she announced, "and I will beat you."

Of course she did not beat him. Or, rather, she beat him when Ulyanov allowed her to. Her father had taught her to play cards, but clever as she was, she could not compete with the hours Ulyanov had spent at gaming tables, gambling dens, and private high-stakes parties for interested gentlemen, the cheroot clamped in the corner of his mouth adding its smoke to the fog that hung already in the room as the gamblers played on through their fatigue and into morning. However, Ulyanov allowed her to win often enough to reinforce her vision of herself as a merciless card sharp, staring him down from her position across the desk, from behind her fan of cards, and daring him to draw. He pretended to be afraid, to be very afraid.

After this night, Ulyanov began to attach himself to the group of junior officers of which Alexandra considered herself the leader, accompanying them on their nightly rounds, their jaunts through the city. Lopukhin, who had been distressed by Ulyanov's defection from the group, by his loss of interest in all his favorite pursuits, was delighted at this change at first, but he saw that Ulyanov, though sitting at the head of the table in some cafe or disreputable restaurant, talked little, drank less, and ate nothing, and Lopukhin thought he detected an undertone of disapproval in the captain's demeanor. He seemed, if anything, *watchful,* as if waiting for some disaster to befall the merry group. And Lopukhin began to perceive that his watchful gaze was aimed primarily at young Karpatsky.

In fact, the captain treated the young cornet with an oversolicitousness Lopukhin found puzzling as well as inappropriate. For instance, the captain himself would decide when the boy had had enough to drink, fixing a look of disapproval on anyone who tried to pour the young cornet another shot. Further, he denied Karpatsky participation in some of the more daring stunts the junior officers performed (walking on the ledges of balconies high above the street while tipping a bottle down one's throat was a particular favorite) and would not permit the boy to enter an opium den, not even just to look around, though Lopukhin argued that the boy should be allowed to experience a wide range of manly pleasures and to decide for himself which ones he wished to pursue. The captain had simply gazed at Lopukhin coldly and ignored the remark. Worst of all, on those late nights when Karpatsky was having an especially good time, having managed to sneak an extra shot of vodka or another glass of champagne while the captain was visiting the lavatory, Ulyanov, perceiving the young cornet's slight increase in inebriation on his return, would rise from his seat, go over to Karpatsky, place a firm hand on the back of the young man's neck, and announce to the group that the boy had had enough and needed his rest. To the groans of the group, he would steer the protesting Karpatsky through the crowd and out the door while champagne corks were still popping all around the room and there were still hours of fun to be had before the dawn, before the whole lot of them had to stumble over to the barracks for early morning drill and then parade, eyes bleary, uniforms stained with oily sauce, their persons pungent with the fumes of young male bodies that hadn't had a change of clothes perhaps in days.

On those mornings, Karpatsky, fresh from his good night's sleep, would greet them in the riding school with such malicious cheer that they would advance on him with shouts of rage that made their hollow heads ring all the more, ready to pull him from his mount, toss him to the ground, jump on him, and beat him blind. However, a cough and a stern look from Captain Mecklenburg-Ulyanov, who had been leaning his elbows on the railing watching the young cornet as he rode, would dissuade the junior officers from this course, instill in them a certain shame at their own lack of discipline, and inspire a resolve to get to bed at a decent hour tonight, which resolution was later abandoned in the haze of smoke and the fizzing of champagne and the warmth of female bottoms resting in their laps, most of all in the joys of male camaraderie as the junior officers, blended into one being, cavorted round the town, a capering, frisking, slobbering amiable mongrel set loose upon the city.

Why the captain disapproved of young Karpatsky's participation in these cheerful debauches was to Lopukhin a mystery, as were certain expressions that appeared on Ulyanov's face when he looked at the boy, expressions that suggested to Lopukhin that his former idol might not be quite what he had thought, that he harbored, perhaps, desires Lopukhin did not care to name. Not that there was anything wrong with that, but it did call for a reevaluation of the captain and his supposed powers. However, it occurred to Lopukhin that perhaps those very powers had led him to this pass. Ulyanov had seemed to lose interest in women entirely some time ago and, to the disappointment of the men, forgotten completely his vow to sleep with every woman that he met. It had been months since the numbers of the tally had been changed—oddly, since just about the time Karpatsky had arrived. Lopukhin hadn't even seen the captain *near* a woman recently. Could it be that the captain, frustrated that he had no more worlds to conquer, disappointed in the ease with which the women fell to his assault, had turned his attentions to the other sex, hoping to find more challenging quarry?

Lopukhin could not believe it. No, surely the captain regarded the young cornet with the qualified affection of an older brother for a younger. The captain was only molding the boy, training and guiding him, though so far as Lopukhin was concerned his education in manhood was being mishandled.

"Wait, Captain," he intervened one night, having had far too much to drink, "let the boy have his fun." But Ulyanov only stared at him, his hand still firm on the back of Karpatsky's neck. Lopukhin, feeling his liquor, rose to his feet and stuck out his chin, hand on the hilt of his sword. "Let the boy become a shman, I mean, a man, sir," he mumbled, swaying on his feet. "You coddle him."

"I coddle him?"

"That's right!" said Alexandra, throwing off Ulyanov's hand and jumping to her feet. In truth, she enjoyed more than she liked to admit Ulyanov's supervisory demeanor, his watchfulness and care, especially on those nights when he accompanied her home, the carriage rides through the cold November streets while she drowsed against his woolen shoulder and he chafed at her fingertips through the leather of her gloves to keep them warm. Once when she was drunk, he had carried her up the steps of the palace and loaded her straight into Nikifor's arms, though she had only been pretending to be drunk, just to see what he would do. "You're coddling me! Stop doing it! I want to stay!" Actually, she was rather drunk tonight at that, having sneaked two extra shots of vodka while Ulyanov was detained in conversation with an officer of another regiment.

The captain looked at her a long moment. Then he made his way to his seat at the head of the table, sat down, and lit a cigar. "Suit yourself, Cornet," he said, folding his arms across his chest so that the smoke from his cigar seemed to pour directly from his heart, "but if you are tired tomorrow, don't complain to *me*."

"I am not *fragile*!" Alexandra, shouted, unsteady on her feet. "I am not *delicate*."

"So who's throwing up all the time?" said Ulyanov.

"That was only a few times, before I got used to drinking vodka."

"Who gets tired and falls off his horse?"

"*Once!*" cried Alexandra, who, feeling it imprudent to stand, fell into her chair.

Everyone watched the captain to see what he would do at this demonstration of insubordination. He said nothing, however. Instead, he threw the lit cigar to the floor, waved the waiter over, ordered a bottle of champagne, and, when it was brought, popped the cork himself and placed the bursting bottle to his lips. The wine frothed and bubbled down his chin, soaking darkly into his chest. Then he smiled and wiped his mouth.

A cheer went up from all the junior officers. It seemed the old Ulyanov had returned.

"I thought you were going to leave," said Alexandra, who was not so delighted as the junior officers to see the reappearance of the old Ulyanov.

"Oh no," said Ulyanov, "I'm enjoying myself too much. The night is still young."

"You'll get drunk."

"That's the idea." Throwing his head back, Ulyanov raised the bottle to his lips again, and the company watched in admiration as his Adam's apple shifted up and down. He was draining the bottle. When he had finished, the front of his tunic was soaked. He tossed the bottle on the floor and wiped his mouth with the back of his hand.

Lopukhin's suspicions of the possibility of an irregular relationship between the captain and cornet were reawakened. He had not liked the sound of that conversation. It sounded like . . . he did not want to admit it to himself.

I am drunk, Lopukhin told himself. So drunk that Karpatsky had begun to look and sound . . . but how could that be? Still, the cornet had used that supercilious tone of voice that women utilized when you were doing something that they disapproved of—that self-righteous, snippy tone, as though they've appointed themselves your conscience, or, even worse, your mother! Karpatsky, though, could not be a woman. He was much too tall. Was he then indeed Ulyanov's lover? Was that the secret of that proprietary tone? That too-intimate interference?

Lopukhin shook his head so violently he felt his stomach swaying in his belly as the room began to spin. What a bad idea that had been, to shake his head! He lowered himself to his chair and placed his head upon the tablecloth to steady it, to keep it fixed and safe. In a moment, he was snoring loudly. Around him the party stirred and frothed.

"Karpatsky!" shouted someone from across the room. It was Durinov, drunk and staggering toward the table, dragging with him a young woman dressed in frills. "Karpatsky! Kinsman of my goddess!"

"Oh, go away," said Alexandra, but he did not hear her. Finding an empty chair, Durinov placed it next to Alexandra's and sat down. The frilly woman sat on his lap, laughing when Durinov's hands reached up to grab her breasts.

"Karpatsky, tell me, have you heard from her? When does she return?" Durinov abandoned one of the woman's breasts and gripped Alexandra's arm.

Ulyanov, alert at the appearance of an acquaintance of Karpatsky's he was not himself familiar with, turned to Durinov. "When does who return?" Ulyanov asked. "Kinsman of what goddess?"

"Sir, I have not made your acqaintance," said Durinov.

"Andrei Mecklenburg-Ulyanov," said Ulyanov, rising from his seat and snapping smartly with his heels, "Seventeenth Hussars, and you are?"

"Ulyanov!" cried Durinov, who was really very drunk. "A legend! A myth!"

"No," said Ulyanov, "it is I who am Ulyanov. Who are you?"

"Is it true," said Durinov, "that you have bedded every woman in the city?"

"Would that it were, dear sir," said Ulyanov, sitting down again and stowing his booted feet upon the table, "but even I do not pretend to possess the superhuman energies such an undertaking would require."

"You are too modest, sir," said Durinov, bowing his head, "but let me introduce myself to such as you. I am Oleg Durinov."

Ulyanov nodded. "But tell me, sir, who is it whose return you are awaiting? You mentioned a kinswoman of our dear Cornet Karpatsky."

"The exquisite Countess Korvin!" Durinov cried, while Alexandra slumped lower in her chair, fearing the consequence of this.

Ulyanov picked at a front tooth. He frowned and cocked his head. "The Countess Korvin?" said Ulyanov. "Hmmm. I know her well."

"You do?" said Durinov, eyes popping widely with anxiety. "Surely you're not telling me that she . . ."

"Is one of my conquests?"

"I would never presume to allow even the thought to enter my head that this goddess might be dishonored in that way."

"You certainly implied it," said Ulyanov mildly, taking a cheroot from his case and inserting it between his lips. He lit it and leaned back. The company waited to see what would happen.

"I think," said Alexandra, seizing this lull in the conversation to try to turn it away from the topic of herself, "that my cousin Alexandra Korvin would be most shocked to know she was being discussed in this sort of place."

"Your cousin?" said Ulyanov. A smile appeared and widened quickly.

"We all know that one does not discuss a lady in such a place as this, under these sorts of circumstances," said Alexandra, looking first at Ulyanov and then at Durinov.

"Your cousin, a lady?" said Ulyanov. "I would say a lady is just what she is not." He snorted and looked at Alexandra with a meaning he was sure she knew the meaning of.

Durinov jumped to his feet. The frilly woman scrambled for a purchase on the table, failed to get it, and tumbled to the floor.

"I challenge you, sir!" cried Durinov, swaying slightly, but clenching his fists to show his strength. Alexandra, who was helping the frilly woman to her feet, closed her eyes.

Ulyanov, looking not at Durinov but at Alexandra, began enumerating on his fingers. "She often eats far more than is seemly; I have seen her. She will not go to bed when she is tired. And her drinking we will not discuss. She refuses to listen to those who offer her sensible advice. She is unpleasant, selfish, even cruel at times. Is this the behavior of a lady?"

"She is an angel," said Durinov.

"In point of fact," Ulyanov went on, "she is not a lady in ways that you cannot even imagine." A chuckle escaped him. He blew out a stream of smoke.

This statement, however, with all that it implied of secret, intimate knowledge of the countess's person, seemed to drive Durinov mad. Eyes bulging, he tore his hair, then launched himself at Ulyanov. Scrambling and kicking forward on the table, sending forks flying and china smashing to the floor, Durinov reached out for the captain, who looked back at him indifferently and did not even flinch. Durinov was caught under the arms by a pair of junior officers and firmly held.

"Karpatsky!" cried Durinov, struggling, "I call on you as Countess Korvin's kinsman to serve as second in my attempt to force this scoundrel to his senses, or wipe him from the face of the earth!"

Oh boy, said Alexandra to herself. Durinov, breathing hard, glared at her, his mouth working as if he were chewing on his anger. Ulyanov was looking at her too, head cocked in curiosity to see what she would do. The eyes of the junior officers were shining. Only Lopukhin, still asleep with his head on the table, was unaware of the drama.

This is madness, she wanted to say. Alexandra Korvin is certainly no lady, not at this time at least. Ulyanov is absolutely right. To fight a duel over this is madness. I, Alexandra Korvin herself, forbid this. Ulyanov is only teasing, and Durinov belongs, well, we know where. But she knew could not stop them with her words. Perhaps as second in the duel she might negotiate some compromise. Yes, that was the best way to control this.

"I agree," she said.

"My second, Count Karpatsky," said Durinov, "will call on you in the morning, Captain Mecklenburg-Ulyanov."

"I will await him with great pleasure."

When Alexandra stepped into the hallway of Ulyanov's house in one of the less fashionable quarters of the city, the shoulders of her greatcoat were white with snow, and she was holding a wooden box. She had spent the morning in consultation with both Durinov (her hand shaking so hard when she took her cup of tea, she spilled the hot liquid down her chin) and Lopukhin, who, awake at last, was both Ulyanov's second and her guide through the complexities of dueling protocol.

"Good. It's time. It will help to make a man of you," Lopukhin had said.

When Alexandra had suggested to Durinov that perhaps this challenge might be invalid, considering the fact that he really did not know her cousin Countess Korvin and she, Count Karpatsky, could assure him that everything Ulyanov had said of her was true, she was met with a blank look. She had understood then that Countess Korvin was irrelevant. This had nothing to do with her and everything to do with Durinov himself. It was a question of his honor, not hers, of his ability to impose on the world his definition of it, in other words, of his manliness, his very being. So.

Lopukhin had instructed Alexandra that, as challenger, Durinov would have the choice of weapons, but if pistols were chosen, which they were, a pair of pistols exactly matching must be obtained, tested for action in the firing, and agreed upon. Furthermore, they must be pistols that neither of the duelists was familiar with, pistols newly bought or borrowed from someone else. The procuring and testing of these pistols was the responsibility of the seconds.

It was also the responsibility of the seconds to find a spot for the duel with unobstructed views of the horizon, so that the combatants could see clear outlines of each other's bodies in the light of dawn. There was the question of the number of paces that would separate the combatants and the number of exchanges of fire that would be allowed. All this must be negotiated and agreed upon according to a complicated set of rules prescribing a certain number of paces and exchanges according to the level of insult, the seriousness of injury to honor.

Leaving Durinov's palace with Lopukhin, who had been waiting in the carriage while she met with Durinov alone, she proceeded to the home of one Prince Vlezko, who possessed a pair of pistols Lopukhin said would fill the bill. Alexandra endured the formal call upon Vlezko, signing for the pistols to relieve him of any liability in the event of a death caused by one of said pistols. Then she and Lopukhin had ridden over to the regimental firing range to test the pistols and after that had driven out of the city to a spot that Lopukhin said was "perfect, and very popular." It was then Alexandra's duty, as Durinov's second, to pay a formal call on Ulyanov himself. She had the carriage drop Lopukhin at his home before she proceeded on to the captain's residence to meet with him alone, as protocol required. Later, Lopukhin would pay his own private call on Durinov.

It was a Saturday morning, and Ulyanov had been breakfasting in his bathrobe when she was conducted into his study at home to speak with him.

"Have some," he said from his seat at the table, which held pots of jam and plates of bread, a basket of boiled eggs, a dish of pickled fish.

Alexandra shook her head.

"Not even a cup of tea? Where's your famous appetite?" he teased, and, as if to emphasize his indifference to the danger he was facing, bit lustily into a slice of bread that was covered with sour cream.

Her hands shook as she opened the box to display the pistols, as Lopukhin had instructed her to do. Her throat was so dry she could not speak and only gestured at them, although she was supposed to say "For your approval."

"Fine. They look fine. I wouldn't presume to question Lopukhin's judgment. He knows best!" said Ulyanov gaily, his cheeks plump with food. He swallowed, smiled, and gestured with both hands outstretched that she be seated.

Alexandra sat across from him.

"Do you accept the challenge?" She pronounced flatly and slowly the words she had practiced in the carriage.

"Why not?" said Ulyanov. "Sure."

"But why?" she said, asking the question that had been building inside her all morning long. "Why do you do this? Why?"

Ulyanov leaned back in his chair. "Because what I said is true. The Countess Alexandra Korvin is not a lady."

"You mean you would die to prove that I am not a lady?"

"Perhaps I don't have to die," he said, "if the countess will prove she is a lady. If she did, then my honor as a man would not be compromised by my refusal to accept the challenge, as the refusal would be an implicit admission on my part that she is."

Alexandra understood instantly what he proposed. She sat up in her seat and grabbed the arms of the chair. "You mean you want me to resign from the regiment."

"Exactly," said Ulyanov.

Alexandra slumped. Ulyanov had set the whole thing up, or rather seized an opportunity, clever as he was. He had known very well that Durinov would challenge him for insulting Alexandra Korvin, just as he had known she would priggishly refuse to drink to herself that afternoon, those many months ago, when he had arrested her.

"Yes," said Ulyanov mildly, crossing his arms over his chest, leaning back, "you are now in the position of being responsible for someone's death, either mine or his. This is what your stubborn folly has brought you to. Unless, of course, you wish to prove you are a lady."

Alexandra shook her head. "So you threaten me. That is not fair. Because you don't want me in the regiment, because you think it is improper for me to be there, you will risk death to impose your will on me? It's insupportable. I will not have it. I will not resign from the regiment. I don't care if you die."

"Do you care if Durinov dies for this? Is your self-importance so great that you would have a man die so that you can continue to amuse yourself with your charade?"

"He issued the challenge. It is not my affair."

"Oh, Alexandra," said Ulyanov, "you are indeed becoming a man. This is ruthlessness. Where is your womanly softness? Your sympathy, your tenderness for life?"

"I don't understand why it is so important to you that I resign. Whom am I hurting?"

"No one at this time," said Ulyanov, opening a cigar case and offering a cigar, which Alexandra took, "but have you thought of what would happen if we were called to battle? Do you think the army is nothing but parading around in a fine uniform and giving orders?"

Alexandra did not concede his point. She asserted that Nadezhda Durova herself had fought and acquitted herself in battle very well.

"That was years ago," said Ulyanov, lighting first Alexandra's cigar, then his own, "many years ago. Before the new artillery. Do you know what the new weaponry can do to the human body? Have you seen it?"

She hadn't. But what did that matter?

"It is my affair if I want to risk it," said Alexandra, "not yours."

"Not quite," said Ulyanov. "You will put others at risk."

"Just because I am a woman? You don't trust me to be courageous?"

"You may turn out to be a coward, you may not. None of us ever knows before we go what it is we're made of and how we will behave under fire, whether we will run to try to save ourselves or stand and fight. Durova was certainly courageous, and I've seen plenty of manly cowards in my time. But this is not the issue."

"What is it then, the issue?"

"It is the men under my command whose lives you will put at risk," he said. "Do you think I would be able to discharge my duties responsibly while worrying about your safety? Do you think I would not risk my own life and the lives of every man under my command in order to save you from danger?"

"But why?" said Alexandra. "Simply because I am a woman?"

"Yes," said Ulyanov. "No decent man who calls himself a man would do any less."

The two were silent now, at an impasse.

"If it bothers you so much," said Alexandra finally, "I will join another regiment."

"I will prevent that."

"What difference could it make to you then?" she cried. "You are the only one who knows I am a woman, and if I were to serve in another regiment, I would put no one at risk but myself."

"But you see, Alexandra, I could not allow that to happen."

"Why?" she asked. "The responsibility is mine, not yours."

"You forget that I am already liable for the death of one woman. I will not see another one endangered if there is anything I can do to stop it. It is now within my power to force you to resign from the regiment, and that I will do, at risk to my own life and the life of another man. The choice is yours. If you wish to prove you are a lady, possessed of the tenderness for life that is a woman's special gift, you will resign. Otherwise one of us will die. And you will have proven you are truly a man."

Alexandra thought a moment. How she loved the cavalry! Oh, she couldn't give it up!

"I will remain in the regiment until we are called to battle, and then I will resign."

"So you wish to play at soldiers, like a child?"

"Shut up! Shut up!" said Alexandra, leaping from her seat. She swept her hand across the table, sending the dishes smashing to the floor.

"Like a child."

Alexandra clenched her teeth. "I will resign," she said, "but I will never speak to you again." She took her coat and left the room.

Durinov, however, refused to withdraw the challenge. "It is too late for that," he said. "The words were spoken. He must die."

"But perhaps it will be you who will die," suggested Alexandra.

"If I do, it will be a glorious death in the service of my lady."

Alexandra threw up her hands and turned away. "He is insane," she said to herself, then turning back to him, said, "You do not even know her."

Durinov looked at her as if it were she who was insane.

"I know her in my heart," he said.

"What can I say to convince you to stop this madness? I know that my cousin would not want this."

"What she wants is not at issue."

Alexandra turned and put her hand on the doorknob. "I know that very well," she said before going out the door.

By the time she had returned to Ulyanov's house, she was dripping with sweat inside her coat. Ulyanov himself opened the front door, ushered her in, led her to the study.

"He refuses to withdraw the challenge," she said, panting, as soon as the door was closed.

An obscenity burst softly from Ulyanov's lips.

"You will simply not appear tomorrow morning, then," said Alexandra, placing a hand upon his arm. "Durinov is irrational. There is no shame in it. You will simply leave the field to him." She had worked out this solution in the carriage, repeating it over and over to herself: "It is simple. Ulyanov will simply not appear."

Ulyanov threw himself into a chair.

"It is too late for that. To back down would be . . . impossible."

"You are all insane," she said.

"And you wanted to be one of us?"

Alexandra lowered herself into a chair and dropped her chin.

"No matter," he went on. "I'm not worth so much. If anything, I deserve the bullet. There's a certain justice in it, don't you think? A life for a life?"

"Wait," she said, raising her head as she understood the implication of what he had just said. "Are you saying you will simply stand and let him shoot you?"

"Of course," said Ulyanov.

"You will not defend yourself?"

"No," he said, "I can't. By conceding his point, I have forfeited my right to shoot at him is my way of looking at it. Of course I still have the right to defend myself if I want to. I just don't want to. It would not be honorable. I've gotten what I wanted out of this, your resignation. To kill the man would not be fair."

"Then this is suicide."

"Oh no," he said, "not suicide at all. He might miss, you know. It's more like gambling. I've always been good at that."

"But it's your life you're gambling with."

"The highest stakes of all. Makes it interesting, doesn't it?" He was incomprehensibly cavalier about his approaching death as he sat smoking and tapping his foot on the floor—the only sign of tension that Alexandra could perceive. Outside the window it was nearly dark, although it was only midafternoon, and the wettish snowflakes made light tapping sounds on the glass, as if something were trying to get inside, get to him already.

Alexandra's tears gathered, broke free, and dripped down the sides of her nose.

She moved across the room and put a hand on his arm. "I beg of you," she said, "do not do this. Withdraw. It is not worth it."

"It isn't a question of being worth it," said Ulyanov, patting her hand. "It's the rules. Without the rules, we are only animals."

"I don't understand."

"No," he said, "you wouldn't. You're a woman and not subject to these rules. You see, they were put in place to show us how little we matter. Our lives . . . pffft. Blown away by the wind. It's the force of idea that matters, the substance of our souls. If we cannot sacrifice ourselves in order to maintain a code or to uphold a principle, we are no better than animals, whose only function is to live, whose only purpose is to survive. There are some things more important than living." Ulyanov took her hand and held it a moment. "You must go now. I have much to do— my affairs to put in order, so to speak."

He led her to the door.

"Alexandra," he said in mock astonishment, "where are your gloves? You came in without wearing them! You will catch cold!"

Alexandra could not speak. She turned her face away and tried to hide it in the massive collar of her greatcoat.

"Are they in your pocket? Let us see." She felt his hands rummaging through the pockets of her greatcoat. He found the gloves and held them out while she inserted her shaking hands inside the tightness of the leather. He smoothed her gloved fingers.

"Now go home and eat and sleep," he said, still holding her hands and bending his head to get a look at the face she was trying to hide from him, "and tomorrow we will see what happens. Remember you have your duties to Durinov. You must be at his home at dawn. And give the pistols to Lopukhin. I am afraid you might forget them."

Alexandra suddenly threw her arms around his neck, but Ulyanov pushed her away and stood looking down at her face, which she was holding up to him now to show her tears, as if that would finally persuade him. An odd smile appeared on his lips, quivered a moment, and vanished. His face was solemn, blank.

"No more of that," he said. "It's the worst you can do to a

man who's facing death. It makes him want to live too much. Go," he said, and pushed her out the door.

Of course she did not sleep, but lay in her bed all night looking up at the ceiling. When the window began to whiten with dawn, she got up, lit a candle, and sat at the small worn desk in her room with her elbows on the wood, her chin in her palms. From time to time she looked up at the icon on the wall, which the light of the candle did not reach, so it was hidden from her, its shapes indistinct.

After a few moments, she got up from the table, called for Praskovia to bring her tea, which she could not drink, and break-fast, which she could not eat, then washed, dressed with the help of Nikifor, and went slowly down the staircase of the palace, through the halls, and out the door, where her coachman was waiting in the sledge. With a scream she remembered she had forgotten the box of pistols and ran up the steps again before remembering she had given them to Lopukhin after all.

She arrived at Durinov's and stood waiting in the hallway of his palace. The very sight of him as he came striding down the hall to meet her turned her stomach sour, and she wanted to beat him round the head and face. Durinov's valet helped him insert his arm inside a fur-lined greatcoat, buttoned it up for him, then handed him his high silk hat. They were just about to exit through the door when Durinov stopped before a mirror to adjust the tilt of the top hat. He fiddled with it, Alexandra tap-ping her boot, until he found the angle he was seeking and smiled at himself in the mirror.

"Have you the pistols? I'd like to get the feel of mine again," said Durinov, smoothing his gloves as he continued to stare at himself in the mirror.

"Lopukhin has them." The consonants of the name exploded from her lips.

"Ah yes, ah yes," said Durinov, stepping away from the mirror. He strode through the door and down the steps of his mansion and stopped a moment to breathe deeply of the morning air. Alexandra, behind him, folded her arms over her chest against the cutting wind. Her greatcoat was heavy and thick, but still no proof against the massive cold. They climbed into the carriage and set off, Alexandra putting her hand up from time to time to see that her hat was holding to her head, as if forgetting she had a chin strap. The shako in its gray linen bad-weather covering felt ridiculous. She would have liked to throw it under the runners of the sledge, watch it be crushed and broken, the silly thing. Sliding along the snowy streets in the sledge, neither of them spoke.

The road grew lonely. They had left the city. Endless empty fields of white on either side, in front of them a looming forest. Raising herself from her seat, Alexandra saw another carriage standing in the road up ahead. It grew bigger as the sledge rushed toward it. In one motion both the driver and the horse of the other sledge turned their heads, and Lopukhin came out of the forest to meet them in the road.

Grabbing at the boughs of the pine trees to keep from slipping in the snow, Alexandra followed Lopukhin into the forest, Durinov behind them. They approached the clearing, now thick with deep snow, that she and Lopukhin had chosen the day before. Ulyanov, she saw, was leaning against a tree smoking a cigarette. She merely brushed him with her eyes before turning her head away, not able to bear to look at him, thinking *he does this for my sake. Mine.*

"Let's pace it out!" cried Lopukhin, who seemed excited, but she saw his Adam's apple move above his collar in a nervous swallow. He was not wearing a scarf. In his arms he cradled the case of pistols. "Forty paces," he said, drawing a line in the snow with the toe of his boot, "from here."

The two seconds began to walk side by side, matching their bootprints in the snow as they counted out loud. After fifteen paces, Lopukhin shifted the box of pistols under one arm, drew his saber with a scraping sound, and thrust it into the snow. The metal was dull in the morning light. "First barrier," he shouted.

"Ten more paces to the second barrier," he said to her.

Alexandra's hand shook so much she could not draw her saber. Lopukhin had to do it for her, sliding the metal out of its leather scabbard and then handing it to her so that she could shove its point down into the ground.

"Second barrier," he shouted. "Just fifteen paces more," he added to Alexandra.

"All right," he said when they were done, "that's forty." He squatted down to check if the barriers were properly aligned, then straightened up again and stood with hands on hips, nodding to himself and breathing hard, his breath making frosty shapes in the air.

"I'm so pleased that Ulyanov chose me as second for this duel," he said, taking a cigarette-case from his sabretache and holding it open toward Alexandra who, deeply grateful, selected one with shaking fingers and carried it to her mouth, glad to have something for her lips to gather round to steady them, "It proves to me there's nothing wrong between us. Good." Lopukhin searched for a place to light his match and ended by doing it on a scratched spot on the buckle of his belt.

"How many duels has he actually fought?" Alexandra's voice rose in pitch.

"Five, I think. No, six."

"Has he ever killed anyone?" Alexandra searched among the

trees for Ulyanov and found him still leaning against the tree far away from her. It had not occurred to her that he'd done this before, though, knowing of his reputation, it should have. All those angry husbands.

"Sure," said Lopukhin, "two, I think. The others were just woundings. He got it once himself, too, in the leg." Lopukhin slapped his thigh to indicate the spot.

Alexandra stared at the figure leaning so casually against the tree. He had killed before and clearly thought nothing of it. She was suddenly in awe of him as she had never been before. However, the knowledge that death, *his* death, was really possible today was spreading through her veins until the icy blood had reached her heart, which seemed to stop. She clutched at Lopukhin's arm, just to feel the warmth of another human presence near her.

"It's all right, Karpatsky," he said, patting her hand. "All part of learning to be a man. We're all frightened at first—it's nothing to be ashamed of. This is where we find our manhood. We don't matter, you know, we're all just dust. This is how we prove it. If we're not willing to die for something bigger than ourselves, we are nothing."

"What's so big about this? A foolish man has quarreled with a stubborn one," said Alexandra.

"Oh, it's not about the quarrel," said Lopukhin, "it's the principle behind it."

"That's an abstraction."

"Exactly," said Lopukhin. "That's the point. The grandeur of it, if there's any. To throw your life away for an abstraction, not even for something real. Rather dashing, don't you think?"

"It sounds like foolish waste to me," said Alexandra. "I don't think I want to learn to be a man."

"Too bad, " said Lopukhin, "you have no choice. None of us does. Now let's get started. Into the jaws of death, you know. Let me see ..." He scratched his nose with his gloved hand. "What next? Yes! We must each approach our men and ask if they wish a reconciliation. Then we can begin."

Alexandra scanned the field for Durinov, found him pacing back and forth at the edge of the clearing, then took off running in that direction, her empty scabbard slapping against her thigh, the snow slipping under her feet.

"I have to ask," she said breathing hard, her hand on her waist, "if you will withdraw the challenge."

Durinov, looking rather foolish in the top hat, which was actually too small for him, sneered. "The scoundrel must be erased from the human race," he said.

"Oh please," said Alexandra, rushing her words, breathing even harder to get it out, "you don't mean that. He's a human being just like you. You cannot throw your lives away for something so trivial as this quarrel. It's senseless. It's evil."

"The evil," said Durinov, raising his chin, "is to allow him to continue to exist!"

Alexandra grabbed Durinov by the collar with both hands. "Listen, my little man," she said, shaking him, "Alexandra Korvin is no lady. I know her well. She's selfish and cruel, completely unworthy of this action. You are mad to risk your life for her."

Alexandra released him. He staggered and righted himself.

"It is you who are mad. I will not withdraw the challenge."

"Oh God." Alexandra turned away. She dropped her head and covered her face with her hand. Lopukhin, who came toward her running, bent down to try to see her face. "Did he withdraw the challenge? Sometimes they do, you know."

Alexandra didn't answer.

"I see," said Lopukhin, "he does not withdraw the challenge. All right. Then they will have to take up their pistols and move to their positions."

As challenger, Durinov had first choice of weapon. He hesitated over the case Lopukhin was holding open, hemming and hawing like a child picking out a chocolate from a candy box—this one, no, that one, no, this one. Finally, he reached out and grasped a weapon, drew it from the box, and held it up to admire its gleaming barrel. "This one, yes," he said, "a little beauty."

Lopukhin turned to Ulyanov, who had been standing near him with a bored expression on his face, smoking another cigarette. He took up his pistol without even looking at it. "Take your places, gentlemen," said Lopukhin.

Each man walked to his end of the track of footprints marking the forty paces in the snow; each man unbuttoned his coat to present an unobstructed target. Lopukhin and Alexandra took up positions to the side, exactly centered between the barriers.

"Now say it. What I told you," Lopukhin said, bending his head to her.

Alexandra cleared her throat and tried to speak. Nothing came out but a tiny squeak of the sort one produces in a nightmare. Lopukhin elbowed her.

"Inasmuch," she said loudly, "as the adversaries have refused a reconciliation, please proceed..." She knew there was more but could not remember it. Lopukhin nudged her again.

He whispered, "Take your pistols..."

"Take your pistols!" shouted Alexandra.

"And at the word *three*..."

"And at the word *three*," she continued.

"Begin to advance..."

"Begin to advance!"

"One..."

"One!"

"Two . . ."

"Two!"

"Three . . ."

"Three!"

The two men advanced toward the barriers, Durinov stalk-
ing, Ulyanov sauntering, both with their arms outstretched, the
pistols' long barrels lengthening their arms into the oddest
shapes. While he advanced, Ulyanov continued to puff on his
cigarette. Lopukhin laughed.

"It's an old duelist's trick," he said, leaning over toward Alexandra. "Intimidates the adversary, shows him that your hand
isn't shaking."

Alexandra didn't answer. She was staring at Durinov to see
what he would do. She watched him raise his arm higher to aim
his pistol, and she saw that the barrel was shaking. On he went,
now staggering through the snow, the ends of his open coat
whitening, the barrel of the weapon continuing to oscillate at the
end of the trembling arm. She heard the cracking of a pistol shot
and did not know which one of them had fired until she saw the
smoke that spurted from the end of Durinov's gun.

She squeezed her lids shut over her eyes.

"I see," said Lopukhin drily, "that Durinov's aim has not
improved."

"What did you say?" Alexandra opened her eyes.

"I said his aim has not improved. He couldn't be wider of the
mark if he'd aimed at the Peter and Paul."

Durinov had fallen in the snow facedown, and he lay there
kicking in frustration. Ulyanov, who was still smoking, had lowered his pistol and was simply standing there.

"Captain Mecklenburg-Ulyanov," Lopukhin called, "discharge
your weapon! You know the rules!"

With a careless gesture, Ulyanov shot his pistol at the ground and threw it there.

"Go back to what you said before, about Durinov," said Alexandra through gritted teeth.

"You mean about his aim? Oh yes! It's such a waste of time for him, these duels, but he insists. He's always challenging someone, you know, and everybody knows he can't hit a barn door, so they all just shoot at the ground and leave it at that. We all keep hoping he'll improve and make it interesting, but he hasn't yet, poor man. We have to take it seriously though, every time. But every time it turns out the very same."

"Thank you," said Alexandra, advancing with determination in Ulyanov's direction. Puzzled, Lopukhin watched. Karpatsky was supposed to be going to Durinov's aid—he was the little man's second, after all. Karpatsky should have been helping Durinov up, brushing him off. Durinov was now sitting up in the snow looking stunned, but Karpatsky walked right past him and up to the captain. The cornet began to push the captain backward, pushing with his hand at Ulyanov's chest. The captain seemed to be laughing.

How very odd, thought Lopukhin, looking down to rummage in his sabretache for his cigarette case.

Karpatsky smacked Ulyanov in the face.

Lopukhin's head snapped up. Had he seen what he thought he had seen? An offense against the military law, warranting court-martial, possible execution? The captain, however, seemed unconcerned. He laughed openly now, throwing out his hands, and when Karpatsky turned his back on him, the captain grabbed the cornet by the arm, talking at him with a worried expression, serious now. Karpatsky jerked his arm away, but the captain held on to him. Then Karpatsky broke away and began to walk quickly away from the captain. Ulyanov followed, intensely arguing, but Karpatsky reached up and covered his ears with his hands. How childish. How unbecoming of a man, an officer.

Durinov rose unsteadily to his feet and stood bewildered in the middle of the clearing, blinking in confusion, before leaning over to retrieve the top hat that had fallen from his head.

I will not resign, and if you ever come near me again, I will kill you" was the last thing Alexandra had said to Ulyanov before seizing Durinov by the arm and marching him through the woods and back to the sledge, where she found her shy driver engaged in serious conversation with Ulyanov's, both of them waving their whips in the air for emphasis and shouting at each other cheerfully.

"Your honor, my master . . . ," said Ulyanov's driver, straightening up when he saw her.

"Should have died but didn't," Alexandra said to him, pushing Durinov up onto the seat and jumping in beside him, where he began immediately to replay the fight, analyzing his mistakes, questioning his choice of weapon, the angle of his stance, his speed of approach, the position of his arm. When they reached his palace, Alexandra pushed him out again onto the street, where he continued muttering to himself, shaking his head, before he turned and walked wearily up the steps.

Weary herself, Alexandra stood swaying in the hall of Korvin palace, feeling she could not walk another step. Her body, with the sensation of inner dryness that comes from sleeplessness, felt hollowed out, and she wondered if her head, with its dessicated brain, might snap from her neck and roll along the floor, rattling like a gourd.

She could kill him. She could really kill him this time. But thoughts of Ulyanov's satisfying murder were interrupted by a scream, the sound of which, coming from somewhere in the upper regions of the building, echoed through the empty palace before reaching the inside of her skull. She rushed up the stairs.

The sound had come from her bedroom. Opening the door, she saw that the screams were coming from something monstrous on the bed, something swollen that struggled and kicked and swore. It was Matryona, her labor begun. Praskovia and Nikifor were on either side of her, their faces tight.

As if I really need this now, thought Alexandra, tossing her shako wearily onto the floor and beginning to unbutton her enormous coat. "And why," she said, pointing to the squirming body, "did you have to put her in my bed?"

"Only bed in the house, little countess," said Praskovia. "She deserves that, doesn't she?"

"I suppose," said Alexandra, dropping into a chair.

"And you can make your own tea, little mistress," Praskovia added, "since I am busy here."

"I will make the tea," said Nikifor, rising up from his crouching position by the bed.

"You will not," said Praskovia, shooting him a look. "I need you here. I need your strong arms to hold her down so she will not go running through the palace and out to the street to try to leave her pain behind. I have seen this happen."

"I will do as his honor directs me," said Nikifor pompously.

"You will do as I direct you," said Praskovia. Nikifor looked at her with such adoration that Alexandra wondered if the two of them might be in love. And what would be the result of this? she thought bitterly. Why, more of that!

Matryona's face swelled with pain, growing larger and redder until Alexandra thought it would burst. Her enormous belly seemed to have a life of its own, moving to its own rhythm as it clenched itself, stiffened, and relaxed again, but of course it really did have a life of its own, and one that the owner of that belly could not control—the child would fight its way out, the woman's own body its ally in this bone-stretching war between two organisms, each desperate to achieve its separateness. Never had the full horror of womanhood come before her with such force, its character of suffering and sacrifice, its bondage to the flesh, which served to succor others, designed to be poked and prodded, sucked and drained, emptied of warmth and life until it hollowed out and dried and blew away with the wind.

"That baby will kill her," said Alexandra, standing up and clutching at the hilt of her sword as if ready to battle biology itself, "as surely as I killed my mother. We must get a doctor."

"Such hysteria!" said Praskovia. "You did not kill your mother. A doctor is not needed. We don't have the money for it, even if we needed him, which we don't. She's doing fine," said Praskovia, laying her ear against the struggling mound, "she's doing fine. The baby tells me so. He's digging with his hands, digging out his tunnel into life." Praskovia stared at the belly with a look of pride and satisfaction, stroking it gently.

"He will kill her," Alexandra insisted, unable to understand why Praskovia was so indifferent to the danger, mystified by the old serf's equanimity, as if this were a natural event, a part of life and not the end of life itself.

"If he does, so be it, but he has to come out," said Praskovia. "He can't stay in forever, as much as he would like to. But he will have his chance to get back in again, or part of him. Won't he, Nikifor?"

To Alexandra's disgust, Nikifor, so courtly, so refined, laughed crudely at the joke, but, seeing Alexandra stare at him, he stifled his laugh and stiffened his face into a mask.

"I will make your tea, your honor."

"No you won't," said Praskovia. "The little countess will

make it for herself. It will give her something to do instead of standing there being frightened and distracting me and upsetting the little mother who is working hard."

Alexandra, who could not take her eyes from the monstrous belly that bounded and leaped with inner life, did not move.

"Go! Out of here! Go!"

Alexandra ran out into the hallway and down the stairs to the kitchen, eager to be away from the room that smelled of blood and sweat, of coming death. She would not be a witness to that death, would not, for she felt it was her mother's death, her mother who lay there struggling on the bed, and she herself the cause of it.

She paced the kitchen, back and forth, covering her ears. Then with trembling fingers she buttoned up her coat again and went out.

She urged her driver to hurry, hurry, and then, although his long face told her he was eager to be home for the birth of the baby and that she should send him back and get a cab when she was ready to return, she told him he must wait for her, and she did not bother to watch as he pulled his head down into his large collar like a turtle, hurt, pulling back into its shell.

In the dining room of the Officers' Assembly there was no one. It was Sunday morning, a fact that she had forgotten, and the officers would be with their families, or, if unmarried, home in their beds sleeping off the effects of the previous night's debauch. The room was empty but for the table and chairs and the long sideboard that stood against the wall, covered with plates of food and bottles of vodka. Alexandra felt she could drink them all. But she must eat first.

She ate standing up, in the fashion of Russian men, or rather tried to eat, but found that the ham and sausage turned dry in her mouth. Still, she forced the food down so that she could drink, which she did, slopping the vodka into the glass and tossing it past her tongue and into her dry throat, where it burned its way down into her stomach.

Alexandra took two apples from a bowl and walked out across the courtyard and into the stable, where she found a sentry lying with his head on the table sleeping soundly. The horses, who were eager for the exercise they would not get today, snorted and stamped their feet at the sight of her, hoping to attract a rider, but she was interested only in Hercules, who turned his long head at the sound of her footsteps and drew back his velvety lips from his long curved teeth, which seized the apple she offered him and crunched it efficiently between their flat surfaces. The stiff short whiskers on his muzzle tickled her palm.

She wanted to ride him. There was no one about to do it for her, so she saddled and bridled him herself and led him out into the courtyard, where she mounted him. She walked him to a snowy field, where a series of posts with small pyramids of clay on top were ranged in two long rows. Alexandra unsheathed her saber, spurred Hercules into a canter, and, with slashing gestures first to one side and then to the other, cut the tops off the pyramids as she galloped past, her mouth set in a tight grimace as the chips of clay flew around her. She would have liked to do it again, and again and again, but there was no one to set up more of the pyramids for further practice in wounding and dismembering. She cantered round the field, then, bored, walked Hercules around a bit to cool him down and took him back to the stable, where she unsaddled and groomed him.

What now? What else was there to do? She supposed she could practice with her sidearm, the small pistol she was required to carry at all times, though she had never quite been able to understand its purpose. Whom was she supposed to shoot? Deserting soldiers? Captured officers cheating during a game of cards? Herself? Ah yes, herself. She remembered now. An affront to the honor of the regiment required death. If someone touched her epaulets or—God forbid—tore one of them off, she was supposed to shoot to kill or, failing that, to shoot herself.

On the firing range, she raised her arm, shot over and over and over again at the target, though it was difficult to see it clearly in the blinding brilliance of the snow, which bounced back at her the searing light of early afternoon. Reloading with bullets from the pouch she wore on her belt, she shot again at a walk, firing as she went, walking in leisurely pace toward the looming target, a straw-stuffed figure of a man. She tried to hit his heart. But then she grew bored with that too.

Still, she refused to go home. The sun blazed up and began to sink again, and surely her driver was growing thirsty and cold and hungry while he waited, eager to be home again, but she refused to think of him. Refused.

She went back to the dining room and sat for a while smoking, hoping someone might come in, but no one came. She drank some more vodka, cleaned her pistol with a cloth, ate a slice of ham. Aha, she remembered, the duty officer! There should be someone here. Yes, she saw the schedule on the door. Young Lieutenant Vorontsov was assigned today. He would be someone to drink with. But where was he? He would likely be in the museum, and if he wasn't, she could look at the exhibits, dull as they were. But going to the door, she found it locked; placing her ear to the wood, she heard the sounds of voices, one of them a woman's. The woman was laughing, the silly giggling that women did when in the company of men, and why? It wasn't as if men had anything interesting to say. Their conversation was so dull. Discussions of different types of guns, their relative merits and demerits—the firing action of one, the stiff trigger of another, length of barrel, caliber of bullet, rifling action versus smoothbore, all of it tedious. All of this interest in things and how they worked. Who cared how they worked and why as long as they did? Men. And this fascination with putting things inside other things and taking them out again. Bullets inside guns. Swords inside sheaths. Metal parts inside other metal parts to make a structure. She supposed it was this drive to make things fit that had given rise to architecture, science, other things like that, but so what? Once she had seen the junior officers spend several hours seeing how tall they could make a pyramid of vodka glasses by inserting each inside the other; now what was the point of that? But of course they couldn't leave it that way. Having assembled this structure of things inside other things, they smashed it so that they could build it up again.

No wonder they sought the company of women. Clearly an attempt to relieve their boredom by finding someone interesting to talk to. Putting her ear to the door again, however, Alexandra had to admit that she did not hear much talking going on between Vorontsov and his girl, and wondered if the drive to insert things inside other things might play a more decisive part in their pursuit of women than a hunger for good conversation.

And women! They only conspired with men in this activity of putting things inside other things, themselves the thing that things were put inside so that other things came out of them again, a vicious circle. If only they would stop it before it started.

Alexandra longed to sleep. She was so tired. But she could not go back into that house. She went to the sideboard, filled a glass with vodka, and tossed the liquid down her throat, after which she wiped her mouth crudely with her hand. She stuffed her mouth with a piece of ham. But it was no good. As hard as she had tried to forget the driver, she could not. She filled a large glass with vodka, piled a napkin with sausage, cheese, and bread for him, and went out of the dining room.

His name was Piotr. Alexandra sat with him up on the box, from which she could see the long bodies of the horses, their long donkeylike ears. It was three in the afternoon, and nearly dark by now.

"Why didn't you tell us your name?" she asked him, listening for the striking of clocks all over the city, the booming of bells that told her, to her discomfort, time was passing.

"Too hard for me to say," he mumbled, his mouth full of sausage.

"Then we'll think of another," said Alexandra, "one that is easy to say." She thought for a moment. "Pavel?"

"Too hard," he said. "It's the *p*'s that mess me up."

"Grisha?"

The driver swallowed his sausage and then mouthed the name, trying it out on his divided upper lip. "That I can say."

"Good," said Alexandra, "good. We have given you a name. Rebaptized you, like a new baby, and you will have new life."

"Mistress," he said, swinging his whip back and forth, "the new baby. I want to go home. I want to see it. I love babies."

"I do not want to see the baby," said Alexandra, "and the mother will be dead by now."

The newly christened Grisha turned his face to her. One eye was turned out, looking in another direction, but the eye that was fixed on her face was clear. "Why don't we just see?" he said.

"Do we have to?" said Alexandra, but they did.

Alexandra found Matryona propped up in her bed with the gold light from the gas lamp glowing on her face—a small round sun in the dark and wintry room, a smaller and even rounder bald-headed moon pressed against it, a tiny new planet lately exploded out of the dark universe inside its mother's body. Alexandra stepped closer to see, while Grisha followed her to the bed, and Praskovia and Nikifor smiled their benevolence, two sweaty, bloodstained gods of childbirth.

The little creature's face, bright red as if thoroughly boiled in the cauldron of its mother's belly, seemed folded in on itself, just a bud of a face still unopened, its petals tight, but miraculous in its miniaturization, possessed of tiny features all in perfect imitation of the real.

"A boy!" exulted Praskovia, lifting aside the piece of cloth to display the proof of this amazing fact, and again Alexandra saw the perfect imitation of the real, the miraculous miniature, amazing in its detailed craftsmanship. "His feet!" Praskovia cried, revealing them, "his hands!"

"And Matryona?" Alexandra asked, though she could see the woman's healthy glow. In fact, Matryona seemed herself to be newborn, a fresh being just lately come into the world and amazed at all she saw.

"Fine," said Praskovia, "just fine."

"So he did not kill her as I killed my mother," said Alexandra slowly, herself amazed.

"You did not kill your mother," said Praskovia with a sigh.

But Alexandra turned away, strode into the next room, and settled herself down to sleep wrapped up in her greatcoat, her boots sticking out beneath her coat in the fashion of a true hussar.

To demonstrate her defiance of Ulyanov, Alexandra began to behave recklessly. Of course, Ulyanov respected her rather vehement request that he stay away from her, but this only seemed to incite her to further outrageousness. Even Lopukhin, looking on in puzzlement, was unwilling to follow where she went.

With her new friend, the Polish lieutenant, Prince Sapieha, who had been watching her with admiration in his eerie eyes from the distance of another squadron for many months, studying the moment when he'd get close enough to scent the freshness of young Karpatsky's flesh, Alexandra spent a great deal of time. It was not that the prince wanted Karpatsky for himself. Karpatsky would belong to others more worthy, to those of both sexes who would relish the young count's ambiguous charm, the bloom of childhood still clinging moistly to him in a way that would appeal to the most refined of sensibilities. Sapieha himself wanted only to stand in the background watching, knowing what would happen when the door closed, so to speak, so that he could carry the knowledge away in his mind to think about when he was by himself, imagining the progressive exposure of more, and more tender, flesh, each cry of pleasure, each moan of joy, as he lay in his bed at night. This would be a satisfaction deeper than the crudely sensual.

The prince liked to display for the young Karpatsky the myriad faces of the city, in particular the most degraded—the results of God's injustices. The poor of the city bore this out most clearly. Poverty had reduced their humanity to its animal essence, he liked to point out to her as he tossed a handful of coins onto the floor of a filthy tavern and watched the drunks who had been hiding themselves in pots of beer reveal themselves as insects scuttling along the floor to snatch the rolling coins. He would often engage the inebriates in conversation, weeping along with them as they related their tales of wives run off, positions lost, children dead and dying, legacies squandered, educations abandoned, ambitions thwarted, dreams destroyed. To the prince, these revelations were nourishing. He made a meal of others' miseries, clucking his tongue and drawing a coin or bill from his purse for his informant, who would grow tearful and thankful and protest that the money would be used for "the children," and the prince would watch with satisfaction as the children's bread and shoes transformed themselves into vodka and beer and made their way down the desperate throat.

"A miracle," the prince would say to Alexandra, "water into wine, bread into vodka, shoes into beer."

"That is blasphemy."

"And all the more wonderful," said the prince.

Once, while listening to another tale of woe, the prince drew from his pocket a large pearl, which gleamed in the palm of his soft white hand as he passed it under Alexandra's eyes. "Now watch," he said, waiting until the drinker's head had dropped and his eyes had drifted shut. The prince then passed his hand over his neighbor's mug of beer and sat back to watch what would happen. In a few moments, the hairy hand groped for the pot of forgetfulness. The prince and Alexandra watched as the man drank deeply of oblivion. By way of ordering the man another pot, the prince showed Alexandra the empty bottom of the mug. The pearl had disappeared. The man had not noticed that he'd drunk it down.

The prince, getting up to go, leaned over and whispered in

the drunkard's ear, "Salvation lies within," and Alexandra and the prince struggled to contain their laughter at the idea that the answer to the poor man's prayer was marinating at this moment in his stomach and would, sometime tomorrow, be found in the bottom of a latrine.

"As you see," said the prince as they walked the streets, placing their boots into the footprints frozen in the filthy snow to make their way across the uneven crust that covered the sidewalks and bridges, sinking their faces inside the collars of their greatcoats to shield them from the wind, "their religion gives them nothing. They get more from liquor. What a sham it all is, holding out to them promises of eternal bliss if they abide by arbitrary rules that prevent them from finding bliss here on earth."

Alexandra was not listening. She was leaning her elbows on the railing of the bridge watching the cold-thickened water struggle in its attempt at forward motion, fail. A body rolled in the water. She huddled herself deeper into her coat, as if to hide herself.

"It is by the crossing of man-made boundaries," said the prince, coming up beside her to look down into the water, "that we find out who we really are."

"Are they man-made?"

"Does it matter? Man is God," said the prince, "all laws thought to be God-given are made by man. By us."

"How? If God made us in the first place?"

"Yes," said the prince. "He gave us free will to defy Him, so he could please himself by punishing us. Only animals are exempt from this, amoral. So pure in their being, animals, without artifice or guile. Pure instinct. Pure desire."

"But not pure in love," said Alexandra. "That is human."

"Is it?" said the prince.

Tears welled in Alexandra's eyes, froze instantly in the bitter cold, and dropped as tiny jewels into the waters of the Neva far below.

Alexandra appeared every morning at the mess with deeply shadowed eyes, and looked out of them to Ulyanov, who did not look back at her or comment on how tired she seemed. So, with the Polish prince she laughed softly behind her hand, their heads together, but Ulyanov did not seem to notice that either. He did not come to the ring to watch her riding practice any longer, to set one booted foot upon the lowest rung of fence, to chew a piece of straw in meditation while frowning at her progress. Nor did he appear at target practice to check the balance of her pistol, fire it, hand it back, and grunt with approval when she hit the mark. He did not stand with his arms crossed to observe her training of recruits, or follow her through the barracks advising her on how to deal with a homesick boy, or one who shivered with fever, or one who staggered, drunk, along the halls. His shoulder no longer appeared beneath her head when she was tired.

Ulyanov ate his meals at the Officers' Assembly quickly and left upon finishing, not lingering to talk or drink with the other officers, as he had used to do. Where he went in the evenings no one knew. Nowhere, the men guessed. Probably stayed at home with his mother. This only incited Alexandra to a desire for further indiscretions, more smoking of opium and drowning in champagne, more adventures in the darkness of the city's heart. Anything to irritate him, rub his nose in her independence, though the sound of Ulyanov's voice often moved her to confusions of swallowed tears.

"The plague ball, what is that?" she asked the prince when he suggested to her one afternoon at lunch that she accompany him to this event.

"A place where God is punished for his torments of the human race," he said, "where boundaries are crossed, and freedom found. Where we worship ourselves."

I'm all for that, thought Alexandra, looking round at Ulyanov, hoping he had heard. But Ulyanov was speaking to another officer. He did not return her gaze.

Not long afterward, it was the night of the plague ball, and Alexandra walked beside the prince through one of the city's enormous empty squares, a palace blazing in the distance across the square and a pale Venetian moon above their heads. Black figures in snapping, twisting cloaks were being blown across the square ahead of them. With cold hands they anchored their masks to their white-powdered faces. In this square, the prince explained, it was Venice in time of plague. The figures, blown from another time and place, landed in the palace and disappeared.

Where had the black-cloaked figures gotten to? There was no one inside the palace that Alexandra could see. A polished hallway stretched into the shadows, but the prince beckoned her, holding back a rich carpet that hung on the wall. Behind this carpet was a door. Down a narrow staircase, round and round she went. Faint puffs of music drifted up to her like smoke. A hot point of light grew larger as she sank deeper.

She found herself inside an enormous space that glittered like a diamond, as if the weight of the city up above had crushed it into hardness, clarity.

The prince licked his finger, touched the shimmering wall, and dipped his fingertip into the astonished O of Alexandra's mouth.

"It's salt," she said, spitting out the finger.

Columns carved in the shape of human figures towered up from the uneven floor. Dancers skipped between the titanic feet, but a few intrepid guests had climbed the colossal legs and hung there, one of them with his legs around a glittering breast and his mouth sucking at the snowy nipple. Others clustered round the ankles and seemed to be licking them.

Alexandra danced. Her partners were tall and elegant women whose waists were curiously thick, whose shoulders were strangely heavy, and these women danced with men whose hips were oddly wide. They all stared out from behind their masks at no one, at nothing in particular, their gaze turned inward. Except for one, who was staring from behind a velvet mask at young Karpatsky in particular, and exchanged a nodding glance with Prince Sapieha, just as the prince had planned.

"When will you sell this pile of rubble?" asked Praskovia, holding on her shoulder, which was already wet with fragrant spittle, the bald little head of the baby, tender and round and fuzzy as a small, soft peach.

"Never," said Alexandra. "It is who I am."

"Who you are is in your heart," said Praskovia. "You don't need a palace."

"Says you," said Alexandra, "who has never owned a palace, so how could you know?"

The palace seemed to be fading round her, though. Stripped of its former functions (as gathering place for the nobles of the city, as venue for balls, soirees, and dinners), its rooms were dark and empty. It was no longer a palace, but merely an arbitrary structure built of cold marble and useless stone, pointlessly large, pointlessly grand, an enormous burdensome weight on its mistress's shoulders. The family huddled into the one room that Alexandra could afford to heat against the cold that poured into the cracks that had opened long before in the palace walls. Matryona had gone again—one good thing, as there was one less mouth to feed, but she no longer provided free milk for the baby, which must now be bought with coins counted carefully from Alexandra's purse, which had been nearly emptied by her insistence on paying her entire mess bill by herself. The day after the duel, she had demanded its delivery into her very own hands so that Ulyanov could not interfere with it.

One day the prince watched as Alexandra, standing at the sideboard in the Officer's Assembly, ignored the vodka and champagne and placed onto her plate one thin slice of ham. She sat down at the table and cut the ham into bits to make it last, chewing slowly at each fragment, sucking out its flavor before swallowing the drained shard of meat. Exultantly, he noted that she looked thinner, that her boots had not been polished and her uniform not cleaned in several weeks.

"My dear Karpatsky," said the prince in his softest voice as he seated himself beside her, "I know of someone who might assist you in your career, someone who is dedicated to the support of our country's officers, particularly those for whom service is a sacrifice. This individual enjoys great satisfaction in helping the young who are in need."

"I am not in need," said Alexandra.

The prince snapped his teeth together.

"I did not say you were in need. But any of us could benefit from the influence of a sponsor, a protector, someone with influence at court who would promote our interests. How else do you expect to progress, to rise? How else do you think it is done?"

"Through competence? Ability?"

The prince closed his eyes, shook his head.

"My dear Karpatsky, one glance at our command will tell you that ability is irrelevant. Connections are what count. Am I incorrect in suspecting something of a lack in that area in your case?"

"I suppose not," said Alexandra. "Yes, I am alone in the world." She spread her fingers to admire her clean, short fingernails and the large strength of her hand before placing it firmly on the table. "But I can take care of myself. And intend to do so."

"Not alone," said the prince, covering her hand with his, "not alone."

Alexandra dragged her hand out from underneath his.

"Won't you meet this person at the very least?" insisted the prince. "I could arrange a dinner."

"A dinner?" said Alexandra, thinking that it had been very long since she had had something good to eat, and enough of it.

"Oh, a marvelous dinner," said the prince, "oysters, charlotka, the very best wines."

Alexandra stared at him dubiously, which led the prince to believe that the suggested menu did not please her.

"Lobster in sorrel, pheasant glacé, roast venison, assorted fruits?"

Alexandra drummed her fingers on the table, thinking. A tornado of snow was swirling outside the window, and she thought of the cold inside the palace pinching at the tender tip of the baby's minimal nose. She was not certain the little one was getting enough milk, though the adults ate less than ever so they could buy him more. At that moment, Ulyanov entered the mess hall with a group of junior officers and, on seeing Alexandra, threw back his head and laughed gaily, as though something marvelously funny had been said to him, though the discussion in fact had been centering on the distressingly high rate of casualties in the war that was always going on in the Caucasus.

"Yes," said Alexandra loudly, "I would *love* to have dinner with your friend. I would love to."

• • •

There was no doubt that the waiter who served the private dining rooms of the Grand Hotel enjoyed his job. He was a man
who loved beauty and here, in these dining rooms without doorknobs, he witnessed beauty of many kinds. The silk-smooth
sheets of linen that sheathed the tables were a delight to him as
he snapped open their stiff folds and sent the cloth flying into
the air only to settle as softly as snow on the tabletops, across
which lovers would gaze at themselves in the mirror of the
other's face. Lovingly he placed the heavy silver instruments of
dining on the field of white, lined up the many-shaped goblets
and flutes in order of use, and decanted wine into crystal con-
tainers, leaning over to sniff with his pointed nose the expensive
perfume of the liquid—ah. A sparkling city of glass had risen on
the table, and in placing the napkins he was careful not to disturb its symmetry. With hands on hips he surveyed his work
with satisfaction, pleased at his contribution to the night's ritual
of beauty and its worship. He turned to the chaise, which he saw
as the very altar of this religion of love, a long couch open at the
sides for ease of access, its moss-green velvet worn exactly in the
middle by the bumping and sliding of many pairs of buttocks
and knees. He dimmed the lamps to a flattering half dark,
understanding that some of the celebrants did not welcome the
exposure of various wattles and wrinkles. He raised the silver
covers from the dishes that stood on the sideboards and sniffed
deeply at the truffles and roasted birds.

A knock on the door! One of the celebrants had arrived! O
beauty, thought the waiter, confronting the frown of the blond
cavalry officer who had been groping the outside of the knobless
door for some means of access. The young officer entered the
room, pulled his shako from his head, shook the snow from the

deep dark folds of his greatcoat, and stamped it from the surface of his wet boots until the carpet was littered with delicate clumps of snowflakes that melted into the lush pile, leaving spots of wetness in their wake. How like beauty itself, those delicate snowflakes so quickly vanished, thought the waiter, bowing repeatedly from the waist and suppressing his urge to gaze adoringly at this young Adonis, to drink his freshness.

"I'm supposed to meet someone here," said Alexandra, flopping down on the chaise in a way that made the waiter wince at the disrespect shown this sacred piece of furniture, "but I don't know who it is."

Even better, thought the waiter. A procurer had been at work. He preferred the term *matchmaker*, and wondered why this ancient profession should be held in such disdain. What harm was there in a third party's intervening in the name of love to satisfy desire, put two together who might otherwise never have met? What harm in the mentorly relationship that would develop, the elder trading his wisdom for access to the youth of the other? And if money entered in? Were not youth and wisdom currencies themselves? Were they not indeed more precious than conventional specie, than rubles and francs and pounds?

"Do you know who it is that is coming to meet me?" said Alexandra to the waiter. "My friend would not tell me. I suppose it's to be a surprise." She shrugged and fiddled with her sabretache, feeling for her case of cigars. "Some surprise," she said, trying to strike a match on the wet bottom of her boot until the waiter, hurrying over with a flint, solved her problem.

"I'm afraid I do not know the identity of your dinner partner, sir," said the waiter nervously, as if suddenly aware he was involved in a process somewhat unsavory to the outsider's eye. "We are discreet here. We keep our eyes shut. And our ears."

This admission brought no signal of approval from Alexandra, who puffed aggressively on her cigar, skewering the waiter with her eyes. "And what is it," she said, "that you would see were you to open them? I'd like to know what goes on here. What sort of place this is."

This was actually the last sort of question the waiter wished to answer, because in answering it for the boy, he would have to answer it for himself. He stood mute and confused, unwilling to think about anything, when he was saved by the sound of a light knocking at the door. The waiter, relieved, rushed to open it, and Alexandra, on seeing who entered quietly, who handed his hat to the waiter and shook the snowy cape from his shoulders into the waiter's waiting arms, leaped from her seat and allowed the cigar to slip smoldering from her fainting fingers as Rybynsky himself advanced on her with public smile and outstretched hand.

How they found themselves seated on the couch Alexandra would never be able to remember: a blur of vocal pleasantries, the too-intimate touch of a hand upon her arm were all that penetrated her mind at that moment. And the sickly sweet odor of Violetta di Parma, an expensive Italian scent that emanated powerfully from Rybynsky's position beside her, as if the perfume ran through his veins like embalming fluid, his blood replaced by this transfusion of the artificial, the luxuriant, the expensive. Bought with Olga's money.

This isn't true, she tried to tell herself. This is not happening. Or if it is, it means something other than what it seems to mean.

"Tell me about yourself," Rybynsky was saying. There was a shifting in the pressure of his body on the couch as he apparently crossed his legs, and out of the corner of her eye (as she sat up stiffly staring at the floor) she could see the polished tip of his shoe tapping tensely at the empty air, impatient to get on with it.

But perhaps this was all a misunderstanding. Perhaps this place was not what the waiter had implied it was, what she had known perfectly well it was, but which she had entered willingly, pressed by curiosity, and now wished she hadn't.

"Why do you do this? What do you want of me?" she cried out, her hands bursting from her lap with the vehemence of her desire to be reassured by him that what he wanted of her—or, rather, him—was not what she knew very well that he wanted.

"No need to be nervous or upset," said Rybynsky in his smooth, polished voice. "I want to help you. I like to help young people. It gives me great satisfaction. Whatever I can do for you, I will gladly do. Prince Sapieha tells me you need some assistance in your career. Which regiment was that?"

It cannot be that he does not recognize me, she told herself. He must know who I am, that I am Alexandra Korvin. This must be his way of helping me, by subterfuge, in secret, out of his former regard for me, perhaps his love, even. To test this supposition, she turned her head and looked him full in the face, her eyes engaging with his. But Rybynsky was looking at her as he had never looked at her before; the normally glacial eyes were melting, oozing all over her face and running down her body as if to seep inside her, occupy every cavity and cranny of her person.

"Ah," he said softly, "I see we are getting somewhere. You must relax, young man, relax. I am no one to be afraid of. Let me get you something to drink. And then you will tell me all about yourself."

He stood up, the couch bouncing lightly as it was relieved of his weight, and Alexandra heard the sound of his footsteps going across the thick rug, the rustling of the crushed ice in the bucket, the soft pop of a stopper, the chink of crystal, the rush and splash of liquid against the bottom of a glass. That look he had given her had been pure in its voraciousness, nothing but appetite alone. No, he did not know her, saw not Alexandra Korvin, with whom he had talked and laughed quite pleasantly on many occasions, but a young man in the uniform of a hussar, and she wondered suddenly if he knew anyone at all, if anyone in the world existed for him at all besides himself.

Oh, my poor Olga, she thought, remembering the pleading letter from her friend. Rybynsky was making his way toward her, two glasses of champagne swaying and spilling their liquid as he walked, an expression of false concern with undertones of greed on his handsome face, but a face that now looked so different to her that she could not believe he was the same man that she had known.

The couch creaked again as Rybynsky seated himself, and Alexandra was conscious of the presence of the towel spread across the cushions under her and why it was there and how Rybynsky's fingers lingered in touching hers as he handed her the champagne and how his hand dropped oh-so-accidentally onto the thigh of what he believed to be a strange young man whom he had never met before but whom he was meeting now in the back room of a disreputable restaurant, all his highest hopes centered on his peculiar satisfaction, his high position turned to common currency to buy assent, cooperation.

Alexandra dropped her head to hide her tears. Rybynsky was talking now, eagerly, intensely, as if he sensed the imminent escape of his favored prey. He spoke of the other young people he had helped, of placing this young man in that position in the Ministry of Justice, or securing a promotion in rank for this young officer, or taking care of a problem with the police for this boy's family, and eagerly, desperately, his voice ran on, ran after this young man who was withdrawing, moving back in horror or confusion or fear or what, Rybynsky didn't know.

Alexandra got up. She extended her hand to thank him for her drink, but Rybynsky's eyes were pleading as if to say, just a touch, a touch is all I need, don't go until I have a touch, and he took that touch, without permission, without assent, as if it were his due. Not pleading any longer, not even asking leave, he reached out with his hand and squeezed her buttock, held its flesh tight between his fingers, and closed his eyes, not caring for his dignity or hers, and Alexandra thought, all right, all right, if that is what you need, poor soul, but then she thought, Olga, was it only your money he wanted? Then she remembered how she herself had tried to do the same and thought, I am no better than he is in the end, poor soul, he can't seem to help himself. Look at him, just look at him, and look at me. How sad the world is, sad. She was immobilized by her sudden grief and allowed his groping, squeezing hand to grip her tighter, did not even whimper, though he was hurting her, for what did it matter anymore?

A pounding at the door reached Alexandra's ears, and, tearing herself from Rybynsky's increasing iron grip, which showed he was about to finish, she sprinted across the room, snatched up her coat, and ran to the door, blessing the intrusive waiter. But it was not the waiter at the door. It was Nikifor, who stood breathing heavily as if he'd been running, face reddened by the wind and shoulders flaked with snow.

"Come at once," he said, "not a moment to lose," and without a backward glance Alexandra left the room, left Rybynsky and thoughts of him behind forever, and closed the door.

"But what? What is it?" she demanded, climbing quickly into her coat as her and Nikifor's booted feet padded down the carpeted stairway of the restaurant. "The baby? Is the baby sick?"

Nikifor did not answer her, only grabbed at her sleeve to hurry her along until he was nearly pulling her through the side door of the restaurant and into the alleyway and through it onto the pavement of the street, where she saw a strange carriage waiting, one that was not hers. Nikifor pushed her toward it. The door opened suddenly on its own, as if there were someone inside who had been waiting, which there was. Alexandra clambered in and the door was shut behind her.

"Good evening, Countess," said Trenyakov, who was sitting inside in high top hat and white silk scarf, as if he were on his way to a formal occasion. "I am sorry to have been so presumptuous as to call you away from your engagement, but there's no time to lose. Your mother has asked to see you."

"My mother!" cried Alexandra. "My mother's dead!"

"Not yet," said Trenyakov, tapping with his walking stick on the side of the carriage to signal the coachman to move off.

Alexandra and the lawyer Trenyakov galloped in their carriage through the nighttime streets of Petersburg, Alexandra opening her mouth to ask question after question and Trenyakov shaking his head or holding up a black-gloved hand for silence: "You will find out soon enough," he said. "It is not my place to tell you."

The carriage stopped. The door was opened. The long lip of tiny stairs snapped down, and Alexandra, followed by Trenyakov, exited. She looked up at the building in front of her, its face blank and cold, its features indistinguishable, faint in the darkness, though on one of the upper floors a light was burning. The form of this house, this palace, was familiar. She sensed she had been here before—there was something about the shape, the height, the shadowed decorations that corresponded vaguely with an imprint in her memory. An image floated up in her mind: a rain of diamonds dropped upon the floor, and a figure, once as tall as she, folded down upon itself, old before its time.

Of course. As if she hadn't known it all along.

The portraits of her mother that her father had destroyed,

his bitterness, the unaccountable visits to the princess in her childhood. *The flame that burned but did not warm.* Why had her father lied to her? Why had he created that false image of perfection? Why hadn't he simply told the truth? She knew.

"I am the daughter of a whore," she said suddenly out loud.

"Courtesan is a kinder way to say it," said Trenyakov, and grasped her sleeve to get her moving. "Hurry, we must hurry. She is dying and will not last the night."

Alexandra gripped his arm. Trenyakov drew back, tried to pull his arm away, but Alexandra held it fast. Another thought had struck her.

"Tell me," she cried, shaking the lawyer's arm, "tell me. Were they married? Tell me, were they married?"

"We must go. Not a minute to lose." Trenyakov, though smaller by a head, began to drag Alexandra through the snow, toward the steps leading up to the palace.

"No!" she cried, "no! You must tell me. You must tell me now."

Trenyakov looked at her. He pulled his arm away. "For pity's sake, Countess, have you no heart? Your mother is dying. Your rights of inheritance and title are of little consequence."

"They're of consequence to me," said Alexandra. "And what heart did she have for me?"

"Very well." Trenyakov dropped his gaze to the ground. "The answer is no."

"Then I am a bastard."

"Illegitimate is a kinder way to say it."

"Oh, damn your kindness," said Alexandra. "I only want the truth."

"The truth is yes. You are illegitimate."

"Then I am not the Countess Korvin at all."

"Legally, no."

Alexandra dropped her chin into the stiff, heavy collar of her coat and sighed. "Then I am nothing," she said, shaking her head, "the countess who is not a countess, daughter of the princess who was not a princess." She raised her head. "And my father? Was he really my father? Or doesn't anyone know?"

Trenyakov was shifting from foot to foot. "No! Of course he was your father. When your mother left him . . . oh, we haven't time! We haven't time!" Trenyakov lifted his eyes to the upper window far above, the light that glowed small in the darkness. He took her hand. "We must go, Countess, we must go."

Alexandra let him lead her through the door, up stairs and more stairs in the darkness, along musty corridors, and then up stairs and more stairs. He stopped at the door of a small room, knocked, and was admitted.

Something was lying on the bed in the dim room. It looked to be a bundle of bedclothes, but it was moving. The old serf who was the princess's only servant stood over the bed, and behind her was a man in black, presumably the doctor or undertaker. Alexandra approached the bed and saw among the folds of cloth a face as white as linen and a pair of eyes, one of which was clouded, gray.

The old serf took Alexandra by the hand and drew her closer to the bed. She leaned over it and said to the face, "She is here. She has come, my lady." Alexandra felt the servant press her hand against the princess's, which felt thin and dry as paper, though hot with fever. Alexandra tried to pull her hand away, but the old serf pressed her fingers down upon the princess's and held them there.

"There," said the serf to the princess, "she has come to you. She has come."

Alexandra did not want to look at the figure lying in the bed, but the old serf would have none of it. She explained to the frightened girl that death was good, death would bring the princess peace and that Alexandra must not be afraid to look.

Alexandra could see no peace, only struggle. But what kind of struggle? To escape the grip of life or hang on to it? Life was leaking from the princess's one good eye, the other already dead.

"Now say you are sorry, mistress," said the serf. "Tell your daughter you are sorry, and this will bring you peace and then you can go."

The figure on the bed seemed incapable of any speech at all. From its lungs issued long, tearing groans, and its feet seemed to scrabble under the bedclothes, as if trying to run from something, or toward it.

"Now say it, mistress, say you are sorry for leaving her, a little baby all alone," said the peasant woman in an oddly cheerful, singsong tone, "then you can go. Then you can rest."

Horribly, the word came out. Pushed out of the struggling lungs by force of physical effort, a "sorry," barely distinguishable from the groans, but distinguishable nonetheless—a grunt of a word, but formed of the proper sounds—emerged.

"There now," said the serf, "you've done it!" She turned to Alexandra. "Now tell her you forgive her. Hold tightly to her hand. And say it."

I do not forgive her, Alexandra thought, but said it anyway, squeezing the skeletal hand in hers.

"Forgiveness will come to you," said the peasant woman, who had noticed the insincerity in the young woman's voice but was undisturbed by it, "and now see how you've brought her peace." The serf waved her hand above the bed, her lips moving in prayer, and it was true. The body on the bed, working to die, had succeeded, or would before long. The long groans had dwindled into gasps, shallow, shortened breaths, as of a runner at the end of the race.

"Father Zosha!" cried the peasant woman. From behind the door, where he had been hiding, a priest appeared in gorgeous vestments that glowed in the half-lit room, and he carried an enormous book bound in gold. Chanting the majestic song of death and resurrection, of redemption and forgiveness of sins, he opened the book and pressed it down upon the woman's face for her to kiss, but the bony hand came up and scrabbled with its nails, trying to push the book away, as if she feared its suffocation. Still chanting, the priest lifted the book away, closed it, and laid it on the woman's chest. He held his hands above her head in final blessing. The figure in the bed was still.

"It's over. She's gone," said the serf, "and a fine death it was, but I wish she hadn't pushed the Holy Book away. Perhaps God will forget that. Perhaps he didn't see. No, I'm sure he didn't see."

Gone? Alexandra hadn't seen it. One moment the princess was alive, and then she wasn't. Alexandra turned away, and Trenyakov came up to put his hand upon her shoulder and guide her away.

"I would rather you had not known," said Trenyakov as he walked her down the stairs. "We always tried to keep it from you, all of us, but a child's duty to a mother, no matter what kind of a mother she has been, is a sacred thing. Especially at her death."

Alexandra did not speak but concentrated on keeping herself upright and walking.

"She was an unusual woman," said Trenyakov, "voracious in her vanity. She fed it with the admiration of many men, but it turned on her in the end, devoured her too."

"To whom does my palace belong?" said Alexandra suddenly, "I may have no right to it."

"Oh, not at all, not at all!" cried Trenyakov. "Your title of countess is one thing, but the property is legally yours!"

"Such as it is, which isn't much," said Alexandra. "In fact, it's nothing at all. Just a pile of stones, empty of meaning, like me. A palace that is not a palace for a countess who is not a countess, daughter of the princess who was not a princess, but a whore."

"No one need know that."

"But I know it."

In silence, they drove back to Korvin palace. Trenyakov helped Alexandra down and, standing on the pavement, held her hand a moment in his.

"I wish I could tell you that the princess had left you something at least to ease your situation," he said in parting, his hat in his hand and the night wind stirring the arrangement of hair that covered the bald spot on the top of his head, "but her estate is eaten up by debt as well. I am truly sorry. But I remain, as always, at your service." He replaced his top hat carefully and turned away. She heard his footsteps crunching in the snow, the creak of the carriage as he mounted, the clopping trot of the horses as he drove away.

Alexandra stood staring at the front door of her palace as if she had never seen it before. She stood there until Nikifor, who had occupied the box with Trenyakov's driver, appeared beside her and asked her something that she did not hear, did not answer. He turned the knob, the door swung open, but Alexandra did not enter. Instead, she turned around.

Down the snowy steps she went, her black boots sunk deep in the wet layer of white which had grown over the steps like weed. Snow was dropping down all over the city, spinning down out of the dark sky to distort the myriad rooftops, to dull the golden domes, to load the windowsills and harden into plaques of slippery ice beneath the hooves of the horses, the boots of the citizens, who, huddled silent in their coats, made their way carefully along the slippery streets. Alexandra, walking hard, realized that, boots or no, she could not hear her footsteps on the ground, could not feel her feet at all. She felt as if she were about to disappear entirely, about to fade into the wet and heavy air from the bottom up, dissolving into the the city like the others, swept away on its filthy tide.

Throwing up her arm, she hailed a passing cab, an open sledge, and, climbing up inside, she called out an address she was surprised she could remember. She pulled the lap robe up to her chin, settling under it for comfort. Her heart was thudding in her ears, which were closed to the sounds of the night in the city, and she wondered again why the address had risen so quickly to her consciousness.

Climbing out of the sledge, she called for the driver to wait, and ran heavily through the snow and up the steps of a house more modest than her own, no palace at all, but a home, clearly a home. She rang the bell and stood waiting, pacing round and round, unable to stop herself from moving.

"Not home" was the answer she received from the butler, who, casting his eyes up and down, noticed that the visitor was dressed in the uniform of his master's regiment, and added, "Try the headquarters."

She took off running again, through the slippery snow and back to the sledge, which she urged through the streets with shouts. "Hurry, hurry," she cried, and when the sledge reached its destination, she jumped down, threw a wad of money at the driver, and ran toward the only shelter that she knew.

On duty for the night, behind the desk in the regimental museum, Ulyanov looked up at the sound of running steps and rose from his seat. When he saw the expression on her face, he opened his arms and, when she reached him, gathered her into them.

It was dawn when Ulyanov woke and reached out for Alexandra, who should have been beside him on the cot. But she was gone. Dressing quickly, he ran through the quarters of the regiment, the Officers' Assembly, the stables, the barracks; she was not there. What did this mean? Had what happened really happened in the first place? Oh, it had. He felt a soreness at that point where his body had met the barrier between them, driven through—it had happened indeed. Not as he had wanted it to, but there it was. It had happened.

He felt remorse.

Now back in his bedroom at home, he walked the floor, sorting and sifting his thoughts.

Had she wanted to? Or had he forced her? Had he, in his excitement and his urgency, overborne the subtle signals of her hesitation, drowned them in the roaring river of his own emotions? Or had it been the other way around? Had she been the one to do the drowning, himself the one swept up and carried away? He honestly could not remember, for in those moments he had not been able to distinguish himself from her, so mixed together had they been, as if their very nerves were tangled up and interlaced so that he could not tell where she began, where he left off.

The sick hollow sensation in his stomach, however, told him he had done something wrong. No, this was not the new Ulyanov. Or rather, he told himself, cheering up for a moment, this was indeed the new Ulyanov. The old Ulyanov would have exulted crudely at having so easily seduced a respectable young woman, well brought up and sheltered and pure as newly fallen snow. Or would he have? It was something he had never done, certainly not in the guise of his old identity, when such women, such pure-eyed girls, had been off-limits. That much of honor he had had, confining his seductions to the already broken-in, to those types of married women whose eyes were warm with the impure thoughts that emanated from their boredom and, gaze lighting on him across the room and knowing, to his shame, of what he was, had glowed hot with recognition of one who would solve their problem. To those actresses and ballet girls in search of a protector to lavish upon them the clothes and jewels they could not provide themselves. To those seamstresses on the lookout for another ruble, respectably received as a post-love gift, which would enable them to pay their rent without resorting to the streets. To the house serfs and lady's maids delighted to put one over on those mistresses of theirs, respectable young girls, who had hoped to catch his interest and trap him into marriage. And so, he suddenly wondered, who had seduced whom? Who had been using whom?

Yes, she had been the one! To throw herself at him, to eat at his lips with exciting desperation, twining herself around him, going boneless, making sounds. And he had been in love with her so long. What else was he to do? Was he made of marble? Was he not a man? How could he have withstood her onslaught?

He sat heavily on his bed, gripping his head in his hands.

Still, it wasn't right, what he had done. As the older and wiser party, the more experienced in these matters, he ought to have restrained her, and himself. He had ruined her! Ruined her! But what was to be done?

His head snapped up. He knew. And why had he not thought of it before? So simple, so obvious, so right.

Ulyanov ran out of the room and down the stairs, leaping

impatiently down the last three steps to land lightly on the tiles of the hallway floor. He felt purposeful, on his way to do what he would do, which was only what he had done once before, but maybe this time it would work.

A few moments later, seated at the desk in his study, he studied his instruments and set them in order. A sharp pen, a pot of black ink and not blue, as was appropriate to the solemnity of the occasion, a sheet of snowy paper, pure. He smoothed the paper gently with his hand and took up his pen.

My dear Alexandra, he began firmly. Yes, the letters flowed from the pen and onto the paper most gracefully, without a break, without a blot, without a hesitation. *In the light of what has happened between us we have no choice but to marry immediately. It is my duty and my privilege. You cannot refuse me.*

He signed himself *Mecklenburg-Ulyanov* and slashed the pen beneath, creating a thick, strong line to emphasize the signature. He blew on the note to dry it, folded it carefully, and rang for Tikhon.

It was not two hours later that Ulyanov received his answer. He had spent the intervening time drawing up a household budget, calculating how much for her clothing, her food, the support of her dependents, the added expense of the entertaining expected of a married couple, which would include one "at-home" a week when they would receive those of their social circle, and this ought not be expensive, for it was not grand, this social circle. He added to the budget a box at the opera, as was appropriate to their dignity as married people, a new coach and pair (his own carriage had a broken spring and had not been used for some time, and one of the matched pair of unfashionably sorrel-colored horses had died of a surfeit of herring affectionately but unwisely fed to him by an inexperienced stable boy), not to mention the nursemaid and the governess when the babies . . . perhaps he was getting ahead of himself, but no matter, he added them in. And the regiment, of course. He must resign. Too frivolous an occupation for a married man, he had decided. He ought to look for a position at court, or something in the government. Perhaps he might begin by taking a post as secretary to some important figure, a man of power and influence. Many who had risen high had begun their careers in such a way. Kakhutin, for instance, that prig he had gone to school with, had begun his career as secretary to one of the Princes Sheremetiev. And now look at him! In his court uniform, he lorded it over his former schoolmates when meeting them at winter balls, though he was not as irritating as that hypocritical Rybynsky, who had managed briefly to turn the head of his darling Alexandra, before, of course, she had found herself a real man—himself, that is.

He was so absorbed in the wording of his letter of resignation to the regiment that he did not hear Tikhon's knock at the door, so that the old butler was obliged to enter and proceed to his master's side and stand there coughing delicately until Ulyanov, suddenly startled, turned his head.

"Porfiry has returned!" said Ulyanov.

"Porfiry has not returned," said Tikhon, shuffling his feet nervously.

"Then tell me when he does," said Ulyanov, turning back to his letter. But Tikhon continued to stand at Ulyanov's elbow and coughed again.

"I am busy," said Ulyanov without looking up. "Tell me when Porfiry returns. He is most likely drinking somewhere. You'll have to speak to him."

"Master," said Tikhon, hanging his head, "Cornet Lopukhin

has arrived and presents his compliments. An urgent matter, he says."

"What? Lopukhin? I haven't time for him! Tell him I am not at home."

"He insists."

"Insists? Presents his compliments? What silliness is this? If he wants a drink, why doesn't he say so?"

"I do not think," said Tikhon, twisting his hands, "he wants a drink. He is waiting in the vestibule. In full dress."

Ulyanov frowned and scratched his head, depositing a smear of ink at his hairline. Irritated at the interruption of his planning of his life, he got up from his seat and went out into the hall, where Lopukhin, in full dress as reported, was gazing at his feet. On seeing Ulyanov he suddenly snapped to attention, clicked his heels, and sliced the air with a sharp salute. He then informed Ulyanov that as second it was his duty to issue a challenge from Cornet Count Karpatsky to meet this very afternoon on the field of battle, unorthodox as this was, to settle a matter of which he, Lopukhin, must confess he did not know the particulars.

Ulyanov's mouth dropped open. "You mean Karpatsky is challenging me to a duel? This afternoon?"

"He is indeed," said Lopukhin.

"Why, this is madness! Impossible, insane! I can't believe it! After I just . . . why?"

Lopukhin threw up his white-gloved hands.

Ulyanov turned on his heel. "I'm going over. To speak to . . . him," he said. Lopukhin, however, placed a restraining hand on Ulyanov's arm. "You know the rules," he said, "no personal contact. You choose a second. Your second does the talking."

"All right, all right," cried Ulyanov, who was now breathing hard. He shook his head, rubbed his forehead again, smearing the ink more messily. "I choose you!"

"Impossible," said Lopukhin, wild-eyed, "there must be two. You must have your own."

"Listen, my friend," said Ulyanov, placing a hand on Lopukhin's shoulder and gazing deeply into his face, "this must not get out. This must be contained. This could ruin him. Lead to court-martial, exile, disgrace. To challenge a superior. It isn't done. You know it. Persuade him. Beg him if you must. Whatever I've done, whatever he thinks I've done, I'll make it right. But this duel must not take place. Now go and talk to him."

The skirts of Lopukhin's dress coat swirled out as he turned on his heel to go.

"Wait!" cried Ulyanov, grabbing his arm, "I understand now. Yes, I understand. He did not receive my message."

"Message?" said Lopukhin.

"He did not receive the message. It's all in the message. Yes, his anger is justified. He has the right to kill me for what I have done to him. But the message will make it right. The message will solve it all. Just wait. I'll give it to you again. I'll write it again. That Porfiry, yes! He's always been unreliable."

Dashing back to his desk, Ulyanov rewrote his proposal with trembling hand, adding this time his protestations of respect and love. Of course she was angry. Of course she wanted to kill him. What woman wouldn't, having been seduced by one such as he? Yes, it would be all right. She would get the message. And, not long from now, be in his arms.

"Now go! Now run!" Ulyanov cried, thrusting the folded note into Lopukhin's pocket.

"That Porfiry, I will kill him!" Ulyanov shouted at no one in particular as Lopukhin slammed the door. That his darling could think . . . that she had to endure the humiliation of believing that he didn't care, that what had happened had meant nothing. This was surely the source of her vengeful anger, yes. And perfectly justifiable.

If I were she, I'd try to kill me, too, Ulyanov told himself, feeling immensely better. Not an unreasonable reaction at all. In fact, there had been many women who had tried before, and not a few men, outraged husbands mostly. Still, Alexandra was more determined than most, and more skilled in the use of arms. However, he was confident that his note would placate her, and, suddenly jubilant that she was within his grasp at last, Ulyanov went to his mother's room across the hall and knocked softly at the door.

Closing the door quietly behind him, Ulyanov walked across the thickly carpeted floor to where his mother, eyes closed beneath her ribboned cap, lay drowsing. He stood looking down at her wasted face, and bent to kiss her forehead.

She smiled and reached out to grasp his hand, opening her faded eyes.

"Mother dear," said Ulyanov, squatting down beside the couch on which she lay, "I have important news I hope will make you happy."

She only continued to smile at him, as if any happy news he had were superfluous to the triumphant fact of his existence in the world.

"I am to be married soon," he whispered, careful not to shock her heart with this extraordinary information.

His mother murmured her delight and surprise, but questioned him on why she had not met the girl and who she was.

"The loveliest girl, the most wonderful," said Ulyanov passionately, "the most spirited, the best-hearted, an extraordinary girl!"

Ulyanov's mother, already tired, smiled indulgently and

closed her eyes again, satisfied that he felt as he should about his bride.

"But penniless," Ulyanov added.

"Good, my dear, that's good," his mother sighed. "I did the same myself, you know, don't you know?"

Ulyanov nodded that he knew.

"Oh so much money I gave up!" She laughed softly. "So much money! The greatest moment of my life! When I stood before my father and told him what his money meant to me, which was nothing, that I would not miss the empty life to which he tried to hold me. The greatest moment. You know that, don't you? Did I tell you?"

Ulyanov nodded that he knew, having heard many times the story of her defiance and disinheritance, how she'd climbed inside that coach in the dead of night, the sounds of horses' hooves beating the dirt as they carried her away. The glory of that moment would never die in her; she seemed to have lived on it ever since.

"Five thousand souls was all I had when I went, those small estates from my mother," she said, her voice dwindling, growing sleepy, "when I might have had five hundred thousand. Now what would I have done with five hundred thousand souls? Too many to know. Too many for anyone to know."

Her face lit with the memory of the serfs and the lands they lived on that she had given up, she was young and fresh again, and then asleep, her fingers fading from his own. Slowly Ulyanov rose to his feet, tiptoed out, and closed the door behind him. His eyes on the clock in the hall, he began to pace, his hands behind his back, his footsteps dignified and firm.

Lopukhin came bursting in, breathless, too bold to knock.

"He will not withdraw the challenge!"

"Not withdraw it?" said Ulyanov, "but what about the note? You gave him the note!"

"I gave him the note and stood there as he read it."

"And?"

"He did not receive your message in the way you might have hoped," said Lopukhin, lowering his eyes, reluctant to describe how Count Karpatsky, flint-eyed, had torn the letter in pieces with great deliberation and scattered the bits of paper on the floor.

Damn her, said Ulyanov to himself.

"At three," said Lopukhin, "in the riding school. The choice of weapon being his, as the offended party, it will be swords." Lopukhin stopped, wrinkling his forehead with thought and silently moving his lips as if matching his intended words with a things-to-remember list that he held in his mind. He began to count on his fingers. "Now first, you know you cannot wear your tunic. You must wear a shirt, you know, that's loose and white, unbuttoned halfway down your chest to show first blood. Swords? Swords? What about the swords? I'll bring my father's dueling pair. They're matched and balanced." Looking confused, as if he could not remember any more from his list of things to do, Lopukhin stood frowning. "I'd be careful," was all he could think of to add. "He's good with the sword, Karpatsky, you know."

"Oh, I know," said Ulyanov, nodding violently, having himself seen Alexandra at drill with the maître d'armes of the regiment and now beginning to suspect her ultimate aim. He shook his head, not able to suppress a bitter smile.

Of course there was a way to stop it. He had only publicly to reveal the true sex of Cornet Count Karpatsky, thereby invalidating the challenge immediately. But was he willing to do this? Standing in his room before the mirror, Ulyanov thought it over as he buttoned up his loose white shirt and unbuttoned it again with trembling fingers. What would it bring down upon her head? Disgrace, ridicule, not to mention prosecution for the crime of impersonation of an officer. And who knew what else? No, he could not put her to that risk. And if he refused the challenge, his own reputation would be ruined. He'd rather take his chance at talking her around.

However. Alexandra did not seem to be interested in talk. Lounging against the wall in the riding school, looking, he could not help but notice, exquisite in her tight black trousers and loose white shirt with a suspicion of a small soft breast swelling near its opening, she stared at him with a look of murder in her eyes, her arms crossed firmly over her chest.

Ah, the mystery of woman, he thought, throwing off his coat and stretching his hard-muscled arms to their full length in hope of gaining the advantage of intimidation. His arms were longer and stronger. He outweighed her by sixty or seventy pounds at least and topped her in height by four or five inches. These things must count for something against the deftness of her footwork, the precision of her swordplay as he'd watched it many times, admiring and encouraging, without thinking that one day she would turn her sword on him. Oh, why hadn't he bothered to practice more? Why had he ignored the regimental regulation for working out with foils and saber with the fencing-master? Oh no, he had preferred to spend his time at cards. At drinking with Lopukhin and Golovanov. At fiddling with his lists and papers while all the while Alexandra, clearly preparing for this day, had been sharpening her skills in readiness. Why, he might even think she had planned it! Yes, planned the seduction of the night before, rubbing against him with her skin that smelled of violets to lure him into love that she might have her moment of revenge—revenge for what?

For loving her, of course! Oh the mystery of woman.

Lopukhin, who had been standing in the center of the riding ring studying a piece of paper (raising his head, closing his eyes, and moving his lips as if he were memorizing its contents), suddenly crumpled the paper and threw it on the ground, unsheathed his saber. Directing Ulyanov to stand against the wall opposite Alexandra, Lopukhin began to mark out the boundaries of the dueling space with the tip of his sword. When he had finished this, he proceeded to his original spot, squatted, laid down his saber, and opened the long leather box that had been sitting there on the ground.

A matched pair of rapiers emerged into the white winter light that poured through the dusty windows. Lopukhin, carrying them point down, his arms held up so that their tips did not graze the ground, approached Alexandra to give her first choice of weapon.

"They are exactly alike," he said, "but you may choose."

"Which one," said Alexandra loudly, "has killed?"

Lopukhin said he did not know, that the swords had belonged to his father, and that he had not been aware of his father's ever having used them.

"Ah," said Alexandra more loudly than before, "virgins. Which one of them is more anxious to lose its maidenhead? Which more eager to plunge into the body of my opponent?" She reached to the left. "This one. She seems to tremble with eagerness."

"That's just my hand," said Lopukhin drily, and turned on his heel to approach Ulyanov, who snatched from the air the sword Lopukhin lightly tossed at him.

Lopukhin took up his saber from where he'd laid it on the

ground and gestured to the combatants to take their places between the lines he had drawn in the dirt and sawdust that formed the flooring of the ring. Then, measuring a space of about three feet, he drew other lines to mark the standing spots and called the combatants forward to their marks. Lopukhin then withdrew to a distance of fifteen feet or so and stood there a moment grimacing, his face turned up to the ceiling as if trying to remember.

"Ah yes," he said, nodding quickly, "inasmuch as the combatants have refused a reconciliation—"

"I have not refused a reconciliation," Ulyanov called out, his eyes on Alexandra. "It is Karpatsky"—he spat the syllables—"who insists on carrying through with this unnecessary madness, Karpatsky whose anger is unreasonable and unfounded, who has suffered no insult at all. If he would only listen to me, if he would only talk to me a moment, I would make him see that this is true." He gazed pleadingly at Alexandra. She gripped the handle of her sword more tightly and swished its blade through the air so it made a menacing sound.

"Shut up!" said Lopukhin. "It's too late! No reconciliations now! You've had your chances, both of you. Now let's see, what else? What else? Oh yes, the handkerchiefs. You are each allowed a handkerchief to wrap around your hand to absorb the perspiration and keep the sword from slipping. I brought them. Yes, I did." He reached into his pocket and drew out two white bits of cloth, which he tossed through the air. Ulyanov caught his, wrapped it carefully around his hand. Alexandra, with an arrogant smile, watched hers float to the ground before she kicked it away.

It was the sort of nonchalant gesture Ulyanov might have performed himself, had he not been so disconcerted. She's learned, he thought. She's learned her lessons well.

Lopukhin, searching his memory again, found nothing, gave up, and leaned down to retrieve the paper he had dropped on the ground.

"The rules," he said, uncrumpling the paper. "First, you are not allowed to use your left hand. If I see you using it, I will tie it behind your back. Second, no grappling of the blade. If I see you grabbing, I will stop you. No going outside the lines or I will stop you. The signal to stop is my blade, when I raise it in the air. Watch for this. If this happens, you will take one step back and resume. At first blood you will stop at once and wait. That's it. I'll keep reminding you if I have to. Now take your guard, and on the word *allez* you will begin."

The combatants took their positions. "*Allez!*" Lopukhin shouted.

A vicious attack began the bout as Alexandra, with rapid crossover steps, drove Ulyanov back and back and back until his back was to the wall. She leaped forward, arm extended, to thrust at his breast. Sweating already, Ulyanov caught her blade with his, pushed it away, and keeping control of her blade by counterpressure, pushed her back.

"Darling, dear," he whispered, leaning toward her, "why are you so angry?"

"I hate you," said Alexandra, her sword still locked with his.

"You love me," said Ulyanov, "you are only frightened."

"You have turned me into a whore."

"Becoming a woman does not make you a whore."

Alexandra slid her blade away from his by retreating with rapid steps; Ulyanov, much to her surprise, did not keep pace with her, but remained standing where he was. Alexandra spat on the ground.

"Why don't you fight?" she said. "Attack! Attack me!"

"I will not attack you," said Ulyanov. "I will only defend myself."

"Aha!" said Alexandra, bouncing lightly on her feet, "so you refuse to see me as your equal and will not attack me. What an insult! Another insult!"

"You mean," said Ulyanov, "to prove you are my equal I have to be willing to try to kill you?"

"That's right!" said Alexandra, driving in on him again, feinting toward his left and evading his parry with a cut to her opponent's side.

Lopukhin shouted, "Stop!" and raised his sword, then dropped it and ran.

A small but spreading stain of red appeared on the whiteness of Ulyanov's shirt, a tiny swelling Valentine heart of blood. Lopukhin inserted his hand inside the capacious shirt and pressed his handkerchief against the wound. The handkerchief turned quickly red. "First blood," he murmured, and called out behind him, "Count Karpatsky, have you achieved satisfaction?"

"I have not," said Alexandra, swishing her sword back and forth in the air.

Lopukhin sighed and shook his head. "Captain Mecklenburg-Ulyanov, are you willing to continue?"

"In a minute," said Ulyanov distractedly, "in a minute." Having used a second handkerchief to sop up the blood, Ulyanov looked around for something else to use to stop the warm streaming from his side.

He pulled off his shirt, crumpled it into a wad, and held it to the wound.

Alexandra's eyes were dazzled by the polish of his skin, the sculptured molding of his arms, the muscled flatness of his chest, which only the night before she had worshiped, trembling, sighing, with her lips. The sword twitched in her hand, eager to begin again.

"You know," Lopukhin interjected, "it is highly improper for me to second this conflict when I don't know the first thing about what it's all about! It's up to me," he added, stamping his foot for emphasis, "to adjudicate the matter. There must be sufficient cause, but how can I judge the sufficiency of cause without my knowing it?"

"Shut up," said Ulyanov, throwing down the shirt. The red-lipped wound had cut across the faint rippling of his ribs, but the bleeding had stopped. "We start again."

"The rules—" Lopukhin began.

"Go check again," said Ulyanov, flexing his knees and extending his sword toward Alexandra with a smile. "You'll see there's a provision for secrecy of conflict. Go check. I swear it's true. You missed it. It's in the book. Go check the book. It's under the buffet in the dining room; we keep a copy there for quick reference."

"I know where it is," Lopukhin said. "I checked it all this morning."

"Check again."

"If you promise not to kill each other in the meantime . . ." And he was off at a run—a man who took his responsibilities seriously indeed.

"Now, darling," said Ulyanov, turning toward his adversary, who raised her sword and scurried backward.

"Don't come near me or I'll kill you," she said, breathing hard, menacing the air with her blade.

"You're just confused," he said, stepping toward her, his voice soft and low.

"I told you I'd kill you if you came near me again," she said, her own voice softening, tears coming into her eyes. "Why didn't you listen? Why didn't you?"

"But it was you," he said gently, "who came near me."

Wrong answer. Alexandra leaped forward with sword extended and delivered a cut to his arm with a flick of her wrist.

"Don't use that voice on me," said Alexandra, "don't use that voice."

"Do you know," he said, "that it is against the code of honor to fight a man who cannot defend himself properly?"

"It's not my affair if you refuse to defend yourself. That's your choice."

"But it's not my choice," said Ulyanov, "it's my duty."

"Like marrying me's your duty?"

"Bad choice of words on my part," Ulyanov observed to no one in particular, "though of course the two issues are entirely separate. No, my duty as a man is to honor women and protect them. I admit I have been somewhat remiss in this respect, but I believe I have shown improvement recently, don't you think?"

Alexandra spat on the ground again. But her sword arm, which she was holding in what was called the high guard, was growing tired. The sword glittered, trembling in the light. Ulyanov saw this and advanced a little closer.

"You value your honor highly," he said, thrusting the point of his rapier into the ground, "and that is good, but you dishonor yourself in fighting me because I cannot risk injuring my opponent, which hobbles my own defense, and so this contest is not fair. I appeal to your honor as a hussar."

"If I were a man, you would fight me properly," she said, lowering her guard, "and this contest would be fair, but now you say it is not fair simply because of my sex? I am as brave as you are, I am as skilled, so why should you not fight me as an equal?"

"Because I might injure you, or kill you, even."

"So what? If that is my choice? If I am willing to have that happen?"

"But I am not," said Ulyanov, "willing to have that happen. I would no longer be a man, but a creeping, savage thing that crawls along the ground, to kill a woman."

"Be a person, then," said Alexandra.

"I am both a person and a man. I cannot separate the two."

"Your tenderness toward the fairer sex is admirable," said Alexandra officiously, "but that very tenderness is the condescension of the superior toward the inferior. The strong for the weak. Noblesse oblige."

"Not condescension," said Ulyanov, thinking hard, leaning on his sword. "It's something else, something more like . . . reverence. To kill a woman . . . it's like killing a bird that only sings."

"So that's what we do? *Sing?*"

"Oh no," said Ulyanov, "much more than that. To kill a woman, it's like killing gentleness, goodness, beauty—all that makes life worth living. Everything we do, you know, we do for you."

"Spare me your poetry," said Alexandra. "I'd be happy to be simply a hussar and be treated as one."

"And that I cannot do."

"And so I will kill you."

"Dishonorably," said Ulyanov. "It is so like a woman to set herself above the rules. Inferiors! Ha! There is no one so arrogant, so egotistical, as a woman."

Alexandra was contemplating an immediate thrust through Ulyanov's undefended heart when Lopukhin came running in.

"I looked and looked," he said breathlessly, his face red and moist with his recent exertions, "and I didn't find it. I didn't find anything about keeping the reason for a contest secret, and I looked and looked. I'm afraid I have to declare this conflict at an end."

"No!" said Ulyanov, who had thought of yet another tactic. "I can tell you this. I dishonored Count Karpatsky. He has the right to satisfaction. But to tell you the facts of the offense would dishonor him again. So he'd have to challenge me again anyway, so we might as well go on."

"But I don't even know if it's a first-level offense, involving verbal insult, a second-level offense, involving physical contact, or a third-level offense, involving violence, and all of these have different rules, and if I don't know which it is—"

But the clash of swords had begun again, Alexandra driving in, catching Ulyanov's blade with her own and backing him against the wall. Ulyanov beat her blade away, ducked under it, and circled round in back of her.

"No, no, no!" cried Lopukhin, who was ignored as Alexandra leaped to face Ulyanov from the other side. A thrust from her and the point of her blade had pierced Ulyanov's chest, its tip buried in the muscle to the depth of a quarter inch. She had only to apply a few pounds of pressure to send the point into the struggling heart itself, to master him completely, as he had mastered her.

Ulyanov opened his hand and let his weapon drop to the ground, concentrating on remaining completely still, while Lopukhin, his responsibilities forgotten, simply stared and did nothing to stop it. And why not, she thought, feeling through the blade the hard flat muscle of his unfettered chest, for then she would be free of him forever, her bondage to him broken, free to be a man! To test her courage, earn glory and distinction, make her mark upon the world. And if not, what was left to her? Only to drag after him, an appendage, a secondary creature standing in the shadow of his larger life, begging for his kisses and his love, listening for his step, her life submerged in his forever and ever until she disappeared from sight.

But of course she could not kill him, just as Ulyanov knew,

just as Ulyanov wished to prove to her. She loved him. Of course she did. She always had.

"Of course!" Lopukhin cried, having just noticed for the very first time the soft swellings within Karpatsky's open shirt. Karpatsky was a woman! He had sensed it all along! And now he could not help but laugh. No wonder she wanted to kill the captain! She and a hundred others! Good old Ulyanov, up to his old tricks! Lopukhin's faith in the world was now entirely restored. Boy, he wanted a drink to celebrate.

Alexandra dropped her sword and ran. That very day she pressed into the weeping Praskovia's hands the contents of her purse and enlisted as a common soldier in the cavalry of the Army of the Caucasus.

The Caucasus! The wild south of the Russian Empire, its new frontier, wild as the Wild West, whose endless flat plains might have been upended here on the other side of the world, stood on end in endless rows of mountains whose rocky passes teem with brigands, chieftains, outlaws, robbers, spies. Not to mention those maidens with night-dark eyes of whom the Russian boys are dreaming. They dream, too, of abductions, seductions, wild rides through the skittering rocks of the mountain passes as bullets whiz and ricochet around their heads. Adventure. Violence. Daring. Boy stuff. Alexandra, however, was not dreaming of these things at all.

Alexandra was dreaming of a bath. Posted as sentry on a miserable mountain pass in cold so deep it froze the hairs inside her nostrils and turned the air inside her lungs to glass, she was squatting and rocking to warm herself, carbine hard and heavy in her hand, hair oily, face grimy, teeth coated with scum, a heavy woolen scarf drawn up over her lips and nose to protect these delicate organs from frostbite. At this moment, she was homesick for her womanhood. She dreamed of lace and satin, high-heeled shoes, gloves, embroidered napkins, the firmness of a masculine hand about her waist as she flew across a polished floor. Of fine tea drunk and pastries eaten under crystal chandeliers, mirrors reflecting back at her herself, her lovely self. Art. Elegance. Household comforts. Cleanliness. Civilization. Girl stuff.

But she would not give in. Play at soldier? Ha! I'll show you who's playing soldier, she said in her mind, her lips moving in silent argument with you know who. She stood up, hoisted her carbine, squeezed off a shot into the wide, high darkness, and squatted down again.

A footfall in the dark. The scrambling sound of stones underfoot. Then silence. Who? Heart beating loudly, Alexandra rose. Stupid of her to discharge her weapon needlessly to indicate her presence. The tribesmen moved so silently, her throat would be open and vomiting blood before she even felt the knife.

The silence did not break again, and Alexandra attributed the sounds to the wind or animals or perhaps the roiling of her own brain, which remained at the same slow boil of fear at every moment, all the time.

Her knees ached, her arms ached, her head ached with boredom and lack of sleep. Boredom alternating with terror. That was the life of the common soldier. There were no snapping, cracking salutes, no glittering parades, no convivial evenings in the Officers' Assembly, only the nights in the crumbling barracks where cracks in the walls let in the icy mountain winds, the light of an alien moon.

Toward dawn, the stars fading and the sky growing transparent and the mountains showing through it, Alexandra heard the soft whistling signal of the soldier who had come to relieve her at her post.

"Anything?" he asked her.

"Nothing. Uneventful," she said, rising from her squat, "an uneventful night. Like every night."

"Oh, not so uneventful," said the soldier, squatting in her place and grappling in his pocket for the pouch from which he would fill his mouth with a mess of cheap tobacco. "We've found them."

"Found whom?" said Alexandra irritably, eager to get to her

smelly bed and pull her sheepskin coat around her for a paltry touch of warmth.

"The camp. And I hear the infidels were filling their bellies with the meat they stole from our supplies and boasting of how they'd cut our throats in our very beds."

Oh boy, thought Alexandra, wishing very hard to be at home, her feet on Praskovia's lap, growing warm and toasty there, and the sound of Praskovia's raucous voice inside her ear.

"But they won't, you know. They won't get to us again. We're moving against them today. A raiding party!" He sounded jolly, happy in a way that made her blood run cold. How could they enjoy this? she wondered. What did they get out of it?

"Of course, they've got a lot of our ammunition. And the carbines they filched, the filthy pagans. Artillery too. But that's the fun part, isn't it?"

She dragged her aching body back to the barracks, sat on her cot and without removing her heavy sheepskin coat or her furred cossack-style hat, threw off her gloves, pulled the woolen scarves, wet and partially frozen with her melted breath, away from her face and put her fingertips into her mouth to try to warm them. At least she had an excuse to keep her coat on all the time—that was something. It hardly mattered, though. The men here were so concentrated on surviving, strung tightly as wire all the time with watching, that they had little attention left over to give to the question of whether one of their company was actually a woman.

She fell asleep while sitting up, the coat so thick with padding it made a bed around her body.

She woke with a jump to the sound of doors banging, horses squealing in protest at their introduction into the cold air outside their stable, and of voices shouting outside the barracks. Someone had pinched her on the nose, the only part of herself showing outside her coat beneath her hat, the only part accessible to touch.

"Wake up, wake up," the sergeant grunted, pinching her again, "what's yer name, you, whoozits, get your ass up and out and in the saddle now." And he was gone.

Battle. A raid. So this was it, she thought, slowly inserting her hands again into the giant, muffinlike mittens that so reduced her manual dexterity that commands were given to the horse with the leg alone. Thank God she had not brought her Hercules, thank God he stood in his warm stall in Petersburg behind the palace, crunching oats between his giant molars and thinking of nothing. And Praskovia, what would she be doing now? And Matryona? Had she come back? And the baby? And Nikifor? And Grisha the driver. Her family. Odd to think she had one. She had never realized that before. Each face came before her, surfacing quickly from the bottom of her mind and fading down again. She supposed she loved them all. Had never realized that before.

And so, she thought, getting heavily to her feet, I go perhaps to die. What would it feel like? Pain and then nothing, she supposed. A mystery, the greatest mystery of all.

Don't think, she told herself, don't think about it. Do. Just do. For the first time, she thought she felt what it really was to be a man. She thought of all the millions who had gone along this path before her, young men still fresh with life who were going to throw that life away. What were they thinking of? Nothing, she supposed. Nothing was best. Don't think. Just do.

In a few minutes, she had saddled her horse, a cossack pony straight from the savage steppes, thrown herself up upon her saddle, and wheeled herself into the formation, where she was one among many, not individual any longer, but an interchangeable part of some larger force. There was something heady in it, in the submergence of the self into the power of the group—it filled her body like the bubbles of champagne, lifted up her spirit, made it light, this eagerness to be one with something larger than herself.

Their carbines strapped to their saddles, two hundred horsemen went pouring out the gates of the stone fortress, trotting quietly along the winding mountain road in single file. None looked up at the morning sky or off to the side at the majestic mountains, or downward toward the valley that stretched out beneath them with its thread of silver river winding through the smooth unbroken green.

Round the mountain they went, down toward the valley, that pocket of springtime within the permanent winter of the mountains. At the bottom of the mountain they discarded their heavy coats, tossing them one by one onto the towering pile of sheepskin as they trotted past, revealing underneath their cossack garb the elegant cut of their uniform coats. They tossed off their massive cossack hats to bare their heads in the misty sunlight, flung their mittens in the air, expanded their constricted chests and drew into their lungs the rich valley-bottom air. The gathering of horsemen grew, swelled, as each one tripped down off the mountain to join it, one by one, drop by drop. A horseman, the last of all, a laggard bringing up the rear, a coward, it seemed, refused to surrender his cap and coat, perhaps believing the layers of animal skin would intercede for him between himself and bullets. But he took his place with the others.

An architectural square of men and horses moved in one piece across the valley, trotted up a hill and stopped there. There the square was split and spread, and then re-formed into three long lines with large spaces in between them. First wave, second, and reserve. No trumpet blare interrupted the quiet morning of the village in the distance, from whose tents and huts fragrant smoke blew through the flower-scented air in the direction of the soldiers.

"Nice morning for a raid," said the soldier to Alexandra's right.

Alexandra could barely hear him for the beating of her heart. From the third and last line, where she was, she could see nothing but the backs of the men ahead of her, and horses' bottoms dancing back and forth in place, eager to get going. And then there was the multiple sound of horses' hooves galloping upon the ground. The first line was off. The second line moved up.

Looking through the spaces between the straight backs of the soldiers ahead of her, Alexandra could see the horsemen spreading out across the plain, pouring toward the village in the middle distance. The booming of a cannon shook the air. More blasts of smoke poured out over the horsemen and covered them, hiding them from view.

"There they go, the filthy infidels," said the soldier, "and they're using our own artillery, the thieving bastards."

Horses squealed in the distance, men shouted and screamed. Then the smoke melted from her clouded field of vision. Horses were lying on the ground, others running riderless. The second line went off now, pounding down the hill and across the plain. The line of reserves moved up to the top of the hill.

Alexandra could see it clearly now, could clearly hear the sounds of weeping, the wails of pain, the shouting of confusion, the squeals and screams of the horses whose bellies were blown open and dragging their spilled contents in twisted coils along the ground. Other horses, panicking, dragged their dead riders, still stuck to a stirrup, through the dirt. The tribesmen were in the field now, hacking with their swords, shooting with their guns from atop their tiny lethal ponies, or, leaping from their mounts, fighting hand to hand with the Russians, bits of steel glinting. Knives. An arm, blown off, sailed through space. A head exploded into particles of blood that formed a pinkish cloud and then melted in the air.

"Get ready," said the soldier off-handedly, rising in his stirrups to survey the field.

I'd really rather not, Alexandra wanted to answer.

Never had the privileges of womanhood come before her with such force. I don't have to do this, it occurred to her; others will do it for me. Men. It was what they were for, as Lopukhin had tried to tell her, as Ulyanov had tried to tell her. It was men who sacrificed their lives for others, men who ran into burning buildings, men for whom the willingness to treat themselves as valueless, to throw their lives away, was proof of their own value.

I can do this, she wanted to say; I just don't want to.

It was not a question of bravery, she explained to herself, tightening the reins and squeezing her horse between her knees until he took a step backward, and another one. Nor was it that women were not heroic in their way, did not sacrifice themselves for others. Just not so literally. In any case, childbirth itself was enough of a risk to life. There was no need to do more.

No, she did not feel in the least bit guilty at deserting her brothers in arms. The arrogance of women? Of course! Upon their preservation rested the preservation of the world itself.

Quietly she backed her horse away, unnoticed by the others, some of whose hands trembled, some of whose throats were dry, some of whom were also thinking, I'd really rather not. But they had no choice, as she did—they were men. Of course they could desert, but only to spend the rest of their lives knowing they'd failed to justify their own existence, were not men, but creeping things that crawled upon the ground. A woman did not have to justify her existence. A woman *was* existence, the conduit of life itself.

Focused upon the possibility of impending death, the soldiers did not notice as she left the line and turned her horse away, except for one, the coward, hidden within his cossack hat and muffling coat. He rose in his stirrups and turned his head to watch the deserter go, cocked his ear to the sound of the hoof-beats that carried the deserter away, envying him perhaps, or considering his own escape. But he only sank back in the saddle, sighed, dropped his chin upon his chest, and waited like the others.

PART 3

The Korvin palace on the Neva sold easily—all two hundred rooms of it, with its stables and greenhouse and orangery and assorted tiny buildings littering the grounds of many acres. The money it fetched was enough to enable Miss Korvin, who no longer called herself a countess, to buy a small estate near Moscow that held only as many serfs as her former palace had had rooms, but which would provide herself and her family with a permanent, if modest, living from the farming of oats and flax.

So they went—Alexandra, Praskovia, Nikifor (who had resigned from the regiment and whose marriage to Praskovia was celebrated with a small cake and much joy), Grisha, who carried the baby always in his arms, and Matryona herself, who had lately returned, and, in a last act of pointless malice, discharged the small responsibility given her by her mistress of locking the main door of the palace by dropping the enormous key down a drainage hole and claiming to have lost it "somehow." This act necessitated a grounds-wide search and a last-minute visit to the lawyer Trenyakov, who wished Alexandra well and agreed to engage a locksmith for her so that she didn't miss her train.

Alexandra was always in black now, in mourning for the mother she had hardly known, but welcoming the excuse to spend a large amount on one and only one elegant dress, which would suffice for a year of wear at least, that year the socially accepted period of mourning for a relative of the first degree. The shortness of her hair would not be questioned, since it was common for women of the time to shear their skulls during an illness, the medical theory behind this practice having something to do with relieving the brain of its extra burden to enable it to heal the body. Anyone seeing the young Miss Korvin would assume she had only lately recovered from a sickness, a thought that Alexandra found amusing, since it was, in a sense, quite true.

Settled in her new home—a crumbling manor house so heavily coated with ivy it was quite literally in the process of being eaten alive by the malignant plant—Alexandra spent her first days staring mournfully out the window of the kitchen at the melting world outside, her sharp elbows planted on the table and her cheek resting in the palm of her hand. The top of the table was crowded with plates of uneaten food and glasses of tea going cold, undrunk. The weight dropped off her so quickly, she began to look as if she had indeed suffered a serious illness. Praskovia, worried but unable to afford a doctor, sent for the local medicine woman, a fat serf from the estate who bustled in on her soft white shoes of birchbark, pressed a gold amulet to the patient's forehead, closed her eyes, and pronounced her verdict: lovesickness, a very serious case. Without relief, the pretty young mistress would die.

"Nonsense," said Praskovia, "no one dies of love. It has a very pretty sound to it, and that is why you say it." Whereupon a fierce argument erupted between Praskovia and the medicine woman, which escalated quickly into slaps, kicks, and punches, ending only when Nikifor pulled the women apart and escorted the field serf out the door and into the yard, where she spat on the ground and marched off in the direction of her village, muttering curses about the insult to her expertise.

As skeptical as Praskovia was, however, she thought the diagnosis was as good as any. At least it was a place to start. Lovesick, but for whom? Some handsome young officer she had known in the regiment, no doubt. What a bad business that had been! Too many men around her mistress for her health. No wonder she was sick. Rubbing her feet that night against Nikifor's larger ones, Praskovia scratched him with her toenails until he admitted to knowing the truth.

"I know that one," said Praskovia, who had seen Ulyanov at the Andreyevs' house party. "A bad business he is, too. Like all of you."

Nikifor protested that he was not a bad business, and Praskovia insisted that he was, and the quarrel continued until they fell asleep and resumed when Praskovia opened her eyes, poked Nikifor awake to continue the argument, and continued to grouse at him until it was time for her to get up to fire the stoves and make the tea. Carrying a chipped tray that had, like all the furniture and housewares, come with the house, she walked barefoot through the dark rooms, distributing the glasses of restorative liquid to all the sleepers in it, beginning with her own husband, continuing into the room where Matryona lay in bed with Grisha and the baby, and on to Alexandra's room, where Praskovia shook her mistress awake, propped her up against the pillows, and held the hot glass to her lips, watching with satisfaction as Alexandra drank. Then she sat heavily on the bed, her legs crossed under her. She suggested to Alexandra that perhaps she might be in love and that since this condition was not very different from drunkenness, the only cure for it was "a hair of the dog that bit you."

"And what do you mean by that?" said Alexandra, roused.

"Well," said Praskovia, "if you are in love, the only way to cure yourself of him is more of him than you can stand. Marriage is a good place to begin."

"I think less of him would be better. Besides," she added, sinking back into the pillows and turning her head, "I wouldn't give him the satisfaction."

But then she did. That very day she sat at the small desk in the drawing room and gritting her teeth so that the muscles of her cheeks twitched and jumped, she wrote the following:

> *Ulyanov,*
>
> *Your insults to me are not forgotten. Though I failed in my attempt to achieve satisfaction, having taken seriously your arguments that my methods were dishonorable, I must remind you that the insult remains.*
>
> *Yours sincerely,*
> *Alexandra Korvin*

What exactly Alexandra hoped to accomplish with this note remains a mystery. But she was certain it would achieve some result, though exactly what she didn't know. She folded it, pounded it flat with her fist, applied a dab of sealing wax, and stamped it with her seal. She addressed it to Ulyanov at the regiment, St. Petersburg, and, having handed it to Nikifor to mail, she ran up to her room, vaulted onto the bed, and pulled the pillow over her head to hide the redness of her face. Then she vaulted out of bed again, ran downstairs, ate an enormous lunch, and, with an expression very different from the sadness on her face the day before, stared out the window as if expecting Nikifor's immediate return with Ulyanov's instantaneous response.

However, though she sent Nikifor into town many times each day to get the mail, he returned each time empty-handed. A month went by. Birds returned to the trees around the house; the brown grass, though still drowned in melted snow, began to show its green; and the narrow light of the end of winter widened into spring. There was still no answer. Alexandra began to droop.

How could he answer that, she asked herself, after I tried to kill him? No, I must do more. I must say more.

Again she sat at her desk, took out her pen and ink, and stared at the white sheet, which stared back at her from its place atop the table.

My darling, she wrote. She crossed it out. Too much. No need to go that far. She crumpled the paper, threw it on the floor, and took another sheet.

My dear Ulyanov, she wrote this time, *Though I believe my challenge was entirely justified, it may be that my refusal to accept your apology was unreasonable. I am willing to admit this. Yours sincerely, Alexandra.*

Convinced that this would do the trick, Alexandra awaited a response with utmost confidence. There was none. Another month went by. Spring had fully taken hold, and the world around the house was yellow with daffodils. The air was sweet with them, and with the sound of the spring lambs peeping as they made their way around the barnyard on trembling legs. Again she drooped. In fact, she wept, and, staining the paper with her tears, she wrote this time: *My darling, I love you so. Why do you not come to me? Is it because I tried to kill you? I apologize. On my knees I beg for your forgiveness.* To the tears that stained the paper she added tiny kisses, knowing he could not see them, but hoping that he would somehow sense them in his heart.

Summer came. Flies buzzed and drowned in the milk that was souring into cheese in pots on all the windowsills. The baby's head, popping up from his stiffly swaddled body, presented a tender target for bug-bites. Alexandra and Grisha fought the bites incessantly, bathing them in oil or mollifying milk, and Alexandra, vigilant against the settling of the flying insects on the sweet soft flesh, would hold the tightly packaged infant for hours, savoring the soothing, satisfying weight of him against her shoulder, her hand waving in the air around his head. When his eyes were open, she would stare down into the perfection of the miniaturized face, marveling at his nostrils, at the amazing existence of his eyebrows, at the tiny lashes that furred his incredible eyes, which, in the hard density of their newness, as yet unworn by years of looking at the world, resembled semi-precious stones.

One day while staring down into the baby's face, she asked Praskovia to tell her about her mother.

"Oh, her," said Praskovia, making a face, "that bitch."

Alexandra suggested that the term was inappropriate. "She was my mother, after all."

"Not much of one," said Praskovia, "hardly a mother at all."

"What would have made her more of one?"

"Love," said Praskovia.

"Maybe she loved me a little bit."

Praskovia snorted. "She loved herself more."

"Don't we all love ourselves more?"

"Yes," said Praskovia, "but we make room. She made no room for you. Or for your father."

"Perhaps," said Alexandra, thinking, "it was because she loved herself less that she had no room."

"That's no excuse," said Praskovia.

"I think," said Alexandra, "there's something of her in me. I know it."

"God forbid," said Praskovia.

"No," said Alexandra, still staring at the baby, "there is. For so long there was no room in me for anyone but myself."

"If that is so," said Praskovia, "it was because there was too little of your mother, not too much."

"That makes no sense."

"Too little of a mother's love, I mean. A father's love alone is not enough."

"I had *you*," said Alexandra, suddenly raising her head and looking at Praskovia as if she'd never really seen her before.

"Oh no," said Praskovia, but smiling, "I'm no substitute."

"But you acted as my mother, you did a mother's duties," Alexandra insisted.

"I'm just a servant. A slave. I did what was there to be done."

"But you loved me."

"Who could help loving a baby?" Praskovia took the baby from Alexandra and scrutinized his face. "They have only to look at you but once, and you're theirs forever."

"Yes," said Alexandra, "I suppose I am the baby's slave now. All of us, except for Matryona, who's his mother in the first place. Why is that?"

"She's like your mother. No room."

"My father," said Alexandra suddenly, "I'm like him too. I like the impossible. To do the impossible."

"Little countess," said Praskovia, bouncing the baby in her arms, "we may fail at the impossible, but sometimes by trying for it, we find the possible, which we may not have noticed before."

"I suppose," said Alexandra, sighing and sinking into thought. She waved her hand to indicate the rotting house. "This is what was possible." She plucked at her black silk skirts. "And this."

The one luxury Alexandra had allowed herself was Hercules, although he was really much too valuable to be kept as a hack and should have been sold to the regiment. Still, she rode him every morning and every afternoon, perched on a dried-out old sidesaddle that she had found in the barn on the property. Some afternoons, after making her way through the waist-high fields of rye and along the muddy country paths that served for roads, she would find herself trotting toward one or another of the houses of a neighoring estate, where one of the serfs, lounging on the front steps in the heat and fanning himself with a large leaf, would leap up and run toward her on dirty feet to lift her down from her mount, take Hercules' reins, and lead him into a barn for water and the admiration of the stablemen, who had never seen such magnificent horseflesh in this backwater of a province a hundred miles south of Moscow.

At first Alexandra had avoided the local gentry, refusing their invitations with excuses of recovery from recent illness, but eventually her boredom got the better of her. She liked best to take tea in the afternoons with old Countess Gregorian, who had once been a belle of Petersburg, but who had married badly and found herself stuck here while her husband's estates and her own had been drunk up and gambled away until there had been nothing left but this, a holding even smaller than Alexandra's, whose peasants were much lazier. She was a pleasant old soul, a small, round woman who wasted her afternoons dozing on the front porch of her peeling old house, tea cooling on a small table next to her. She usually had a lapful of embroidery that she worked and reworked—like Penelope, she would pick out the accomplished stitches every evening so that she would have something to do on the morrow, besides the fact that it saved money on cloth and thread. Therefore, she never finished anything but went on working and reworking the same piece of cloth until it went to pieces in her hands and she was forced to start another. Absentminded, the old countess called all her male peasants by the name of Prokhor and all the females Petra, which simplified her life enormously, though she sometimes called the females Prokhor and the males Petra and they, laughing to themselves, affectionately stole her blind.

Countess Gregorian was as well an incorrigible matchmaker,

and as the days went by and Alexandra had no answer from Ulyanov, she began to listen to the countess's suggestions with an ear and a mind more open than before.

"There's young Menshikov, although he's thin," the countess would say, beginning her litany of eligible men, "and Strupinsky, who is fat. If only we could blend them, we'd have a fine figure of a man, wouldn't we?"

Alexandra, who had never met either, would nod and listen for more.

"And there's Bakhtrin, and there's Berg, who has five thousand souls, not bad, and Babkin. Although perhaps it's Babkin who has the five thousand souls. It's hard to keep them straight, all those B's. And that does it for the young ones. But perhaps the old ones would be better. They're broken in already, well trained. There's one who's had five wives, and all of them have died in childbed. But you look strong. A big girl, you are. Perhaps you could survive him. He's killed all the others with his lusts." She shook her head.

Alexandra commented that he did not sound like a good prospect and that perhaps the countess could suggest another.

"There's old what's-his-name, who has never married. Oh, what is his name? Botkin! That's his name! Another B! Old Botkin. He putters here and everywhere all around his estate. Plants. He loves his plants. He names them, you know."

"How very eccentric," commented Alexandra, who found the countess's own eccentricities delightful.

"But you shall meet them, you shall meet them all," said the countess, grasping Alexandra's hands in hers and squeezing them, "a lovely girl like you, Miss Korvin. A Petersburg belle! Just like myself! Though I was not so tall as you. Did I ever tell you . . ." and the countess would be off on another of her memories, of the time she had dazzled such and such a prince, had danced with the French ambassador and been pinched by him behind a curtain, had received five proposals of marriage in one day, had seen her own glove displayed in a glass case as a precious specimen by a charming doctor who had been too poor to marry her but whom she thought of to this very day.

"As you will someday, my dear, find pleasure in remembering the past and past admirers. Oh my, how many I had! How handsome they were! Well, perhaps not all of them were good-looking but they were young men and handsome by definition, as brides and babies are beautiful."

Alexandra was thinking her own thoughts then. With the cracked china teacup and saucer resting on the palm of her hand, she was in fact remembering her own extraordinary past, measuring against the monotonous summer fields outside the window the beauty of the Caucasus and the feel of Hercules' giant battle-driven heart pounding between her thighs and the shouts of the hussars in her ears and the thundering of a thousand hooves against the earth.

One day not long afterward, as Alexandra sat with the old woman, the countess suddenly started up from her seat with a cry, tottered across the room to a desk, and returned to her seat waving a letter. It seemed the old countess, although no longer a member of the high society of Petersburg, still had ties to it and, having received a letter from one of her old Petersburg friends, thought that Alexandra, so far from home, might be interested in news of her former world.

"Let me see, let me see," said the countess, who had perched a tiny pair of spectacles upon her nose and was riffling through the pages of the letter in search of the relevant passages. "Ah, here. Olga Rybynsky. Did you know her?"

Alexandra admitted that she had and hoped that the countess would probe no further.

"Well," said the countess, her magnified eyes bouncing back and forth across the lines of text, "it's quite a scandal. She's been divorced! Of course, the legal proceedings were very much behind closed doors, but everyone knows the reason, and everyone's talking. There's not a tea dance, cotillion, or card party where it isn't discussed to death. Nonconsummation! Fancy that! Poor thing. What humiliation for her, to be unwanted by her husband, and so publicly too!"

Alexandra pointed out that the husband's rejection was hardly public but had been made so by a cityful of gossiping mouths greedy for discussion of others' misfortunes but who disguised their malice as sympathy. Alexandra's reaction, so vehement, brought the countess's eyes to young Miss Korvin's face, and the countess speculated for a moment on the surprising strength of the young woman's emotion. Countess Gregorian's mind, however, was too porous to sustain the impulse to investigate, which quickly fell into one of the many crevices and crannies that honeycombed her charming, distracted brain. Distracted, she forgot about it.

"Oh! And her father!" the countess continued. "Prince Andreyev, that poor, tormented man with the money he can't get rid of. Well, he's given up! He's renounced it all! He's dressed himself in rags and is going round the country with bags of gold and rubles, just throwing it away! Pouring it over the heads of the peasants, stuffing it into their pockets. They think he's a saint. He has a thousand followers, picks up more in every town, and they drag themselves after him in a train that goes for miles behind him, carrying icons and flowers and chanting and singing. And with him he has his old African majordomo, who has converted to Christianity at last and has dressed himself as a monk. How very odd. Everyone is wondering what happened, the old pagan. Oh, how handsome that African was when he was young! You know, many, many ladies of Petersburg tried to seduce him. His dignity drove them quite out of their minds. And now the peasants, who have never seen an African before, are convinced that he is some magical being and further proof of the prince's sainthood!"

In listening to this news of the Petersburg milieu, Alexandra's nerves began to tighten. At any moment she expected news of Ulyanov's marriage or engagement. He had clearly forgotten her. So many months had gone by, and she had received no answer at all from him. But the countess went on to news of Princess Sherbatiev and her most recent miscarriage, and then the Austrian ambassador's scandalous love affair with the beautiful wife of a dentist, a woman well known for her promiscuity with anything in trousers, and then there had been a great quarrel between two factions of the government over a proposal for a new tax on windows. Although with each new item Alexandra's nerves stretched tigher, anticipating a mention of Ulyanov, none came. How very odd. He had been such a fixture in that world, one of the greatest gossip fodders of all, always doing something scandalous. The fact that there was no scandal connected with his name was more ominous than ever. Surely he had married and given up his old ways. Still, as much as Alexandra had conviced herself that Ulyanov must be forgotten, this brief contact with his milieu had left her breathless, for each piece of news from the world in which he lived had been suffused with him, radiant with his proximity.

When, not long afterward, Alexandra met the young men whom the countess was pressing upon her as possible suitors, the dazzle of Ulyanov's memory drained the men of color, faded them, rendered their distinctions indistinguishable as if they were standing in a blinding sunlight. They were all the same to her, insignificant collections of features with arms and legs, none vivid enough to dent her consciousness, and she forgot that Ulyanov himself had once been to her as insignificant, as unimportant, as annoying, as pathetic, as callow and unattractive as these young men.

The blaze of her love was intense. But though it flamed high, fed by his sudden and unexpected indifference, it could not survive indefinitely. He had not deigned even to throw a tiny twig upon her fire. The fire subsided, cooled, and shrank to an irritating ember embedded in the center of her heart, which pained her enough that she sought now to douse it completely with the attention of other men.

So when the countess announced to her, in a state of high excitement, that she had received news of an extraordinary event about to be visited upon the neighborhood, that old Prince Durashvili was coming with his new secretary, and that Prince Durashvili, old as he was, was as yet unmarried, not unattractive, and one of the richest men in Russia, not to mention a figure of power and influence, adviser and friend to the emperor, well, the ember died and turned to ash.

Why, she asked herself, had she been willing to throw herself away on such a man as Ulyanov in the first place? Womanizer, rake, libertine! And insignificant, too! Belonging only to the lower stratum of the aristocracy, untitled, of modest fortune, modest intellect, modest prospects.

Yes, the thought of Prince Durashvili and his millions perked Alexandra up considerably. The palaces she might have, the parties she might give, the gowns from Paris houses, the jewels, estates, and carriages. A carved and painted troika would be nice. Sets of German porcelain, a thousand covers matched, with bowls and cups and soup tureens all gilded, flowered, jeweled. All of it flooding back to her, the restoration of her birthright, her status, her pride.

Standing before the broken mirror in her bedroom, in which her image was reflected back to her with a crack running down through the middle, so the two halves of her did not quite match, she weighed her assets and wondered if she were still pretty enough, still woman enough, to get him. Her hair, which now curled to her chin, was coming along, but she wondered if she wasn't still half a man in some sense. She had worked at being masculine so long that she wondered if she hadn't lost the knack of femininity. And she had no clothes and no money to buy them. She would have to do the best she could, relying on the stateliness of her figure unadorned. She hoped it would be enough.

The impending arrival of the great prince excited many fantasies among the provincial aristocracy, dreaming on their modest farms of a brilliant marriage for a daughter who'd been difficult to dispose of, or of the prince's sponsorship of a good-for-nothing son for a leg up onto the bottom rung of a civil service career in the glittering capital, far from the dust and dirt and boredom of the provinces. Unrealistic as these dreams might have been for all of them, Alexandra included, they provided a sizzle of excitement, a delicious spice to the dull round of ill-cooked dinners and somnolent card parties, awkward amateur theatricals and out-of-tune musicales that constituted the social life of the gentry in a provincial backwater in the Russia of the nineteenth century.

The prince's tastes, his likes and dislikes in food and music and decor, were endlessly discussed and argued over, and the question of who was to host him during his visit ignited a feud between the Countess Gregorian and Madame Soubritsky—each of whom considered herself the leader of local society—that continued well into the next decade.

It was naturally the countess who won out, her experience in high society and her status as the only titled personage in the area giving her the edge. Her manor house, its dilapidation newly concealed under masses of indoor plants carted in to obscure a crack in the parlor wall or an area of water staining in the dining room, exerted a gravitational pull on all the local inhabitants of a standing sufficiently high to warrant an invitation to a dinner with the prince, or, if their status was lower, to an afternoon of tea. Hoping to be invited, the wife of the local physician offered to the countess her precious porcelain, bought ten years before on a honeymoon trip to Berlin, and the countess, whose own collection had been depleted by the necessities of squaring her husband's debts, accepted gladly. A magnificent, if untuned, piano owned by Monsieur Malabarque, a Frenchman who had arrived twenty years before to serve as music master to the children of a local family and had never left, now occupied the empty space left by the departure of the countess's own piano at about the time the Frenchman had arrived so many years ago. Lamps, chairs, pillows, linen, and china knickknacks were contributed by other aspirants to invitations, until the countess's home was upholstered with their hopes, decorated with their dreams.

The day of the prince's arrival had come, but the prince himself did not appear at the appointed time. Of course, the prince had written of the important business he had in the province, where he was to oversee the progress of some industrial projects he had established several years before at the emperor's suggestion, but the local notables and officials who had gathered to greet him at the countess's waited with growing frustration, stamped their feet with anger at the affront of his lateness, banged their heads against walls with hyperbolic Russian expression of the tragedy of his nonappearance, shouted loudly, drank too much vodka, ate too much herring though their wives grabbed their arms to restrain them, and ended by collapsing snoring in the too-many chairs that crowded the reception rooms on the first floor of the house, so that at the shouts from the servants of "He's here! I see him now!" they staggered to their feet disoriented, frightened by the changes in the light, and wondering where they were.

Alexandra, who had charge of the prince's and his secretary's rooms, was upstairs arranging a bunch of wildflowers in a cracked vase she had wrapped in a piece of yellowed lace, an effect she thought quite elegant. She placed the vase on a scratched mahogany dresser that already held a set of silver toiletry articles that had belonged to the countess's husband. Their presence there had been the subject of a quarrel between Alexandra and the hostess. Alexandra had suggested that because the toiletry articles were placed so prominently on the dresser, the prince would feel that he was expected to use them, when he had certainly brought his own, and besides, the items were far too personal and might affront the prince's modesty. The old countess, on the other hand, had insisted that she wanted the prince to see that she owned them, but Alexandra had said that the prince wouldn't care. On seeing the expression of disappointment on the countess's face, however, Alexandra gave up the argument immediately, admitted that the articles were fine in quality, and agreed that the prince was sure to be impressed.

The prince's valet was to be accommodated in the small dressing room that adjoined the dead count's bedroom, and Alexandra made sure she placed a pot of flowers there as well. The bedroom of the prince's young secretary, who was sure to be a gentleman, this sort of position being a common one for young

men of the aristocracy who were embarking on a career in politics, was down the hall. Alexandra was just smoothing the linen
on the pillows of the bed and fluffing up the lace in the secretary's bedroom when she heard the clattering of the hooves that
announced the prince's arrival and the shouting from the excited
peasants outside. Running to the window, she pressed the tip of
her nose against the glass.

A grand traveling coach, of the sort that she herself had
owned at one time, accompanied by several smaller carriages,
presumably containing the remainder of the prince's retinue, had
appeared in the long, curving drive before the countess's house.
The horses, a quartet of muscular matched grays, switched their
tails in impatience, anticipating the water and oats that were
waiting for them in the barn. The liveried coachman, also dressed
in gray, and his gray-coated assistant had already descended from
the box and opened the gilded door. The coachman flipped the
tiny stairway down to receive the prince's feet, which appeared
upon the instant, pattering quickly down the steps. And there
he was.

A handsome man of not more than sixty—gray-haired, but
vigorous and virile and richly dressed—he looked about him with
a smile, filled his strong chest theatrically with the country air,
and clapped his coachman on the arm. Then, turning back to the
door of the coach, he put out a hand, which was ignored by the
person who was emerging, whose feet rested only briefly on the
tiny staircase before he jumped down a foot or so to land lightly
on the ground. This young man, clearly the secretary, his lower
status signified by his simple costume of black, did not stop to
breathe the country air, but, looking worried, proceeded directly
to the house, as if he had urgent duties to perform, and it took
Alexandra but a moment to see who he really was.

Her heart turned over, burst into flame. Forgotten quickly

were the palaces and carriages and sets of china a thousand covers matched, the painted troikas, Paris gowns, her birthright, her status, her pride.

Alexandra ran out of the bedroom and down the stairs. Arriving at the bottom of the steps, the hallway nearly bulging with those waiting for their presentation, she tried to push her way through the crowd but failed to budge the local dignitaries and officials and their desperate, waiting wives and daughters. She hopped up and down and craned her neck.

The old prince and his young secretary stood side by side next to the countess as the old woman, in her glory at last, made her presentations to the prince. Alexandra could see nothing but the rising and falling of women's bodies as they curtsied, the inclinations of the heads of the men. She moved up and up in line, feeling feverish—oh, what would he say when he saw her? And then it was Alexandra's turn. But she could not raise her eyes to Ulyanov's face. She turned to the prince.

"Your highness," said the old countess, "I present to you Miss Alexandra Korvin." Alexandra sank to the ground, her black silk skirts whispering around her, but the silent smile that answered her curtsey, the respectful inclination of the head, the hand that helped her to her feet, as he had helped all the others, were Ulyanov's.

"Oh my," said the countess, reaching out to steady the unsteady Alexandra, "I'm afraid I got it all mixed up. It's not the *old* Prince Durashvili with his *new* secretary, it's the *new* Prince Durashvili with his *old* secretary. But you know how I am."

What had happened was this: when Ulyanov's mother, of the great aristocratic clan of Mecklenburgs, had forfeited nearly all of her inheritance upon her marriage to Ulyanov's father, a kind man, and handsome, too, but a representative of the lower echelon of Russian nobility—whose holdings were nil, though his virtues were considerable—her vast inheritance had passed to the young Prince Durashvili, a distant relation but a man of scruple so pure he had vowed on the spot that he would not keep this windfall for his own descendants. This Prince Durashvili had decided that he would never marry, so there would be no such descendants, and that he would hand the enormous legacy over to its rightful heir upon his death. Nor did he wish to spoil the young Ulyanov with the sorts of expectations most likely to thoroughly ruin an already undisciplined young man. Instead, he kept the gift a secret until he knew his end was near, that is, until just a few months ago. Laid out on what he knew to be his deathbed, old Prince Durashvili had sent for the young Ulyanov, adopted him legally so there would be no question of his rights in the eyes of the many squabbling relatives he knew would make a fuss, and ceded to him both the title and the fortune, with the attendant powers and privileges that that prince had accumulated in a long and fruitful career in the service of his emperor.

"But why didn't you write back to me?" asked Alexandra.

"I was busy," said the prince. "I knew you'd wait."

"Who's arrogant now?" said Alexandra.

"Well," said the prince, "when you tried to kill me, I knew you loved me very much."

"I thought it was when I *didn't* kill you that you knew I loved you."

"That confirmed it."

"But if you loved me, why didn't you follow me to the Caucasus? How could you have allowed me to risk myself that way? Me, a woman?" she teased.

"I did follow you," said the prince, explaining how Nikifor, his spy, had told him where she was going, and how he'd traveled at once to the Caucasus, camped out in the hills near the fort, nearly lost his toes to frostbite, chased her around the mountains, shadowing her every move, and how certainly she would have been wounded in the battle against the tribesmen, which had been a fierce one, and how relieved he had been when she had withdrawn, and how he had felt obliged to take her place in the line of battle, prepared to give his life in place of hers, "a life for a life."

"But why didn't you reveal yourself? All of that could have been avoided. The risk to you! You might have been killed."

"I thought you would be angry. You wanted to prove yourself a soldier. I thought you would resent me if I tried to stop you."

"I didn't exactly prove myself a soldier," said Alexandra with a grimace.

"No," said the prince, "you were a good soldier, a good officer. One of the best I ever served with. I didn't want to tell you that for fear you'd try to make general, or join the general staff. And then where would I be?"

Of course there were gowns and jewels and palaces and estates and carriages and sumptuous dinner parties. A set of porcelain with a thousand covers matched. A painted, gilded troika, even a villa on the island of Capri. But such was the burden placed upon her shoulders by the heavy weight of these holdings (the hours spent with accountants and business managers, her back aching from sitting for so long, her eyes swimming with the millions of hard black marks on the thousands of pages of the ledgers, the logistical nightmare of running a number of large households simultaneously, designing menus, keeping track of supplies, ministering to the illnesses and complaints of dependents, as well as managing the jealousies and intrigues of social life at the very pinnacle of the empire) that she understood how a life could be dedicated, as her father's had been, as Prince

Andreyev's was, to ridding oneself of it all, to unloading the burden from one's shoulders through extravagance or charity, it
didn't matter which. And some days, seeing how crushingly it all
weighed upon her husband, and feeling the futility of her
attempts to lift at least some of that burden onto her own
shoulders and of overcoming the obstacles such enormous
responsibilities placed in her path to him, she would think with
great nostalgia of the poor and simple room in which she had
once imagined, with horror, her life with the rake Ulyanov.

Nevertheless, Princess Durashvili managed to overcome the
obstacles in her path to her husband often enough to produce
seven children—six enormous boys and one tiny girl, her father's
favorite, the six boys representing, in the opinion of the prince,
the component of the princess's character that was masculine,
the girl a small but perfect droplet of her femininity. This theory
was not looked upon with kindness by the princess, who found
it insulting and expressed herself warmly on the point whenever
the prince brought it up, which was often, since he had not
exactly conquered his delight in mischievous teasing of the
princess. On these occasions, it was not unlikely that the princess
would treat her husband to an exhibition of the deftness of her
swordplay, which would always send the servants running to the
kitchen, the pantry, the servants' quarters, and the stables to
gather an admiring audience of onlookers who seized upon the
occasion to wager large sums of money upon the outcome, that
is, on which of the two would pin the other to the wall, while
the nursemaids and nannies and governesses and tutors, also
alerted, would come running down the stairs with the children at
their heels to see what Mama and Papa were up to.

The friendship of Princess Durashvili and Princess Andreyev resumed shortly before Alexandra's marriage to the prince,
and the two young women rushed back into each other's arms,

Alexandra tactfully declining to discuss what she knew of the character and predilections of Olga's husband, though Olga admitted to these herself, or what she knew of them. Rybynsky himself continued in his position at the pinnacle of the civil service but considerately never married again, the settlement from his divorce from the Princess Andreyev being quite sufficient to provide for all his needs, since Prince Andreyev had leaped joyfully at the opportunity to unload an enormous sum into the councilor's elegant lap. As for Prince Andreyev, though he never succeeded in his goal of completely divesting himself of what he thought of as his obscene and offensive pile of wealth, he was able to make a large enough dent with his policy of random generosity to reduce his holdings to an amount he considered tasteful.

Olga married again, and happily this time, to a man who, in contrast to her first husband, would not leave her alone, often chasing her through the palace in pursuit of the physical delights she had on offer, to her great joy and satisfaction.

Of Nikifor and Praskovia there is little to say—Praskovia, freed, lived happily with her husband in a sumptuous home provided for them by the prince. Matryona, who married Grisha, would not accept her freedom, having tasted enough of it, and served her mistress with as little devotion as before, but more affection. The baby, named Piotr-Grisha, thrived, grew, was educated at the university, and became a partner in the office of the lawyer Trenyakov, who found the woman he was looking for one night on the streets of the brothel district of the city and married her.

Alexandra never lost her taste for fine tobacco. And, though admired and envied throughout the capital for the stateliness of her figure, the exquisite taste of her clothes, the grace and plenty of her table, the generosity of her purse, the kindness of her heart, the politeness of her children, and the devotion of her husband the prince, she was at least as famous for the high quality of the Cuban cigars she always offered to her male guests after dinner, never declining to take one for herself.

Notes

A number of characters from nineteenth-century Russian novels appear (without being named) in this book. In some cases they speak, and so dialogue from the novels in which they appear is used. These quotations appear on the following pages:

pp. 37–38   Prince Andrei Bolkonsky from Tolstoy's *War and Peace* asks Alexandra to dance. The words he speaks and the paraphrased description of his interaction with Pierre and Natasha are from the Signet Classic paperback edition of the book, p. 556, translated by Ann Dunnigan (1968).

pp. 43–44   Rasputin appears at the ball. His words are taken from a letter Rasputin wrote to Empress Alexandra, quoted in *Tsar: The Lost World of Nicholas and Alexandra* by Peter Kurth (Little, Brown and Company, 1995), pp. 118–19.

pp. 139–40   Alexandra dreams "a Russian dream." The dream is based on Tatyana's dream in Stanzas XI–XX of the Babette Deutsch translation of *Eugene Onegin* (Modern Library, 1936).

pp. 180–85   Alexandra and Trenyakov go to a restaurant, where they encounter Levin and Obolensky from *Anna Karenina*. The cashier and waiter who appear in this scene are also from *Anna Karenina*. All dialogue spoken by the Levin and Obolensky figures is from the David Magarshack translation (Signet Classics, 1961), pp. 49–58.

pp. 316–21   Alexandra goes to a brothel, where she encounters Sonya, the prostitute from *Crime and Punishment*. Some of Sonya's dialogue is a paraphrase of Marmeladov's conversation with Raskolnikov about his family situation, pp. 15–16, Constance Garnett translation (Bantam, 1981).

pp. 350–58   The setting and ritual of Ulyanov's duel with Durinov are loosely based on the duel between Dolokhov and Pierre in *War and Peace*.

All in all, eleven characters from these four novels appear.

Nadezhda Durova, the Cavalry Maiden mentioned in the book, was a real woman who did disguise herself as a man and serve in the Russian cavalry in the early part of the nineteenth century. She published her memoirs in 1836, and her story can be read in the Indiana University Press edition of her journals, *The Cavalry Maiden: Journals of a Russian Officer in the Napoleonic Wars* (1989), translated by Mary Fleming Zirin.

The Righteous Procopius of Vologda, Fool-for-Christ and Wonder-worker, mentioned on page 271, appears in the Russian Orthodox calendar of saints. His day is July 21.

Vladimir Littauer's fascinating memoir of his years in the pre-revolutionary Russian cavalry, *Russian Hussar: A Story of the Imperial Cavalry, 1911–1920* (White Mane Publishing Company, Inc., 1993) provided invaluable details about the life of a cavalry officer. *Bayonets before Bullets: The Imperial Russian Army, 1861–1914* (Bruce W. Menning, Indiana University Press, 2000) provided general background on the nineteenth-century Russian military organization. Priscilla Roosevelt's marvelous *Life on the Russian Country Estate: A Social and Cultural History* (Yale University Press, 1995) provided the revelation that no matter how opulently I had depicted life at the Andreyev estate Pandemonium, the real Russian aristocrats were even more extravagant (you can't make this stuff up, though I tried). Details about the conduct of Russian duels were found in *Ritualized Violence Russian Style: The Duel in Russian Culture and Literature* (Irina Reyfman, Stanford University Press, 1999). *Dueling: The Cult of Honor in Fin-de-Siècle Germany* (Kevin McAleer, Princeton University Press, 1994) provided general background on the cult of the aristocratic duel. The creation story told by the Armenian prince on page 199 is based on one found in the chapter "The Caucasus: A Mountain World," from *Russian Cooking,* by Helen and George Papashvily (*Foods of the World* series, Time-Life Books, 1969).

The name Ruslan comes from *Ruslan and Ludmila,* the narrative poem by Alexander Pushkin, Russia's greatest poet, who set the old fairy tale in verse. The hero Ruslan, a legendary Russian prince, faces many obstacles (including a battle with a gigantic disembodied head) in order to win the hand of the princess Ludmila.

ACKNOWLEDGMENTS

I would like to thank my agents, Simon Green and Dan Green of Pom, Inc., who nursed me through the writing of this book, giving support and many valuable suggestions—I couldn't ask for any better. Thanks also to my editor, Kristin Kiser. Her skill and taste have been a wonder, her kindness and tolerance a reassurance. Stephen Koch, my thesis adviser at Columbia, has remained a source of advice and encouragement. My sister, Susie, my trusted "general reader," who read the book as it was being written, offered her typically pure and unpretentious response, as well as enough enthusiasm to keep me going. My brother-in-law, Graham, kept asking, "Are you done yet?" and never stopped encouraging me. Thanks also to Eileen Tomarchio, who has listened to me endlessly, patiently, for many years, providing much wisdom and insight. And to Amanda Filipacchi, who came to my rescue when I had nearly given up, the greatest thanks of all.

About the Author

BARBARA SCRUPSKI is a graduate of Rutgers College. She has studied at the University of Konstanz in Germany, at Cambridge University, England, and at the Institute for Polish Language at Jagiellonian University, Kraków, Poland. She holds an M.F.A. in writing from Columbia University.